He stood behind her, her scent wrapping around him in a sensual cocoon, and he realized he was in serious trouble

The stance was too intimate, their bodies way too close. There was no way he could prevent his reaction to her as she wriggled to get into shooting position.

When her gun sagged in her hands, he clenched his teeth in frustration at their enforced proximity but reached around her to help hold the gun. "This time, don't close your eyes. It'll make it easier to see if you hit your target."

"How will I know if I'm on target?" Kelly demanded and he realized she was playing word games with him. He didn't know if he wanted to turn her around and kiss her or turn and walk away.

"You'll know."

She aimed again, and shot. And when the bullets rang out, she flung herself around in his arms, a pleased grin on her face. "I did it!"

"But you didn't hit anything."

"Not yet." And that's when she planted a kiss on Wade's lips.

Dear Harlequin Intrigue Reader,

We have another month of spine-tingling romantic thrillers lined up for you—starting with the much anticipated second book in Joanna Wayne's tantalizing miniseries duo, HIDDEN PASSIONS: FULL MOON MADNESS. In *Just Before Dawn,* a reclusive mountain man vows to get to the bottom of a single mother's terrifying nightmares before darkness closes in.

Award-winning author Leigh Riker makes an exciting debut in the Harlequin Intrigue line this May with *Double Take.* Next, pulses race out of control in *Mask of a Hunter* by Sylvie Kurtz—the second installment in THE SEEKERS—when a tough operative's cover story as doting lover to a pretty librarian threatens to blow up.

Be there from the beginning of our brand-new in-line continuity, SHOTGUN SALLYS! In this exciting trilogy, three young women friends uncover a scandal in the town of Mustang Valley, Texas, that puts their lives—and the lives of the men they love—on the line. Don't miss *Out for Justice* by Susan Kearney.

To wrap up a month of can't-miss romantic suspense, Doreen Roberts debuts in the Harlequin Intrigue line with *Official Duty,* the next title in our COWBOY COPS thematic promotion. It's a double-murder investigation that forces a woman out of hiding to face her perilous past...and her pent-up feelings for the sexy sheriff who still has her heart in custody. Last but certainly not least, *Emergency Contact* by Susan Peterson—part of our DEAD BOLT promotion—is an edgy psychological thriller about a traumatized amnesiac who may have been brainwashed to do the unthinkable....

Enjoy all our selections this month!

Sincerely,

Denise O'Sullivan
Senior Editor,
Harlequin Intrigue

C-1

OUT FOR JUSTICE
SUSAN KEARNEY

 HARLEQUIN®

TORONTO • NEW YORK • LONDON
AMSTERDAM • PARIS • SYDNEY • HAMBURG
STOCKHOLM • ATHENS • TOKYO • MILAN • MADRID
PRAGUE • WARSAW • BUDAPEST • AUCKLAND

Special thanks and acknowledgment are given
to Susan Kearney for her contribution
to the Shotgun Sallys series.

ISBN 0-373-22774-4

OUT FOR JUSTICE

ABOUT THE AUTHOR

Susan Kearney used to set herself on fire four times a day. Now she does something really hot—she writes romantic suspense. While she no longer performs her signature fire dive (she's taken up figure skating), she never runs out of ideas for characters and plots. A business graduate from the University of Michigan, Susan writes full-time. She resides in a small town outside Tampa, Florida, with her husband and children and a spoiled Boston terrier. Visit her at www.SusanKearney.com.

Books by Susan Kearney

OKLAHOMA

NEW MEXICO

ARKANSAS

• Mustang Valley

Dallas •

Fort Worth •

LOUISIANA

TEXAS

N

MEXICO

Gulf of Mexico

All underlined places are fictitious.

CAST OF CHARACTERS

Kelly McGovern—The great-great-granddaughter of Shotgun Sally and Mustang Valley's most infamous citizen. Kelly is determined to pierce the veil of secrecy around her brother Andrew's death, even if it means moving in with the town's bad boy to protect her.

Wade Lansing—Mustang Valley's original bad boy and Andrew's best friend.

Sheriff Ben Wilson—Honest law enforcer or man with his own agenda?

Jonathan Dixon—A law school colleague of Andrew's with a chip on his shoulder and a grudge the size of Texas.

Mayor Mickey Daniels—He'll do almost anything to win his reelection—but does that include murder?

Debbie West—Andrew's fiancée and woman with a secret past.

Niles Deagen—Oilman extraordinaire or a man on the verge of bankruptcy?

Lindsey Wellington—New to Mustang Valley and Lambert & Church, she's determined to get to the bottom of Andrew's mysterious death, especially if it helps out her new friends Kelly and Cara.

Cara Hamilton—A fledgling reporter and Kelly's best friend.

Andrew McGovern—Kelly's brother lost his life much too soon. But was the fire that caused his death really an accident…or arson?

Shotgun Sally—The legendary frontierswoman influences the lives of Kelly, Lindsey and Cara in their quest for the truth!

For Phyllis and Sy Dresser

Prologue

"Hi, short-stuff. What's up?" Andrew McGovern answered his sister, Kelly's, phone call with such enthusiasm that if she hadn't known better, she wouldn't have guessed he'd just worked an eighteen-hour day.

"It's after midnight," Kelly pointed out with sisterly affection. Andrew might amuse himself with his gadgets, like the caller ID that had told him she was on the line before he'd picked up the phone, but she'd bet her new diamond-bezel Rolex her parents had given her for a college graduation present that her brother hadn't checked the time in hours.

Papers rustled. She pictured Andrew behind his battered desk in the annex of his law office of Lambert & Church, his tie and jacket thrown over the back of a spare chair, his desk a mountain of papers, his file cabinet half-open, his eyes bleary despite the numerous cups of black coffee he'd drunk to keep him awake.

"And?" he asked.

"Don't you have anything better to do than work on Saturday night?"

"Nag. Nag. Nag." Andrew chuckled. "Short-stuff, if you aren't careful, you'll start sounding just like Mom. And if, like her, you want to know if I'm still engaged to Debbie, I am. In fact, I'm bringing her to breakfast at the house tomorrow morning."

Kelly sucked in her breath. Mom and Dad didn't approve of Debbie West's family and they certainly wouldn't be pleased about his engagement. Andrew's fiancée lived on an impoverished ranch just outside of Mustang Valley, Texas, about an hour north of town, with her alcoholic father and no-good brother. While Andrew seemed oblivious to his parents' reservations about his current relationship, Kelly's stomach knotted. She didn't like discord. Doing what her parents expected of her was so much easier than butting heads.

She'd always enjoyed her parents' approval, making straight As, being popular in school and avoiding trouble. Sure, sometimes she'd rather have been out partying than hitting the books on a regular basis, but she had discipline, something the brilliant Andrew, who often worked through the night but then didn't go into the office for another two days, knew nothing about. And she'd never understood why her older brother seemed so intent on riling up the folks by choosing friends from the other side of Mustang Valley. Like Andrew's best friend, that renegade Wade Lansing, who owned the Hit 'Em Again Saloon, and Debbie West, a high-school dropout who worked at a local diner.

Daddy had worked hard to buy the biggest house in Mustang Valley, and Mama had spent half her life decorating it. Kelly had enjoyed teen parties by the pool during high school and had been proud to bring home college friends to stay during vacations. Her best friend Cara Hamilton might not be as wealthy as the McGoverns, but she came from a middle-class home just a few streets away and now lived in a new apartment complex with nicely landscaped grounds and all the amenities, including a spa and security system. And she had a respectable career as a fledgling reporter. While her brother turned up his nose at the McGovern life-style, Kelly liked having her own horse and the pretty Jaguar Daddy had bought her after graduation. She saw nothing wrong with appreciating the finer things in life.

However, Andrew seemed to take pleasure in thumbing his nose at convention and the family. He hung out with whomever he pleased and rarely brought them home. Although he'd never been in serious trouble, Andrew had enjoyed racing his souped-up Mustang with dual chrome exhausts down Main Street and spying on the girls skinny-dipping at Half-Moon Lake. All harmless pranks— but ones that could have led to more serious trouble. Then, after finishing law school, instead of joining their father's oil company, he'd chosen to work at Lambert & Church, happily taking pro bono cases and mixing with all kinds of lowlifes, even criminals, as well as high-paying clients.

''Andrew! I think the only reason you date Debbie is to rile Mom and Dad.'' Kelly's older brother might hang out with some unusual people, but nevertheless the siblings were close. She enjoyed teasing him, especially about his friends. ''I thought

I should warn you…Dad still wants you to work for him. He's going to make you another offer.''

"I wish he wouldn't. I'm happy here. Busy. Needed." More papers rustled, and she suspected she had only half his attention. "In fact, I'm working on something real interesting."

His car alarm interrupted their conversation.

Andrew swore. "That stray cat must have jumped on my car, again, no doubt leaving sandy paw prints all over it, never mind waking everyone within a quarter-mile radius. Gotta go. See you tomorrow."

"Bye." She set the phone back in its cradle with a shake of her head, turned off her light and pulled up her covers. She wouldn't have fallen asleep so easily if she'd known that was the last time she and her brother would ever speak.

Chapter One

"Andrew's dead." Though Cara spoke to Kelly in her brash, no-nonsense reporter's voice, there was a catch in it. "And whatever you do isn't ever going to bring him back."

"I know." Kelly hugged her friend. If not for Cara's support, she didn't know how she would have made it through the past forty-two days. "Just hear me out."

"Okay." Cara plunked herself down on Kelly's bed, ran her fingers through her short red curls and stared at her through hazel eyes filled with concern and sorrow. A few years ago, Cara had been engaged to Andrew, but they'd mutually ended their relationship and remained friends.

Kelly tried to shove down her own grief over Andrew's death long enough to put her thoughts in order, thoughts that hadn't left her since the morning Andrew's body was found. "According to Sheriff Ben Wilson's report, an eyewitness saw Andrew chase the cat from his car, turn off his alarm and return to his office. But there was no witness to the fire that started in the annex of Lambert & Church sometime during the night.''

''Word is it was an electrical short, though the fire department is still investigating. Any reason you're suspicious it was something else?''

''Nothing concrete.'' But Kelly just couldn't let go. Not when the facts didn't add up. Kelly might have grown up the pampered princess of well-to-do parents, she might not have the bold brashness of Cara, but she had her own kind of genteel determination that had seen her through college and had left her with her pick of law schools.

She liked to believe that her toughness came to her from her grandmother's grandmother on her mother's side. Shotgun Sally had been a legend around this part of Texas for well over a century. Dozens of stories about her abounded, and one of Kelly's favorites was how the aristocratic-born widow lady had come out west at age twenty to start over and make a new life for herself and her sons. Now Kelly had suffered the loss of a dear family member—just like her famous ancestor. Somehow she would survive because surely a smidgen of Shotgun Sally's toughness ran in Kelly's blood.

Thoughtful, Kelly twisted a finger around a blond lock. ''There was no witness to Andrew's death.'' A death probably from smoke inhalation since his badly burned body had been found still sitting in his chair. That he'd died in his sleep was little consolation to Kelly and her devastated parents.

Andrew might have been a rebel, but he'd been well loved. The entire town of Mustang Valley had turned out for his funeral and to pay their respects, including Debbie West, who'd arrived with her eyes red and swollen from crying. And Kelly had never seen Andrew's best friend, saloon owner Wade Lansing, so somber as when he acted as one of the pallbearers. Dressed in an immaculate black suit, shirt and tie that she wouldn't have suspected he owned, Wade had looked forbidding and dangerous, but had done Andrew proud, standing tall and strong beside her daddy, Sheriff Wilson, Mayor Daniels, and Donald Church and Paul Lambert, senior partners of the law firm where Andrew had worked.

Her father had tried and failed to remain stoic during the funeral, and he'd aged ten years in the past six weeks, his white hair thinning, the circles under his eyes darkening. Beneath her Vera Wang veil, her mother had wept copiously and Kelly should have been crying, too. But she couldn't. She was too angry at Andrew for dying. Too upset with the sheriff who couldn't give her any explanations why her brother hadn't even tried to get out of the first floor of a burning building.

Her world no longer made sense and she needed to put it in order before she could go on with her life. Finding answers for Andrew and herself might not be her specialty, but she was a fast learner and she fully intended to search for the truth.

"If someone else had been around, they would have gotten Andrew up and out of there." Cara's special brand of reporter logic made her good at figuring things out.

Kelly picked up a brush and ran it through her hair, not because her shoulder-length hair needed brushing but because she found the action soothing. "That night when I spoke to Andrew he was awake and excited. I have difficulty believing that he fell asleep so soundly that the smoke didn't wake him."

"The fire broke out at two in the morning. He must have been exhausted." Cara stood, took the brush from Kelly and tossed it on the marble and gold cosmetic table.

Kelly frowned at her. "Andrew was always the lightest of sleepers. Remember how picky he was about his sheets?"

"Huh?"

"Surely you haven't forgotten our sleep-over back in middle school when you put your puppy in Andrew's bed and she left a little sand behind."

Cara nodded with a chuckle. "Who would have thought a few grains of sand would keep Andrew tossing and turning all night? Or that he'd retaliate with an ice cold glass of water at 7 a.m."

"My brother required six pillows to sleep, propping up his knees and back. And now the sheriff expects me to believe that Andrew fell asleep in an uncomfortable office chair? It's just not possible."

Cara's eyes glimmered with interest. "*You* questioned Sheriff Wilson?"

Kelly shrugged. "Yeah. And he gave me a patronizing hug and told me he would look into my suspicions. Then I asked Paul Lambert what Andrew had been working on, and he just patted me on the head and told me the work was confidential. I don't know how you investigate your stories. People don't take me seriously."

"That's because you're..."

Kelly raised a perfectly arched brow. "What?"

"Polite."

"There's nothing wrong with good manners."

Except that six weeks after Andrew's death, Kelly had no more answers than she'd had the morning she'd been told he'd died. But she was determined to find out exactly what had happened that night. She just wasn't sure how to go about investigating.

However, Cara did know, and Kelly would eventually learn from her friend how to obtain the information she desired. Kelly might be polite but she knew how to get around Cara. "So you studied investigative journalism. Where should I start? What should I do? How should I act? What should I wear?"

Cara rubbed her forehead. "What if there's nothing to find? Can you live with that?"

Kelly stood, appreciating her height that allowed her to look down on her shorter friend. Andrew might have called Kelly short-stuff because she was a good eight inches shorter than his six-foot-two, but now she looked down her nose and used her most charming grin on Cara. "I just want to find out the truth. You of all people should understand."

"Of course I do, but... Look, Kelly. It's like this. While I was working for the high school newspaper on that exposé of the football coach and the school secretary, you were the head cheerleader. And in college—"

"Hey, I studied damn hard."

"I know you did, sweetie. Maybe you could investigate the society page or the travel section or—"

"Give advice to the rich and famous?"

"Exactly."

Kelly fisted her hands on her hips, careful not to wrinkle her silk blouse. "So you think all I can investigate is fluff?"

"If the hat fits…"

"…I'd wear it only if it were in style. But so what if I like fashion and gossip. That doesn't mean I didn't love my brother enough to find out what happened to him. Are you going to help me or not?"

Cara nodded. "I just don't want to see you hurt even more, but the last time I saw you this determined was the day you took your LSAT's." Cara looked her up and down, frowning at Kelly's elegant blouse and frilly, ladylike skirt that ended at midcalf. "I'd say a trip to the mall is our first stop."

"IF ANYTHING HAPPENS to me, look after short-stuff." Andrew's words reverberated in Wade Lansing's mind as he walked down Main Street and spied Kelly McGovern.

Kelly looked different from the out-of-his-class woman that she always presented to the world. Instead of the feminine silk blouses and lacy skirts or designer dresses she favored, she was wearing jeans, boots and a tucked in blouse with a blazer. She'd done something to her standard shoulder-length blond hair, pulling it back softly with a clip that showed off her blue eyes and model cheekbones.

Wade wished he'd questioned Andrew more fully during the short phone conversation the night of his friend's death, but the bar had been packed and he'd been shy two waitresses. Still, he'd taken the time to ask Andrew why he thought anything might happen to him, but Andrew had told him it was probably nothing.

Nothing, my ass.

Andrew wasn't prone to panic or exaggeration. He'd stumbled onto something he shouldn't have and it had gotten him killed. And as much as Wade had liked and respected Andrew, his friend had grown up protected from the harsher side of life. Andrew trusted people, whereas Wade did not. Andrew always gave people the benefit of the doubt. Wade expected the worst, so he didn't need evidence to listen to his gut, which told him Andrew had been murdered. He'd been around trouble too many times not to trust his instincts.

As a kid, those instincts warned him to hide on Saturday nights so that his drunk father couldn't find him until he sobered up. The few times he'd forgotten to hide had taught Wade to never let down his guard. He had few friends, but Andrew had been a good one, and Wade owed him more than one favor.

Besides, watching Kelly's back and cute little bottom was certainly no hardship. With her long slender legs, she should wear jeans more often. She'd always been attractive in that don't-touch-me-I'm-off-limits-to-the-likes-of-you kind of way, which he'd accepted out of respect for Andrew. But today she actually looked approachable—if he could discount her five-hundred-dollar boots and the designer bag she'd slung over her saucy shoulder.

The sight of Kelly's new look not only reminded Wade of his promise to his friend but had his instincts screaming. He and Kelly didn't patronize the same kinds of establishments or reside in the same part of town. Kelly probably hung out in Dallas's or Fort Worth's fanciest malls or perhaps at Mustang Valley's finest steak house, but he'd rarely seen her on grounds he considered his turf. And why was she walking instead of driving her spiffy new Jag? What the hell was she up to?

His curiosity aroused, he followed her down Main Street past the post office and the pharmacy, keeping his distance and a few shoppers between them, considering possible destinations. Kelly didn't date guys from this side of town. She picked proper and preppie college boys with impeccable credentials and a family history as tony as her own. She'd only visited his saloon once to pull Andrew home during a family emergency. He recalled how out-of-place she'd looked in her lacy skirt and soft, sophisticated blouse, and yet she hadn't hesitated to enter his rowdy bar alone, shoulder past several inebriated cowboys to demand that her brother accompany her to the hospital. Her granddaddy had had a stroke. She'd looked sassy and sad then, letting neither Andrew's drunken state nor his lost cause of the moment, who'd been clinging to her brother's arm, deter Kelly from her task.

On the sidewalk in front of Wade, Kelly suddenly spun around and made a bee-line straight at him with that same determined pout of her lips that he so vividly remembered from years ago.

He braced for a confrontation. "Hey, short-stuff. What's up?"

"Don't call me that, please."

Kelly was always ultrapolite, but with him she usually sounded so irritated that she couldn't quite hide that annoyance. In return, he couldn't help feeling gratified that he was getting under that *Cosmo* girl skin. Maybe it was a remnant from his teenage years, but he loved bringing out the spark that she kept so carefully controlled. Watching her suppress all those simmering passions, he cocked one hand on his hip and pulled off her sunglasses.

She maintained a cool, superior tone, but vexation and perhaps a gleam of fury shined in her vivid baby-blues. "What are you doing?"

"I've missed your gorgeous green eyes," he teased.

"They're blue." She snatched back her sunglasses, her pretty polished pink nails shimmering in the sunlight. "Are you trying to distract me from the fact that you're following me?"

Ah, she might look like a fairy princess, even in those hip-hugging jeans, but she had a brain almost as sharp as Andrew's. Wade reminded himself not to get so caught up in the glisten of her lip gloss that he underestimated her. "You caught me in the act."

She chuckled, her lips absolutely adorable and way-too-appealingly kissable. "It wouldn't be the first time."

If she was trying to embarrass him with the memory of her walking up to the car her brother had lent him and her getting an eyeful of him and Mary Jo Lacy in the back seat, she wouldn't succeed. Of the three of them, she'd been the embarrassed one. Funny, he could barely recall Mary Jo's expression, but Kelly's had been a sight to behold. Her blush had started at her shapely chest, risen up her delicate neck, flowered over her cheeks and forehead. Her teenage-innocent eyes had widened in surprise before her lips had parted into a big round *O*.

"So what are you up to?" He eyed her from the tips of her new boots to the designer sunglasses she'd grabbed and thrust up high on her forehead.

"Nothing."

"Yeah, right. When I see Miss Kelly McGovern sashaying down Main Street on this side of town in blue jeans, I know something's up. If I didn't know you better, I'd think you had an assignation at the Lone Star Lodge."

"I don't sashay. I don't frequent that establishment. And I have better things to do than stand here and—"

"Better things to do? That doesn't sound like 'nothing' to me."

"My business is no concern of yours." She turned around to dismiss him.

He fell into step beside her. "Aren't you even a little curious why I was following you?"

"Not particularly." She yanked down the sunglasses.

"Okay." He matched her, step for step, and didn't say another word. He tipped his hat to a few of the townsfolk and waited. Wade hadn't always been this patient. In his younger days he'd been known for his hot blood and his blazing temper. But he'd mellowed during his midtwenties. And he had the advantage here. She wanted to be rid of him, so she would either have to speak to him again or accept his company. He looked forward to either decision.

Her floral scent floating between them, the sunlight shimmering off her blond hair, she stopped on the sidewalk and peered over her sunglasses at him. "What do you want, Wade?"

Her respect? Her trust? Damned if he knew. "It's not what I want but what Andrew wanted."

"Don't play word games with me about my brother." She almost snapped at him, and he realized that the unhealed wound in her heart was responsible for the rawness in her voice. She'd adored her brother, tagging after Andrew into her midteens, shooting hoops with them in the park and getting underfoot. Andrew hadn't minded, and Wade had enjoyed teasing the prickly princess. But they hadn't run into one another that often. Andrew hadn't brought his friends home much, and as Kelly's popularity increased into her late teens, she'd found her own group of friends. Wade and Kelly might not ever have even spoken if not for Andrew—and now he was gone.

"I'm sorry. I miss him, too." Wade ran a hand through his hair. "Let's start over."

"From ten minutes ago? Or eighteen years ago?"

She was referring to the first time they'd met. At ten years old, Wade had been the terror of the schoolyard and a class-A bully, copying his father, his only role model up to that point in his life. Wade had caught a stray ball from a group of kindergarteners playing kick ball. No one dared ask him for the ball—except five-year-old Kelly. She'd skipped over in her immaculate yellow ruffled dress, smiled at him like an angel and had plucked the ball right out of his hands, murmuring a sweet thank-you. He'd been so stunned at her audacity that he'd just stood there and let her get away with it.

Wade didn't answer her rhetorical question. "I spoke to your brother the night he died."

"And?" she prodded.

"He said that if anything happened to him that I should look after you."

Her tone turned all businesslike. "What do you mean—if anything happened to him? Are you saying my brother expected trouble?"

"I'm not sure. He sounded more excited than concerned. I didn't question him thoroughly."

"Why not?" Her voice turned sharp enough to slice and dice, and he refrained from wincing, especially since he'd asked himself that same question a hundred times.

"The saloon was packed. I was shorthanded and I expected him to be over within the hour."

She stood still for a moment, clearly thinking. "Have you mentioned your conversation to Sheriff Wilson?"

He shook his head. "I've spoken to Mitch, Deputy Warwick. He's looking into it for me on the QT."

"Why on the QT?"

He squared his shoulders and it only helped a little to know that she wasn't prying into his personal life but trying to understand the situation with her brother. "Sheriff Wilson isn't exactly a fan of the Lansing family. Deputies don't like answering domestic squabbles." And his folks had habitually fought every Friday and Saturday night. Deputies had stopped at his house as often as the local coffee shop.

He refrained from mentioning that he'd never liked Sheriff Wilson, but Mitch was an all-right deputy. The man had compassion, probably learned the hard way since growing up half Native American wasn't easy in these parts.

To give her credit, Kelly didn't fault Wade—at least out loud. "If you hear anything from Deputy Warwick, you'll let me know?"

"Sure." He wished he could see her eyes that she'd hidden behind those sunglasses.

"You needn't worry about looking after me. I'm fine."

Once again Kelly dismissed him, her booted feet taking the steps, two at a time, up Doc Swenson's front porch. Wade almost left her to her business. But when Doc opened the front door and stepped onto the porch, Wade decided this meeting had nothing to do with a personal medical problem.

At eighty years of age and Mustang Valley's only doctor, Swenson conducted his business inside where he'd converted two downstairs bedrooms into patient consultation rooms, or in the former dining room where he now performed autopsies for the sheriff's department.

The town desperately needed a younger doctor but like most small towns, Mustang Valley didn't have the population to support one of the medical facilities to induce a physician to move here. Doc had delivered most of the townsfolk around these parts, including Kelly and Andrew. When Wade's folks couldn't pay the bill, Doc had treated the thirteen-year-old Wade's broken leg for free. These days, for more serious problems, folks usually made the one-hour drive to Dallas or Fort Worth.

Kelly shook Dr. Swenson's hand. "Hi, Doc. Thanks for agreeing to talk to me. I know you're busy." When Wade stepped up on the porch beside her, she stiffened. "Excuse me, but I don't remember inviting you to join us."

Doc put his hand on Kelly's shoulder. "It's better if Wade's here. Just two hours ago, we had a couple of kids throw a rock through the front window. Probably just a prank." He jerked a thumb at a broken pane temporarily fixed with duct tape. "But I'd feel better if Wade walked you back."

Wade nodded. "Yes, sir." But he thought it odd that Doc believed she needed protection against a couple of juvenile delinquents and wondered if he had an ulterior motive.

Kelly looked up at the porch roof as if seeking heavenly patience, then back at Doc and ignored Wade. "Fine. Doc, I wanted to ask you about Andrew's death."

Doc gestured to a swing on his front porch. "Please, sit. I need to rest these old bones every chance I get—which isn't often enough these days."

Kelly settled on the swing, careful to leave Wade plenty of room so they wouldn't be touching. Normally he might have deliberately crowded her—just to irritate her some more. But he couldn't do that with her looking so distressed about Andrew, and behaved himself, sitting on the opposite end of the swing.

"Doc, the sheriff said my brother died of smoke inhalation."

Doc sat in a rocker and lit his pipe. "I assure you, he didn't suffer any pain."

"You could tell that from the autopsy?" Wade asked.

"Yes."

Kelly twisted her hands in her lap, noticed what she was doing and then grasped one hand firmly in the other. "I don't see how Andrew could have fallen asleep at his desk. When I spoke to him at midnight, he was wide awake and excited and told me he was working on something interesting."

"Did he say what?" Wade asked.

"No." She focused on he doctor. "What else did the autopsy reveal?"

Doc puffed on his pipe and blew out a ring of smoke. "Nasty habit. Don't ever start. Smoking causes cancer, you know."

He took his pipe from his mouth and pursed his lips, eyeing her with a scowl. "I didn't want to mention this at the funeral, and I'm not supposed to tell you this now, but Andrew didn't die from the fire."

"He didn't?"

"He died from a bullet to his head."

"Oh…my…God." Kelly turned white. "Andrew was murdered?"

Chapter Two

Murdered?

Kelly's suspicion had proven correct. Still, having her hunch confirmed proved a shock. Her nerves jerked as if a bomb had gone off and rattled her to the core. At first she feared she might faint, but then, with an inner fortitude, she inhaled a deep breath, squared her sagging shoulders and looked Doc straight in the eyes, listening to his explanation.

"A bullet indicates Andrew's death was an accident, suicide or murder," Doc told them bluntly.

Wade defended his friend. "It wasn't an accident. Andrew didn't keep a gun in the office and he certainly didn't kill himself."

"Why was this kept a secret?" Kelly demanded with unconcealed bitterness. She might have turned white but she hadn't fainted and her brain was working perfectly as the question burst from her.

"Sheriff Wilson wanted me to keep the particulars quiet while he investigated."

"Is this the usual procedure?"

"No, but it's not that *unusual*, either. If the shooter thinks we've attributed Andrew's death to the fire he started, to cover up the shooting, then the sheriff might have a better chance of catching the killer.''

''That may be so.'' Kelly stood, trembling with shock and indignation, wishing she hadn't been so wrapped up in her grief, that she'd followed up on her suspicions sooner. ''But he had no right to keep this from our family. I'd say the sheriff has some explaining to do. Thanks for the information, Doc.''

''Anytime. And be careful. I don't want anything happening to you.''

''I'll be fine.''

''I'll make sure she stays that way.'' Wade shook Doc Swenson's hand and walked down the steps with her. She half expected Wade to try to talk her out of going to the sheriff, but he remained quiet.

''What are you thinking?'' she asked him.

''I was making a mental list of all the people we should talk to.''

''We?''

''I'm not letting you do this alone.''

''I appreciate your wanting to look after me, but…''

He looped his arm through hers. ''It's not necessary?''

''I'm not sure about that.'' She wasn't going to turn down help from any quarter. Wade could be useful. He knew about a side of Andrew that her brother had sheltered her from. He also heard things at the saloon that might be handy. On the other hand, he was big and strong, and she didn't trust herself around Wade. Years ago she'd had a schoolgirl crush on him, but hadn't even considered there could be anything between them since her parents had clearly disapproved of Wade.

She trusted her parents' judgment, so she really didn't like the effect he had on her now. She liked the way he'd looped his arm through hers. She liked his intention to follow through on his promise to her brother. And she liked the concerned look in his eyes. Mix that with his flat-out determination to stick with her, and the man was downright irresistible. Yet never once in all the years she'd known him had he indicated even a smidgen of interest in her beyond as his friend's kid sister.

Considering her interest in him, she should keep her distance. He was all wrong for her. Yet she owed it to her brother to seek justice and, to be fair, she'd have a better chance of success if she accepted Wade's help. Although she'd lived in Mustang Valley all her life, he knew people that she didn't.

As long as he proved helpful, she'd let him stick around. But if he interfered, tried to dissuade her or tried to take over, she'd dump him so fast his head would spin. Satisfied with her plan, she picked up her pace.

Just to keep him from getting too familiar, she removed her arm from his. His touch might be gentlemanly and brotherly, but she didn't relish the way she reacted to him. "Andrew was murdered. If I start poking my nose in where it doesn't belong, the wrong person might notice."

"I'm glad you're going to be reasonable."

She bristled. "I'm always reasonable."

"I'm sure that's true—from your perspective."

"What's that supposed to mean?"

He didn't answer, which infuriated her. Sometimes she had the feeling they came from not just different parts of town but different planets. Maybe that was why he'd always fascinated her. He was so different from the college guys she'd dated.

Wade's voice remained soft but was threaded with steel. "Just so we're agreed. When you go talk to the sheriff, we go together."

She nodded. "Who else is on your mental list?"

"The short list? The fire chief. Andrew's associates at Lambert & Church. Debbie West. And Mitch, the deputy I told you about."

"I vote we start with the sheriff. But I have to meet Cara for lunch." Kelly checked her watch. "Why don't I meet you at the sheriff's station at two?"

"What? You don't want to invite me to do lunch?"

She rolled her eyes skyward. "You wouldn't be interested in our girl talk."

"You'd be surprised what interests me."

She waved him down the street. "Go away, Wade." Knowing from experience that there was no faster way to discourage his company, she added, "Besides lunch, I have some shopping to do."

OVER TUNA SALADS and Dr. Peppers in Dot's sandwich shop, Kelly filled Cara in, recapping her conversation with Doc about her brother's murder and Wade's offer to help figure out what had happened. The high-backed booth gave them some privacy, but Kelly kept her voice down below the croon of a Garth Brooks song over the speaker system, well aware that in small towns like Mustang Valley gossip traveled faster than e-mail.

"So Wade and I are talking to Sheriff Wilson next," Kelly told Cara, pleased with her progress and more determined than ever to keep asking questions.

Cara snapped a bread stick and swirled it in her dressing. "Back up. Slow down. What's with the Wade-and-me stuff?"

"He offered to help. I accepted."

"This is Cara you're talking to, sweetie." Cara crunched down on the bread stick and swallowed. "I happen to know you've had a crush on that guy since practically forever."

"*Had* being the operative word."

"Yeah, right."

The two friends exchanged glances and both chuckled. Kelly saw no point in hiding anything from Cara. Her friend might disapprove, she might speak her mind, but they always backed each other up.

When they were teenagers, Kelly's parents had been a big factor in the boys she'd chosen to date. But perhaps she should reconsider their influence. After all, she was no longer a kid but a college graduate.

"Okay. Wade's still got these very cool gray eyes. I admit it, there's a certain spark there. At least on my side. However, he's still treating me like Andrew's little sister."

"And you don't like it?"

"I like the way his chest and shoulders fill out his tacky T-shirt in all the right places." She held up a hand to stall Cara's protest. "But that doesn't mean I can't accept his help without becoming...involved. I don't judge a man on just his looks."

"Wade's not like those college guys you go with. He's dangerous. I don't like the idea of you and him together. It's like trusting a hungry wolf to guard a newborn calf."

"Andrew trusted him," Kelly countered.

"And look where he is now."

Kelly didn't bother to hide the pain that statement caused. "I can't believe you said that."

"Sorry. My reporter instincts took over. Going in for the kill to win an argument is my specialty." Cara reached over the table, her eyes filled with remorse, and patted Kelly's hand. "But hurting my friend is unacceptable."

Kelly shoved her half-eaten salad away. "Apology accepted. I guess I'm overly sensitive these days."

"Of course you're overly sensitive. Who wouldn't be after losing their brother? You're not yourself and that's one of the reasons I'm worried about you hanging out with Wade. I'll admit he can be useful. He knows almost everyone, and he and Andrew were tight."

"But?"

"But you're especially vulnerable right now. These last weeks have been rough. And you know Wade's reputation is..."

"Just say it."

"He's a hard man to read, and at the same time he's a gifted observer. I've seen him at work behind that bar. He can fix food and serve drinks and act totally absorbed in his work, but now and then it pops out how he's exceptionally aware of his customers. It's almost as if he senses trouble before it starts—like he has sensory antennae, alerting him to what is awry, out of place or simply off.''

''Those aren't bad traits.''

''Yeah, but he keeps his own counsel and runs that saloon like it's his own private kingdom. He's always in charge. I've seen him toss out three-hundred-pound drunks without breaking a sweat or resorting to pulling the knife he keeps strapped to his ankle.''

''He's a skilled marksman, too,'' Kelly added, recalling the picture Andrew had taken of Wade holding a trophy. ''He wins the skeet-shooting competition at the state fair every year. But so what if he doesn't need a bouncer at that saloon of his? Andrew says—said—Wade could be trusted. I figured if there's trouble, he's a good person to have on my side.''

''Yeah, as long as he's not gunning for you.'' Cara drummed her fingers on the table. ''Trouble has a way of finding that man. And the women, old and young, are still attracted to him like mares to a stallion.''

''Give me a little credit. We won't do anything that I don't want.''

Cara shot her a skeptical grin. ''And what exactly do you want from him?''

Kelly paid for their meal with a credit card. ''We can discuss it while you help me pick out a thoroughly intimidating new outfit.''

"You changing outfits for the sheriff or for Wade?" Cara asked.

"Stop grilling me," Kelly half demanded, half complained, knowing her friend meant well but would try to boss her until she put a stop to it. "I know what I'm doing."

"Sure you do." Cara checked her watch. "I don't have much time. Some of us have to work for a living."

Kelly rolled her eyes. "You love that job so much, if the *Mustang Gazette* didn't pay you, you'd work there for free."

"And I've got an interview lined up with Mayor Daniels over his election campaign."

"You're not working on one of your exposés where you've got to go undercover?" Kelly asked.

Cara shook her head. "Not this week, but stay tuned. Anyway, how about I catch up with you later?"

"Okay."

"And Kelly…"

"Yes?"

"Be careful."

"Would you please stop worrying? I'll be fine."

SURELY THAT COULDN'T BE Kelly waiting for him in front of the police station, wearing an outfit Wade classified between summer-break bragging and *Vogue* good-looking? He swallowed hard and reminded himself that his friend's little sister was taboo territory. The fact that Andrew was no longer alive to remind him didn't entitle Wade to forget she was off-limits.

Still, keeping his eyes above her neck was going to be more difficult than controlling a rowdy Saturday night crowd at the Hit 'Em Again Saloon. The contrast between her lace V-neck blouse and string of pearls that dipped between her breasts and her classic smile was almost enough to make Wade spin around and head elsewhere—except he'd promised Andrew to watch out for his little sister.

Wade sighed and kept walking with his teeth gritted in determination. He considered himself fairly knowledgeable about women and their clothes, but Kelly had knocked him off balance for the second time that day.

What in hell did she think she was doing? After working behind a bar he'd learned to recognize that the way a woman dressed said quite a bit about her personality and her mood. Kelly always wore classy, expensive, designer stuff that said hands off. Now her expensive fitted lace blouse stretched across a chest that had suddenly grown ample—no doubt due to some clever underwires designed to tease and entice.

Judging by the heat shooting directly south, he was ''enticed'' all right. *Down boy.* Kelly was still Kelly. First and foremost she was one high-maintenance lady. Her manicures alone likely cost more than his electric bill.

He had no doubt she was dressing this way for a reason. If she thought the sheriff might be distracted, she would likely be proven correct. No red-blooded male could possibly look at her without his mouth watering. She still wore her hair up, but some of it now tumbled down, curling around her face, one jaunty lock over the corner of her left eye. And those knotted pearls that tucked into the hollow of her breasts taunted his fingers to touch.

She waved at him and the movement caused her breasts to rise, drawing his gaze to her chest. "Nice."

She eyed him with a glint of amusement. "You think I look good in blue?"

"I wasn't talking about your shirt."

"Oh." For a moment her eyes widened as if startled, then she eased into a dangerous smile and looped her arm through his. "Good."

He didn't know what he thought when she didn't act the least insulted by his direct reference to her assets. On the one hand, she seemed more touchable by showing a hint of skin, but contradictorily, he wanted her more than he ever had before. Sure, he'd noticed that Kelly was cute, but he'd never really considered getting together with her. First, there had been Andrew who wouldn't have been pleased, and second, there had always been this unbreakable wall between them. However, the wall had cracks, ones he couldn't seem to stop himself from peeping through.

He frowned at her. "You going to tell me exactly what you're up to before we go inside?"

"Sheriff Wilson already thinks I'm a piece of fluff." She didn't sound resentful, just stated the obvious. "So I went out of my way to reinforce his attitude by buying this shirt."

"Why?"

"Suppose he's hiding more than the fact that my brother was murdered?"

"Like what?"

Wade didn't believe that just because the sheriff wore a badge that he was an upright citizen. But he had no quarrels with the man, either. Wilson's deputies left the saloon alone and Wade took care not to give them reasons to hassle him or his patrons. And he'd like to keep it that way.

"I don't know," she said. Together they entered the Sheriff's Department. "That's why we're here. To ask questions."

"Okay." He wondered if she had a plan or intended to play this by ear. He also wondered if those tight jeans made her hips appear to sway more than usual or if she'd deliberately changed her walk to a sexy swagger.

Kelly headed straight to the front desk, seemingly unaware of the attention several deputies gave her. "We're here to see Sheriff Wilson."

"You have an appointment?" asked a male receptionist who wore a headset and didn't look up from his computer.

"No, sir. But it's real important that I talk to him."

"I'm sure it is." The male officer looked up, then looked again before dismissing her. "He's busy, but if you care to wait..."

Kelly leaned forward and whispered loudly, "You don't understand, sir. This is *personal*. My brother died and I have so many unanswered questions. Sheriff Wilson would much prefer hearing what I have to say in private. However, if you insist, I could go public..."

Wade clamped his teeth together to prevent himself from grinning. Kelly had insinuated that she had crucial information about Andrew and if the desk officer knew what was good for him, he'd give them immediate access to his boss.

The officer pushed a few buttons on a speakerphone, then mumbled into his microphone before jerking his thumb down the hall. "The sheriff will see you now. Third door on your left."

Sheriff Wilson sat in a loose gray uniform behind his desk, a burning cigar in his hand despite the No Smoking sign on the building's front doors. In his fifties, tall and rangy, he had tough, leathery skin that bespoke a hard life-style.

His gaze wandered from Kelly's face to her chest and stayed there until Wade cleared his throat. But that only earned Wade a scowl from Kelly before she turned a high-wattage grin on the sheriff.

"What can I do for you, Kelly?"

"Sheriff, I just wanted to thank you for all your help. It was kind of you to come to my brother's funeral."

"I'm truly sorry for your loss."

Wade wondered where she was going with this conversation. He could tell Sheriff Wilson was just as curious and antsy. No doubt he had more important things on his plate.

Kelly's tone turned weepy. "My brother…he was very special to me. Everyone loved Andrew. I just don't understand why anyone would have wanted to murder him." She opened her purse, removed a tissue and dabbed at her eyes that brimmed with tears.

"Murder?" The sheriff looked from Wade to

Kelly, ignoring his smoking cigar. "Who said anything about murder?"

Wade didn't say a word, but marveled at how she was manipulating the sheriff with her antics. Kelly was just full of surprises. He recalled Kelly had starred in a play during her senior year of high school, but she hadn't displayed this kind of emotional depth back then. Obviously, her acting abilities had improved and Wade wondered if she was playing him, too. But since he'd already agreed to help her, what would be her angle?

Kelly sobbed and her chest quivered. "Wasn't Andrew shot with an 11 mm gun?"

"No, 9 mm." The sheriff's gaze snapped upward from her chest as he realized what he'd just admitted. He raised the cigar to his lips and puffed, probably stalling as he considered his options. "May I ask how you learned—"

Kelly let the tissue trail over her neck. "I want to know who did it."

"The case is under investigation."

"Sheriff, I know you must be doing everything you can, but it's been weeks and weeks. My parents will be devastated to learn that Andrew's death wasn't an accident and that his murderer is still free."

The sheriff didn't exactly squirm in his seat but a bead of sweat broke out on his brow. Kelly's father was a powerful man in Mustang Valley and the sheriff needed his support to keep his job. That he'd kept a secret about Andrew's murder from Mr. McGovern wouldn't sit well with Kelly's father.

The sheriff stubbed out his cigar in an ashtray,

reached across his desk and patted her shoulder. "Look, there's no point in telling your parents what really happened until I find Andrew's killer."

"I don't understand. His family knew him best. Surely we can help, and you haven't even asked us any questions." Kelly's eyes opened wide. "Unless you consider us suspects?"

"Of course not." The sheriff spoke soothingly, patronizingly. Police procedure dictated that everyone would be a suspect until proven otherwise. "Sometimes it's better to keep an investigation quiet. We don't want to scare away the suspect. We want to catch him, right?"

Kelly sniffled. "Yes."

"So let me do my job, okay?"

Wade figured he'd been silent long enough. "Sheriff, I believe Kelly would like you to keep her informed of your investigation."

"Yes, please," Kelly piped in, twisting the screws some more. "That would make me feel ever so much better in keeping a secret from Daddy."

Sheriff Wilson shook his head. "I'm not at liberty to share the facts in this case with you. However, after we catch your brother's killer, Kelly, I assure you that you'll be the first to know."

"Just how long do you expect that to take?"

"I wish I could tell you. I'd like nothing better than to solve this case and put a murderer behind bars, but I won't make you a promise I can't keep. I just don't know how long our investigation will take."

Kelly stuffed the tissue back into her purse, her eyes once again dry. "Thank you, Sheriff. I guess there's no reason to upset Daddy. For now. But promise me...you will place your best deputies on this?''

''Absolutely.''

Wade shook hands with the sheriff and escorted Kelly from the building. ''That was quite a performance.''

As soon as they strode out, she dropped the sexy walk. Her voice turned tart. ''I'd hoped to learn more. A 9 mm is a real popular gun, isn't it?''

''Yeah. And considering this is Texas, that information may not help us much.''

''Maybe I'll learn more at Lambert & Church. I'm heading there next.''

''Uh, Kelly.''

''Yeah?''

''You changing clothes again?''

She winked at him. ''Absolutely.''

Chapter Three

Kelly didn't know if any of the partners would be in at Lambert & Church, but she assumed one of the associates would have time to talk to her—even if she and Wade arrived without an appointment. She'd changed into the conservative navy suit with gold buttons that she'd picked out that morning and added hose, shoes and a bag to match before pulling her hair back and up into a severe bun. In the rest room at the *Mustang Gazette*, she wiped off most of her makeup and peered at herself in the mirror. She looked like one of those clueless summer law clerks whom Andrew had always liked to tease. In other words, perfectly unremarkable.

With Wade waiting for her to exit, she took a deep breath, hurriedly stashed her jeans and lace top in Cara's office, then headed through the front doors of the busy building. Outside, the humidity had risen along with the temperature into the mideighties. Gray clouds scudded across the sky, threatening a May shower. Azaleas and bluebonnets bloomed in hanging baskets along the sidewalk. And the townsfolk nodded friendly hellos or tipped their hats to passersby.

They strode past Mayor Daniels's campaign headquarters where red, white and blue balloons attached to parking meters outside whipped about in the wind. A banner had come loose and flapped, a broken cord dangling.

"Andrew told me you were a fashion plate, but I thought he exaggerated," Wade teased as he walked beside her wearing the same jeans and dark blue shirt he'd worn since this morning.

"Dressing for the part gives me confidence."

"You look like confidence personified."

"Thank you," she said as self-assurance welled up in her.

Kelly was surprised his patience with her investigation hadn't worn thin by now, but although his long legs ate up a steady pace on the sidewalk, he didn't hurry her. He also didn't pepper her with questions. Unlike the men she'd dated, some of whom could have filled up the Grand Canyon with their compliments, Wade's simple words touched her. That he actually seemed willing to let her take the lead, she appreciated even more.

Wade opened the door for her at Lambert & Church and the cool air-conditioning caused goose bumps to form on her skin. Or perhaps it was the stench of the burned annex out back where Andrew had died. Although a construction company had cleared the burned timbers, the scorched earth still reeked of smoke.

Kelly headed straight for the receptionist. "Hi, Wanda." She greeted the friendly woman who answered the phones and guarded passage to the inner sanctum. "I'd like to speak with Mr. Lambert or Mr. Church, please."

"Sorry, Kelly. Mr. Lambert's in court and Mr. Church has a meeting with Mayor Daniels." Wanda spoke softly. "I want to tell you again how sorry I am about Andrew. We all miss him."

"Thanks."

Beside her Wade squeezed her hand as if he realized how difficult it still was for her to talk about the loss of her brother. But for Andrew's sake, she had to be strong.

"If there's anything I can do—" Wanda's phone rang and she answered it, then transferred the call. "If you like, I can make you an appointment for next week."

Kelly was considering the time slots Wanda offered her just as Lindsey Wellington breezed through the front doors. Kelly recognized the woman lawyer as one of Andrew's co-workers but didn't know her well. A newcomer to Mustang Valley, Lindsey wore her blouse buttoned up to her neck and a long-sleeved jacket as if she still lived in Boston, where Kelly knew she was from.

"Kelly McGovern." Lindsey shifted her documents and stuck out her hand, shaking Kelly's then Wade's as Kelly made introductions.

Lindsey shoved back her shiny brown hair and surveyed them with piercing blue eyes. "I didn't expect you so soon. But please come into my office."

"You're expecting me?" Kelly looked at Wade, who shrugged and appeared puzzled, too.

"Would you like a cup of coffee, tea or a soda?"

Lindsey asked as they followed her into her office where stacks of legal documents perched on top of file cabinets and flowed in a river across the floor. In contrast, her desk was immaculate.

"No, thanks," Kelly answered for both of them.

Lindsey walked behind her desk, opened a closet door and spoke over her shoulder. "You didn't get my phone message?"

"I'm afraid not."

"Well, I'm glad you came." Lindsey picked up a carton and set it down on her desk right in front of them in a forthright manner. "Before I moved in here, Andrew had this office. When he relocated to the annex, he forgot to take some of his things. I thought you'd want them."

At the familiar smell of Andrew's faded brown leather jacket, Kelly's throat clogged and her voice hitched. "Thanks."

"There's not much here." Lindsey's tone, although brusque and polite, still managed to convey sympathy. "A few family pictures. Some work notes. Just old memos and junk he forgot to move."

That old junk was all she had left of her brother. Oh, God. Kelly hadn't known this would be so hard. Dealing with his death struck her at the oddest and most unexpected times.

She grappled for self-control. Wade had taken a chair beside her, seemed to understand her difficulty and inserted himself smoothly into the conversation. "Lindsey, did Andrew have any enemies here?"

Lindsey's eyes widened. "At the firm? Everyone gets along."

"What about clients?" Wade persisted. "Surely

Andrew might have had a few criminals who believed he could have defended them better?''

"Possibly. But they're in jail." Lindsey frowned, her gaze cutting from Wade to Kelly with sharp suspicion. "What's all this about? And why are you here if you didn't get my message?"

Kelly finally collected herself by ignoring that box of Andrew's. "We don't think the fire was an accident." She didn't reveal that the killer had used the fire to cover up a shooting. If the sheriff wanted to keep his investigation quiet, Kelly would abide by the man's wishes.

"You're implying the fire was deliberate?" Lindsey spoke in her strong Boston accent. "We're talking murder?"

"Yes," Kelly admitted. "But please keep this to yourself. The sheriff wants it that way."

"All right. I always liked your brother." Lindsey sounded both sympathetic and careful. Clearly cautious and holding back, she peered at them as if trying to make up her mind about something.

"What?" Kelly's heart hammered her ribs. "If you know anything that might help us figure out who killed my brother…anything at all," Kelly pleaded, "tell us."

"I probably shouldn't—"

"—but you will."

"—give you this." Lindsey opened a file cabinet and used a key to unlock a compartment. "Andrew was working on these papers right before he died. It's a copy of a file." Lindsey spilled the rest. "I think Andrew left this here for safekeeping, but I have no idea why."

"What is it?" Wade asked.

"It's a contract offer to buy the family ranch of Andrew's girlfriend."

Debbie's family was moving? Andrew had never said a word to Kelly about it, but then, he didn't like to talk about his girlfriend since the family had clearly disapproved of her. And due to that lack of communication, Kelly had no idea if this file could be important. Perhaps Wade knew more than she did, and she made a mental note to ask him about Debbie and her family later.

Wade reached for the documents. "Is there anything unusual about the offer?"

"None that I can see." Lindsey frowned at them. "But maybe you should talk to the family."

"We will." Kelly stood. "Everything you've told us is confidential. No one will know where those papers came from. After all, Andrew could have left them at home."

Lindsey motioned her to sit. "There's one more person you might question."

"Who?"

"I shouldn't be telling you this." Lindsey shrugged, then sighed. "But I'd like to see justice done."

"I don't want to compromise your position, but any help you can give us would be appreciated."

Lindsey gestured with her hands. "It's nothing that wasn't reported in the *Mustang Gazette* just a few months ago."

"I was away at college then," Kelly told her.

"Andrew represented Sean McCardel during his divorce last year. Apparently the client wasn't satisfied with his representation. When the judge awarded full custody of the kids to his wife, he blamed Andrew. Apparently the man blew up on the courthouse steps, vowing to get even. Of course, it may have just been talk.''

Kelly would ask Cara. If her friend hadn't covered the story, she would know who had. Kelly stood, walked around the desk and hugged Lindsey. ''Thanks so much for all your help.''

WADE DIDN'T WANT to be impressed with the way Kelly had handled Lindsey, but he was. As he carried Andrew's box to her pretty new silver Jaguar and stowed it in the trunk, he realized that Kelly had displayed the exact right mix of sympathy and determination to elicit Lindsey's help. Kelly might look and act like a fashion plate, but she had keen instincts about people. While he wouldn't call her tactics outright manipulation, he would call them brilliant. The way she won people to her cause, Mayor Daniels would have been smart to have hired her on his campaign staff.

Already today she'd learned from the doctor that Andrew hadn't died in an accidental fire but from a bullet. The sheriff had admitted to her that the gun was a 9 mm, and now Lindsey had just given her several new leads. And they hadn't yet had time to go through Andrew's box.

Kelly glanced up at the darkening thunderclouds. ''I want to change back into jeans before we head out to Debbie's ranch. Could we please take your truck?''

''Good idea.'' Not only would Debbie's family

resent her pulling up to their struggling ranch in her nifty new sports car, but with the storm brewing and the roads slick, he'd rather have four-wheel drive. "I'm parked behind the saloon."

Ten minutes later the storm broke, drenching his truck, but they were ensconced safe and dry inside. He switched on his lights and wipers, almost turned up the country station but decided he'd rather talk to Kelly instead—which rocked him back in his seat. Wade had always liked women. He liked their scents, their smiles, the way they moved. And he especially enjoyed how Kelly sugarcoated her determination with an ultra femininity that conveyed a strength he'd never suspected.

He found her too damn attractive and wondered if she was playing him just as she'd done with the doc, the sheriff and Lindsey. He didn't like that idea at all, but he also didn't understand why it bothered him as much as it did. What was it about her that called to him? Perhaps she was simply his last living tie to Andrew, his best friend since high school.

Wade turned onto the highway. The heavy downpour had caused several cars to pull under the overpass to wait out the storm. With the large-size tires on his truck, he had good traction and the large cab gave him decent visibility, so he proceeded with caution.

"Tell me about Debbie," Kelly requested, her eyes focused before them on the road, her tone firm—and yet he sensed a hesitancy to pry into Andrew's private life.

He risked a glance at her. Her eyes looked troubled. "What do you want to know?"

She rested her hands loosely in her lap. The air-conditioning cleared the moisture from the windshield and carried her scent to him, making the cab seem intimate and cozy, especially with the rain pattering the roof.

"Andrew was going to bring her home to Sunday breakfast. He didn't care what our folks thought. He was certain of his choice and determined to marry her. But did he love her? Or was he rebelling against my father?"

Astute questions and ones Wade wasn't sure he knew the answers to. "He didn't talk much about her to me."

"But you saw them together?"

"He brought her to the saloon most Saturday nights."

"And?"

"And what?" Distinct discomfort about answering her questions made him stall.

"What was your impression of her?"

He reminded himself that betraying Andrew wasn't possible. The most he could do for his dead friend was help his sister seek justice. "If you're asking me if Debbie was with Andrew because he was successful and had a bright future or because she loved him, I wouldn't know."

"You're holding out on me," Kelly complained. "I'm not asking you for facts—just your impression. Certainly you must have given some thought to Andrew's choice in a wife?"

"Frankly, I thought he could do better." Wade swerved around fallen debris on the highway. "But you know Andrew—"

"He wanted to fix the world."

"Exactly. He liked to be needed and therefore he tended to pick women in distress."

"What did Debbie need from him besides legal help with her property?"

Kelly obviously didn't know much at all, and Wade found himself reluctant to reveal his friend's secrets. First, he didn't want to cause the McGovern family more pain. Second, he had to remind himself once again that Andrew was dead and talking to his sister wasn't a betrayal. Still he knew his revelation would come as a shock and braced himself before speaking sympathetically. "Debbie had been married and divorced."

"You're sure?" Kelly's brows lifted in surprise and consternation.

"Yeah."

"How could I not know that? How could my *parents* not know that? Mustang Valley is simply too small for gossip not to have reached us. Daddy has all kinds of connections and not even Cara knew Debbie was married, because she would have told me."

"According to Andrew, Debbie married Niles Deagen after she got pregnant her sophomore year in high school."

Kelly gulped. "She has a child?"

"She had a miscarriage. So the hush-hush elopement and Vegas wedding were unnecessary after all. She wanted the marriage annulled, but Niles wouldn't agree to it, although he did keep it quiet to avoid looking like a fool."

Trouble seemed to follow Debbie like a dark

shadow. While Wade had nothing against her personally, he always had felt she came attached to too many problems. Which was exactly why Andrew no doubt had found her irresistible. His friend had a thing for the underdog, while Wade preferred to keep things simple.

So what was he doing with Kelly? Because sure as hell, there was nothing simple about her. She came with her own set of problems that slowly but surely were becoming his. But even if he could withhold his help, he could never deny Andrew the justice he deserved.

"Why would he look foolish for marrying Debbie?" Kelly asked with an innocence that made him realize once again how protected she'd been. Her folks had made sure she'd only seen the better side of life. Wade didn't blame them. Kelly had a special spark around her that caused optimism in others. She saw the up side in people, expected the best and was rarely disappointed.

"Debbie was sixteen. Her husband was thirty-eight."

"Oh."

"Andrew finally helped her obtain a messy divorce. I heard that Niles still wants her, but that's rumor—not fact."

Kelly didn't let the nasty facts deter her from plunging right in to find out more. "Niles Deagen. Why does that name sound so familiar?"

"He's a big-time Dallas oil man, with a penchant for teenage girls."

"But Debbie's no longer a kid."

"She still looks like a kid. She's flat-chested and

slender-hipped and has that round baby face that makes her appear about twelve.''

Wade didn't understand the man. Wade liked his women full-grown and grown-up. While Kelly would fit his physical requirements, he usually dated women who wanted nothing more from him than a good time. Instinctively he knew that when Kelly hooked up with a man, she would be thinking about the possibility of happily ever after.

Kelly shot him a sharp glance. ''You think Niles could have had anything to do with Andrew's murder?''

''That would be pure speculation.'' But the thought had occurred to Wade. More than once. However, he didn't have a shred of evidence to back up that hunch.

''If he's an oil man, he has the means and a motive.'' Kelly sighed. ''I never thought finding Andrew's killer would be simple, but the more I learn, the more complicated this seems. I keep adding suspects to my list and haven't eliminated anyone.''

He didn't like the idea of Kelly getting discouraged. Not when she'd done such a good job of keeping herself together.

''Hey, chin up. Today's only the first day. You're doing great.''

''Maybe I should ask Daddy to hire a private investigator.''

''You could.''

''But?''

''He'd be a stranger to Mustang Valley, and the folks here don't open up to outsiders.'' And then

Wade wouldn't have an excuse to spend more time with her.

"I imagine you hear all kinds of gossip in your saloon." She hit him with one of those innocent-sounding, sideways comments that made it difficult to anticipate where she was taking the conversation.

"We've been busy lately. That means I have to draft lots of beer and rustle up my Texas-famous chili. You stop by sometime and I'll serve you up a bowl—on the house."

"Thanks." As if uncomfortable with the notion of them spending time together for any reason other than Andrew, she changed the subject. "So what hot buttons have stirred up the town lately? Does Tony Barker have a shot at defeating Mayor Daniels?"

"I doubt it."

"That's what Cara said, too. Tony was a friend of Andrew's, I should probably stop by and see him."

"Even Andrew, as much as he liked the underdog, didn't think Tony had a chance of defeating the mayor. Daniels's contributors have deep pockets, and the town isn't much interested in local politics these days. Folks are more concerned about the price of beef, land, oil and—"

"What's wrong?"

"Maybe nothing."

She caught him scanning his rearview mirror, glanced over her shoulder, spied the tow truck with its flashing yellow lights. "It's Aaron's Towing. Probably someone broke down in the rain."

Wade checked his speedometer. Fifty-five. The tow truck must be barreling down the highway at eighty mph to be closing the distance between them so fast. It wasn't as if the truck was an emergency vehicle with lives at stake, so to be driving at that speed in the stormy weather wasn't just reckless, but brainless.

Wade pulled over, steering his tires onto the shoulder to give the big truck ample room to pass.

"Wade! He's not passing." Kelly tightened her seat belt and braced her feet on the dash. "He's going to hit us."

Wade overrode his first instinct to hit the brakes. A collision at a slower speed would cause a more forceful impact. Instead he jammed his foot on the gas and took satisfaction as his truck lunged forward.

Kelly tugged on his arm. "Are you crazy?"

"I'm not racing him. I'm trying to avoid a crash." In his mirror he glimpsed the tow truck gaining on him and shook her hand off his arm. "Let me drive."

"He's catching us. I thought this truck was fast."

"It is. But he had a head start." Wade checked the mirror. The tow truck couldn't be more than a few car lengths behind. "Hold on."

"Like I have something else to do?" she muttered.

Wade prayed his truck could pick up enough speed to avoid a crash. But he hadn't recognized the threat soon enough. His late reaction might get them both killed.

"Do something else," Kelly insisted.

He yanked the wheel. Tires screeched and burned rubber. He steered the truck off the road and thanked God for the flat and rolling land of Texas. They smacked through the guardrail and suddenly the truck was airborne. Kelly let out a gasp. He braced for impact, praying the truck wouldn't roll. Praying the tow truck wouldn't come down on top of them. Praying Kelly and he would survive.

Before death, one's entire life was supposed to flash before him. But all Wade could think about was failing in his promise to Andrew—that he'd failed to take care of Kelly McGovern.

The truck bounced hard. Rolled. Crunched. A vortex of metal spun them and then spit him out.

WADE DIDN'T REMEMBER the truck stopping. Why was he out of the truck when he'd been wearing his seat belt? He'd come to, flat on his back with the rain pelting his face. He had no idea how long he'd been unconscious, but he was soaked to the skin and shivering. The thunderstorm still raged full force, and the sky had darkened with the sun setting behind the clouds.

For a moment he was tempted to just lie there. But then the accident came rushing back. Kelly. He had to find her. She might need him.

He tasted blood, sat up and spit. Despite his seat belt, he'd been thrown out of the truck. Every muscle in his body roared in pain, but he forced himself to his feet, staggered to his truck.

His truck lay upside down, the cab crushed inward, the windshield a spiderweb of cracks on one side, the passenger's window long gone. Bending and dreading what he would find, Wade peered inside. Between the rain and the fading light, he wondered if he could be hallucinating.

The truck was empty.

Just to make sure, he crawled inside, praying her body wasn't wedged against the floorboards. His hand caught on the seat belt strap and tugged free. The end had clearly been slashed with a sharp object, probably leaving just a few frail threads intact, which had torn during the crash.

The chance of one seat belt failing had to be astronomically high. The chance of both of them failing at the same time meant that someone had wanted them dead.

A prickle of ice stabbed down his spine. Wade crawled deeper inside the cab. He felt around, ignoring the bits of glass that sliced his flesh.

Nada.

He wriggled back out, confused and breathing hard.

Think.

His cell phone had been crushed. Calling for help wasn't an option.

The tow truck was nowhere to be seen. The highway stretched empty ahead and behind as far as he could see.

Perhaps Kelly had been thrown out of the vehicle like he'd been. She could be lying by the road hurt...or worse. Wade pried open his toolbox and retrieved his flashlight.

After a thorough search, he slumped next to his truck in despair.

No one had passed by in all that time, and he hadn't found any sign of Kelly at all. She was gone.

Chapter Four

Dazed and wet, Kelly shivered in the front seat of a passenger car. She couldn't recall climbing inside the vehicle, couldn't recall the driver's name, couldn't remember anything that had happened since leaving Lambert & Church over an hour ago.

Her head ached, and every time she turned it, a sharp pain sliced down her neck. Her palms stung from road rash and each whipped muscle in her body smarted when she breathed.

The friendly woman driver said she'd found Kelly stumbling down the highway, but Kelly didn't remember that, either. With her scraped palms and wet clothes, she must have been in an accident. Thank God she didn't have total amnesia. She knew who she was and recalled her entire life, everything except the last hour—no doubt due to the golf ball-size knot near her temple.

Kelly looked at her clothes for clues. She wasn't dressed for riding her horse. Jasper hadn't thrown her and left her for greener grass. As Kelly tried to recall what had happened, the pain in her head sharpened, but she forced herself back to her last coherent memory.

She and Wade had been about to...Wade. Something must have happened to him. And suddenly it all came back, the tow truck, Wade's truck rolling, her smacking her head and awakening in the rain. Wade was probably back at the accident site.

"Please, turn around," Kelly requested.

"I need to get you to a doctor," the Good Samaritan driver insisted with gentle firmness. In the dim light of the car's interior, the woman's white hair fluffed around her face in an attractive manner.

"You don't understand." The driver's name came back to her in a flash. "Peggy, I was in an accident. And I wasn't alone. We have to go back."

Peggy plucked a cell phone from her purse. "We'll call 911 and they'll send police and an ambulance."

"But we're closer." Kelly fought down rising panic. "Suppose he bleeds to death. I can't just drive off with you and leave him lying there. Please, turn around."

"Okay, but I didn't *see* any accident." Peggy called 911 and reported the situation, then spoke calmly to Kelly. "When I found you, you were all alone."

Kelly's panic subsided a little as Peggy pulled a U-turn. "Wade swerved off the road to avoid the tow truck." And now, in the dark, they could ride right by and not see him or the truck. "Can you find the spot where you picked me up?"

"I doubt it. This road looks the same for miles

and miles. But we can try, dear. Tell me about your fellah. Is he a good man?''

''He's not mine. He's a friend of my brother's, and yes, he's a good man.'' Funny how she'd answered without hesitation. Wade might have a dangerous reputation, he might have lived a rough life, but he could be counted on, and she instinctively trusted him. ''He was trying to help me....''

Oh, God. If anything had happened to him because he had been helping her, she might never forgive herself. She shouldn't have gotten him involved. Her hands shook and she twisted them in her lap, peering through the dark windshield, praying she might spy his truck. A taillight. Something.

She tried to tell herself she would have had the same nauseous worry in her gut over the welfare of anyone who'd been riding with her, but Kelly wasn't accustomed to lying to herself. She liked Wade. Really liked him.

Perhaps someone else had picked up Wade and even now he was back in Mustang Valley, taking a hot shower. No. Wade wasn't the kind of man to leave her behind. If he'd been able, if he'd been conscious, he would have found her. He wouldn't have left her.

If only she had remembered what had happened sooner.

Please let him be all right, she prayed.

The driver began to slow. ''I think I found you around here.''

In the dark, this part of the highway looked exactly the same as the rest to Kelly. ''Can you please pull onto the shoulder and turn on your high beams?''

"It would help if we knew which side of the road you crashed on,'' Peggy suggested, but did as Kelly asked.

Oh, no. Kelly almost smacked her forehead, but memory of her head injury stopped her hand in mid-motion. "I'm not thinking clearly. We were on the other side of the road, heading *out* of town.''

"You're sure?''

"Yes.''

"All right. Let's stay on this side for two miles,'' Peggy recommended. "I'll keep track on the odometer and then I'll turn around and head back again. But if we don't see anything, I'm taking you into town. Deal?''

Kelly knew Peggy meant well, but she wasn't leaving. Not until she found Wade. She peered up ahead and across the highway and saw movement. Then a light flashed on and off, then back on again. A headlight? A reflector?

"Look!'' Kelly pointed.

Peggy angled the car and slowed even more. "That's a man with a flashlight waving us down.''

"It's Wade.'' They were too far away to make out his features, but she knew it had to be him. And the fact that he was well enough to stand by the road and signal made her heart thump wildly against her ribs. He was alive.

The future suddenly seemed brighter. As relief and delight raced through her, she realized that she didn't want to waste more time playing silly games. She wanted to get to know Wade better, and she didn't mind in the least making her feelings clear to him. But she also feared that her growing attraction to Wade might be her way of hanging on to memories of her brother. Andrew had been such a great guy and she'd hated losing him. She didn't understand how anyone would have wanted to kill him. But Andrew, of all people, would have wanted her to be honest with his best friend.

Whatever happened between her and Wade—she wasn't going to hide. Not from herself. Not from him. Life was too precious to squander their days. Or their nights.

A moment later Peggy pulled another turn and stopped. Kelly slid out of the passenger seat and ran toward him, her adrenaline rushing, her mouth dry, her pulse pounding. "Are you all right?"

"I'm fine—now that you're here." Wade's arms closed around her. His shirt was soaked and bloody, but he didn't hesitate to draw her to him. His skin was icy cold, and she snuggled against him, trying to give him some of the warmth she'd gained from the car's heater.

Her parents must have been wrong about Wade, since being within the circle of his arms seemed so right. And perhaps it was time to make her own decisions. She would no longer live solely for her parents' approval. She was a grown woman and could make her own choices. Kelly wanted to tell Wade about her epiphany about him, how she'd realized she'd been suppressing her feelings for no good reason other than a schoolgirl habit, but with Peggy there to overhear every word, she couldn't say what she wanted to.

Wade hugged her for what seemed like much too short a time before stepping back. "I've been searching for you since I woke up."

"After I hit my head, I was dazed. Peggy picked me up as I walked along the highway. It took a while until my memory of the accident came back."

"And then she insisted we turn around and find you," Peggy told him. "I've phoned 911 and the deputies and emergency medical should be here soon. Why don't we all wait in my car where it's warm?"

It seemed like forever until the police wrapped up their investigation. Kelly sat in the back of Peggy's car, snuggling against Wade's side. He tried to move away, but after she claimed she was chilled, wrapped his arm over her shoulder and allowed her to snuggle against him.

After Wade told her about the slashed seat belts, she should have been alarmed. When the deputy informed them that the tow truck had been reported stolen just hours ago, she should have felt doubly unsafe, but she didn't. With Wade's comforting arms around her, she relaxed amid an overpowering belief that they would be all right, that they would find Andrew's killer.

After the paramedics checked her and Wade and they both refused further medical care, they learned that another deputy had found the tow truck several miles up the highway.

And there was no sign of the driver.

DEPUTY MITCH WARWICK gave Wade and Kelly a lift back to Mustang Valley. Kelly had thanked

Peggy for all of her help. A tow truck would haul Wade's totalled vehicle back in the morning. However, Wade's primary concern was not his truck but Kelly's safety.

Maybe he was overreacting, but Wade preferred for Kelly to stay with him rather than go home to her parents' house tonight. Before he broached that controversial topic, he wanted backup, and Mitch seemed just the level-headed guy to agree with him.

In the back seat of the deputy's car, Wade spoke to Kelly, but loudly enough for Mitch to hear, too. "Our questions about Andrew's death today rattled someone badly enough to attempt murder."

"Mustang Valley doesn't have enough law enforcement to protect anyone 24/7. Have you considered leaving town?" Mitch asked from the driver's seat.

The early-evening storm had come and gone, leaving behind a chilly drizzle and even more questions than Wade had that morning. And more suspects. He'd thought he'd known Andrew fairly well, but if he hadn't known Andrew had been murdered, he would never have believed his friend could have stirred up this kind of animosity against him.

"I do have a business to run," Wade answered. Although he had a manager to take care of the saloon when he wasn't there, his personal touch was required to keep things running smoothly.

"I live here," Kelly added. "I can't just turn tail and run. I owe it to my brother to find out what happened."

Mitch took the highway's exit to Mustang Valley.

"Your brother wouldn't have wanted you in danger."

So the level-headed Mitch believed Kelly might still be in danger, too. That confirmation was all Wade required to speak his mind. "Kelly, I'd feel better if you spent the night with me."

"I'm sure you would."

Wade couldn't see her face but heard the amusement in her tone and chuckled. "I'm serious."

"So am I."

"You'd be safer with me. And you don't want to endanger your folks, do you?"

"I could stay with Cara." Kelly didn't sound sure, as if she hadn't considered her plans until now and had yet to make up her mind.

"You really believe two women alone would be less of a target?"

"What kind of target would I be at your place?" Kelly asked, her tone cool.

At her smart comment, Mitch choked back a laugh and Wade had to restrain one as well. However, if the situation wasn't so serious, he would have enjoyed teasing her right back.

Instead, he kept his voice thoughtful. "This isn't about you and me."

"Now I think I'm insulted," she muttered.

This time Wade definitely heard a chuckle from the front seat. How unbelievable that she could feel snubbed when he wouldn't make a move toward her. What nonsense. Out of respect for Andrew, he would keep his hands off her. In fact, if she hadn't claimed to be cold, he wouldn't have allowed her to nestle up against him like a sunbathing cat. "Would you care to elaborate?"

"If you can't admit the basic chemistry between us, you aren't ready for the advanced class."

"You go, girl." Mitch egged her on.

"Enough comments from the peanut gallery," Wade snapped at the deputy before turning back to Kelly. "In case you've forgotten, someone murdered your brother. Probably that same someone tried to kill us this afternoon."

"And we survived. While I understand the need to be careful, I refuse to let my life be dictated by a killer." Wade opened his mouth to interrupt but she kept talking. "Daddy bought me the cutest little Saturday night special for my birthday and I keep it in the glove compartment of my Jag."

"Do you know how to use the gun?" Wade asked, wondering if Andrew had been aware that his little sister carried a gun.

"It's loaded. Daddy said all I needed to know was how to point it and pull the trigger."

"You've never fired the gun?" Wade asked, keeping his voice mild while his anger spiked at her father's irresponsibility. Without practice, the first time she fired the gun, she was as likely to shoot herself as her intended target.

"I've never needed to even take it out of the special pink leather case." She drew herself up proud and straight. "I don't exactly hang out with the kind of people who need shooting."

"And I do?"

She patted his shoulder. "Now I've gone and ruffled your male feathers. I didn't say anything about who you hang with. How could I, when I don't even *know* your friends. Ever since we met up at Doc's this morning, I've known I felt safer with you than going on alone.'' Aggravation edged her tone. ''That's why I accepted your help in the first place. So I think, yes, I'll spend the night with you, Wade. Now make me a happy woman and tell me I can have the bed.''

Hmm. Talk about smooth. She was accepting his invitation and setting rules at the same time. ''What about that great chemistry you said we shared?''

''That's all we're going to share—for tonight, anyway. I'm not in the mood for romance. I have an ugly knot on the side of my head and God knows how many bruises. My blouse is ripped and my shoes scuffed so badly I don't know if I can ever wear them again. Right now a hot bath, clean sheets and a good night's sleep sound like heaven.''

''I can do better than a hot bath.''

''Really?''

''My back deck has a hot tub. If you're not going to let my fingers soothe away your aches and pains, the jets should do the trick.''

She winked at him. ''I didn't bring a swimsuit. But then, I don't suppose that matters, does it?''

DESPITE ASSORTED CUTS and bruises the thought of a nude Kelly in Wade's hot tub caused an immediate and disturbing tingle, then blood surged south. He unlocked the front door of the ranch house that his uncle had left him along with the saloon, hoping her interest in his home would distract her from his too-tight jeans.

He flicked on a light, then adjusted the dimmer to low. "Home, sweet home."

She spun around, taking in the wooden-planked walls, the old two-man hand saw hanging above the sofa, the tan furniture and the shelves of books that lined the wall opposite the stone fireplace. She inspected the only picture he had of his parents, another of him and Andrew and grinned at the blooming white orchid in his kitchen window.

"I'd never have suspected that you liked flowers."

He raised an eyebrow. "There's probably lots you don't know about me."

No doubt she didn't even suspect that he'd read every book on his shelves, either. But then again, he'd seen her father's vast library in his home office and had thought the same thing of Mr. McGovern. But while her father's collection of thick leather volumes looked shiny and new, the pages uncreased— at least, the few he'd thumbed through—Wade's books were worn and frayed, comfortable and familiar friends to get him through some hard nights.

"What would you like first? Food? Coffee? A hot bath?"

"Do you have any juice?" Her eyes sparkled and she headed through the living room and straight to the double glass sliding doors, curiosity in her expression. "This where you keep the hot tub?"

"Yeah." He turned on the DVD, wishing Reba's rich croon would calm his traitorous body, then poured two glasses of juice. Pretending that Andrew was here wasn't working. Neither was pretending that she was simply a woman he'd brought home from the saloon. Because there was nothing simple about Kelly McGovern. Another woman might be moaning and groaning over her bruises. Another woman might run home to daddy. Another woman wouldn't make herself so damn at home that he felt as if he was the intruder. "Give me a minute to get robes and towels."

Retrieving the items only took seconds, but he took a moment to lean back against a wall in his darkened hallway, close his eyes and calm his pounding pulse. He drew in a deep breath, and Kelly's tantalizing scent, both feminine and earthy, wafted in through the open doors on a breeze. Reminding himself that she wasn't there for romantic purposes did nothing to cool his ardor.

He wished he could attribute his reaction to the near-death experience. But the truth was that he'd liked her a long time. Although he'd never expected to entertain her in his home, his body seemed to be acting on an accumulation of moments they'd spent together over the years. Moments he hadn't given much significance to until now.

He heard a splash and envisioned her trailing her perfectly manicured nails through the heated water, dipping in a delectable toe and ankle before lowering herself inch by delectable inch into the water. Most likely he had no trouble envisioning her, since he'd seen her swimming at Half-Moon Lake. Was that a sigh of contentment he heard over Reba's melody?

But sharing lake water and his hot tub were two different things. Having her in his home guaranteed he wouldn't sleep tonight. But he'd had no choice.

At least here he could offer her some measure of

protection. The house had a decent alarm system, and if anyone showed, they'd have to go through him to get to her. He wouldn't have allowed her to go outside alone, except the backyard was fenced. Besides, whoever had been after them this afternoon probably didn't yet know their plan had failed. While he fully expected another attempt on their lives, he figured their enemy wouldn't regroup this soon.

Still, he intended to be prepared. His skilled fists and the knife he kept strapped to his ankle might not be good enough protection. Carrying the towels and robes over one arm, two juice glasses in his hands and a shotgun under his other arm, he headed out onto his deck.

It was black outside with low, threatening thunderclouds blocking any sight of the moon. But the deck lights that absorbed solar energy during the day and emitted soft blue lighting after dark allowed him to see her. Just as he'd suspected, she was already soaking in the tub, her head tilted back, her chin pointed upward, her eyes closed. Every inch the pampered princess, she spoiled the image by shoving a lock of hair from her eyes and revealing a dark smudge that at first he thought was a shadow, but upon inspection proved to be a bruise. She'd be lucky if she didn't have a gigantic shiner under her eye tomorrow.

What was he thinking? She was banged up and hurting and here he was standing salivating over her when she required medical attention. Alcohol to clean her cuts. At the very least, some painkillers.

"I'll be right back." He set the robe and towels

nearby, braced the shotgun within easy reach of the tub and headed inside. Opening his freezer, he grabbed a handful of ice which he wrapped inside a clean hand towel.

What else? Aspirin.

When he returned to the patio, she hadn't moved one inch. But her lips parted into a grin. "This is heaven."

No, heaven would be taking her into his arms, tasting her lips, massaging her shoulders. He'd been about to climb into the tub and join her but found himself hesitating.

While he couldn't see her body, just knowing about her lack of clothing had heat flushing his neck. He didn't want her to know how he was reacting to her, but hiding his arousal didn't seem possible without his body cooperating.

And for some reason that part of his anatomy had developed a sudden rebellious streak. *Down boy.*

He stalled for time and sipped some apple juice. He rarely drank alcohol. With his family's drinking history, he preferred not to test his susceptibility to addiction, so he was perfectly happy with the juice and handed her a glass of her own.

"Thanks," she murmured, her tone throaty and low.

When their fingers touched just briefly, the heat from her flesh darted up his arm and then swooped straight to his lower regions. Gritting his teeth, he backed away, determining that surely distance would allow him to regain a measure of control.

She peered over her juice glass. "Aren't you joining me?"

"One of us has to stand guard."

She sipped her juice and rested the glass on the edge of the redwood tub. Her hold on the glass might be delicate but her tone was anything but. "Let me get this straight. You're standing guard because you think I'm going to attack you?"

He chuckled. "That thought never crossed my mind."

But at her erotic suggestion, his thoughts frothed enthusiastically. What he wouldn't give to have her attack him. He imagined wet, slick flesh pressing him down, her mouth, hot and seeking, taking exactly what she wanted.

She frowned at him. "You're standing guard because you want to impress me with your... equipment?"

Her husky voice and her sweet scent had made him forget that she possessed a truly sharp mind and that the double entendre had no doubt been deliberate. Of course, his forgetfulness might also have something to do with knowing that she sat fewer than two feet from him—without a stitch of clothing on. Or it might be that he knew she wouldn't object to him climbing right into the tub with her, sitting so close their breaths would mingle, their thighs would touch.

No, he couldn't risk it.

Beads of sweat broke out on his forehead and he took another sip of juice. "In case you've forgotten, someone wants to kill us. We can't let down our guard."

"Oh, really?" Her voice tied him in knots with her skepticism. "You thought it was safe enough to let me come out here without you, and now you're trying to tell me that you need to stand guard, like my ancestor Shotgun Sally's lover, Zachary Gale, once did when he protected her from Indians? I don't think so.''

''What's with your family's obsession with that particular ancestor?''

''What do you mean?''

''Andrew told me he wanted to fall in love with the same passion that Zachary loved his Sally.''

''Some families can trace their ancestors back to kings and queens. Some claim fame by tracing their genealogy back to the Mayflower. In my family we're proud to be descendants of Shotgun Sally.''

''But she wasn't nobility. Legends say she was a rebel. You really think you're one of her descendants?''

''Yes. And stop changing the subject.''

She'd caught him. ''Huh?''

''Don't 'huh' me. You know I find that particular ancestor fascinating, so you deliberately tried to distract me from your lack of courage.''

He choked on the juice and set it down. ''Excuse me?''

''I'm finding your illogical statements absolutely fascinating. Admit it. You don't want to climb into this tub with me.''

He shrugged. ''Okay. I don't want to climb into the tub with you.''

''Ah,'' she sipped her juice, her delicate neck tempting his fingers to stroke. ''What about if I promise not to bite?''

He didn't answer with words but gave in to temptation and placed his hands on her shoulders. The pulse at her neck leaped, but she held perfectly still as if a movement might break the mood. Standing behind her, he allowed himself the pleasure of kneading away the knots and the tense muscles, soothing sore tendons. Her skin beckoned him to touch, to smooth, to soothe.

"Mmm," she sighed. "You feel so good, I'll give you an hour to stop that."

"And when the hour's up, you'll be putty in my hands?" he teased.

"Something like that." She swirled the liquid in her glass. "So what's the real reason you won't get in this tub with me?"

No way was he answering her question. He removed his hands from her shoulders, stopping the massage. His fingers tingled with sorrow at the sudden lack of her warmth, but he forced them to reach for the washcloth filled with ice instead.

"Where's that knot on your head?"

She touched the tender spot and winced. "Here."

"This should keep down the swelling." Gently he placed the icy cloth on the lump.

"It's cold."

"Ice usually is," he agreed.

"I liked the massage better."

"I'm sure you did. After a while we need to move this to the bruise by your eye."

"But—"

"Think how bad you're going to feel when you look in the mirror at your big black eye or if this lump swells to the size of a grapefruit."

"Not funny. We could have died today, and I decided that since we lived, we should really live." She smiled and sipped her juice. "Maybe you should kiss me where I hurt and make me all better?"

Chapter Five

Kelly stretched and then winced at several sore muscles. But as she awakened in Wade's guest room where she'd slept alone, and recalled last night, she frowned over her behavior. What had happened to the conservative college graduate who was supposed to be spending the summer deciding between a career in law or real estate? Andrew's murder had not only devastated her but taken her to another place.

She couldn't blame a nonalcoholic beverage for her behavior toward Wade, but she must not have been herself or she never would have been so forward. She'd played reluctant to spend the night at his home while riding in the back of the squad car, but Wade hadn't pursued her flirtation as she'd hoped. So she'd changed tactics, and never had she acted so boldly in her life. She wished her excuse was that it wasn't every day she came so close to dying. However, instead of her entire life passing in front of her eyes, she'd seemed able to momentarily set aside everything but her building feelings for Wade. She'd heard of men and women who tossed away their value of abstinence before a partner went off to war. But she didn't even have that excuse. She'd made all those inviting remarks to Wade *after* she'd known she was safe.

On top of the danger, the hot tub had relaxed her to a state where she'd cut loose her inhibitions like a thirty-pound anchor and sailed onward steered by nothing but pure feminine instinct. Okay, she wasn't surprised that she had those impulses. The real shocker was that she'd acted on them while right in the middle of trying to find out who had killed her brother. She felt guilty as hell for reaching out to Wade when Andrew was dead. And yet her brother would have understood her need to connect with a man she liked and respected at a time when she was emotionally shaky. If Andrew had still been alive he would have told her there was nothing wrong with giving and receiving comfort. And while she'd once wondered if her attraction to Wade might have been a longing to hang on to memories of Andrew, she now knew better. She liked Wade, liked the way he treated her.

Her feelings toward Wade seemed to have done a complete 180 in a very short time. Until Andrew's death, Wade had always irritated her, but perhaps she just hadn't recognized the simmering attraction between them until now, when they were sharing so much time together. So her boldness hadn't come out of nowhere but was an accumulated buildup that had reached the do-something-about-it stage, allowing her to make the first move. Although she wasn't sure herself how far she'd intended to go, her invitation had been unmistakable.

And then, after she'd gone and overcome inclinations she'd suppressed for a lifetime, Wade hadn't even joined her in the tub.

He'd acted the perfect gentleman. Damn him. She not only felt like a fool, she had no idea how she would face him this morning. Pretend none of it had happened? She could go with that option. Pretend his rejection didn't matter? But that would be a mockery of her own feelings, and she wouldn't do it.

However unaccustomed she was to being the aggressor, however much she'd been taught to play the flirtatious Southern belle and to practice come-hither looks, she'd enjoyed the part of pursuer and wasn't so sure she wanted to give up the role. Failure didn't sit well with her at any time, never mind with something as important as getting to know Wade better. The fact that he was so valiantly resisting only increased her determination.

She needed a game plan. Obviously some new clothes. She couldn't decide which outfit he'd liked best yesterday, the business, the casual or the sexy one. His eyes had seemed to caress her no matter what she'd worn.

Double damn him.

As Kelly sat up in the double bed in Wade's guest room, she marveled at her extraordinary thoughts. Was she really changing so much that she planned to make another move on the guy? More likely she was simply allowing her real self to come out of hiding. The notion both pleased and scared her, and made her think she might have more in common with Andrew than she'd thought. Perhaps going slowly and feeling her way into a relationship with

Wade would be prudent. On the other hand, she'd known him for years.

While she could still recall Cara's warnings about the dangerous Wade Lansing, her friend didn't know the man raised orchids. Or read books. Or acted the perfect gentleman. Besides, that edge of danger added a spark of excitement to their exchanges. She never quite knew what he would do next.

She sighed and padded to the bathroom. Last night, before she'd slipped under the covers, she'd called her parents and told them she wouldn't be home just yet. She'd rinsed out her underwear and hung them up to dry. Only, they were still damp and she couldn't bring herself to wear them. So she used the new toothbrush Wade had provided and donned her shirt and jeans.

Following her nose into the kitchen and the scent of perking coffee, she stepped over to the table. Wade sat tilted back on the rear legs of his chair, reading his newspaper. The moment he spied her, he put down the *Mustang Gazette* and leaned forward, his full attention almost making her self-conscious. He took in her finger-brushed hair and the slight bruise under her eye, and then his gaze swept over her chest, his pupils dilating slightly.

So, he'd noticed her lack of underwear. Served him right. She hoped naughty thoughts sucked the moisture right out of his mouth.

She grinned at him. "Morning."

"Morning."

Whether his voice was usually this husky in the morning or due to her lack of attire, she couldn't say. Pleased with herself, she walked over to the kitchen counter. ''Can I have some coffee or are you going to hog it all to yourself?''

He ducked his head back into the newspaper. ''Mugs are in the cabinet to the left of the sink.''

He might be pretending to read, but she knew her braless state had thrown him, and swallowed down another smile. While she hadn't gone without underwear to distract him, she couldn't have planned better if she'd laid out a seduction campaign.

She filled a mug and sat across the table from him. He handed her the local section and they sat together reading like an old married couple. Well, not quite. Going by her parents' marriage, married people didn't usually have this kind of sexual tension humming between them, especially this early in the morning.

The coffee chased away the last of her sleepiness. ''I'd like to ride out again today and see Debbie West, her family and her ranch.''

''Well, we can't take my truck.'' Was that a blush creeping up his neck? ''It's either your Jag or…''

''Or?'' she prodded, curious about the color in his face.

''The Caddy.''

''You have a Cadillac?''

''I inherited Betsy from my uncle. Actually, Betsy was his wife's car. After she died, he couldn't part with it. And I've kept the car in storage all these years, but she runs just fine.''

He didn't squirm in his seat, but he most definitely fidgeted. A man who grew orchids in his kitchen and was nostalgic over an old car—who would have thought Wade capable of such sentimentality?

She savored the jolt of her morning caffeine and asked, "What aren't you telling me?"

"If we take Betsy, we won't be going incognito. She was built in 1955."

"Oh."

"And my aunt painted her hot pink."

"Wait a second. Isn't that the same car that used to be on the roof of the Hit 'Em Again?" She recalled the ridiculous pink car with the passion-purple banners and balloons that had been a Mustang Valley landmark for the better part of her childhood.

"Yeah." He grinned. "But the city inspectors made us take Betsy down. They said the car could fall on someone. Mayor Daniels probably just thought old Betsy was ugly."

"I didn't know you were so sentimental."

"I'm not."

"Whatever you say."

He scowled at her. "Stop that."

"What?" She kept her eyes wide and, hopefully, innocent looking.

His mouth curled upward in one of his irresistible bad-boy smiles that she couldn't help but find charming. "How can I argue with you if you stubbornly insist on agreeing with me?"

She raised her coffee cup to him in a toast. "You've made your point. But if you think that wisecrack remark is going to get me to agree with everything you say, then you don't know me very well."

"I know you better than you think."

"Really?"

"I know that you have a much better brain than

most people give you credit for. And while you take pleasure in your fashion-plate clothing, substance is more important to you than image.''

''What else?'' Her curiosity burned. What woman could resist hearing what a guy thought of her—especially a man who'd known her for years? A guy that was sending he-was-interested-but-wasn't-going-to-do-anything-about-it signals. A guy who had a reputation of playing fast and loose with other women, but who backpedaled away from her. They'd never been close, but she'd always been underfoot, and while she wasn't stunned by his perception, she was surprised that he'd turned the conversation so personal.

''You have determination and courage but wrap it all up in such a tidy, feminine package, you don't intimidate men who should feel threatened.''

''Men like you?'' she asked, recalling once again how he'd refused to join her in the hot tub. That he could refuse her at all rankled. And not because she couldn't take rejection, but because she couldn't ignore his blatant interest followed by resistance to her. Couldn't ignore his cool gray eyes meeting hers so frequently. Couldn't ignore the pleasure his hands had given her neck during his too-short massage. His interest was obvious, jolting and oh, so delicious—and yet she wanted to smack him upside the head for refusing to acknowledge where they were headed.

She felt as though she was three steps ahead of him. And not only had he no intention of keeping up, but he kept lagging further and further behind.

''Women like you scare the hell out of me,'' he

admitted with a bold grin that said just the opposite. "Now I suggest you stop fishing for compliments and get ready. Are we taking the Caddy or your Jag?"

She dug into her purse and pulled out her keys. "I think I'd like to be in the driver's seat today."

WADE SUSPECTED Kelly was irritated with him. However, he didn't expect her to turn up the music, then ignore him for the entire half-hour drive to the Wests' ranch. If she'd been a man, she would have been brooding. He preferred to think of her giving him the silent treatment as pouting. Pouting because she hadn't gotten her way.

Tough.

Kelly might be smart and courageous but she was also one very spoiled piece of work. He'd always thought she was a happily-ever-after kind of woman who wouldn't indulge in a fling. He'd been wrong, since her current behavior had proved otherwise. However, he didn't feel like letting her use him to scratch an itch with the town's bad boy during her summer break before she returned to law school and forgot all about him. Nope. Wade knew better than to knuckle under and give her what she so obviously wanted.

Not that he wouldn't enjoy making love to her. He would have enjoyed it immensely. Just the thought of him being the one to draw soft moans of pleasure from her throat, of skimming his hands over her silky, pliant flesh, of finally tasting those sultry lips could heat him hotter than sizzling oil in a hot skillet.

But the thought of her exploiting him held him back. She only had one use for a man like him, and if he gave her what she wanted, he wouldn't just be going back on an implied promise to Andrew, he would be selling himself short. Just because she might require comforting to help her get past the loss of her brother, didn't mean that Wade would let her trample his own esteem in the process. His blood might not come from the illustrious Shotgun Sally of McGovern fame, but he had his standards—ones that most definitely didn't include Ms. Kelly Mc-Govern.

So he let her drive and sulk. Let her stay miffed with his refusal to play the dating game.

He tipped his hat over his closed eyes and pretended to sleep, but surreptitiously he kept checking the side-view mirror. No menacing tow trucks appeared on the highway. This road was as clear as the morning air without a cloud in sight.

Wade had never been to the Wests' homestead before. But the overgrazed forty acres didn't appear much different from the other mom-and-pop ranches that were all slowly going out of business throughout the West. The little guys couldn't compete with the large corporations that used all the newest technology, who herded cattle by helicopter and bought in volume and were managed by a team of agricultural experts.

Kelly slowed down considerably before turning onto the dirt drive, which nevertheless shot up choking dust. She shut off the engine, but neither made a move to exit until the dust settled. Outside, the bright sun glared and he kept his sunglasses on.

Kelly did the same. He saw her taking in the yard overgrown with weeds, the peeling paint on the sagging front porch, the curling and worn shingles on a lumpy roof.

The air smelled of sweat, dirt and manure from the cows behind the barbwire fence. Two rusty bikes, both with flat tires, and an old wheelbarrow rotted next to a barn that had been old twenty years ago. He didn't blame the Wests for selling their ranch. Surely they could do better elsewhere than this overbaked piece of dirt.

Kelly stood still for a moment, taking in the poor land, ignoring the buzzing flies. Looking as out of place as a fairy princess in a sweatshop, she nevertheless squared her shoulders and headed up the front porch steps. Clearly, she didn't want to be here, but true to form, she would press on until she had the answers she sought.

He admired grit in a woman, but wished she'd confided in him. He had no idea if the Wests would welcome them or not. The few times he'd met Debbie, she'd been with Andrew, who tended to overshadow her. And the only time he'd seen Debbie and Kelly together had been at Andrew's funeral where they'd kept their distance from each another.

A barking dog announced their presence, but Kelly rapped smartly on the front door, anyway. Still giving him the silent treatment, she didn't even glance his way.

With one hand wrapped in the pit bull's collar, Debbie opened the door. She wore a tank top, cut-off jeans and her hair tied back in a bandanna. No shoes. Her chestnut hair was streaked with dust, cobwebs and grime. But her eyes, dark with sorrow and puffy from too many tears, told of her misery and revealed her surprise to see them.

"Hey, come in." She shoved a rag into her pocket and tugged the barking dog back inside. "I was just cleaning the windows."

The inside of the ranch house had cheap tile floors that were immaculate. A threadbare carpet lay in front of a worn sofa. However, the coffee table gleamed with a silver tea set and white doilies. And not by one twitch of her lips or change of expression in her blue eyes did Kelly reveal that she was unaccustomed to these kinds of surroundings. In fact, if he hadn't known her better, he would have sworn that she was as comfortable here as she had been at his place.

He wondered why he found her adaptability so surprising when Andrew had exhibited the same trait. Wade supposed he made those assumptions about Kelly because of her clothes that always had a style that set her apart, that said, "I'm special." And he'd been fooled by her airs and her outfits like just about everyone else in town, except Cara. He should have realized the brash and smart reporter had befriended Kelly for her inner qualities—qualities he couldn't help admiring as much as he did the more visible ones.

"Would you like some sweet tea?" Debbie asked, offering Southern hospitality that would have been rude to refuse. "I just made some this morning."

"Thanks." Kelly fearlessly held out her hand to let the pit bull have a sniff, then slowly patted the dog on the head. "What's his name?"

"Brutus." Debbie stepped into the kitchen, placed a pitcher of tea on a tray next to mismatched glasses with ice, then carried everything to the living room. "If you know anyone who might want him, we need to give him away before we move. He's a great watchdog and he's never bitten anyone. I can't keep him with me at the new apartment."

"So you're definitely selling?" Kelly asked, her tone casual, but Wade sensed she would soon come to the real reason for their visit.

"I have a job in town." Debbie settled in a chair next to her dog. "With the mayor. I'm working for city hall. He wants me to liaise with the ranchers and farming community."

"That's great." Kelly crossed her legs and folded her feet under the sofa, seeming genuinely happy for Debbie. "And your father?"

"The mayor's offered to find him a job, too—if he can stay sober." Debbie poured the iced tea. "Andrew set up the sale of this ranch as well as the new jobs for us before he died."

"That's why we came," Kelly spoke gently. "Are you up to talking about Andrew?"

Debbie's eyes narrowed on Kelly. "I suppose."

"Did Andrew have any enemies that you know about?" Wade asked. Although he knew Kelly was perfectly capable of asking the right questions, there was a tension between the two women, almost as if Andrew were still alive and they were fighting over him.

Debbie's sharp gaze sliced to Wade, then back to Kelly. She set down her tea and folded her arms over her chest. "What's this all about?"

''Yesterday Kelly and I were asking a lot of questions around town about Andrew,'' Wade explained. ''On our way here, a stolen truck ran us off the road. My truck was totaled. We think someone tried to kill us.''

Debbie's eyebrows arched. ''Because you were asking questions about Andrew?''

''Yes.'' Kelly also set down her practically untouched tea. ''If there's anything you can tell us, I'd be grateful.''

By unspoken agreement, neither Kelly nor Wade wanted to tell Debbie that Andrew had been murdered. She or her ex-husband could be connected to the killing and if so, Wade didn't want her leaving town—not before they figured out what was going on. Since she had no motive, Wade didn't believe Debbie had anything to do with Andrew's murder, but she could have accidentally given information to someone else who did.

''Well, Niles, my ex-husband has hated Andrew since Andrew and I got together. Andrew's handling of our divorce didn't help.''

''Exactly how angry was Niles?'' Kelly asked, and by her tone Wade could tell she hated prying.

Debbie sighed. ''Niles has a temper, but he's not usually violent—if that's what you're asking—and I've never known him to get his hands dirty.''

She left the statement hanging. Kelly and Wade knew that Niles had the funds to hire people to do his dirty work.

''Anyone else?'' Wade asked. ''What about your father? Did he and Andrew get along?''

''At first Daddy wasn't too keen about Andrew,

but after he did such a good job negotiating the sale of our land to those big lawyers, Daddy changed his thinking. Andrew got us a better price and a faster closing date.''

''Did my brother ever mention any clients who were angry with him?'' Kelly asked.

''Not really.'' Debbie frowned and then pressed her lips firmly together as if remembering something she didn't want to reveal.

''What is it?'' Wade asked.

''Probably nothing.''

''Can you please tell us anyway?'' Kelly prodded.

''Andrew asked me never to repeat it…but… Promise me that you won't tell anyone else?''

Wade nodded. ''I promise—unless it turns out that this person is trying to kill us—then our deal is off.''

''Fair enough.'' Debbie picked up her tea, drained half the glass in two gulps, then twisted the tumbler in her hands. ''During Andrew's last year in law school, he was involved in an unpleasant incident.''

Wade glanced at Kelly, who shook her head, indicating she knew nothing about what Debbie was about to reveal. Neither did Wade.

Debbie sighed again. ''Andrew saw another student cheating on a final exam. Now, the code of honor at law school made him duty bound to report the cheater, but Andrew didn't want to. He knew that his coming forward would cause the other student to be expelled, and likely the cheater would never attain his law degree.''

''Andrew must have been torn up over that decision,'' Kelly muttered.

Her brother, always the rooter for the underdog, would hate to end another person's career before it had begun. And yet Andrew's personal code of honor wouldn't allow for cheaters, either.

"What did Andrew do?" Wade asked, his gut already churning because he knew his friend well enough to know the decision must have given him many sleepless nights.

"He turned Jonathan Dixon in. Sure enough, the school expelled the man two weeks before graduation. And it's a good thing Andrew turned him in, because the professor had also seen the man cheating and suspected Andrew also knew. If Andrew had kept quiet, he too could have been expelled for failing to report the incident."

"Jonathan blamed Andrew?" Kelly guessed.

"What do you think?" Debbie downed the rest of her tea. "It got ugly. Jonathan issued threats, and the campus police had to physically remove him from the classroom. But you know Andrew. Instead of being angry for being put in that awkward position, he wanted to help the guy. So he told Jonathan that if he ever needed a job, to come to Mustang Valley and look him up."

Kelly groaned, clearly annoyed that her brother had tried to befriend someone who might be dangerous—which was probably why Andrew hadn't mentioned the incident to either Wade or Kelly. Both of them would certainly have advised him to just forget the unpleasant episode and move on. Some people couldn't be helped, but Andrew had never seemed to understand that. Odd how he and Kelly thought alike on the matter.

Kelly kept her tone neutral. "And this Jonathan, did he come to Mustang Valley?"

Debbie nodded. "Andrew got him a job working for the mayor, too."

"When?" Wade asked.

"The week before Andrew died."

A week? Now that was a huge coincidence that needed looking into.

"Seems like the mayor is in a hiring mood," Wade commented, his thoughts churning. Mustang Valley had been growing large enough that he didn't necessarily recognize every stranger in the Hit 'Em Again Saloon. And city hall was growing by leaps and bounds. Between Daniels's reelection campaign and the growth of Mustang Valley, Wade supposed the city employed quite a few people, who all technically worked for the mayor. But Wade still knew most people in town, and, as far as he knew, Jonathan had yet to frequent his establishment.

"Jonathan's job is only temporary. Just until the election. Andrew was trying to line up something else for him for afterward." Debbie sighed. "I have to tell you that Jonathan seems like a really nice man. I can't imagine him stealing a tow truck and trying to run you down."

Kelly frowned. "Wade told you that the tow truck ran us off the road, not tried to run us down."

Debbie shrugged. "Same difference."

But was her wording an assumption? Or did she know more than she was telling? And what about her Jonathan story? Was that to throw them off track? It seemed suspicious that someone who had a motive for revenge had shown up in town a week before Andrew's death.

"Oh, I almost forgot. Jonathan is going by the name of Johnny. He claims he wants to make a new start."

"Johnny?" Facts clicked in Wade's mind. "Is Johnny about five-six with black hair and a mustache?"

Debbie's eyes widened. "You know him?"

"Yeah. He's been in for a few drinks." Wade rubbed his knuckles in recollection of the last time Johnny had a few too many. When Johnny turned surly and obnoxious, Wade had cut the man off and Johnny had staggered from the bar, furious. He'd slammed into another customer and a brawl had broken out. Six broken chairs and one cracked mirror later, Wade had thrown out the drunk and restored order.

Johnny hadn't returned again.

Wade didn't find it odd that Andrew hadn't introduced him. But he did find Kelly's accusing eyes on him uncomfortable. He hadn't said a word, but she seemed to know he was holding back. Yet she clearly understood that he didn't want to say more in front of Debbie and gave him a slow nod and a we'll-talk-later look.

Who would have thought the bartender and the debutante could work so well together? Almost like a team.

Chapter Six

"Mom. Daddy?" Kelly walked through the front door of her home with Wade beside her. The stubborn man had insisted on sticking to her like mascara. Unlike her makeup, she couldn't just wash him away. So she was forced to make explanations to her parents, which she never found easy, with Wade right there to hear every word. Why did men and parents have to be so difficult? "I'm home."

"Don't shout, dear. We're in the breakfast room."

Kelly checked her makeup in the foyer mirror, smoothed lip gloss that didn't need smoothing with her pinky and enjoyed the fact that Wade stood there trying to look patient and unable to look away. Just for spite, she fluffed her hair, knowing it would both annoy and fascinate him, then swallowed down a grin. Seemed she did that a lot around Wade.

Annoyed that he'd refused to stay in her car while she picked up a few changes of clothes and some necessities, she entered the breakfast room with trepidation. Her mother had recently painted the walls a rich burgundy, and contrasted the woodwork trim with a creamy white that supposedly encouraged dining enjoyment by setting the right tone. The octagonal airy space with windows overlooking the garden was usually one of Kelly's favorite rooms. In fact, her folks often ate informal dinners there as they were doing right now, but today she dreaded going inside.

After Andrew's death, she didn't want to cause her parents any more pain by having them worry over their remaining offspring. And knowing Mustang Valley's gossip network as well as she did, by now half the town had either spied her driving with Wade or had actually seen them together and reported it to friends, co-workers and family.

However, she'd loved her brother way too much not to seek justice. She wanted to put behind bars the person who'd murdered him. She wanted his killer to pay for his crime, and if that made her as bloodthirsty as Shotgun Sally, then so be it.

Her parents had to know she'd been keeping company with Wade, and they wouldn't be pleased—less pleased if they knew what kind of trouble she'd stirred up. Trying to make the best of an awkward situation, she pasted a cheery grin on her face, looped her arm through Wade's and escorted him to meet her parents.

Of course, they'd all met before through Andrew. But Daddy wouldn't be happy to see her hanging out with the man he derogatorily called the saloon keeper, and Mom wouldn't necessarily back Kelly up. But then again, she might. Like all the women in the McGovern family back to Shotgun Sally, Mom had a mind of her own and she could be ever so unpredictable.

"Mom. Daddy. I brought Wade over, and we don't have time for dinner." Kelly leaned over and kissed her father on the cheek. He raised his smooth, aristocratic cheek to her, but his dark hazel eyes were shadowed with concern.

Her mother, a petite blonde with Kelly's blue eyes, stood and took two plates out of the china cabinet and set additional silverware. "Of course you'll eat. We're going to sit down together like a family and have a discussion."

"Yes, dear." Her father agreed, nodding his head with a firmness that told Kelly they might even know more than she'd suspected.

She and Wade were about to be ganged up on with all the Southern politeness that should have had them running in the opposite direction. But leaving without making some explanations wasn't an option, though she felt like a child who had done something wrong and was about to be scolded and punished.

"Sit down. Have some steak." Her father passed the platter to Wade.

"Thank you, sir."

"Serving you dinner is the least I can do since you're protecting my little girl."

Protecting? Uh-oh. She shot her mom a how-much-do-you-know look.

Her mother rolled her eyes at the ceiling. Obviously, Kelly had really underestimated them this time. To say her mother was smart was an understatement. She could complete the *New York Times* crossword puzzle in thirty minutes flat. Daddy always consulted her on his oil deals, and Kelly suspected her mother could have run the company better than he did.

Not that Daddy didn't do a fine job. But like Andrew, he tended to see the good side of people and overlooked the bad, and she loved him for it. Besides, as a good family man, when it came to protecting his loved ones, he could be ferocious.

Kelly filled her plate with char-grilled steak, shoestring French fries and jalepeño stuffed olives. Her father poured them both a goblet of rich Bordeaux, then set the crystal wine decanter on the white linen tablecloth without spilling a drop.

Her mother passed the salad. ''We know Andrew was murdered.''

They knew? Kelly almost dropped the platter her mother was handing her.

She and Wade exchanged glances, and he subtly shrugged, which she took to mean as, this is your family, I'll let you handle them. Great. She'd always avoided confrontations by doing pretty much what her parents wanted. Early on, her idea of rebellion had been to carry lipstick and eye shadow in her purse and apply the cosmetics after she left the house for school. So she was accustomed to her parents' approval and disliked causing discord. And deep down she knew that they wouldn't be pleased with her spending time with Wade looking into Andrew's murder or for putting herself in danger.

Normally she might have obeyed their wishes, but Andrew was too important to her to let the comment slide. His loss had shaken her safe world in a manner that had her questioning her life, her values, her goals. First and foremost in her mind was getting

Andrew some justice, and she no longer knew if she wanted to attend law school, when staying in Mustang Valley near her parents, her friends and Wade seemed much more appealing. At least she needn't make that decision right now.

"Sheriff Wilson told Mayor Daniels, who then told me." Her father sliced his steak, but didn't raise the meat to his mouth. "Your mother and I wanted to keep the news from you because we feared you'd go looking into Andrew's death and put yourself in danger."

"Which is exactly what you've done," her mother said with both vexation and sympathy. "Did you think we wouldn't hear about that stolen tow truck almost running you down?"

"I never could keep secrets from you guys," Kelly muttered. "I only tried because I didn't want you to worry."

"We're always going to worry about you," her mother said.

"I'm not a little girl anymore."

"Age has nothing to do with it. I'll worry about you when you're sixty." Her mother paused, her eyes tearing, then she regained control of herself and continued. "Andrew was our son and we loved him very much. The pain of losing him will never go away. Never. It'll be there whether we talk about him or not. It'll be there whether we find out who killed him or not." Her mother dabbed at her tearing eyes with a napkin. "And we don't want to lose you, too. I just couldn't bear it if anything else happens to this family."

Fresh guilt stabbed Kelly and made her stomach

quiver. "Mom, I could stop asking questions right now—"

"But it's too late for that," Wade said, inserting himself into the family conversation. "I don't believe Kelly will be safe—not until we find out what happened to Andrew."

"We agree." Her mother reached across the table and squeezed her father's hand. "That's why we want to send both of you out of town."

"Both of us?" Kelly's pulse pounded with uncertainty. She'd always thought that her parents hadn't liked Wade, hadn't liked Andrew hanging out with him. Then she realized that they thought of Wade as protection for her. They didn't know that she liked him in other, not so simple, ways.

"We don't want you to be alone," her father said, confirming her suspicions, and she did nothing to clear up their misconception.

Her mother outlined their plan. "We'll hire a private investigator—"

"That won't work and you know it, Mom." Kelly picked up a stuffed olive and popped it into her mouth, chewed and swallowed, giving her time to form her reply. "People in Mustang Valley don't talk to outsiders."

Her father frowned. "Our first priority is *your* safety."

"Look, if someone wants me dead and I leave, who's to say they won't follow me?" Her parents traded a long glance, and she could see they were worried about that possibility, too. "Besides, if I'm in danger, I'd rather be on my home ground with friends around me I can trust. Seems to me the best way for me to be safe is to find Andrew's killer and turn him or her over to the authorities."

Her father gave up all pretense of eating, threw down his napkin and shoved his chair back from the table. "Have you thought of giving the sheriff time to do his job?"

"If he hasn't found anything by now, he probably won't." Wade kept his tone even and firm, but he sure didn't seem to mind standing up to her father, which she appreciated, especially since he did it respectfully. "And I don't trust the sheriff."

She thought her father might rant. That he might throw Wade's background in his face for not believing the law would help. But Daddy surprised her.

He swirled his wine in his glass, then shot a piercing stare at Wade. "Why don't you trust Wilson?"

Wade held her father's stare. "Our sheriff's more concerned with the mayor's reelection campaign than in solving Andrew's murder."

"Is that your only reason?" her father asked.

"Yes, sir." Wade hesitated, as if choosing his words very carefully. "That's the only reason I'm willing to state out loud."

"SO THEN WHAT HAPPENED?" Cara asked while the two friends met in the reporter's office the following day at the *Mustang Gazette*.

Kelly sighed. "We finished dinner without coming to any agreement. When we left the house Mom looked ready to burst into tears again and Dad looked…defeated. They want me to leave Mustang Valley, but I'm not going."

"Good. So what's next?"

''Wade had to order supplies for his saloon and pay a few bills. He dropped me off here, escorted me to your door and made me promise not to leave until he returns. We're going to check out Jonathan Dixon, the guy who cheated in law school and now works for the mayor. Then we may head to Dallas, if Niles Deagen will talk to us.''

''Niles Deagen? The oil man?''

''And Debbie's secret ex-husband.''

From behind her desk, Cara started typing on her keyboard. ''I've got a file on him. Last year I was researching a story about oil and his name came up.''

Kelly came around Cara's desk and peered over her friend's shoulder at the monitor. ''You have anything interesting?''

''Depends what you mean by interesting. I have Deagen's home phone number and the address of his last lover.'' Cara used her mouse. ''Here it is. I'll print out the file.'' While they waited for the printer to spit out the information, Cara drummed her nails on her desk.

Kelly recalled going through Andrew's box of stuff last night. Nothing seemed sinister, but the mayor's campaign literature she found reminded her that Jonathan needed watching. Any guy that tried to cheat his way through law school obviously didn't have good character. While cheating on a test was very different from murder, she felt Jonathan was their best lead.

''Do you have any information on the mayor?'' Kelly asked.

''Like what?''

"His scheduled speeches and campaign agenda might help us track down Jonathan without asking too many questions and drawing more attention to ourselves." Kelly checked her watch, wishing they had more time to chat. "Wade should be here soon."

"Hold on and you can have the mayor's stuff, too."

"Thanks, Cara. Oh, yeah, I almost forgot. When Wade and I were over at Lambert & Church, Lindsey Wellington told us that Andrew had a client who wasn't satisfied with my brother's representation after he lost custody of his kids."

"That would have been Sean McCardel."

"Yes. Does he still live in Mustang Valley?"

"I have no idea but I'll pull up the *Mustang Gazette's* articles about him. And while we wait for the printouts, why don't you tell me more about what's going on between you and Wade."

Had Kelly just wished for more time? Suddenly she couldn't wait for Wade to arrive.

Kelly liked having parents and friends who were concerned about her—at least most of the time. This wasn't one of them. Especially since last night had been a complete disaster. Wade had spent the entire evening trying to talk her into hiding while he tried to solve Andrew's murder alone. His chauvinistic attitude had riled Kelly's normally easy-going nature.

Kelly's voice came out sharper than she intended. "Must you always be the inquisitive reporter?"

"I thought I was being the inquisitive friend,"

Cara snapped, her temper clearly simmering, but her eyes showing Kelly's unthinking remark had hurt.

"Damn, I'm sorry. Really, sorry. I shouldn't take out my frustration on you."

"No problem." Cara's eyes softened with sympathy. "You've been through a lot."

Kelly realized that, as much as she tried to tell herself that her life was still normal, she was stressed out and had every right to be. She'd lost her brother. Someone had tried to kill her, and she and Wade...there was no "she and Wade." "After I fought with my folks, Wade and I argued. Or rather he lectured and I refused to listen."

"I take it you didn't end the fight by making mad, passionate love?"

"I wish." Kelly almost smiled at Cara's sarcasm. "That man is so stubborn that I want to smack him almost as often as I want to kiss him."

"Wow. You've got it bad. Maybe you should just take him to bed and work him out of your system."

"You don't understand."

"So educate me."

"He doesn't want me." At her admission, Cara's lower jaw dropped, and Kelly held up her hand before her friend could press for more information. "I take that back. He wants me. He just won't do anything about it."

"No wonder you're frustrated."

"I'll straighten myself out. I have a plan of sorts."

"So what are you going to do?"

Kelly saw Wade entering through the office door

and grinned at Cara, not caring if he overheard. "I'm planning a Shotgun Sally moment."

Cara signaled her with a thumbs-up. "You go, girl."

WADE WAITED until they were safely out of the *Mustang Gazette,* off the street and inside Kelly's Jaguar before letting loose his curiosity. Kelly had this just-swallowed-a-rich-creamy-chocolate look on her face, and it stayed with her as they'd said goodbye to Cara and exited the building.

He strapped on his seat belt, glad he wasn't driving so he could study Kelly's face. "What's a Shotgun Sally moment?"

"My ancestor had her own ways of dealing with men." Kelly slipped on a pair of sunglasses, put the Jag into gear and merged with Main Street's traffic. "She was a real aristocratic widow lady who ran a saloon for a few years. She stored a shotgun behind the bar, but she kept all those rowdy men in line without ever taking down the gun."

"That's hard to believe." Wade had run the saloon since he was eighteen years old and was skeptical of a genteel lady keeping order among a bunch of wild cowboys, especially more than a century ago when times were even rougher. "But maybe the men were more chivalrous back then. Still, a drunk is a drunk, and most have no manners."

She pushed the sunglasses high up on her nose. "Legend says Sally only fired her shotgun once. And that was a warning shot to keep her lover Zachary Gale from trying to run away from his promise to marry her."

"And this is a woman you admire?"

"Absolutely. She's a woman who knew what she wanted and wasn't afraid to go after it. Since Sally didn't have a father to make Zachary live up to his word, she did the reminding herself."

Kelly seemed to find the legend amusing. Either that or she had something else in mind. Something she intended to keep secret, and he wasn't sure how he felt about that. On the one hand he didn't expect her to tell him every thought in her head. On the other, he didn't like her holding back on him, either.

That he was worried about what she was thinking when he should have his mind on solving Andrew's murder told him she was getting to him. Despite the sunglasses that hid her vivid blue eyes, and the way she didn't seem to want to share what was on her mind, he suspected her Shotgun Sally moment had something to do with him.

What was she planning? Obviously, she wouldn't tell him until she was good and ready.

So he picked on Shotgun Sally to test Kelly's patience, just as she was testing his. "If Sally had to force Zachary to marry her, he couldn't have been much of a catch."

"Oh, he was," Kelly insisted. "Zach just didn't like commitment or the idea of giving up his freedom—at least that's what my grandmother told me, and she heard the story from her grandmother."

Wade chuckled. "Seems to me the ladies in your family may have romanticized things."

"Sally was just being practical. She was pregnant and the baby needed a father." Kelly defended her ancestor with a zest that made him believe her enthusiasm wasn't so much about the story she told but about her planned Shotgun Sally moment—whatever that was.

A flying rock, followed by the sound of shattering glass caught Wade's attention. He glimpsed kids fleeing the damaged storefront. "Turn left at the corner."

Kelly frowned, but steered the car as he directed. "But campaign headquarters are—"

"I know where they are. I just saw a couple of kids throwing rocks."

Kelly kept going, but mumbled something about having better things to do than chase down a few juvenile delinquents. But Wade thought he'd recognized a certain tattered green backpack on a skinny kid with short black hair.

The Jag turned the corner and the boys split into three directions. "Stop the car."

Wade unsnapped his seat belt, opened the door and set off through the park at top speed. It took him a full sixty seconds at a flat-out run to catch the kid by his backpack and shove him up against the wall.

Wade pushed his face right at the kid's. "Damn it, Rudy. Are you part of the group that threw rocks at the doc's place, too? What the hell do you think you're doing?"

"Nothing."

"You call throwing rocks nothing?"

Rudy shrugged. "You gonna let me go or not?"

"Not." Wade gripped his shoulder, hard enough to make Rudy wince. "We're going back to that store. You're going to apologize and work off the damage you did."

"And if I don't?" The son of Wade's dishwasher shouted with defiance, but Rudy was trembling so hard that Wade knew he was a hair's breadth from bursting into tears. Rudy wasn't a bad kid, but he hung out with the wrong crowd. While Wade wanted to give him a break, he knew the kid had to take responsibility for his actions.

Rudy drew his skinny shoulders back straight, waiting for Wade's answer.

And of course Wade knew the kid wasn't half as scared of the law as he was of his parents. So he spoke mildly. "Then I'll just have to tell your father."

The kid caved. His shoulders sagged and the fire went out of his eyes just as Kelly came running up, her eyes worried. "What happened?"

Rudy took one look at Kelly and his eyes turned crafty. "I'll make you another deal instead."

Wade yanked him toward the broken window. "You're in no position to bargain."

"The lady might think otherwise."

"Do I know you?" Kelly peered at Rudy. In his baggy jeans and overly large T-shirt, he looked younger than his fourteen years. But Wade doubted they'd met.

"This is Rudy Waters. His father works for me."

"I know you," Rudy spoke up with a determination that surprised Wade. "You're Kelly McGovern, and your brother got himself murdered—at least that's what the sheriff told the mayor."

Wade didn't think the kid was making up lies to save himself. Unlike his hardworking father, Rudy habitually sneaked out, but the kid liked to eavesdrop. Wade had caught him doing so several times in the Hit 'Em Again's pool hall. From experience, he knew that people never paid attention to what they said around kids.

"What else did the sheriff say?" Wade demanded.

"If I tell, you'll let me go?"

Wade reached into his pocket, pulled out his wallet and slipped out a few bills as if he was going to pay Rudy. "Depends on what you have to say."

"The sheriff told the mayor that Kelly McGovern was stirring up trouble, and if she wasn't careful she might get herself killed."

Kelly's eyes went round. Wade shook his head slightly, signaling for her to remain silent.

Rudy shook off Wade's hand on his shoulder and tried to snag the cash.

Wade pulled the money just out of reach of Rudy's fingertips. "What else?"

Rudy eyed the bills hungrily but dropped his hand to his side. "Ain't that enough?"

Wade tried to draw out more information from the kid. "When the sheriff was talking did he sound worried or did he sound like he was making a threat?"

The kid hesitated as if deciding which answer would earn him the money faster.

Wade shook his shoulder. "I want the truth."

"I don't know." Rudy's voice was surly. "They kept their voices way low."

"Where did you hear this conversation?"

"At the mayor's headquarters."

Wade wished they had more to go on. The sheriff's remark could have been perfectly innocent. The man could be legitimately worried over Kelly's safety, especially after the tow-truck incident yesterday. And then again, his words could also have more sinister implications. Either way, Wade didn't have time to fool with Rudy.

"This money is to pay for the window you broke." Wade stuffed the money into the boy's hand, grateful the broken pane had been a small side panel of glass and not the main one. "Now go pay for the damage. We'll be watching."

"Wait." Kelly stopped the boy. "If you hear anything else I might be interested in, you come to me and I'll reward you for your time. Understand?"

Wade's admiration for Kelly spiked up another notch. She hadn't interfered with his holding the kid against the wall. She'd kept her mouth shut at the right time. Yet she might have gained them a snoop, one whom no one would suspect.

He only hoped that the boy's avaricious nature didn't put him in danger. But Rudy was a street-smart kid and would protect himself first and foremost. He knew how to stay really quiet so that people didn't notice him. And if he'd been hanging out around campaign headquarters, his presence there a second time wouldn't be suspicious.

Rudy licked his lips greedily. "Yeah, lady. I understand. You're in even more trouble than me."

Chapter Seven

Think positive.

Kelly tried to put the kid's words out of her mind as Wade opened the door to Mayor Daniels's campaign headquarters for her. Red-white-and-blue banners, buttons, posters and literature dominated the formerly unleased storefront. Inside, a surprising amount of activity hummed. Three people manned phone banks. A fax machine spat out paper. A man ran copies and a group of women congregated around a coffeepot in a makeshift kitchen.

A kid like Rudy wouldn't have been noticed among all the bustle, and his words haunted Kelly. Had he been telling the truth? Kids exaggerated. Yet ever since he'd mentioned the sheriff and the mayor's discussion, she'd felt unsettled. Even Wade's teasing her about Shotgun Sally on the ride over hadn't distracted her from the possibility that Andrew might have been involved in something that other people didn't want known. Something for which he'd been murdered.

"It's hard to tell who's in charge." Wade walked

over to a woman wearing a button that read Vote for Daniels.

The harried redhead looked up with bleary eyes from the newspaper ads spread out on a folding table and appeared to recognize that they didn't belong here. As if on cue, she smiled politely. "Hi. I'm Rebecca. Are you two here to deliver flyers?"

Wade kept his voice low. "We're looking for Jonathan, Johnny Dixon. Is he around?"

Rebecca shook her head. "He didn't come in today."

"Do you know where we can find him?" Kelly asked.

"Not only is Johnny absent today, he didn't call, either." Rebecca frowned. "And that's not like him."

"Ma'am, do you have his phone number or home address?" Wade asked.

"I'm sorry. I can't give out that kind of information. However, if you'd like to leave a message, I'll give it to Johnny when he arrives."

Mayor Daniels walked out of the back room, and the flurry of activity in the room heightened as everyone busied themselves. At fifty, his signature gray hair and friendly green eyes had won him many votes. Popular with both the townsfolk and the ranchers, the mayor would likely be reelected for the fourth time.

He stuck out his hand to welcome Kelly. To add warmth, he clasped his other hand over hers, too.

Kelly didn't know if the combination of sympathy and warmth in his eyes was genuine, but played along as if he was an old friend of the family. In truth, she didn't know the mayor well. But her daddy did, and Daniels had been at Andrew's funeral with most of the other of Mustang Valley's leading citizens.

"Welcome, Kelly."

Rebecca left them with the mayor and returned to sorting newspaper ads. Mayor Daniels shook Wade's hand in the same friendly manner as he had hers. "Wade. Have you two come to volunteer for my campaign?"

"I'm afraid not." Kelly understood why the man was so good at his job. After she turned him down, he didn't show any disappointment. Instead he maintained the same expression as she continued, "But we could use your help."

"What can I do?" he offered, his lips narrowing just a bit.

"We're looking for an old friend of my brother Andrew's. Johnny Dixon."

"He's a great kid. Hard worker." Daniels peered around the room. "He doesn't seem to be here, but Rebecca can tell you where she's sent him."

"Rebecca just told us that he hasn't come in today," Wade said.

The mayor's eyes shifted from Wade to Kelly and back around the room, almost as if he were acting. She wondered if the mayor already knew that Johnny wasn't there, and wondered if he had any reason to lie.

Kelly leaned forward and touched the mayor's arm. "We were hoping you could give us his phone number and address." At the hesitation in his eyes she repeated, "Johnny was a friend of Andrew's."

"I know." The mayor lost his smile. "Andrew introduced us, but you aren't going to do anything dangerous, are you?"

"You heard about someone running us off the road yesterday?" Wade asked.

"Yeah. The sheriff doesn't think it was an accident, and we're both concerned about you two playing amateur detective. One unexplained death in this town is already one too many. Mustang Valley is a safe place, and we don't need a reputation for violence. It's not good for the residents or the corporations thinking about investing here, and it's not good for my campaign."

"Gee, Mayor. I'd hate to get myself murdered and hurt your campaign," Kelly muttered.

"Look, I didn't mean to sound that cold and you know it. I don't approve of you putting yourself in danger. Let the sheriff do his job."

He sounded concerned. But he was a polished politician, and his voice was probably trained as well as an actor's and could convey whatever he wished.

Kelly forced herself to keep her tone light. "I just wanted to talk to Johnny about law school. I've been accepted for fall semester."

Daniels's grin came back. "Congratulations."

Kelly wondered if his cheeks hurt from all his smiling or if the muscles were accustomed to it. At least she seemed to have turned the topic away from her investigating and the danger. "I'd always figured that Andrew would be around to show me the ropes, but…"

She let her sentence dangle in the air between them unfinished, feeling not the least bit guilty for misleading the man after almost dying yesterday. A girl had to do what a girl had to do. And right now, everyone was a suspect.

Wade put a protective arm over her shoulder. "You'll be fine."

The mayor headed for a file cabinet. "I guess Johnny won't mind my giving out his address to the sister of his old friend." He fingered through file tabs, stopped and read. "It's 22 Mustang Road. Apartment 1C. It's that brick building on the corner with the flat roof across from the gas station."

"Thanks. I know where it is." Wade offered his hand to Daniels.

Daniels shook it. "Johnny's phone number is under new listings in the phone book, but I'll save you the trouble." He wrote on a piece of notepaper and handed it over.

Kelly folded the paper and slipped it into her pocket. "Thank you so much."

"I hope you find what you're looking for." Daniels started to step away and then turned back. "And, Wade?"

"Yes, sir?"

Daniels's tone hardened. "Keep her out of the way of Sheriff Wilson's investigation."

"I'll try, sir."

Kelly smiled sweetly at the two men towering over her. "Did you two forget what century this is?"

"Huh?" Wade muttered.

"What are you saying?" Daniels asked.

"Women have voting rights these days," she pointed out.

Wade scowled at her. The mayor recovered more quickly. "Of course they do. I'll be counting on your vote."

WADE DIDN'T LIKE politicians. He supposed it had something to do with someone else earning a living off his hard-earned tax dollars. In addition, Daniels's smooth-talking ways irritated him. He couldn't read the man and therefore didn't trust him. Which probably meant that Daniels was simply very good at his job.

As they walked down the sidewalk back to her car, Kelly plucked from her purse the cell phone her parents had given her before she'd left their house. Wade didn't blame her folks for wanting to keep tabs on their daughter and reminded himself to replace his own ruined phone. Between keeping his business afloat during his absence and investigating Andrew's murder with Kelly, Wade hadn't had much free time. Nor did he have any family members to worry about him.

His mom had split when he was just a kid. His father had drunk himself into an early grave. An aunt and uncle had taken him in and tried to raise him but by then he'd been accustomed to complete freedom and doing things his way. He now regretted what a tough time he'd given them. After their deaths in a car accident, he'd inherited the Hit 'Em Again and that had probably saved him.

He'd been forced to take on the responsibility of running the business or lose the roof over his head. And he'd worked damn hard to make the place a success. At least he had a good manager to stand in for him. Since he hadn't taken off more than one day a week since he'd inherited the saloon, Wade figured he was due a vacation. If he chose to spend that time with Kelly, and check in once in a while, that was his call—one of the advantages of the self-employed.

Kelly unfolded the paper with Johnny's telephone number and dialed. She held the phone to her ear but didn't say a word for a minute, then snapped it shut with a sigh.

"No answer?" he asked.

She shook her head. "No answering machine or voice mail, either." Kelly plucked the car keys from her purse and tossed them to Wade. "Would you mind driving?"

He snatched the keys out of the air. "Yeah, it's such a chore to drive a Jaguar."

"Very funny."

She didn't wait for him to open her door for her but slipped into the plush leather seat and donned her seat belt. The lady had something on her mind and he couldn't quite peg her mood. Was she considering the mayor's suggestion that they quit? He didn't think so. Ever since she'd left Cara and the *Mustang Gazette,* her temperament had been…pensive.

She didn't even ask him where he was driving, but since they had a little time to kill until they tried Johnny's phone number again, he headed out of town, leaving the traffic behind. He drove past suburban areas until the houses were farther and farther apart and they finally headed onto a dirt road. When he stopped to open a barbwire gate, she seemed to come out of her trance. To open the gate, he slipped out of the Jag before she asked any questions, but when he returned, she had a what-are-we-doing-here look in her eyes.

He turned down the radio. ''Since Mustang Valley doesn't have a gun range, I though we might do some shooting out here.''

''Whose property is this?'' she asked, taking in the crooked fence posts, the sagging barbwire and the shed on the north quarter of the parcel.

''Mine.''

She looked around curiously at the flat, empty acres that had once held cattle but now stood empty. ''You planning on doing some ranching?''

He snorted. ''I don't fancy going broke, but my father had big dreams. This place is the only thing he left me and it's pretty worthless. But I pay the county fifty dollars a year in taxes to keep it, anyway.''

''You never talk about your family.'' He heard the toned-down interest in her voice.

''Not much to say. Didn't know my mother. She ran off and never looked back. Dad drank himself into the grave.''

He caught the pity in her blue eyes before she stared at the horizon. But she kept her tone casual. ''You don't any have cousins, aunts, uncles? No one?''

''You don't miss what you've never had.'' The last thing he wanted was her sympathy or to speak of the aunt and uncle who'd raised him. He threw the Jag into gear and eased over the bumpy, overgrown pasture.

She seemed to realize he didn't want to pursue the

subject. He didn't mind when she tipped back her head on the seat and closed her eyes. A soft little smile played across her mouth, and he would have given tonight's take at the bar to have known her thoughts right then.

He headed for the shed his father had built almost four decades ago. The structure needed a paint job, but last summer Wade had reshingled the roof. The timbers were sturdy and the chained doors kept out vandals—not that there was all that much inside worth stealing—just a few guns and ammunition, a worn-out saddle and bridle and crates of assorted junk that he'd never thrown away.

"So you're going to give me shooting lessons?" That mysterious grin was back on her lips. He wondered exactly what had so amused her.

"I hope you never have to use the weapon your father gave you, but you should know how."

"Okay."

At least she didn't seem to mind that he'd taken a detour from their investigation. He stopped the car by the shed, opened the combination lock and pulled back the doors. Kelly peered inside, her eyes alight with interest, her golden hair gleaming in the sunlight. If she'd been any other woman he would have considered taking out the blanket he kept in a storage trunk, spreading it over a thick patch of grass and…

Don't go there.

She's Andrew's sister. Untouchable.

"Why don't you take your gun out of the glove compartment?" he suggested, not liking the way the gentle breeze carried her scent to him. A light floral scent that reminded him of orange blossoms and rain-kissed flesh. Reminded him of a hot summer night when he and Andrew and Kelly had seen a movie and shared a bucket of popcorn. Her lips had been the same color of pink that night as they were this afternoon, and just as unkissable, he reminded himself.

While he gathered milk crates, empty milk jugs and set up targets, she returned to the car, retrieved her gun and rejoined him. She held the weapon pointing downward between her thumb and pointer finger, her nose squinched up as if she were holding a dead skunk.

He restrained a laugh. Apparently, not even the ridiculous pink holster could make the weapon an acceptable accessory. She was right in one respect. Kelly was all lean, soft curves and feminine delights. The hard metal gun in her hands was almost jarring.

He took the weapon from her fingers, surprised at the weight. "This gun is no Saturday night special."

"Really?"

"It's a 9 mm semi-automatic Beretta." He should have known that while Mr. McGovern didn't know enough not to give his daughter a gun without instructing her how to use it, he wouldn't buy anything cheap, either. Only the best would do when it came to Kelly McGovern.

Wade didn't blame her father. The woman had aroused Wade's protective instincts, too. And he wouldn't allow her to shoot herself in the foot because he hadn't bothered to teach her how to use the weapon.

"So it's a good gun?" Kelly asked.

"Yeah." He took the gun away from her so she

wouldn't drop it in the dirt and get sand in the clip. "I have plenty of ammo."

She shuddered. "You mean we're going to shoot it more than once?"

"Why don't you like guns?"

Kelly looked up at the sky and rolled her eyes. "Who said I didn't like them?"

He checked the safety, which was on, then slipped out a fully loaded clip which slid smoothly into his hand. The gun seemed well oiled and good to go. He checked the chamber. Empty.

He turned his attention to her. "Let's get you outfitted."

She smoothed her blouse, tightening the material over her breasts. "I don't like the shoulder holster. I tried it on for Halloween once, since I thought it would go with my Annie Oakley costume I had made in a special pink leather to match the holster, but the weight made me lopsided, creased my blouse and was just danged uncomfy."

He pictured her as Annie Oakley in a Stetson hat, a short pink leather skirt and vest with matching fringed boots and restrained another grin. "I meant we need to wear protective gear."

"Protective gear?" She frowned at him. "Are you afraid I might shoot you?"

He chuckled. For a smart woman she could be amazingly dense. He handed her a set of sound-deadening ear protectors. "Here you go."

She took the ear guards from him as reluctantly as if he'd handed her a live snake. "That's going to mess up my hair."

"You really don't want to shoot this gun, do

you?'' He wondered if she was thinking about Andrew's being shot, but he couldn't afford to let her out of this, not with their lives at risk.

''I could think of better things to do.'' Her voice purred like a kitten's.

Better things? Like making love on that old blanket of his in an empty field?

His mouth went dry. Although he couldn't decide if her word choice had been deliberately flirtatious, he knew ignoring it would be best. Taking a moment to calm his galloping pulse, he threaded his fingers through his hair.

''Look. Someone may be trying to kill us, but even if they aren't, it's dangerous to carry a loaded gun when you don't know how to use it.''

''Okay.'' She placed the protectors over her ears. ''You don't need to be mean about it.''

Mean? Had his irritation at the images she brought to life in his mind caused his voice to turn harsh?

He handed her the gun. ''First thing you need to know is that even if the gun's unloaded, never point it at anyone unless you intend to shoot them. Treat the weapon as if it's always loaded.''

''Got it.''

''Here's the safety. When it's in this position, you can't pull the trigger.''

''Got it.''

''All right. Here's the clip. Ram it home.''

It took her three tries but she finally loaded the gun, almost dropping it twice in the process. But at least she never aimed it at him.

''Take off the safety,'' he instructed.

She fumbled around but finally flicked the switch. "Now what?"

"Aim at that milk jug, but don't pull the trigger."

"Okay." She poked the gun in the direction of the milk jug, reminding him of a fencer trying to jab an opponent.

"You're going to shoot the gun, not stab someone with it."

She arched her brow and shot him a sarcastic glower. "Now, how did I miss that?"

Ignoring her fit of pique, he issued instructions. "Look through the sight."

She lifted the gun but it drooped. "It's heavy."

"Use two hands."

"Show me," she demanded, and handed him the gun.

"Like this." He braced the wrist of the hand holding the gun with his other hand and looked down the barrel.

She tried but her hands were positioned all wrong.

"Wait a sec." He took her hand and placed it over the other. Her flesh was warm and soft, her pulse racing.

"All right, now, pull the trigger."

She closed her eyes and jerked the trigger. The gun fired and she fell back flat on her butt and almost dropped the gun. Furious, she yanked off the ear protectors, stood and rubbed her butt. "You didn't tell me it would kick me on my—"

He sighed and bit the inside of his cheek to keep from laughing out loud. He knew damn well that a 9 mm didn't have that much kick but played along with her theatrics. "Sorry."

She glared at him like a hissing kitty cat after a bath. "I'm going to be sore. And I now have a grass spot on my jeans."

"You'll live. Put the ear guards back on and try again. This time I'll hold you."

"Fine." Haughtily she put the ear protection back on. "But if you let me fall again, this lesson is over."

He stood behind her and she leaned against him, her hair brushing his cheek, her scent wrapping around him in a sensual cocoon. And that's when he realized he was in trouble. The stance was too intimate, their bodies way too close. With her back to his chest, her bottom nestled against his front and her hips nestled to his crotch, he couldn't ignore the heat seeping into him. Couldn't prevent his reaction to her wriggling to mimic the stance he'd shown her as his arousal tightened the seam of his jeans.

When the gun sagged in her hands, he clenched his teeth in frustration at their enforced proximity but reached around her to help hold the gun. His cheek brushed hers. Her hair tickled his ear. And her scent drove his pulse crazy. "This time, don't close your eyes."

"Why not?"

"Well for one thing, you'll be able to see if you hit your target." His voice came out huskier than he would have liked and he could no longer tell if his hands were steady.

"How will I know if I'm on target?" she demanded, and he realized she was playing word games with him again. He didn't know if he wanted to turn her around and kiss her or turn and walk away.

"You'll know," he assured her.

"Now what?"

"Pull the trigger."

"Okay."

She shot. And shot and shot, the gun wildly raking the grass or firing harmlessly into the air but never once hitting the milk jug. And when the bullets ran out, she flung herself around in his arms, a pleased grin on her face. "I did it. I did it."

Her laughter was contagious but he shook his head. "You didn't hit anything."

"Not yet." And that's when she planted a kiss on his lips and hugged him so tightly that she cut off his breath. Or perhaps it was his tripping heart that cut off his oxygen circulation, but he suspected it was likely her mouth pressed to his, her breasts flattened against his chest, her hips molded to his. With her arms around his neck, one hand in his hair, her mouth encouraged him to kiss her back with tantalizing boldness, and he did what came naturally. He obeyed what hundreds of thousands of years of male instincts told him to do. He gathered her close and kissed her back.

Hot damn, the woman could kiss. And fire him up hotter than a rodeo cowboy on Saturday night. She teased, she taunted, she nipped and she yielded her soft body to him so that he had difficulty knowing who was taking and who was giving. His thoughts spun, and a heady feeling of happiness swept over him. Holding her in his arms was pure pleasure. She was wonderfully soft, fantastically erotic and so…not…for…him.

Gasping for air, he pulled back and scowled at her. "Just what the hell were you thinking?"

"I was thinking that one kiss isn't nearly enough."

He didn't like the way he'd responded to her, as if hit with a lightning bolt of passion, and he hardened his tone. "One kiss—was one too many. I didn't bring you here to fool around."

She glared at him. "Well I don't know about you, but I certainly hit *my* target."

"This is serious."

She tucked the gun into the waistband of her jeans. "When have I ever indicated that I wasn't serious?"

"I was talking about you learning to use the gun."

"Oh, for heaven's sake. Hand me some ammo."

She removed the clip in one smooth motion. He gave her bullets and she loaded the clip with no instruction, without fumbling once. She rammed the clip home like an expert. Then she placed the ear protectors over her head, spun around and fired. The plastic jug jumped and while it was in the air, she hit it again. And again.

He'd been had.

"I thought you said that your father never taught you to use a gun?"

"He didn't. Andrew did."

"And you let me think…"

"Whatever you wanted."

All her pretending had been to get him to put his

arms around her. Anger and admiration and lust battled within him, and when she turned around he raised his hands in mock surrender. ''Okay. Okay. You win.''

Chapter Eight

"What do I win?" Kelly asked, allowing her happiness to show in her eyes.

Wade's kiss had been fantastic. With all the excitement sparking through her, and her lips aching for another kiss, she had a little difficulty following the conversation. But somehow she didn't think words mattered so much right now. Not with that heat in Wade's eyes that fired a piercing shot to her heart.

Man, oh, man, he was yummy. He kissed like a dream, his eyes turned to smoke and he looked like some kind of dangerous angel who would like to ravish her in one gulp. And still he held back. Maybe he still felt guilty for living instead of dying like Andrew, the way she had at first. Sometimes her feelings for Wade made her feel selfish. But she just couldn't think about Andrew or finding his murderer all the time. His death was still too painful and there was nothing wrong with her and Wade exploring their growing friendship—one that she believed Andrew would have eventually approved of. She had no idea from where Wade summoned so much fierce self-control because she could see the desire in his eyes, feel the need radiating off him in waves, hear the rasp in his words.

His nostrils flared and the pulse in his neck thudded erratically. "You win the best-kisser-of-all-time award."

"And?" she prodded, holding herself stiffly, somehow already knowing he intended to reject her again. Although disappointment washed through her that he wouldn't be reaching to take her back into his arms for another extended kiss, she took heart in the fact that each time he denied her he had more difficulty doing so. She inhaled through her nose, let the breath out slowly through her mouth and braced her feet to steady herself against whatever he said next.

"And it's time to call Johnny again," he reminded her.

Damn him. He just had to go and throw their investigation into her brother's murder in her face. She swatted down the guilt that she was messing around with Andrew's best buddy, while her brother rested in his grave. Andrew would want her to live. She would allow herself to miss her brother, but she would not regret kissing Wade—not ever.

Besides, if Wade was feeling half of what she was, he wouldn't be able to resist her much longer. Their growing friendship and trust in one another wasn't just one-sided. She liked him a lot. She admired his loyalty to her brother and his work ethic, and did as Wade suggested and took out her cell phone again. While she called, Wade collected and stored the crates and empty milk jugs and extra ammunition.

"Johnny still isn't answering," she told him.

"Well, we have two choices." Wade relocked the shed, his strong fingers snicking the chain tight. He moved with such smooth confidence, she wondered what those fingers would feel like on her skin, and flushed at the thought. Wade paid no attention to her, testing the lock. "We can head into Dallas to talk to Debbie West's ex-husband or we can drive back to town and hope Johnny shows up."

"It's kind of late in the day to drive into Dallas. Besides, I'd rather try and line up an appointment with Niles. A businessman like him is bound to be busy, and for all we know he could be out of town."

"All right. We head back to Mustang Valley," Wade agreed, allowing her to make the choice.

She liked the fact that Wade often let her make the decisions. Other men—and their egos—felt threatened by her. She'd never been around anyone as strong or self-sufficient as Wade, or anyone who seemed to have as little to prove. His self-confidence allowed him to treat her as an equal and she liked the way he made her feel valued and special. Wanted.

Oh, he might be temporarily resisting, but he wanted her all right. During their kiss, she'd felt his arousal pressed against her. But she didn't understand his reason for playing hard to get. She wondered if he'd made some kind of promise to her brother to hold back, or perhaps it was more simple. Perhaps he just hadn't had a woman in a long time and, while he was aroused by her, he didn't like her enough to pursue her.

She didn't like that possibility.

However, Wade could be remarkedly close-mouthed when he didn't want to talk. He'd mentioned his family, giving her a brief explanation that was civil, without going into details. Coaxing him to talk about his reasons for rebuffing her wouldn't be easy—yet that didn't deter her one whit. Although she understood that part of his resistance was because she was Andrew's sister, she didn't know his exact reasons. Wade was a man worth putting forth some effort to understand. And she planned to do much more than understand him.

"What are you thinking?" Wade asked on the drive back into town.

"Why do you ask?" she countered.

"You have this mysterious smile on your lips. One corner of your mouth is turned up as if you have a delicious secret and are about to burst into laughter."

"Really? I'll have to be more careful," she told him, seemingly not at all disturbed by his observation. In fact his watching her so closely and asking that kind of question revealed that her tactics this afternoon were working on him on several different levels. And she saw absolutely nothing wrong with thinking about their relationship as they searched for Andrew's murderer. Thinking about Andrew all the time was just so sad that she had to allow herself a respite. And it wasn't as if they weren't already doing everything in their power to figure out what had happened.

"So what were you thinking about?" he repeated.

"You don't want to know." She deliberately evaded the question and challenged him to provoke his curiosity.

He pulled out onto the highway. "I wouldn't have asked if I didn't want to know."

"Okay. I was thinking about you."

"Could you be more specific?"

"I was thinking about how you reacted to our kiss."

He glared at her.

She grinned. "I told you that you didn't want to know. Despite all Southern-belle rumors to the contrary, women do think about sex, you know."

"Did anyone ever tell you that you're incorrigible?"

She sighed. "Maybe that's why I can't seem to keep a boyfriend."

"That's not what I heard. Andrew told me you've left a trail of broken hearts all over Texas."

"Andrew loved to exaggerate. But he also understood women."

He shot her a sideways glance. "Meaning I don't?"

"You don't understand me."

"Well, we can agree there."

"Damn it." Her frustration level rose several degrees until she felt hot enough to turn the air conditioner down to its lowest setting. "Why must you do that?"

"Do what?"

"Agree with me."

"You want me to argue?"

"You agree with me when you want me to shut up."

"Well, it beats the alternative, which would be kissing you."

Now that was insulting. "And kissing me is so terrible because…?"

He chuckled, and she realized too late he'd been teasing her. However, she still wished he'd answer her question. But he let her words hang in the air between them unanswered.

Instead of satisfying her burning curiosity, he kept his eyes peeled on the road and was clearly maintaining his focus on why he was with her. "Why don't you try calling Johnny again?"

JOHNNY STILL HADN'T ANSWERED his phone, so they drove by the mayor's campaign office again. No one there had seen or heard from him all day. Kelly was about to call it quits. After spending the afternoon with Wade, she was both tired and encouraged. She looked forward to a peaceful dinner and evening at his place to wear down his resistance to her a little more. Maybe, if she got lucky—a lot more.

Too bad it wasn't politically correct to use Shotgun Sally's tactic. Kelly had no doubt her ancestor might have just pointed her gun at her man and made him admit that he wanted her. However much that idea appealed to Kelly, she figured that going to such extremes wouldn't be necessary, not after that wondrous kiss that had curled her toes and lightened her heart. Not after Wade had seemed just as stunned as she'd been at the embers they'd kindled and sparked into flames.

Whew. Just thinking about that kiss gave her an edge. Because no matter how cool and disinterested Wade acted, she knew better. Chemistry, lust, attraction, whatever she wanted to call the electric tension between them was there, all right. What she didn't know was if he had any feelings for her.

One thing at a time.

"Let's drive over to Johnny's apartment." Wade clearly had his mind on their search for her brother's "friend." Wade drove from the mayor's campaign headquarters toward a residential section of town. The quiet streets and homes with green lawns along with kids playing tag or riding their bikes seemed to mock the idea that Johnny might be in town for nefarious purposes.

His quadplex was a neat brick one-story where he rented one of the four units in the building. Wade parked the car and they both strode down a brick sidewalk to the front door. She didn't see any interior lights shining through the windows. Nor did she hear a TV or stereo, either.

Kelly's nerves were on edge. Of all the suspects on their list, in her opinion, Johnny was one of the most likely to have killed her brother. His motive of revenge, for retaliation at Andrew's getting him kicked out of law school by reporting him for cheating, seemed a simple reason for hatred. And when all his friends had graduated and gone on to practice law and Johnny had been unemployed, had his anger at her brother erupted into violence? She didn't know, but as Wade knocked on the door, Kelly was very glad to have him by her side.

When no one answered, Wade knocked harder.

Johnny's door remained closed, but the neighbor opened his. A thin man in his early twenties peered at them through thick glasses. He held a baby in his arms and a toddler sat on his foot, her tiny legs wrapped around his ankle.

Wade spoke apologetically. "Sorry to disturb you."

"No problem," the neighbor replied. "The walls are so thin we tend to hear everything. That's why Johnny's such a great neighbor. He's a quiet one."

Kelly couldn't help recalling all the interviews she'd seen on television after a murder where the neighbors claimed the shooter had always been quiet. She shuddered a little.

Observant as always, Wade placed an arm over her shoulder. "You wouldn't know where we could find Johnny would you?"

"Go, Daddy. Go," the toddler demanded, obviously disappointed her ride had ended.

"In a minute, honey pie." The man popped the baby's pacifier back into its mouth and spoke to Wade. "I have no idea where he went, but you're the second person who's asked me about him today."

Kelly covered her surprise and kept her tone casual. "Who else asked?"

"The sheriff came by around three o'clock. I told him the same thing I'm telling you. I haven't seen Johnny all day. I'm afraid I'm not much help."

"Thanks, anyway," Wade said and turned as if to go.

"You said you had no idea where Johnny went."

Kelly took a stab in the dark. "What makes you think he was going somewhere?"

"When I went out to pick up my newspaper, I saw him place an overnight bag in his car trunk. I might have stopped for a conversation, but the baby started crying, so I just waved and headed inside."

"Okay. Thanks again." Wade handed the man one of his business cards. "If he shows up, would you ask him to call me?"

"Sure." The neighbor shut the door, and Wade started to steer Kelly back to the car.

They'd reached a dead end. Kelly wondered what Cara would do if she were on a story. Cara never gave up, which was what made her such a good reporter. Her friend would knock on doors, pester every neighbor.

"Maybe we should question the other people in the building," she suggested.

"Good idea." Wade hugged her a little tighter. "It was also great that you picked up on Johnny having gone somewhere. I didn't catch that."

"Thanks." Wade didn't mind that she'd thought of something that he hadn't. In fact, he seemed pleased by her initiative. Kelly had never realized before how often she'd hid her intelligence when she'd been with other men. She'd learned early in life that men liked to believe they were smarter, and she'd let them, but in doing so she'd suppressed a part of herself that she missed. Using her brain was satisfying, and she appreciated being with Wade because he had enough confidence in himself not to be threatened by her intelligence.

She complimented him in turn. "I'm not sure I'd

have had the courage to knock on his door if you weren't here with me,'' she admitted. ''And now that Johnny's left town, he seems even more suspicious.''

''He could be perfectly innocent. Maybe he had a hot date or went to Fort Worth for a job interview.''

That was another thing she liked about Wade. He could disagree with her, presenting another possibility without putting down her or her idea. He simply mentioned another side of things and he didn't seem to care who was right—as long as they solved the mystery.

They strode around to the other side of the building, and Kelly rang the doorbell. A white-haired lady cracked open the door and peered at them. ''I'm not buying anything.''

Kelly chuckled. ''We aren't selling anything, ma'am. We were hoping you might know where your neighbor Johnny Dixon has gone.''

''Never heard of him.'' The neighbor slammed the door.

''Okay.'' So much for Kelly's polite demeanor making friends and influencing people's help, but she wasn't about to give up. ''Let's try this last apartment.''

Wade knocked, but there was no answer. ''Looks like we struck out.''

Disappointed, Kelly headed back along the sidewalk to where Wade had parked the car. ''We can try again tomorrow.''

But she halted as an old souped-up Mustang pulled into the space opposite the apartment door they'd just tried. A man got out of the car from the driver's side, a woman from the passenger side. With her short, curly blond hair, petite figure and snappy dress style, she would have been pretty without the frown marring her face. The man scowled first at the woman, then at Wade and Kelly who were blocking his path.

There was a tension about the couple that suggested they'd been arguing. The woman had drawn her red lips into a pout, and her eyes brimmed with tears that had yet to escape down her cheeks. The man's body language, his too-stiff shoulders and ramrod straight spine, plus the set of his tense neck told Kelly that she and Wade could have picked a better time to ask their questions. But they were there. The couple probably didn't even know Johnny—after all he had just moved to town several weeks ago.

"Excuse me, sir." Kelly shot the man her best friendly grin. "I'm looking for Johnny Dixon."

"You and every other slut in this town," the man sneered.

Beside her Wade bristled. Kelly took his hand and squeezed his fingers, signaling him to stand down. She wanted information not a fight, and let the insult slide. "You mean Johnny has someone besides…"

"Yeah. You'll have to get in line behind my *wife*." The man barreled around them and went inside. Apparently his wife knew Johnny better than her husband liked.

The woman stared after her husband, clearly reluctant to follow him inside. Kelly strolled over to her, and the woman lifted her chin. "Don't mind Kevin. He's jealous of every man I talk to."

"So you've spoken to Johnny? Do you know where we can find him?" Kelly clued in on the hesitation in the woman's eyes. "Please, it's important."

"He left this morning."

"Did he say where he was going?" Wade asked.

"Yeah. He said he was heading to Fort Worth and that if he returned it might be to pack and leave for good." The woman sighed. "It's probably just as well. Kevin, my husband, and Johnny might have got into a shooting match if he had stayed—but there was nothing going on between us. I swear it."

"Johnny had a gun?" Wade asked.

"Yeah. It was the only thing he and Kevin had in common."

WADE THOUGHT HARD while Kelly thanked the neighbor. He took her hand and pretended to head toward the car until the neighbor disappeared behind his front door. "Why don't you wait in the car?"

She peered at him with suspicion. "You trying to get rid of me?"

For once he cursed her sharp intelligence that let her see right through him. But he didn't bother to lie and hoped she wouldn't give him an argument over his plan. They needed more clues, and right now he saw only one way to obtain them.

He kept his voice low. "Unless you're up for breaking and entering, I suggest you do as I asked."

Her blue eyes narrowed but not before he saw a glimmer of excitement mix with blatant disapproval. "You're going to break into Johnny's apartment? How?"

''That lock is so flimsy, it wouldn't keep out those stone-throwing juvenile delinquents.''

Wade extracted an army knife from his back pocket and opened a thin blade. He picked the lock as easily as if he'd used a key. Striding inside, he perused the living area. The overstuffed chair and threadbare couch probably came with the place. The tiny kitchen that extended off the living area had a peeling linoleum floor but was spotless—probably never used.

''If you're coming inside, hurry up before some-one sees you,'' he instructed.

Kelly stepped over the threshold and shut the door, but just stood there as if she couldn't believe she'd actually accompanied him. ''What are we looking for?''

''Anything connected to Andrew. Anything that might tell us where Johnny went. And I'd like a look at his gun—that is, if he didn't take it with him.'' Wade headed into the bedroom to search, figuring that was the likeliest place to stash a weapon.

Johnny's clothes hung in the closet. He still had socks and underwear in a battered bureau. A stack of law books sat piled on a rickety nightstand. Obviously, Johnny intended to return and pick up his things.

Wade searched under the mattress, in the closet and bureau but he found no sign of a gun. He found no notes in the nightstand. No diary. Nothing to go on.

A quick search in the bathroom revealed a bottle of aspirin, a half-used bottle of shampoo. No razor.

No toothbrush. The man expected to be gone at least overnight, just as the neighbor had claimed.

"Wade."

"Yeah?" He left the bedroom and joined Kelly in the living room.

She pointed to an answering machine. "I played back his messages. There's one from the sheriff, two from campaign headquarters asking his whereabouts. Now listen to this." Kelly pressed a button.

And Wade heard a familiar voice that he couldn't quite identify until the speaker gave them her name. "Johnny. This is Lindsey Wellington at Lambert & Church. Call me back immediately. It's important."

Kelly peered at the machine. "She left that message last night. I think Johnny got the news and forgot to erase it." She looked at Wade. "Did you find the gun?"

"No."

"Neither did I. Maybe he took it with him. Or maybe he keeps it in his car like I do." Kelly looked around, her eyes bleak. "Can we get out of here?"

Wade checked his watch. "If we hurry we might catch Lindsey at Lambert & Church before she goes home for the day. I'd like to know why she called Johnny and what was so important."

When Kelly and Wade caught up with the attorney, Lindsey Wellington didn't look as if she would be heading home for several hours. The last time they'd been in her office, her desk had been immaculate, but now notes covered the surface. She'd taped a plat map to the wall. Obviously she was busy, yet she greeted them with a friendly smile.

"Wade. Kelly. I'm just going over the paperwork

for the Wests' sale of their property. It was Andrew's deal, but I know he was concerned over the details. I figure it's the least I can do for the fiancée and her family. Please. Come in. Have a seat. What can I do for you?''

Kelly took a chair. ''Thanks. Andrew would have appreciated your help, I'm sure.''

Wade could see that Lindsey was busy and got right to the point. ''We're looking for Johnny Dixon. Do you have any idea where he might be?''

''As a matter of fact, I might. Johnny's work on the mayor's campaign was only temporary. Andrew had hoped to find him a permanent job at city hall but it didn't pan out. I happened to speak with a friend of mine in Fort Worth, and she mentioned that her firm was looking for a law clerk and I suggested Johnny.''

''Would you have the address of the law firm?'' Wade asked.

''You're going all the way to Fort Worth to find him?'' Lindsey's Boston accent thickened. ''What's so important that you can't wait until he comes back?''

Wade exchanged a long look with Kelly. He would leave it up to her to decide whether or not to tell Lindsey that Andrew had been murdered. And that one of their prime suspects was Johnny Dixon.

Kelly didn't answer Lindsey but asked a question of her own. ''Can you tell me what Johnny's attitude toward Andrew was like?''

''What difference does it make now?'' Lindsey asked. She paced behind her desk, as if setting her thoughts in order. ''I only saw the two of them together twice. Once here at Lambert & Church and once at lunch at Dot's. Andrew treated Johnny like one of his lost sheep. He seemed to collect people who needed his help.''

"But what was Johnny's attitude toward Andrew?" Kelly pressed.

"If you're asking me if he murder—"

"Who said anything about murder?" Kelly asked.

"I heard a discussion when I was at the coffee machine."

Kelly shrugged. "I should have known. After all, this is Mustang Valley. Word gets around."

Lindsey spun around and headed back in the opposite direction, her quick steps eating up the distance. "Johnny is desperate to get a job. I had to lend him gas money to drive to Fort Worth."

"So he won't be staying overnight in a hotel," Wade surmised, but then, why had he taken his toothbrush?

Lindsey stopped pacing and leaned over her desk, peering at a bunch of notes. "Actually, the company where he's interviewing said they'd put him up for the night."

So much for the missing toothbrush.

"It's odd that he took off without telling anyone at the mayor's campaign headquarters," Kelly muttered, probably recalling the messages on the machine. Wade would also like to know why the sheriff had left a message and also stopped by the apartment but he might be following up on Andrew's case.

Wade went back to a statement Lindsey had made earlier. "So what's your opinion of Johnny?"

"Obviously, I wouldn't have recommended him if I didn't think him qualified."

"I was talking about whether he still harbored any ill will toward Andrew," Wade explained.

Lindsey folded her arms across her chest. "I'm not a mind reader."

"But you have an opinion?" Kelly pressed.

"My opinion is that under extreme pressure any person is capable of losing control of themselves."

"And was Johnny close to the edge?" Kelly prodded even harder.

"I'm a lawyer not a psychiatrist."

"We aren't in a court of law asking for expert testimony. I'd just like your opinion." Kelly walked around the desk. "Please, Lindsey. Is there anything else you can tell us?"

"All I know is that Johnny was broke and dejected about his future." She rustled through her memos and plucked out a piece of paper. "Here's where he intended to stay, the law firm where he interviewed and the name and phone number of my friend."

"Thanks." Kelly took the paper and began to walk toward the office's exit.

"Oh, there's one more thing."

"Yes?" Kelly turned, her forward progress halted.

"Please let me know if you find him. I'm a little worried," Lindsey admitted.

"Why?" Kelly asked.

"He promised to call me back after his interview and let me know what happened. I haven't heard from him."

Chapter Nine

Kelly had mostly stopped feeling bad over enjoying Wade's company. But she still felt occasional stabs of guilt that she was alive and could talk to Wade and enjoy his friendship when Andrew couldn't. Although she was doing her best to find Andrew's killer, her brother would have wanted her to live life to the fullest, and she planned to do that.

If Johnny didn't return to Mustang Valley to work by tomorrow morning, Kelly and Wade would get up early and drive to Fort Worth. With their investigation on hold for the evening, Wade fed Kelly a bowl of his famous chili for dinner. She contributed the garlic bread and dessert, a decadent topping of melted butter and brown sugar, syrup and pecans spooned over rich vanilla ice cream. After cleaning up the kitchen, he'd checked in with his manager at the saloon, and she'd ended up on Wade's back deck in the hot tub, wondering how to get him to join her.

By now she could have supplied herself with a swimsuit, but that would have been counterproductive to her plan to seduce Wade. Except how could she begin to sweep him away when the stubborn man refused to come anywhere near her?

She tilted back her head, allowing the heat to soothe her tense muscles, but she had difficulty ignoring her nipples that pebbled every time she thought about Wade joining her. Instead, he sat several frustrating feet away on the porch swing, fully clothed, his mind clearly set against her.

Backlit by indirect lighting, he peered off in the distance—deliberately she was sure—not looking her way. His dark hair gleamed and his face appeared calm in repose, but the jut of his jaw reminded her of a man gnashing his teeth. And he kept pulling at the neck of his T-shirt as if it were too tight, letting her know that he was a lot more edgy than he was trying to appear.

What would Shotgun Sally do? Pretend to drown and then drag him into the tub with her? At the ridiculous thought, Kelly chuckled.

Or maybe Sally would pull out her gun and force him to join her naked in the tub and then let nature take its course?

She cursed under her breath.

''I heard that,'' Wade teased, his tone knowing, as if he could read her mind and knew exactly what was wrong. ''Did Andrew know that you use language like that?''

''Andrew was my brother. My older, protective brother. And he preferred to think of me as a kid, not a woman with a mind of her own.'' She cupped some water and let it trickle through her fingers, enjoying the feel of the wet heat in the cool night air.

"Andrew didn't take into account that I like to be kissed and held and pursued. Hint, hint."

"I have no interest in pursuing you," he told her with a mix of both laughter and irritation.

"I suppose I should be grateful." She splashed water in his direction, sprinkling him with a few drops.

He moved his chair back another twelve inches. "Why?"

"Because after our kiss, I'd imagine that if we made love it would be…wonderful."

"You aren't making sense."

"Sure I am." She didn't bother to restrain her sarcasm. "Why would you want to feel wonderful when you can sit over there by yourself and brood?"

"I'm not brooding."

She chuckled. "If you say so. But you know shooting that gun caused me to exercise muscles today that I don't ordinarily use. I guess I'll just have to ease that soreness myself. My fingers and palms, all the way up to my forearms, require massaging." She lifted one hand out of the water and rubbed at the sore spots with the other, lingering, playing with the water, allowing the moonlight to glint off the water droplets clinging to her skin, her motions a giant caress meant strictly to entice him out of that chair.

He didn't budge. "You don't play fair," he complained, staring at her, his voice husky.

She took her time, stroking first one arm, then the other, as if she were applying suntan oil. "Too bad you won't join me because I'm sure your fingers could work out…my…aches…better than I can myself.''

He choked on her double entendre. ''You're shameless.''

''I know what I want,'' she countered with a boldness that she must have inherited from her famous ancestor, because she sure as hell had never acted like this before. But she found herself enjoying the challenge of pursuing him—even if it meant throwing caution to the gods of lust and recklessness. She turned in the tub and folded her arms on the top ledge, then rested her chin, keeping the water up to her neck.

''You don't have a clue what I want,'' he said.

And he'd made it clear he wasn't going to tell her, which only egged her on. ''I'm not a virgin, Wade. Nor am I a tramp.''

''I've never thought that.''

''I'm choosy and I want you.'' She laid her words out with brazen abandon—after all, she had nothing to lose but her pride. And yet, even if he turned her down again, she knew every attempt was bringing her ever closer to her objective. He couldn't disguise the raw need in his tone any more than she could hold back her words. ''I suppose if you have no intention of being with me, I'll just have to take care of myself.'' At the same time she told him that, she smoothed a hand along her neck and toward her chest, stopping just above her breasts.

He groaned, no longer able to tear his gaze away from her. ''Stop it.''

''Okay.''

She stood up in the waist-high water. The moonlight glinted off her breasts and the cool night air barely lowered her internal temperature. Never in her life had she acted so boldly, but between the death of her brother and almost losing her own life the other day, she knew life could end suddenly, and she wanted to make the most of hers. She didn't want to hold back her feelings or her desire for this man, and if that took baring her body and coming to him naked, she could do so.

She'd never felt more vulnerable in her life. Or more triumphant as the hunger in his eyes reminded her of a tiger about to leap on its prey. He clenched his jaw, deepening the hollows of his cheekbones and giving his expression a savage sharpness that made her breath catch. At the sight of the bulge in his jeans, she restrained a satisfied grin.

Dipping her hands beneath the water, she cupped a handful, then splashed it over her, enjoying the wet heat and the cool air. "Come play with me, Wade."

"No."

She fisted her hands on her hips. "Why not?"

"I don't owe *you* explanations."

"You don't owe me a thing." She had no idea what made her flatten her palms on her tummy, then smooth them up her midriff until she saw him swallow hard with a fierce longing that he had no reason to deny.

He sucked in his breath and released the air in a slow hiss. "I promised Andrew that I'd look after you."

"So go ahead and look."

"Damn it. Stop playing games."

"What's wrong with playing games?" Ducking

underwater and holding her breath, she cut off any response he could possibly make. Let him stew in his own frustration. Let him wonder if she'd changed her mind. Let him—

The water churned with his arrival. He hadn't stopped to take off his clothes. In the underwater lights of the hot tub, she could see he'd kicked off his shoes, hadn't bothered to take off his shirt or jeans or socks, revealing his impatience. He seized her shoulders with his large hands and jerked her to the surface, and for a moment she considered whether she'd pushed him too far.

Then his mouth crashed down on hers, taking before she offered, demanding, and divulging a need he'd failed to deny.

About time.

She wasn't sure she could have faced him in the morning if he'd spun and walked away. But now that he was here, holding her, kissing her, she reveled in his clean male scent. In his clever mouth and ardent hands that roved over her back and melted her insides.

Sizzling heat pounded through her veins, and she wanted to make this last. She wanted to savor her need and his. But she felt caught up in his power, as if she'd stolen a ride on a runaway train. She wrapped her arms around his neck and hung on, plastered her breasts against his chest and kissed him back until her thoughts whirled and her heart raced on a pure adrenaline rush.

The heady feeling of knowing he wanted to resist her but couldn't had her gulping for air and grabbing his shirt to pull it over his head. He laughed into her neck and let her remove his shirt, and when they finally stood flesh to flesh, her skin skimming over his hard chest, her lips and teeth exploring his jaw and neck, she wanted more.

"Hey. Slow down," he whispered.

She nipped his shoulder. "No way."

"There's no rush."

But there was. She didn't want to give him a moment to think, for fear he might change his mind. And after joining her in the water, after tasting the caramel on his breath from their luscious dessert, after holding him so close, she couldn't bear to risk him backing off.

"Wade."

"Mmm." He nuzzled a path down her neck that left a trail of blazing heat.

"I'm not sure I can stand up while you do that."

"I'm just getting started."

That's exactly what she wanted to hear. Yet, contradictorily, she needed him to hurry. She wanted to take off his clothes, but he seemed more interested in exploring the shell of her ear. And, damn it, his hands hadn't even come close to exploring her breasts. Here she was in his arms, naked, available and he seemed more interested in her neck than getting down to business.

"Wade."

Shamelessly she arched her breasts against his powerful chest, her nipples budding with hot bliss. "Touch me."

"I am touching you. You have the silkiest skin and you taste like nectar."

He ran his lips down her neck and she shivered

in anticipation. At the same she reached for his jeans and fumbled with his belt. If the water ruined the leather, she'd buy him a new one.

Just as she reached for his zipper, his mouth closed over the tip of one breast. She gasped, her fingers losing contact with the metal fastener, her mind losing focus on the task she'd set for herself. His tongue swirled and created a magic aura that wrapped around and blanketed her in a trance, where she could only stand still and ride out the pleasure.

Any reservations she might have had about encouraging him wilted. She couldn't feel this good, this needy, this desperate unless they were meant to have this moment together. A sense of certainty, of rightness, of expectation and hope let her drop her normal inhibitions with Wade in a way she'd never done before.

As he held her in one spot with hands and teeth and tongue, her legs weakened just as her pulse raced.

"Please," she murmured, unsure of what she was even asking him for. She only knew he couldn't keep her so still. She needed to move. To use her mouth on him at the same moment he tasted her.

He bit lightly, then licked away the tingling love bite before attending to her other breast, giving it identical loving. Her fingers tugged his hair, trying to urge him on. But intent on being thorough, he held her fast, his jeans out of her reach.

"You feel too good." She tried to step back, but he kept her captured with his teeth, and the tug of his lips almost had her moaning in frustration.

"There's no such thing as feeling too good," he

murmured, his lips tickling and teasing her breast while his hand ministered to her other breast until desire welled up so hot and heavy that she wanted to pound on him to stop. Only she didn't want him to stop. She wanted more. Her entire body trembled for him, but every time she moved, he nipped and kept her exactly where he demanded.

"Damn you, Wade. I need you inside me."

"Okay." He agreed, but the foolish man kept right on with his sensual assault to her breasts until her head spun and she had to grab his shoulders to keep her balance.

"We need…I need…to take off…your jeans," she told him as a bolt of pure lust shocked her from her breasts to her toes.

"Okay." With his teeth on her breast, and one hand roving over her other breast, she didn't dare move. He had her trapped on the edge of desire, and he seemed intent on keeping her there, teasing, taunting, tempting until she was ready to scream with a longing for release.

His free hand dipped between her thighs, teasing the curls, and she didn't know if she parted her legs for him or if they were already parted. She only knew she'd never felt so vulnerable, so lusty, so ready to explode. Just a few caresses of his fingers between her slick folds would drive her over the edge. She trembled with anticipation, every muscle tensing for his touch.

She waited. And waited, but he always seemed to miss the exact spot where she needed him most. And then it struck her that he was reading her like a book, keeping her right on the edge on purpose, denying her the ultimate pleasure just to drive her crazy with frustration.

''I can't take…much more.''

''Okay.''

To her surprise, he released her. He placed his hands on her waist and lifted her out of the tub, setting her bottom down on the deck with her legs dangling into the water. The cool breeze on her hot skin created a sizzling sensation down her spine, but when his head dipped between her legs and his tongue licked her, she let out a short scream, half panic—half pure pleasure.

And every sensation that he'd created swept her into a tumbling cascade of need. Her head tilted back, her back arched, her breasts thrust wantonly upward at the sky. His tongue on her most intimate place, his hands cradling her bottom, his fingers holding her tipped up and open.

She flattened her palms on the deck and her knees hooked over his shoulders. And then he feasted until she squirmed, until she moaned, until she floundered wildly, caught between where he so wickedly kept her and where she so desperately wanted to go.

And when she could take no more, when every cell in her body demanded release, he pulled back, climbed from the pool and swept her into his arms.

And she didn't know whether to kiss him or curse him because she felt like a wild woman, ready to attack, he'd set her to simmering, heated her until she almost boiled over, and then he'd denied her his heat just when she needed it most. He set her down in the bedroom and made her stand still while he dried her with a towel, taking his time to caress her face and neck and breasts and back and bottom with the thick terry cloth, until she snapped it out of his hands and returned the favor.

The man had a chest that could have been on a fitness magazine. A light dusting of chest hair made him sexy as hell, but it was the heat in his eyes that jolted her into returning the favor.

She might have driven him to the brink when he'd jumped into the hot tub, but he'd just done the same to her. She clung to her sanity just barely, and did her utmost to ignore the out-of-control fire he'd stoked as she dried his back and stomach.

And finally, she tugged down his zipper. Pulling off his wet jeans took more strength than she had, but not even gravity or his slender hips came to her aid. Even with the open zipper, she tugged on the wet material, tried sliding her hands inside the waist and down his buttocks to separate the clinging denim from…bare skin. Wade didn't wear underwear.

As time passed, she regained a little control over herself and now she saw an opportunity for payback. Yes, removing his wet jeans was a chore, but when she could have tugged them down an inch, she settled for less and with each sliver of hips and thighs that she revealed, she stroked, caressed and patted.

And when his jeans finally pooled at his feet, he kicked off his socks and either he tackled her or she tackled him onto the mattress—she wasn't sure which. Nor did it matter, since their actions got them where she wanted to be. On his bed. In his arms.

She'd landed on top and he grinned up at her, his smile utterly charming. "Are you going to have your way with me, woman?"

"I believe I am."

He jerked his thumb at the nightstand. "Condoms are in the top drawer."

She leaned over to open the drawer, and he took her breast back into his mouth. Fire shot through her, and all of her need came raging back. She dropped the first condom on the floor, reached for another. He reached and slipped a finger into her delicate folds, and her hands shook so badly, she couldn't open the packet.

"Would you stop that for a minute?"

"Mmm."

In frustration she used her teeth, ripped open the packet and saw that she'd torn the condom, too. "Damn it. I need another one."

"Mmm." His tongue and teeth made movement difficult. This time she took the entire box and dumped the contents on the bed. She fumbled again, but opened the damned thing. His fingers found her and she groaned.

She needed him inside her, filling her, stroking her. This time she opened the slippery packet more carefully. Unrolled it over him, not an easy task when she couldn't see exactly what she was doing. But from the frantic motion of his mouth and his fingers, he was just as eager to join with her as she was for him.

Her breath came in raw pants. But finally she positioned her hips over him, slid down his erection. And held perfectly still. "Ah, I finally have you."

"Let me introduce you to a concept." His hands clasped her hips. "It's called movement."

"I think we should wait."

"That's not going to happen." He rolled on top of her in one swift movement.

She should have protested. He'd made her wait. He'd said she could have her way with him, but he was taking over. Not that she could complain when he felt so good. And she liked the idea of him losing control, of not being able to keep to what he'd said. Of his having to have her right now.

When he began to thrust, hard and fast, she wrapped her legs around him, drew his mouth to hers. His fullness ignited the explosion and as wave after wave of pleasure washed over her, he kept moving, kept going. She gasped for air, dug her fingertips into his back and hung on as she burst again and then again. This time he was right there with her.

Minutes later, when her galloping heart slowed and her lungs stopped burning for air, she realized that he had his hands clenched in her hair and he snuggled close, yet protectively, keeping his full weight from pressing her into the mattress.

He rolled them both onto their sides. "We need to talk."

"Mmm."

"I'm serious."

"I don't want to talk." She wanted to enjoy every residual effect of their lovemaking. Her body felt heavy and sated, more relaxed than she'd ever known. And with the buzz of multiple orgasms still in her bones, the last thing she wanted was to analyze this marvelous experience.

One glance at the determination in his eyes told

her she wouldn't like what he was about to say. She placed a finger on his lips. "Shh."

"No can do." He rolled off the bed, headed to the bathroom.

She pulled the sheet over her and closed her eyes. Maybe she could fall asleep before he returned. Wade had been absolutely yummy in bed. And his actions, the care he'd taken with her body, told her much more than any conversation could about his feelings.

She might not be able to fall asleep, but she could pretend. He took a quick shower, and by the time he returned, her breathing was steady. She could feel him looking down at her, but kept her eyes closed.

He hesitated, as if deciding whether or not to join her in his bed. When the mattress dipped, she didn't allow her smile to reach her lips. And when he slipped under the covers, she snuggled against him. His arm came around her. And then she no longer had to pretend to sleep.

TOO HYPED TO SLEEP Wade listened to her breathing. He wasn't proud of himself. He'd known better than to take Kelly to bed. He should have held back. But when she'd stood up in that hot tub, the water glistening over her breasts, he'd simply been too aroused to resist.

Instinct took over. Instincts that told him he would never forget this night and that he would regret his weakness for many years to come.

And guilt played into the mixture. He'd promised Andrew to look out for his little sister. Andrew hadn't meant make wild, crazy, awesome love to her.

So he'd disappointed the trust his friend had placed in him. What was more important, he'd disappointed himself. He didn't believe in tasting caviar when one must dine regularly on cheese and bread. One didn't test drive a Ferrari when one drove a pickup truck. But now that he'd tasted the forbidden fruit, he'd have to suffer the consequences.

He deserved the sleepless nights, the comparison of knowing other women wouldn't measure up to what she'd given him. She hadn't held back. She'd kept up. And she'd tasted sweeter than any exotic dessert.

But no way would it happen again. She'd taken the edge off his lust. Now there was no more mystery between them. They'd go to Fort Worth tomorrow, find Johnny and get to the bottom of things. Perhaps they would have to go to Dallas and talk to Debbie West's husband. And even if they never figured out who murdered Andrew, Kelly would return to school after her summer break.

He wouldn't allow himself to become any more involved. And so he allowed himself to enjoy, just this once, the fragrance of her hair on his pillow, the soft silkiness of her breast against his chest, the smoothness of her legs entwined with his.

Shortly before dawn, Wade entered that twilight zone just before falling asleep when a thud brought him to full wakefulness. Had a raccoon climbed on his roof?

Had a neighbor's dog come scrounging around his trash can?

Once again wide awake, he eased out of bed and reached for the gun on his nightstand. He didn't bother to dress but padded silently from the bedroom without waking Kelly.

It was probably nothing.

Nevertheless, he didn't turn on any lights. He stepped quietly and carefully into the living area.

The front door was closed. So was the back. But he hadn't turned his security system on after they'd come inside from the back deck. Other things had been on his mind.

He peered into the kitchen. Checked the front closet.

Nothing.

He was about to engage the system and head back to bed when he heard the creak of shoe leather scuffing across the front stoop. The hair on the back of his neck raised.

If he'd been alone, he'd go outside to investigate. But he had to stay inside to protect Kelly. Because if she ever came to harm, Wade would never forgive himself.

Chapter Ten

A soft knock on the front door followed by a feminine "Kelly, are you awake?" made Wade realize that the female outside didn't mean any harm. However, he had no intention of opening the door stark naked with a gun in his hand.

"Give me a minute to dress," he called out.

He hurried to the bedroom where Kelly remained sound asleep, her face snuggled into his pillow. He put the gun back on the nightstand, donned a fresh pair of jeans and grabbed a shirt but didn't put it on.

Then he shook Kelly's shoulder. "Wake up, Sleeping Beauty."

"Mmm." She barely stirred.

"Wake up," he said again. He shook her a little harder. When she still didn't move, he flipped on the light, appreciating the way the golden rays kissed her skin. "Wake up. You've got company."

Kelly immediately straightened, her eyes wide open. "What do you mean *I've* got company?"

He wondered if she'd been playing possum and had pretended to sleep, but why? He frowned at the only reason he could reach—that she didn't want to speak to him. How ironic that every other woman he'd dated always wanted to talk and he hadn't. Now he needed to have a relationship conversation and in all likelihood Kelly was the one avoiding it. However, now was not the time to delve into her tactics.

He snapped his jeans. "Someone at the front door is asking for you."

She glanced at his alarm clock. "It's 6:30 in the morning." Nevertheless she scrambled out of bed, not the least self-conscious about her nudity. Although he'd seen everything she'd had to offer last night, and she could offer plenty, he couldn't help but appreciate her all over again. He liked her lean lines, her toned skin and the sparkle in her eyes.

"I should have known it was someone who wanted to talk to you," he muttered to cover up his discontentment at his resolution never to make love to her again. "My friends know better than to show up before noon." He neglected to mention that he'd been worried about a dangerous intruder, especially after he saw the fear flash in her eyes.

"Something must be wrong." She yanked his shirt from his hand. "Can I borrow that? Thanks." Then she dashed out of the bedroom. Last night she'd left her clothes by the hot tub, and with nothing to replace them in his room, he supposed she might have run off in just the sheet if he hadn't lent her his shirt.

It startled him, pleasantly, that little Miss Fashion Plate had no compunction at all about revealing her body to him. There was no false modesty about her, yet she didn't show off, either. She just acted quite natural, and he'd never realized that she was so comfortable in her own skin.

With a shake of his head and a slight grin, he trailed her to the front door. If she could greet their guest wearing nothing but a T-shirt, he needn't bother with a shirt or shoes.

Kelly swung open the door. "Cara! What's happened? Are Mom and Dad—"

"They're fine."

Cara stepped inside and shut the door behind her. She took in Kelly wearing his T-shirt and him in his jeans. Another woman might have exhibited a smidgen of embarrassment, but Cara didn't even seem surprised that they'd hooked up.

"Why are you here?" Kelly asked.

Cara glared in his direction, and he suspected she didn't want to speak in front of him, but Wade had no intention of leaving. However, he could be civil. "Coffee, anyone?"

"Thanks," Cara said. "I take mine black."

"Yes, please." Kelly frowned at her friend. "Now tell me what's so important that you had to wake me up at the crack of dawn."

"A story came across my desk last night about Niles Deagen, Andrew's fiancée's ex-husband."

"We were going to try and see him either today or tomorrow."

"That might be difficult."

"He's dead?" Wade asked from the kitchen.

"No, nothing like that. He's in financial trouble."

Cara perched on a chair as if she was ready at any moment to leap to her feet. Kelly sat on the sofa, tucked her feet under her and frowned at her friend.

"I'm not following. What does this have to do with Andrew? Or me?"

"I'm getting to that."

"Today, please," Kelly demanded, and Wade realized that even when she was sarcastic and demanding, she still maintained that polite and ladylike aura that he found so compelling—especially after the way she'd let loose in bed with him last night. She was all lady in the daytime and a tigress in bed—what more could a man want?

She's not for you, he reminded himself once again.

Cara interrupted his thoughts. "Andrew defended a man named Billy Jackson, an employee of Niles Deagen's."

"And?"

"When Niles was arrested for racketeering, Billy Jackson turned state's evidence against his boss. Billy ended up dead in a Dallas Dumpster last week."

"And?"

"The bullet from the autopsy turned out to be a 9 mm."

"The same caliber that killed my brother."

"I know it's a leap because 9 mm guns are so common, but if you could get the sheriff to compare the bullets, it might prove to be the same shooter."

"Good thinking." Wade handed Cara a mug of coffee.

"Thanks."

Kelly smiled her thanks and accepted her mug. "Since Mustang Valley doesn't have a forensics lab, the bullet that killed Andrew could be sent to Dallas for their lab to make the comparison.''

"Do we know what the D.A. has on Niles?" Wade asked.

"I asked. He's not talking. There's nothing in the public records. And the D.A. just put a huge down payment on a piece of property he can't afford.''

"You think he took a payoff?" Wade asked.

Cara sipped her coffee and spoke to Kelly as if Wade wasn't there. "You should keep him. Any man who makes coffee like this…yum.''

Kelly sputtered. "Cara!"

Wade settled his hip against the far end of the sofa, amused by the byplay. He enjoyed the blush rising up Kelly's neck and then her bold I-can't-believe-you-said-that-in-front-of-him stare at Cara.

"It's about time you went after what you wanted," Cara continued, not the least intimidated by Kelly's scowl.

"So what kind of financial trouble is Niles in?" Wade asked to get Kelly off the hook.

"Right now, it's just rumors. Talk about money and sex arouses everyone's interest.''

Apparently, Cara wasn't done teasing Kelly. But Kelly had her own way of coping. She looked at her watch and spoke sweetly. "Don't you have to be at work by seven?"

"Where does the time go?" Cara slugged down a big gulp of caffeine, stood and handed Kelly her empty mug. "Hell, I'm late, but that doesn't mean I don't realize that you want me out of here.''

Kelly stood and hugged her friend. "Thanks for the info. I appreciate it.''

Like the busy reporter she was, she hurried out the door, but then she looked over her shoulder and winked at Wade. "You notice she didn't thank me for my advice."

"I'M CALLING DADDY," Kelly told Wade and picked up the phone. She gave him a chance to protest, but when he didn't, she dialed, repeated the information Cara had given her and asked her father to make the request to the sheriff to compare the bullets that had killed Andrew and his former client Billy Jackson.

The request served several purposes. One, it would free them to track down Johnny Dixon in Fort Worth and Niles Deagen in Dallas. Two, it might take the heat off of Wade and Kelly. Whoever had tried to run them off the road just might believe they'd given up on their investigation and leave them alone. Besides, if Kelly made an outright appeal to the sheriff, she might as well take out an ad in the *Mustang Gazette* to announce their suspicions. Three, the sheriff was a lot more likely to heed a request from one of the town's leading citizens than his just-graduated-college daughter.

Next she tried phoning Johnny's room at the hotel Lindsey had written down for her. No answer. She also tried his apartment. Again, no answer. But for all she knew he was sleeping in. Yawning, she stretched and the T-shirt rose up her thigh several inches. Wade pretended not to notice, but he looked away with such studied disinterest that she knew better.

As she headed to the guest room for some clothes

and to use the shower, she wondered how long she could keep avoiding the conversation he'd wanted last night. She couldn't always pretend to be sleeping or distract him with flirtation. Sooner or later he'd find a way to pin her down and talk, but she figured the longer she could put him off a serious discussion with his telling her how unsuitable they were for one another, the more time she had to work on changing his mind, especially since the more time she spent with him, the more she liked him, as a friend—not just a lover.

Sure they'd been great together in bed, but that wasn't enough. Kelly had always longed for love, for a soul mate, for someone to share her life with, and she believed Wade might just be that man if he'd only give them a real chance.

Kelly plunged under the hot water, recalling how she'd gotten to him last night in the hot tub. He most certainly hadn't intended to make love to her, but she'd won that battle of wills, and she hoped, now that he knew how good they could be together, that his attitude toward her would soften enough to let him acknowledge his feelings. He had to have them. She certainly did. She couldn't have made love to him if she hadn't believed they had a shot at a future together, and she refused to believe Wade could make love with that kind of raw sensuality, yet still maintain that level of concern over her well-being and satisfaction without having genuine emotions toward her.

He just needed a lot of coaxing. Fine. She could do that. Her father had once told her she was a natural-born flirt. In recent years she might have curtailed those tendencies, but Wade seemed to appreciate her efforts.

What if she was wrong about Wade? Suppose he couldn't return the love and the friendship she offered? Life would go on.

Would she be disappointed? Of course. She might be devastated.

It might take a long time to move on and get over this wonderful feeling inside that told her they were so right together. She loved the way he took her ideas seriously. He never patronized her. He was steady and loyal and brave.

She wanted to continue to get to know him better, much better. And whether sharing a drive or a meal or a moonlight kiss, she always enjoyed his company. If he didn't feel likewise, she had the support of her family and her friends and an inner strength that demanded she take this emotional risk or regret that she'd failed to follow her heart. Her powerful feelings toward Wade were simply too strong to leave unexplored. Now that she'd gotten to know him, now that they'd made love and she knew how terrific he could be, she couldn't walk away and pretend he meant nothing more to her than a one-night stand.

She didn't do one-nighters. She wasn't interested in a fling. She never allowed herself to make love to a man unless she believed he had long-term potential. The fact that she'd been wrong twice before, in two other relationships, didn't deter her. The right man would come along someday—that he might turn out to be Wade excited her and propelled her to take a few calculated risks.

After showering, she towel-dried her hair, pulled it back into a ponytail, leaving a few locks to curl around her face, and applied makeup. She donned a sleeveless clingy tank top, a short flirty skirt, comfy sandals and for a touch of professionalism, she grabbed a suit jacket and packed an overnight bag in case they wound up staying in Forth Worth or Dallas.

When she returned to the living room, Wade wore jeans and a denim shirt. He was talking on the phone, something about his inventory and a bar fight, and he mentioned Rudy, the kid who worked for one of his employees and who'd broken that windowpane in town.

Wade hung up the phone. "Ready?"

"Yeah."

"Apparently Rudy has something to tell me. He's outside."

The kid was sitting on Wade's front stoop, throwing pebbles at the trash can. He stood up, shoved his hands in his pockets and mumbled, "Dad found out about the damage to that broken window and told me to come see you. Thanks."

"Apology accepted," Wade said.

As gratitude went, Rudy had spoken most grudgingly but Wade let that slide. He didn't rub the kid's nose in his mistake and she liked him for it.

"I might have some information for you," Rudy said. "But I'm not sure if it's important."

"Why don't you just tell us and let us decide?" Wade suggested.

"Dad said I'm not to bother you—but you did ask."

"That's right, I did. I can pay for information," Wade told him, reaching for his wallet in his back pocket.

"I was hanging out at the mayor's campaign headquarters, waiting for the flyers to come back from the printer so I could deliver them."

"Yes?" Wade prodded.

"Mayor Daniels was talking to Sheriff Wilson about a land deal, and when they said that the Wests were almost ready to make some money, I listened real hard. Because Debbie and Andrew were engaged, I thought you'd be interested."

"I am. The Wests are selling their ranch, and Andrew was handling the lawyering for them, that's common knowledge."

Rudy's face was puzzled. "Is it common knowledge that the mayor and the sheriff are eager for the contract to go through?"

"I have no idea why they would care, except that the West family needs that money." Wade pulled out a five-dollar bill. "Is that all?"

"Except for when they saw me, they stopped talking." Rudy shrugged. "I got the feeling I wasn't supposed to have heard what I heard."

Wade handed the kid the money. "Thanks."

"Was that important?" Rudy asked, his eyes curious as he tucked the money into his front pocket.

"I don't know. We're working on a puzzle, and you just brought us another piece. Until we have more, we can't put the clues together, so we need you to keep listening."

"Okay."

"And, Rudy…"

"Yeah?"

"Keep a low profile. That means don't get caught listening."

"Sure." Rudy strode away whistling and Wade watched him go, a lopsided grin on his face.

Kelly kept her voice down so the kid wouldn't hear him. "If you want to give him money, why don't you give him a real job, like mowing your grass or washing dishes?"

"He's not ready for hard labor."

Kelly shrugged. "It's your money."

"You don't understand."

"So explain it to me."

"On your side of town it's acceptable for kids to take a low-level, low-paying job to earn gas money. Rudy's never going to have a car. His family is too poor."

"But a steady job would earn him the money to—"

"He doesn't see it that way. He thinks working for me in the saloon would be selling out. He's afraid if he takes a job washing dishes then he'll end up like his father."

Kelly realized that Rudy reminded Wade of himself. He could have been that kid. He understood him. Coming from her upper-middle-class world with its work-hard-and-you'll-succeed ethics, she had difficulty following the logic of his statement. Or maybe it wasn't logic so much as a different attitude toward life. Could the way she and Wade looked at the world prevent their relationship from deepening?

With her optimistic nature, she expected good

things to happen, and they usually did. Wade came from a background rooted in poverty, and it affected the way he dealt with the police: suspiciously. The way he looked at life: as one giant roll of the dice. The way he dealt with her: sending mixed signals.

She had no idea what to do about it. Her parents came from similar backgrounds. They had attended the same schools, socialized with the same crowd, attended the same church.

Kelly came from a two-parent upper-middle-class household. Wade had never known his mother, and his father hadn't been there for him. She understood that how she'd grown up had helped shape her into the person she was today. Maybe that's why she admired Wade. He'd had a rough life and he'd made his own way. Successfully.

He wore his self-confidence as comfortably as his broken-in jeans. Yet he didn't come off as someone with something to prove, either. She'd really liked the way she could be herself with him, too. And after last night, she thought they could have a future together—if he'd just give them a chance.

THE FORT WORTH area was congested compared to Mustang Valley. Traffic was stop-and-go, and Wade drove. During the drive, Kelly had received two phone calls. The first had been from her father to check on her as well as to tell her that the sheriff had agreed to send the bullet that had killed Andrew to Dallas for analysis to be compared to the one that killed his client Billy Jackson. The second call had come from a worried Lindsey, who'd told them that

Johnny Dixon had never shown up for his appointment as a legal clerk.

Kelly put her phone back in her purse. ''Lindsey didn't think he would miss his appointment unless something bad happened.''

''I have to agree, especially since he had to borrow gas money to drive here.'' Wade turned right, drove past the hotel's valet parking and backed into a parking spot.

Kelly speared him with a curious glance. ''Expecting to make a fast getaway?''

''Just being careful.''

She didn't say more, but she opened the glove compartment, took out her gun and placed it inside her purse. Then she flipped the visor down and checked her makeup in the mirror. He was beginning to think of her makeup and clothing as battle armor. She subtly changed her looks depending on who they would meet, and he was just as sure she'd done that to him last night, too.

She'd certainly never looked more appealing than she had in that hot tub with the moonlight glistening off her wet skin. She'd set the bait and he'd walked right into her trap. Except, he didn't feel trapped, but fascinated, intrigued and eager to see just what she'd do next.

Only, this time he planned to be ready for her. This time he'd find the willpower to resist. Not just for Andrew's sake—but his own. Wade had to suppress his growing feelings for her with a savage ruthlessness before he got in too deep and drowned. Now that he knew how potent she could be, he would build up his resistance to her.

They entered the hotel through a side door and headed toward the elevator. "According to Lindsey, Johnny reserved room 504."

The elevator arrived with a family of four. Wade and Kelly exited first and followed the hallway signs to Johnny's room. Kelly knocked. Once. Twice.

Nothing.

She turned to him and shoved a lock of hair back from her troubled eyes. "Now what?"

Before he could answer, Kelly caught sight of the maid, and her blue eyes brightened. She headed toward a diminutive woman with dark olive skin, dark hair pulled back in a bun and creased brown eyes.

"Excuse me, I was wondering if you could help us?" Kelly spoke pleasantly.

The maid pushed her cart to the next room. "You need soap, towels, clean sheets?"

"My brother's friend asked me to come visit him. I've driven all the way here to meet him," Kelly improvised, telling mostly the truth but skirting the facts. "Last night he didn't answer the phone."

"He was here last night. He wanted an extra pillow," the maid offered.

"This morning he won't answer the door. I'm afraid something might be wrong."

"I call hotel security."

Kelly looked at Wade and began to protest. "But—"

Wade shook his head and she heeded his silent disagreement. "Security might be a good idea."

The maid used the phone, and two minutes later a uniformed guard joined them. "You think there's a problem in 504?"

"We don't know." Wade placed himself between Kelly and the door. "We expected Mr. Dixon to answer his phone or the door and he didn't show for an important job interview this morning."

"Okay." The guard knocked, and when he didn't get an answer either, he opened the hotel room door. He entered the room and did a quick search of the closet and drawers. "There's no one here. Looks like your friend checked out."

Wade didn't know what to think. Johnny had been desperate for this job. If he wasn't at the hotel, then where was he? "Thanks for your help. Sorry to have disturbed you."

Discouraged, he and Kelly returned to her Jag and she replaced her gun in the glove compartment. "As I see it we have two choices. We check the hospitals, the morgue and the police stations for Johnny or we go on to Dallas and speak with Niles."

Kelly sighed. "What do you think?"

"I vote we drive to Dallas. Johnny might show up later today in Mustang Valley."

Kelly clicked on her seat belt. "It's so strange. He left the mayor's campaign without telling anyone. He comes here and doesn't show for the interview. But the maid told us that she spoke to him last night."

"It's almost as if we're chasing a ghost," Wade muttered. "It's probably just bad luck. Maybe he got a flat tire on the way to his appointment."

"But wouldn't he have phoned his potential employer, who would have told Lindsey—who would have told us?"

Wade grinned. "You know you're scaring me. I actually understood that sentence."

"Why is understanding me scary?" she countered. "Women are simple creatures, really."

"Yeah, right."

"It's true. We just need good friends, a close family, a job we enjoy and someone to love."

"What about fashion accessories?" he teased.

"Them, too," she agreed.

Traffic snarled and he slowed the car. Up ahead he saw red and blue police lights and the intersection blocked. A traffic cop rerouted them.

"Must be an accident."

"Oh, no," Kelly gasped.

"What?"

"That looks like Johnny's car. I saw a picture of it in his living room."

Chapter Eleven

"Is he dead?" Kelly dreaded the answer to her question but knew she had to ask.

Just minutes before, Wade had pulled into a parking lot and they'd walked over to a police officer on the scene. Yellow tape surrounded what proved to be Johnny Dixon's car. Several bushes in the median looked uprooted, and a telephone pole had crushed the car's front end. One officer snapped photographs, and another wrote up the incident while a third measured skid marks on the road.

The windshield in front of the driver was shattered and blood trickled down the glass. Kelly turned her gaze from the scene, her stomach roiling. If Wade hadn't avoided the tow truck pursuing them a few days ago, they might have been as unlucky as Johnny Dixon.

"I can't give out medical information, ma'am," the police officer replied from the other side of the cordoned area. "An ambulance took the driver to County General. You can check on him there."

Kelly didn't see any other vehicles, but a tow truck driver was hooking up Johnny's smashed car, and it appeared another car had been involved but had been removed from the scene. She saw no additional skid marks, no other signs that another car or truck could have caused the "accident."

She tried to phrase her question innocuously and ignore the sweat on her brow from the hot sun. "Was anyone else hurt?"

"No, ma'am."

Wade would understand that she was worried that someone might have run Johnny off the road, just as had been done to them. Yet she hesitated to sound too inquisitive since she didn't want to make explanations to the policeman. "Officer, were there any witnesses?"

The officer's eyes narrowed. "Why do you ask?"

"Just curious," Wade replied. "Did you find a gun in the car?"

"I suggest you take your curiosity elsewhere. You people need to move along and go about your own business."

"But—"

"Ma'am, I've told you all that I can."

At a momentary dead end, she and Wade returned to her Jaguar and the air-conditioning cooled her. She wasn't in the mood to talk. Seeing that wrecked car had shaken her more than she wanted to admit. The sight of the tow truck had brought back their own close escape from death just a few days before, and Kelly wondered if her parents had been right, that they should leave the state and hide out while the sheriff did his job. However, he might never solve the case, and then neither she nor Wade would be safe until they figured out the identity of Andrew's murderer.

"Can I borrow your phone?" Wade asked.

"Sure."

After she handed it over, he dialed and chose the speaker option so she could listen to his conversation. After several rings Deputy Warwick answered, "Mitchell here."

"I was wondering if you could request a look at a Dallas accident report for us," Wade phrased his question as a suggestion, but she heard the urgency beneath his mild tone.

"What accident?" Mitch asked.

Wade gave him Johnny's full name and the street address. "Any news yet on whether the bullet that killed Andrew matched the one that struck his client?"

"We should have an answer this afternoon," Mitch told him. "Mr. McGovern's applying pressure on the sheriff. Oh, and we got the fire chief's report. Your guy used an accelerant to start the fire at Lambert & Church. Gasoline."

"Thanks, Mitch."

Kelly had no idea which information was important. She intended to keep gathering pieces until she could put the puzzle together. Right now she wanted to talk to Johnny Dixon, so they drove to the hospital.

But no one there wanted to release any official information about Johnny's condition to anyone but family. While Kelly sat alone in the waiting room, hoping that Johnny would be all right, Wade sweet-talked a nurse into giving him information, which he promptly shared with Kelly.

"Johnny has a brain injury and is in a coma. He may not make it through the night, or he could remain in a vegetative state for the rest of his life."

"That's terrible."

"Or he could wake up any minute and be fine."

Stunned, Kelly tried to regroup. She'd been hoping for better news. She couldn't get Johnny's "accident" out of her mind. She had no evidence to support her theory that there had been more to it than the driver losing control of the car, and there was too much that they didn't know. Too many bad things had happened lately with people who had been connected to Andrew for this car wreck to be simple bad luck.

"The doctors are doing their best, but we can't do anything for him by staying here," Wade said. "I think we should drive over to Dallas and talk to Niles Deagen."

"Okay."

Kelly had never thought that playing private investigator wouldn't have consequences, but in the last few days she'd come to the conclusion that it could be a very dangerous profession, one she'd have no interest in doing full-time. But if she survived the next few weeks, she vowed that never again would she take her tomorrows for granted.

During this dangerous time with Wade she'd passed a milestone in her life. She'd changed in several ways, one of them being that she trusted her own instincts more than ever. And she now refused to live in a world where the approval of others influenced her decisions as much as she'd allowed in the past. If her parents didn't approve of Wade, that was their problem. She was a big girl and it was her decision whether or not to pursue a relationship with Wade. Or attend law school in the fall.

Right now her primary concern was to fight for justice for Andrew. No way was she backing down. As Wade escorted her into the hospital parking lot and back to her parked Jag, she quickened her steps. The sooner they figured out who had murdered her brother, the sooner she could move on with her life.

NILES DEAGEN WORKED in a penthouse suite of the Deagen Building, an architectural masterpiece of marble and mirrors. Built with oil money, the building had the opulence of a palace, with twice the security.

Kelly had made Wade stop in a department store and insisted they each purchase new clothing before this visit. As a result of the shopping spree, Wade now wore a three-piece dark gray suit and squeaky new black shoes. For herself, Kelly had chosen a conservative blue dress that brought out the color in her eyes. Earlier, Wade had been impatient with the shopping delay, but as he strode past other men and women dressed similarly, he now realized that the time they'd spent had been worth it.

They might be meeting Niles on his turf, but at least they were dressed as equals. On the drive into the city, they'd debated the pros and cons of calling ahead. Wade wanted to risk a surprise visit, but Kelly had insisted that a man of Deagen's stature would be guarded by secretaries and security. Without an appointment, they might not get to see Niles.

So Kelly had phoned and asked for an appointment. Surprisingly, Niles had fitted them in for a three o'clock meeting. They gave their names at the front desk, and a man in a uniform issued them temporary passes.

After riding the brass elevator to the tenth floor, striding down several hallways and receiving directions from two secretaries, they were finally ushered into Deagen's office. Floor-to-ceiling windows overlooked the city. Another wall housed framed works of art. The fourteen-foot-high ceilings gave the office an airy feel, the thick carpet portrayed wealth, while the mahogany furniture suggested old money.

In his early forties, Niles had thick black hair that was showing the first signs of gray at the temples. He wore gold-rimmed glasses and a custom suit. His piercing green eyes surveyed them with an authority that told Wade the man was accustomed to taking charge.

"Mr. Deagen. I'm Wade Lansing and this is Kelly McGovern."

Kelly shook Deagen's hand. "Thanks for seeing us on such short notice."

"No problem. Please, sit down and make yourselves at home, and call me Niles." Deagen didn't sit behind his desk. Instead he pulled up a chair on their side of the desk. "Debbie said you might be coming by."

"Debbie?" Wade asked. Niles's comment startled him. He hadn't been aware that Debbie still spoke to her ex-husband. And even if she had, how had she known that he and Kelly would come here?

"Please. Let's not play games. Andrew handled Debbie's divorce and then he was murdered. Debbie said you asked her questions and would likely want to talk to me, too. I suppose in your eyes that our love for the same woman makes me a suspect. But despite what you might think, I didn't hate your brother. As lawyers went, he treated me decently and I'm sorry for your loss, Ms. McGovern."

"Thank you."

It seemed to Wade that despite the sheriff's wish to keep his investigation under wraps, the news of Andrew's murder had leaked far beyond the confines of Mustang Valley. And from Niles's tone, either he was an extremely smooth liar or he genuinely held no ill will toward Andrew.

"Would you mind telling us where you were the night my brother died?" Kelly asked bluntly.

While Wade admired her tactic, he didn't think taking a head-on approach with a man like Niles was the best of ideas. And yet Niles didn't seem to mind at all.

"I was in Washington, D.C., that night with several senators and two congressmen. I'm sponsoring a bill to open up drilling in the Gulf of Mexico."

The oil executive might have an airtight alibi, but that didn't mean he hadn't hired a thug to do his dirty work. Wade was about to ask Niles about the rumors of his financial problems when the door to the office opened.

Kelly gasped. Niles smiled a welcome.

Wade turned around to see Debbie West entering

the room. She had no makeup on and wore clothes
he considered much too young for her. Although he
was no fashion expert, in her pink shirt and schoolgirl skirt, she looked about fifteen. She strode into
the room, seemingly not the least bit surprised to see
them. She walked directly to Niles and then sat in
his lap.

Kelly and Wade exchanged glances.

Debbie kept her eyes downcast, her voice flat.
"Niles and I are reconciling."

"I see," Kelly said, pain and anger swirling in
her blue eyes at what she obviously considered a
betrayal of her brother. "Did you ever love my
brother or were you—"

"I loved him, but he's gone."

Kelly's eyes narrowed with accusation. "You expect me to believe that you loved my brother, yet
he's only been gone less than two months and you
seem to have moved on easily enough."

Debbie trembled and she refused to look at Kelly.
Niles took Debbie's hands between his, and a tender
look glazed his expression. "And I'm prepared to
take good care of Debbie."

Wow. Wade's thoughts whirled at the multitude
of possibilities. He'd never expected this turn of
events. What bothered him most was that Niles
didn't seem to care that Debbie had divorced him
and then changed her mind after Andrew's death. It
seemed to Wade that Niles's attitude was obsessive,
off-kilter.

But Wade knew that what struck Kelly hard was
Debbie's seeming betrayal of her brother, who had

gone out of his way to help Debbie. That his fiancée could move on so easily had to hurt Kelly.

"Debbie, I wouldn't be so sure you've found a meal ticket," Kelly said with a bite of steel in her tone. "From the rumors I've been hearing about Deagen Oil, Niles has leveraged the business to the max and could lose the whole company."

"What does that mean?" Debbie asked with a wide-eyed-little-girl look that made Wade uncomfortable.

Niles patted her hair as if she were a dog on his lap, not a full-grown woman. "Nothing to worry your head over, sweetie pie."

Debbie stood up. "I know you have work to do, dear. I'll escort our guests out if that's okay with you."

The moment they exited Niles's office and shut the door behind them, Debbie dropped the little-girl demeanor. She straightened her shoulders and held her head up. "I can't imagine what you must think of me."

"I don't know what to think." Pain and distrust mixed in Kelly's tone. "How could you go back to a man like Niles after being with my brother?"

Several office workers who seemed overly interested in their conversation passed by. Debbie raised her finger to her mouth. "Shh. Not here."

She led them down the hallway and opened a door into a conference room filled with a long shiny table and upholstered high-backed chairs. "We can talk in private here."

Wade's curiosity burned, and he vowed to pay close attention to Debbie's words, especially knowing that Kelly, being upset that this woman had betrayed her brother might not be thinking clearly.

Debbie shut the door behind them and bit her bottom lip. ''For what it's worth, I loved Andrew. I think…we could have been happy together but—''

''Right.'' Kelly's tone hardened. ''You loved my brother so much that two months after his death you're back with your ex-husband? Were all those tears at his funeral just for show? Was my brother just another man that you used?''

''You don't understand.'' Debbie sagged against the wall. ''Look, I could have stayed with Niles in his office. I didn't have to volunteer to talk to you, but I did because…''

''Because?'' Kelly prodded, disdain coloring her words. She'd obviously made up her mind that this woman hadn't been good enough for her brother, and Wade tended to agree, although he was more open to hearing the extenuating circumstances.

Still, Wade's sympathy went out to Debbie. Wade had the feeling it had taken all of the woman's courage to speak up and try to explain. Debbie's hands trembled. She spoke quietly, the entire time keeping her head down, her gaze on the floor. ''It's just that I'm not like you.''

''What do you mean?'' Kelly looked clearly bewildered. But Wade figured he had a better handle on Debbie's situation than Kelly did. The two women had grown up in the same small town under vastly different circumstances. Kelly had been born with a silver spoon in her mouth. Sure she'd worked hard in college, but that was a lot easier with Daddy paying the bills than it would have been for Debbie who'd probably never entertained the idea of attending.

"I never graduated high school, nevermind went to college like you. Don't you think I'd like to work and be self-sufficient?"

"How do I know? Maybe you just want to depend on a man for your every need."

Debbie shook her head. "I've learned that to get a decent job, I need skills or an education. I have neither. And I'm broke, too."

"What about the money from the sale of the ranch?" Kelly asked.

"Most goes to the bank, the rest we owe to the credit card companies. I need a friend to help me out. I couldn't make it alone. That's what I meant when I said I'm not like you. You're strong. You can stand alone."

"Did you see my brother for anything more than a meal ticket?"

Kelly headed toward the door.

Clearly she didn't want to listen to Debbie's excuses, but Wade understood what Debbie was trying to say better than Kelly did. Kelly hadn't had to clean the house; her folks had hired a maid. She hadn't had to work two jobs to help put food on the table or arrive at school so exhausted she couldn't keep her eyes open.

Wade started to follow Kelly out the door but paused a moment to squeeze Debbie's shoulder with compassion. He was about to try and think of something comforting to say when Kelly stopped, rooted her feet in the carpet so suddenly that he almost bumped into her. She opened her purse and dug through it.

Kelly pulled out her checkbook and her pink pen, then signed a check that she thrust at Debbie. "Here. Use this however you like."

Debbie took one look at all the zeros and shook her head. "I can't take that."

Kelly rolled her eyes. "Andrew would have wanted you to have a way to survive without turning to a man like Niles."

"I don't know what to do with that kind of money. I'm not smart like you."

"My brother didn't date dumb women." When Debbie still didn't take the check, Kelly folded it and stuffed the paper into Debbie's pocket. "The first thing you have to do is believe in yourself or no one else will."

Tears brimmed in Debbie's eyes. "I don't know how to thank you."

"You can thank me by going back to school with that money. Every woman should be able to support herself. And if you need help, you call me. I'll be there for you."

Grateful tears of apparent disbelief and relief at her good fortune spilled down Debbie's cheeks. "Thank you."

Kelly's change of heart and her generosity kept surprising Wade. After being so angry with Debbie, he hadn't known she could be so compassionate. Or so tough. But that toughness combined with a hefty check was exactly the kick in the butt Debbie might need to regain her self-respect and set her life on a new course.

Debbie opened the door. "Come with me. There's something I want to show you."

They headed down the hall to the elevators, but with other people riding down with them, they weren't free to talk. Kelly and Wade exchanged glances, but Kelly indicated that she didn't have a clue where Debbie was taking them, either. But no matter what Debbie showed them, Wade couldn't have been prouder of Kelly. At first she'd been so angry at what she'd seen as Debbie's betrayal of her brother that she couldn't understand Debbie's position, but once she had she'd offered a hefty check and more importantly her friendship.

They exited into the parking garage, and Debbie headed toward locked double doors by the stairs. "Niles always runs up the ten flights of stairs. He says it keeps him in shape. And yet if he doesn't get the closest parking space to the stairwell he complains like the dickens. However, he doesn't usually park his car in the locked storage area."

"Why are we here?" Kelly asked.

"Niles told me he drove to Fort Worth this afternoon for a business meeting about an oil lease, but then I got a phone call from his manager who claims he never showed up."

"I don't understand," Wade told her.

Debbie shrugged. "Niles has lied to me before of course, but then I saw his car."

She pulled keys from her pocket, unlocked the doors and pushed them wide open. Once inside the dark area, she led them to a dark green BMW parked by the stairwell. The car appeared normal until they stepped around to the front. The bumper was dented, the paint scratched.

"Looks like he was in an accident," Debbie said, stating the obvious.

Wade figured Kelly was wondering the same thing he was. Had Niles run Johnny off the road this morning? Or was Wade letting his imagination get the best of him?

Debbie folded her arms over her chest. "Niles asked a body shop owner to pick up the car at five o'clock. Seems to me he's eager to cover up his accident."

Wade called Deputy Warwick. Since Debbie had been so helpful, he allowed her to hear both sides of the conversation with Kelly over the speaker-phone.

"Hey, Mitch. Did you get hold of Johnny Dixon's accident report?"

"Yeah. Hold on. Okay. I've got it right here."

"Does it mention anything about paint from another vehicle?"

"Dark green."

"I'm looking at a dark green BMW with a dent. The owner intends to send it to a body shop within the hour. If I give you the tag and location of the vehicle, can you have an officer impound the car?"

"Not without a way to tie the car to the accident, I can't," Mitchell said. "Who does the car belong to?"

"Niles Deagen."

"The Dallas oil man? We've got to be real careful. Everything by the book or his lawyers will tear

us up in court. Right now you haven't given me
enough to warrant a search.''

"Was there anyone mentioned in the report who
saw Johnny's accident?" Kelly reminded Wade that
the cop on the scene hadn't been forthcoming when
they'd asked that question. He could have been holding back information that Mitch would give them.

"There was an eyewitness," Mitchell admitted.

"Did the witness say anything about a green
BMW?" Wade asked.

Wade waited impatiently, and Debbie shifted un-
easily from foot to foot. He hoped she wasn't having
second thoughts about helping them. About helping
herself.

"It's right here. A dark green BMW. Okay. I'll
take care of it. Give me the location and I'll ask the
Dallas police officer to impound the car. Then we
can compare the paint on Deagen's car to Johnny
Dixon's and see if we get a match."

Wade moved on to his next question. "Did you
get the bullet comparison done?"

"The bullet that killed Andrew came from a different gun from the one that killed his client. The
case detective thought the client's ex-girlfriend committed the homicide. I heard she confessed about an
hour ago. But don't give up. If the car paint matches,
we'll bring in Deagen for questioning."

Debbie frowned. "Deagen didn't even know
Johnny. Why would he want to hurt him? It doesn't
make sense."

"We don't have any idea," Kelly admitted. "But
without your help, we wouldn't have gotten this far.
Thank you."

"If there's anything else I can do to help, let me know," Debbie offered. She touched the pocket where the check resided. "I'm leaving town. You can get in touch with me through Lindsey Wellington."

"We appreciate it." Kelly hugged her. "And you should leave right away. Niles may be involved in something nasty."

"What will you do next?" Debbie asked.

Kelly shrugged her shoulders. "I have no idea."

However, Wade suspected from the pursing of her lips and the glint in her eyes that Kelly had much more than an idea.

What neither of them noticed as they left Niles's office building was the van following them.

Chapter Twelve

Frustrated that they hadn't yet solved Andrew's murder, Kelly was at least pleased they were making progress. When they'd begun the investigation she hadn't had any leads. Now they had too many. And with clues to follow and more people to question, she was hopeful that she and Wade might eventually get Andrew some justice.

With their investigation going better, Kelly was looking forward to some serious alone time with Wade that evening. When they returned to his house after eating dinner on the road, she poured them both a glass of wine, turned the CD player's volume to low and curled up on the opposite end of the sofa from him, determined to change his mind.

"We need to talk."

He set down the newspaper he'd been perusing and gave her his full attention. "About?"

"Us."

"There's nothing to talk about." When he began to pick the paper back up, she moved closer to him, close enough to smell the shampoo from his shower and a hint of aftershave. She placed one hand on his shoulder and let her fingers play with the hair at his neck.

"We haven't really discussed our making love."

She planted a kiss at the base of his neck where his pulse fluttered erratically. Knowing that her touch affected him gave her the courage to pursue their discussion. Besides, she liked touching him, liked his response to her, liked the way she felt about herself when she was with him.

His hand closed over hers. "You're going to use every weapon in your arsenal to get what you want, aren't you?"

"Uh-huh." Since he held her hand still, she kissed a spot behind his ear.

"Okay. Fine." He shifted around to face her, ending physical contact, but the heat in his eyes warned her to tread with care. "What exactly do you want from me?"

His direct words confused her. First he didn't want to talk about them, then he claimed there was nothing to talk about and now he was asking her a question that was difficult to answer.

What did she want? She wanted him to admit he had feelings for her. She wanted him to tell her that he wanted to make love again. She wanted him to care about her as if she was his woman—not Andrew's sister.

Telling him her thoughts was out of the question, especially with him so guarded. She sipped her wine and eyed him over the brim of her glass, her heart skipping as if it knew exactly how important this discussion was to her future. He'd avoided talking about himself by asking a question first, one she didn't know if she wanted to answer.

She stalled. "Can you be more specific?"

"Do you want a fling with Mustang Valley's bad boy?" he challenged her. "Do you just need someone to console you while you grieve? Are you trying to use me to rebel out of your safe little world?"

He flung the questions at her with a curt aloofness that told her her answer meant more to him than he wanted to admit. So despite the pain he'd inflicted, she kept the hurt pinned down. "You sound as though you think that I'm using you."

"Aren't you?" His gray eyes darkened with fierce accusation. "You've known me all your life, but you've never exhibited any interest in me until now."

"Not true."

He arched an eyebrow in disbelief. "Yeah, right."

She held his gaze and kept her voice level. "I've had a crush on you since I was in the eighth grade and you were a senior in high school and took Cindy Jo Crocker to the prom. You wore that black suit and black shirt that knocked my socks off. I wanted to be Cindy so badly that night that I followed you and Andrew on my bike. You never even knew I was there, and when I lost sight of your car, I went home and cried my eyes out. And do you know why I cried?"

"Because you weren't old enough to buy a gown for the prom?"

"Cute." She shook her head. "I cried because I knew that good girls didn't go out with exciting guys with questionable reputations. You represented everything I couldn't have—excitement, rebellion, freedom. Or at least I couldn't have those things and keep my parents' approval, too.''

"That was your choice.''

"I know that now. Andrew was the brilliant older son, so I gave myself the role of being the polite Southern belle, of sticking to the rules, of making straight As and never, ever embarrassing the family.''

"Exactly my point. You and I should never have happened. We don't belong together.''

"But we do. Because I'm not that anxious-to-please adolescent anymore. The approval of others is no longer as important to me as my own happiness.''

"And now that little Miss Do-It-by-the-Book has come out of the closet, you need to prove you've broken out of your self-imposed box by making love to me? Well, we did it. You can now move on with your life.''

She set down the wineglass with frustration. "Well, I'm trying to move on, but you keep resisting.''

"Excuse me?''

He hadn't expected her to agree with him, and it had thrown him. She wondered if he was ready to hear the words she wanted to say. Wondered if she was going too fast. Wondered if she was about to scare him away. But she couldn't hold back, and if he couldn't deal with her thoughts, then he wasn't the right man for her.

"Do you think I could have made love to you if I wasn't already halfway in love with you?''

He snorted. "You think you're in love with me?"

"Yes."

He stared at her so long that she had no idea what he was thinking. "Just how long do you think your love will last?"

"I don't know." If he kept up his attitude, she might not love him for more than another minute. "I've never been in love before." She wouldn't give him a guarantee. She wasn't ready to commit her life to him. Not unless he met her halfway. And he appeared far from believing her, never mind admitting his own feelings—which she assumed he had for her—but she could be wrong. She might be making a total fool of herself by declaring her love, and he was trying to let her down easy.

Well, she'd wanted this conversation, so now she had to be strong enough to listen to what he had to say. Only, he wasn't saying anything. He just kept staring at her with those smoky gray eyes that made her want to forget about talking, grab the front of his shirt and pull his head down until their lips met.

"You love me?" he asked, this time with less disbelief in his tone.

"Yes. I love you." She eyed him with hope and vexation. He just stared at her, his face stoic as if he'd had to endure some kind of silly prank. "Space to Wade. This is the time where you're supposed to chime in and say that you love me, too."

"What about your parents?"

She lifted her chin. "This is between you and me."

"What about Cara's opinion?"

"Ditto for her."

"And your law degree?"

"What does that have to do with anything?" For a man who'd just heard that she loved him, he certainly was throwing out a lot of objections for her to trip on. She might not have declared her love to any man before, but she was agile and vowed not to go down without a full-fledged battle.

"If you go to law school, you'll leave Mustang Valley."

And then she got it. She understood why he'd been holding back. Not because he didn't have feelings for her, but because he was afraid of losing her.

"My attending law school doesn't mean I'll leave you. Haven't you ever heard of phone calls and airplanes and vacation time?"

"You haven't thought this through."

She fisted her hands on her hips. "No. *You* haven't thought this through. You don't have the courage to take a chance on me. You're the one who's been holding back. I never thought that a man who could toss a mean three-hundred-pound drunk out of his saloon without breaking a sweat, a man who took on a murder investigation to ensure justice for his best friend, a man who doesn't give one whit what the townsfolk think about him would be afraid of me. But you're an emotional coward, Wade."

"What?"

"It's not your background or your reputation or education that's going to drive me away. It's your fear of loving me. And that means you aren't good enough for me."

She marched for the door, her heart heavy, her eyes brimming with anger and unshed tears. She'd laid her heart out for him to take. Instead he'd chosen to crush it. Well, she couldn't make him love her or make him say he loved her. And if he didn't make the effort, it didn't matter either way.

Hoping he might still change his mind didn't make the ache inside her hurt any less.

Damn him.

She brushed away an angry tear. She needed to find Cara. She wanted to talk with a friend she could count on to take her side.

Too full of anger to watch her step, Kelly knocked into a chair. The carton filled with Andrew's papers tumbled to the floor. Great. The last thing she wanted was to delay her departure. She didn't want to spend another minute with Wade right now. Still, she kneeled and randomly stacked the papers that she'd already gone through twice in hopes of finding a clue as to why Andrew had been worried that something might happen to him.

While she piled the papers, Wade squatted beside her. He straightened the tipped-over box. "I need some time, Kelly."

"Take the rest of your life," she muttered as she thrust papers back into a folder.

"I never thought you were serious about me, so it colored my thoughts and my judgment. I suppose I was protecting myself."

"From what?" She stopped fussing with the papers and clutched Andrew's jacket.

"From you," he admitted. "I always considered you off-limits. And I didn't want to be your boy toy."

"It was never like that. I'm not like that." She

didn't like that he thought so little of her. Didn't like that he thought she'd been using him. Didn't like that he didn't think she had genuine feelings.

"I understand. Now," he said, his eyes locked on hers. "But all of this is rather sudden. I could tell you what you want to hear but…"

"But?"

"It would be a lie."

"Great." His words hurt but she couldn't deny the honesty he conveyed.

"I don't want to hurt you." He spoke gently. "As soon as I figure out how I feel I'll let you know."

"So damn nice of you." Insulted and irritated, she straightened the pile of papers in her hands. "You'd better think fast because I don't intend to wait very long."

He held out the box to her to dump the papers. She started to toss the entire stack and frowned at the yellow paper at the bottom of the carton. "What's that?"

"What?"

She gestured with her chin. "I don't recall seeing that before." Kelly placed the papers on the counter, reached inside the box and pulled out the piece of folded yellow notepaper. "This is Andrew's handwriting."

"It must have been wedged in the bottom flaps until you dumped the box on its side."

She opened the paper and flattened it, her mouth dry, her hands shaking. "It's a list of owners in the Ranger Corporation."

"Isn't that the corporation that's purchasing the

West family's ranch?'' Wade asked, setting aside the box and leaning over her shoulder.

''Yeah.''

''Who's on the list?''

Andrew's scrawl was hard to read and she'd had more practice than he had. ''Niles Deagen. Mayor Daniels. Sheriff Wilson. My father, Paul Lambert and Donald Church, plus a list of twenty investors I don't recognize.'' She sighed and put down the paper. ''It doesn't seem important.''

Wade picked up the paper. ''But it might be.''

''How? There's nothing illegal about forming a corporation or the fact that Niles is a major contributor to the mayor's reelection.''

''Lots of voters wouldn't appreciate their mayor siding with big business.'' Wade snapped his fingers. ''Didn't Andrew have the mayor's financial statement in that box?''

''So what?''

Nevertheless she dug out the papers Wade was talking about and handed them to him. He scanned the typed and stapled pages. ''There's no mention of the mayor owning part of the Ranger Corporation in this document.''

She was catching on. ''If he failed to disclose his ownership and Andrew found out and confronted him—''

''It would most certainly hurt his upcoming election,'' Wade speculated.

''So he kills Andrew? It seems far-fetched.'' Kelly wasn't buying the motive.

Wade placed all the papers back in the box and left Andrew's note on top. ''Suppose the Ranger

Corporation invested in other land or businesses. Big money could be involved, and the mayor's influence might be needed to construct roads, change zoning, etcetera.''

"So what do we do now?" Kelly asked. "Go talk to the mayor?"

"That's what Andrew might have done."

And look what had happened to him. Wade's implication rocked her. She hadn't forgotten their earlier conversation or how he'd asked for more time to think about his feelings for her, either. She picked up her car keys. "Before we do anything else I want to speak to Lindsey and Cara."

CARA, LINDSEY AND KELLY met for a late-night snack at Dot's. Wade had refused to allow Kelly to drive there alone, but once she'd met up with her friends, he'd headed over to the Hit 'Em Again Saloon to check on business. Kelly had promised to call Wade when their meeting broke up, and he would come by and take her wherever she wanted to go.

In a corner booth, Cara and Lindsey had listened to Kelly bring them up-to-date while they'd all eaten their sandwiches. Currently they shared a trio of desserts.

Between sips of her diet cola and forkfuls of chocolate cake, Lindsey spoke. "You've got enough proof to nail the mayor for incorrectly filling out his financials for reelection but not enough to investigate him for murder."

"She's right," Cara agreed, breaking a cinnamon-raisin cookie into pieces. "The mayor doesn't even own a registered gun. I checked."

"Did you find anything useful on Niles Deagen?" Kelly asked, ignoring her slice of lemon pie for the moment.

Lindsey checked her notes. "He's been brought up on racketeering charges twice, but so far the charges never stick. The man can afford top-notch lawyers."

Cara brushed crumbs from the table. "There're still rumors going around that Deagen's company is on the verge of collapse. But since he holds the stock privately, I have no way to check the real situation. On another note, when will the sheriff's office finish comparing the paint on Deagen's car to Johnny's?"

Kelly sighed, feeling weary and emotionally exhausted. "It could take days or more. And Johnny's still in a coma."

Cara eyed her across the table. "You aren't giving up, are you?"

The tension in her must have been obvious to Cara, and she tried to make her tone sound less dejected. "What makes you say that?"

"You sound discouraged," Lindsey told her. "But you're doing an excellent investigative job."

"So excellent that all we've found are dead ends." Kelly shoved her hair out of her eyes, cut her pie into pieces but didn't eat. "I'm not sure what to do next."

Cara pointed her fork at her. "What's really wrong?"

"Nothing," Kelly murmured, but Cara knew her too well.

"It's Wade." Cara spoke knowingly to Lindsey. "She likes him. A lot."

"And how does he feel about you?" Lindsey asked the big question with unerring accuracy.

Kelly rubbed her chin, glad to get another take on Wade. "That's the problem. He says he doesn't know."

"That's so typical of men," Cara told her. "Sometimes they are the last to know."

"Sounds like a cop-out to me." Lindsey gazed sympathetically at Kelly.

Cara nodded her agreement. "Seems to me that you need to bait a trap."

Kelly raised a skeptical eyebrow. "To catch Wade?"

Cara signaled her a thumbs-up. "Him, too."

KELLY PHONED WADE to tell them their meeting was about over. He told her he would come by and pick her up within a few minutes. After Lindsey and Cara left Dot's, Kelly paid the check, then used the rest room. She'd promised Wade she wouldn't leave Dot's until he returned and she took her time brushing her hair, refreshing her makeup and checking her teeth for smudges of lip gloss.

She wouldn't give up on solving Andrew's murder, and she wouldn't give up on Wade. Somehow she'd find a way to make her life go in the direction she wanted. She wondered what her ancestor Shotgun Sally would have done if she'd been in her position, but didn't come up with any answers.

Kelly exited the rest room and bumped right into

Mayor Daniels. She teetered back into the wall. "Gosh, you scared me. Where did you come from?"

He reached out and steadied her. "Oops. You okay?"

"I'm fine."

"Good." He didn't release her arm, shoved a gun into her side. "Don't even think about screaming for help."

Oh, God.

Mayor Daniels had a gun on her.

Her weapon was in the glove compartment of the Jag.

Her friends had left, thinking she'd be safe in a public restaurant until Wade came back. But Mayor Daniels had chosen his window of opportunity with a precision that frightened her as much as the gun in her ribs.

Daniels tugged her out the back door, and she doubted anyone had noted her sudden departure or would miss her. People weren't usually that observant.

Daniels hustled her through the door into a back alley, the same way he must have come inside. So it was highly unlikely that anyone had seen him. When Wade arrived and began asking questions, neither Dot nor her waitress would be able to tell him anything useful.

Outside, the garbage bin smelled and the area lacked decent lighting. With Daniels's car parked out back, he clearly intended to shove her inside his waiting vehicle. If she got in, he could take her anywhere, kill her and dump her body. It might be days before anyone found her.

Her thoughts circled in a panic.

She needed to do something. But what?

The idea of overpowering the mayor seemed impossible. And if she struck out ineffectively and he injured her, that would lessen her chances of getting away if a better opportunity arose later.

She dragged her feet, stalling. Her mind racing. *Think.*

She had a cell phone in her purse, but even if she managed to secretly call 911, no one would know her location. She could try and break his grip and run, but his fingers dug into her arm with a strength that told her she wouldn't stand a chance.

Maybe she could play dumb. "What's this all about, Mayor? You already have my vote."

"Shut up."

"Hey, that's no way to talk to one of your constituents. My daddy always says—"

"Be quiet." He shook her so hard that she almost bit her tongue.

Talking hadn't worked. Escape didn't seem a likely option.

Kelly tried the next best thing. She stepped around him, flung her free hand around his neck as if she was embracing him.

She made her voice low and sexy. "Don't you think I'm a mite too young for you, Mayor?"

For the moment he stopped dragging her across the pavement. "What the hell are you talking about?"

At least he was no longer urging her toward his car. If she could just play dumb, delay him for long enough, use up enough precious seconds, Wade would search for her, maybe even look out the back door and find her in trouble.

"I'm talking about you and me, Mayor. I've always found you attractive, but I didn't know you liked me."

"You think I like you?" he sputtered.

"Of course you do," she said. "But I never worked up enough nerve to let you know. I'm so glad you've gone and made the first move." She ran her free hand up and down his arm. "I find powerful men, especially politicians, so-o-o sexy."

Had she overdone it? Would he fall for it?

Hurry up, Wade.

Daniels's fingers clenched her arm even more tightly, and he shoved her against his car. "This is a gun. I'm not fooling around."

Frustration and fear had her trying one last time to convince him that she was interested in him as a man, not as someone who had to fear anything she might know. "Ooh. I always liked Sheriff Wilson's gun. I didn't know that you had one, too."

"I told you to shut up. Do you think I'm an idiot? Do you think I don't know that you've been asking questions about me all over Texas?"

He flipped her around roughly. He banged her against the car and she grunted in pain as her knee struck the door. When he pulled her arms behind her back, she struggled, stomped on his foot.

In surprise and pain, he released her. She ran a few steps, then his hand clamped down on her shoulder. "Take one more step and I'll knock you out, right now."

"Okay."

She forced herself to hold still, trembling as he used a plastic garbage bag tie on her wrists, then he pushed her into the passenger seat of his car.

Fear like she'd never known made her weak, almost sick. Mayor Daniels must have killed Andrew and now he was going to shoot her, too. Only he couldn't do it right in the middle of town where too many people would hear the gunshots. He was going to drive her somewhere else.

She struggled against her bonds, but he'd yanked the tie so tightly her fingers were already going numb. She would have risked a scream except the lot behind Dot's that took overflow parking during the day was empty at this time of night.

Think.

He'd been in such a hurry to tie her up, he hadn't removed her purse, which still hung from her shoulder. But there was no time to dig into her purse for the manicure scissors that she might use to cut herself free. Once he got away, she would be at his mercy.

Daniels slid into the driver's seat and started the car. She had to do something to draw attention to her predicament. Something drastic. This might be her last chance to get attention and the help she needed.

Kelly leaned toward the door, raised her leg and kicked the center of the steering wheel. The horn blared.

Daniels cursed. He struggled with her leg and she slammed the back of her heel into his jaw, then pressed her toes forward and onto the horn again.

Daniels yanked her ankle and twisted. She screeched in pain but she kept kicking.

A fist shot in her direction and struck her temple. Pain exploded in her head and the world turned black.

Chapter Thirteen

Kelly woke up just seconds later. Pain made her thoughts sharp. "You can't kill me and get away with it. I've told too many people my suspicions about you," she lied.

And she would keep lying—especially if it would keep her alive.

Daniels had stuck his gun into the waistband of his pants. He hadn't bothered with his seat belt. Or hers. She wriggled around in an attempt to grab her purse, which had slipped off her shoulder to the floor.

The next time he made a hard right, she slid to the floor and let out a yelp to make him believe that she hadn't changed her position on purpose. Behind her back, she felt around for her purse.

Got it.

She opened the bag just as Daniels reached over and lifted her under the arm and propped her back on the seat. Luckily she managed to keep the purse with her.

"Who have you told about me?" he asked, his glance at her more curious than concerned.

She wanted to name Cara and Lindsey, who he knew she'd just met. He would fear Cara and her reporting, Lindsey with her ties to the law. But in case Kelly didn't make it, she didn't want this monster coming after her friends.

"Wade knows. So does my father," she said, lying some more.

"They'll just think you came off with some goofy idea."

"Not after you plug a bullet in me, they won't," she countered. Meanwhile, she stuck her fingers into the tiny purse. Her wallet was on top, and she dug past her checkbook, hitting a tube of lipstick.

"I have no intention of shooting you like I did your brother."

So he *had* killed Andrew. Until this moment she hadn't known for sure. But why would he have admitted that to her unless he planned to kill her, too?

"You aren't going to shoot me?"

Her fingers clasped the manicure scissors just as he drove out of downtown Mustang Valley. But maneuvering was almost impossible with her weight pressed again her numbed wrists.

"Of course not. You're going to die in an accident. On Wade's land." Daniels sighed. "With him in prison for your death, my election campaign should go just as I planned."

"You're forgetting about my father. I told him about you when I found—"

"Found what?"

"Andrew left me his notes," she told him, trying to stall for time, hoping she could turn the tiny scissors into a cutting tool.

"And what did those notes say?"

"That you own part of a company—"

"Nothing wrong with that."

"Except you failed to declare it on your public financial statement." She hoped her combination of truth and lies might make him reconsider his actions. Her head ached where he had slammed his fist against her temple. And as she maneuvered the scissors, the plastic cut sharply into her wrists. But determinedly, she kept hacking away at her bonds. "The voters won't be happy with you when that information comes out in tomorrow's press."

"Your friend Cara is doing the story, I suppose."

"It's already written and has been put to bed."

Daniels shrugged. "Well then, I guess the *Mustang Gazette* may have a little fire tonight."

Daniels pulled onto the highway, and she glimpsed headlights in the sideview mirror. She prayed that Wade might be following, and sawed all the harder with the scissors. She stabbed herself repeatedly and blood trickled down her fingers. Hopefully, she wouldn't hit an artery and do Daniels's dirty work for him by bleeding to death.

"You're willing to kill just to cover up a lie on a financial statement?"

"That lie could keep me from getting reelected."

"And to keep me quiet, you're willing to commit murder?"

"Running this town is a power to which I've become accustomed. Believe me, I never wanted to kill you. But after you found the note in the bottom of Andrew's box, I knew you wouldn't keep quiet," he said with a sly glance in her direction.

"How did you know about the incriminating evidence against you?"

"The man in the van has been following you for some time. After he saw you find those notes, I knew I had to kill you. And I'm going after Wade next."

Oh, God. He was insane. He'd actually had someone following her, although no one appeared to be following now. Her heart pounded and her mouth went dry with fear. "You can't keep killing people." She said the words to keep him talking, to keep him distracted from her leaning forward to ease the pressure against her wrists.

"What do you mean by people? You'll only be my second victim. It's a shame really. Who would have thought that I would have to do away with a pretty young thing like you. Politics really does make strange bedfellows."

Daniels's voice was cheery, as if he were discussing his summer vacation plans or his advertising scheme to be Mustang Valley's repeat mayor. His tone increased her determination to free her hands. But when the tie finally snapped free, she was unprepared to make her next move.

The scissors weren't big enough to do much damage but they were the only weapon she had. She gripped them tightly behind her back and worked out the numbness in her wrists. Now what? Reach over and wrestle him for the wheel? Should she force the car off the road? There was no guarantee either of them would survive, but at least she had a chance of taking him with her—if she crashed the car.

Oh, God.

She told herself the only way she could protect Daniels from coming after the ones she loved was to grab the steering wheel and yank hard. But she didn't want to die.

She couldn't imagine the pain she would cause her parents if she died. And Wade. He might not have admitted having feelings for her—but she had them for him. She wanted the time to explore where their relationship could go. She wanted more days, more nights. Right now she desperately wanted just a minute in his arms.

But she had no time.

Daniels was taking her to Wade's ranch. Once he slowed down, the possibility of her crashing the car lessened. She had to make her move now while they sped down the highway. This part of Texas didn't have many trees.

And they'd passed the last overpass and bridge abutment several miles back. The telephone poles flashed by too fast for her to aim at one of them. But a billboard was coming up on the right. A billboard with steel-poled, solid legs.

She wedged the scissors into her left hand, crooked her thumb over the edge. Every muscle in her arms and shoulders tensed as she waited for the perfect moment. She saw no cars up ahead. Just one pair of headlights a long ways back.

You can do this.

On three.

One.

Two.

Three!

She slid her hand with the scissors out from behind her back. And she stabbed Daniels' thigh.

He shouted in pain.

The car swerved, knocking into a low wooden fence she hadn't noticed. Fence slats flew into the sky.

Kelly released the scissors and yanked on the steering wheel. Daniels cursed. Shoved her away.

Damn it. They were going to miss the steel poles. Then the car hit a ditch and toppled over.

WADE COULDN'T BE CERTAIN Kelly was in the car he was following. When he'd entered Dot's café and Kelly hadn't been out front, he'd assumed she'd gone to the ladies' room. However, when he'd heard insistent honking from the street out back, he'd hurriedly knocked on the ladies' room door, then checked inside.

No one was there.

And his adrenaline kicked into overdrive. He shoved out the back exit just in time to see a vehicle's taillights making a hard right.

Wade had rushed back inside the restaurant. Neither Dot nor the waitress could tell him Kelly's whereabouts. They thought she'd left with Cara and Lindsey but couldn't be sure. He tried to phone Cara but voice mail answered at the *Mustang Gazette*. He hung up and tried Lindsey at the office. But it was almost midnight. No one answered and he didn't have her home phone number.

While he called information, he unlocked the Jag, drove around the block and searched for the taillights he'd seen disappearing at the corner. Fifteen minutes later he still hadn't caught up with the car he was following. Still unsure if Kelly was in that car, he didn't consider turning around. One thing he knew for sure, the car up ahead of him was traveling at a high rate of speed and the driver didn't want to be caught.

Wade tried Cara at home again—no answer. If Kelly was still with her friends and they'd gone off together without Kelly telling him, he was going to be both relieved and angry at her for putting him through this gut-stabbing fear for her safety.

She probably wasn't in the car he was tailing. And yet, suppose she was?

He pressed the pedal down on the Jag and sped along the country highway. At least he knew the road and its curves well, since he used this route on the way to his property. Up ahead the car careened onto the shoulder of the road, then veered back in a zigzag pattern.

Was the driver drunk? Or was a struggle going on inside the car?

Were his instincts on target? The car rolled over and skidded into the billboard's foundation. He swallowed his panic, jammed on his brakes and ran to the smoking car, which had ended in an upright position.

The sight of Kelly on the passenger side made his heart pound and his mouth go dry with fear. She wasn't moving. And he could smell gasoline amid the smoke.

Yanking open the door, he reached inside, turned the key to switch off the engine and pulled Kelly out. Her eyes were closed. Blood trickled down her forehead. He didn't stop to see whether she was still breathing or had a pulse. He had to get her away from the car before the flames reached the gasoline tank and the vehicle exploded.

Sick with worry, Wade carried her about a hundred yards, sank into the grass, ready to go back for the driver. But the car, whose engine he'd turned off, suddenly revved. The driver must be conscious. But what the hell?

The driver should be getting out of the car, racing from the flames. Instead the idiot was driving, turning.

Aiming straight for them.

Wade didn't hesitate. He scooped Kelly back into his arms, searched for cover. There was none. Except maybe he could place the Jag between him and the oncoming car.

He had only seconds and strained to sprint with Kelly in his arms. His lungs burned in the smoky air. His thighs stung with the effort. Clutching her tightly to his chest, he vowed that if they couldn't both get away, at the last moment he'd thrust her to safety or die trying.

Behind him he could hear the vehicle gaining on him. But he didn't spare a second to look back. He dived behind the Jag, twisting in the air to cushion Kelly as the two of them hit the dirt.

The fall seemed to jar her awake. Her eyes opened and stared at him puzzled. ''What—'' Then he could see memories wash over her. ''The mayor—''

The mayor? Wade spied Daniels turning the car around to make another pass at running over them. Smoke belching from the undercarriage didn't seem to slow him down.

''Can you get inside the Jag?'' Wade asked Kelly, unsure of her medical condition. She had an assort-

ment of scrapes and bruises but no obvious broken
bones. However, after that crash she could have sustained a multitude of internal ailments.

She scrambled awkwardly, and he could tell she
was hurting, but she made it inside. She slammed
the door shut, then reached inside the glove compartment and pulled out her gun.

Wade started the powerful engine. Too late.

From his left the other vehicle slammed into them
hard enough to shatter the driver's window. Kelly
fired two shots.

He had no idea if the window had broken from
the collision or her bullets, didn't know if she'd hit
anything at all, but the gunfire must have frightened
the mayor enough to reconsider trying to crash into
them again. Daniels roared back onto the highway
and sped away in the opposite direction from Mustang Valley.

"Go after him," Kelly demanded, her tone commanding, urgent.

The moment Wade pressed his foot to the gas
pedal, he realized he wasn't attaining full power.
"Something's wrong."

"He's getting away." Kelly peered down the
road, seemingly unconcerned by the blood trickling
down her forehead and cheek. "We have to go—"

The Jag's engine died.

Wade shoved open his door, exited the vehicle
and hurried toward the engine, but he couldn't open
the hood due to the damage from the collision. Without tools he probably couldn't have done much, anyway.

"We aren't going anywhere. But we can call for

reinforcements.'' Wade flipped open his new car phone and dialed Deputy Mitch Warwick.

"Do you know what time it is?" answered a cranky Mitch.

"Mayor Daniels just kidnapped Kelly McGovern, then tried to run us both over."

"What!"

"Wake up. Even as we speak the mayor is heading due south. My guess it that he doesn't plan to stop until after he crosses the Mexican border."

"Is this a joke?"

"Mayor Daniels admitted to me that he killed Andrew," Kelly pitched in.

"What was his motive?" Mitch asked, the sleepiness now gone from his voice.

While Kelly explained that the nondisclosure of his ownership in some land deal coming to light could have prevented the mayor from winning his reelection campaign, Wade looked her over. He'd been so afraid when he couldn't find her at Dot's. Then he'd watched the car roll over, and when he'd run from the smoking car and danger, he'd been ready to plant himself between her and Daniels's car to protect her.

No woman had ever meant so much to him.

And now as she stood in the smoky field after having almost died twice in the last few minutes, all he could do was marvel at her inner strength. She'd fired two shots at the mayor, then, after almost being run over, she'd urged him to chase Daniels down.

Another woman would have been clinging to him, crying, hiding. But she'd been determined to fight for the justice she wanted for her brother, and he suspected her determination might have even been responsible for the initial crash into that billboard foundation. All in all, Kelly McGovern was quite a woman.

Mitch promised to send an ambulance and backup. He said Sheriff Wilson and his deputies would find Mayor Daniels and bring him back to Mustang Valley for justice. Wade figured with the smoke coming out of that car, finding the mayor wouldn't be too difficult.

Kelly hung up the phone and swore. "Damn. Damn. Damn."

Wade hurried to her side, ready to grab her if she toppled over. "What's wrong? Are you hurt?"

"I'm bleeding." She touched the blood on her chin as if she hadn't realized she'd been hurt until just that moment.

"You're going to be fine," he tried to reassure her. "It's just a small cut."

"I'm bleeding on my silk *blouse*. The stain is never going to come out."

He stared at her, his lower jaw dropping in astonishment. "You're worried about your blouse?"

"It's a Donna Karan."

"How terrible." Wade smacked his forehead in mock horror.

"The stain won't come out."

She glared at him, the gun by her side, pointed at the dirt. "Are you making fun of me?"

He held up his hands in surrender and teased. "Not while you have the gun."

Her eyebrows narrowed. "What—"

The sound of a loud boom cut off her words.

Chapter Fourteen

Ambulances, sirens blaring, a fire truck and several deputies in their cars rushed down the road. One black-and-white pulled beside them and stopped. Deputy Warwick exited his vehicle. "Are you two all right?"

"Yeah, but after the explosion we just heard, I'm not so sure about Mayor Daniels." Wade's tone was thoughtful, and all his earlier teasing had disappeared from his demeanor. He stood straight, his face smudged from the smoke, his shirt spattered with her blood, and to Kelly he'd never looked more beautiful. Men weren't supposed to be beautiful but Wade Lansing was beautiful to her. She didn't think she'd ever tire of looking at him.

He'd saved her life, risked his own to rescue her. Without his strength, quick thinking and courage, she might not be standing there right now. Odd how he could commit himself to her with actions but couldn't follow through with words. While she had difficulty understanding where he was coming from, she knew he hadn't had a loving childhood. He might not even recognize how he felt about her, and it could be a long time, if ever, before he could give her what she wanted from him.

And as much as she loved him, she couldn't spend her life waiting for him to make the first move. She wasn't ready to give up on him, either, not after what they'd shared. So, just as she'd seduced him, she would have to lead him to the idea that they could be a permanent couple. Only, she didn't know how to get there from here.

She must have missed some of the conversation between Wade and Deputy Warwick because suddenly his radio blared with information.

"The mayor's vehicle exploded," a deputy reported. "Mayor Daniels is dead. No one else is injured here, but we could use the ambulance to take the body back to town."

"So it's over." Wade took her hand, and then she flew into his arms. His powerful chest supported her, his strong arms closed around her. She'd wanted justice for Andrew and she'd gotten that. But along the way she'd found something else. She'd found the love of her life. The other details could wait. Right now she just wanted Wade to take her home.

Apparently that wasn't going to happen: Her parents drove up and came rushing over.

She hugged both her mother and father to assure them that she was safe. At the same time she wanted to bring Wade into their circle of love. But when she tugged his hand, he resisted.

Standing tall and alone, he spoke with the deputy about towing the Jag back to town. He told her he would hitch a ride with Mitch to give them a run-down of what had happened and suggested she go home with her folks.

If he thought he could get rid of her that easily, he was so wrong. However, now was not the time to have a personal discussion, with all the medical people, Mitch and her folks around.

Tomorrow morning she would give a detailed report to Sheriff Wilson and then she intended to meet with the girls for a plan-of-action session. By the time she was done with Wade Lansing, he wouldn't know what had hit him.

WADE WATCHED KELLY get into the car with her parents. He made himself keep watching as she drove away and wondered at the sense of loss that gripped him. He would see her tomorrow when she came to his house to pick up her things, but he was accustomed to her living at his house, sharing their evenings together.

Hell. He had a business to run. With the investigation over and Daniels dead, she no longer needed his protection. She would be safe with her folks. So why did her leaving him feel so wrong? Why did he have this hollow ache in his chest as if he was making the biggest mistake of his life?

After hitching a ride with Mitch to his ranch, Wade cleaned up in his shower and headed to the Hit 'Em Again, where not even the business details of ordering supplies, hiring a new bartender and paying bills could totally distract him from missing Kelly and worrying about her. By closing time, he'd worked himself up and used his excess energy on a three-mile run back home.

Tomorrow, he'd take care of purchasing another truck, now that the insurance company had come through. He kept checking his cell phone for messages, but there were none. Which meant that Kelly was fine. In her own home, her own bed—back where she belonged.

Wade settled into his hot tub on his back deck, hoping the heat would soothe his thoughts. But he could have sworn he smelled Kelly's unique scent, recalled how she'd soaked in this exact spot, teasing him with her sensuality, taunting him to take one forbidden taste. One taste had led to another and their lovemaking had been so powerful that he would remember her for the rest of his days—and some very long nights.

It was his own fault, of course. He should have resisted her sweet seduction. He should never have even kissed her.

Damn it. He should be satisfied that Kelly was safe and back in her protected world. Andrew would be pleased with their resourcefulness and that they'd both survived. And especially that his killer had been revealed and had paid for the crime with his own life.

Wade should be exhausted after the trying day they'd spent, but he was wide awake. And as he watched the sun rise up over the horizon, the angry streaks of purple and slashes of pink reminded him today would be harder than yesterday.

When his cell phone shrilled, it startled him so much that he almost knocked it onto the ground. The voice on the line was female—but not Kelly's, not the woman whose voice he'd been hoping to hear.

"Sorry to call so early."

"Who is this?"

"Debbie West."

Why was she calling *him* when Kelly had given Debbie *her* number. "What's wrong?"

"The McGoverns aren't answering their phone."

He quickly filled Debbie in about Mayor Daniels and their stressful evening. "They might have just turned off their phone to get a good night's sleep, or maybe it doesn't ring in the bedrooms."

"You're probably right."

"But?" he prodded, not yet too concerned.

"Niles tracked me down to the women's shelter where I've been staying."

"Women's shelter? With all the money Kelly gave you why aren't you at a hotel?"

"Niles has a violent temper. I felt safer here after he tracked me to my new apartment I'd rented in the middle of the night. He was ranting about Mayor Daniels's death and how he could lose everything."

All along Wade and Kelly had suspected that Niles might have been backing the mayor's election, that Niles might have been helping Daniels with some of his dirty work—but suppose it was the other way around? Suppose the mayor had been taking orders from the powerful oil man? That would mean Kelly still might not be safe.

"What do you mean, he could lose everything?"

"I don't know the details, but he borrowed a lot of money and he was counting on a big payoff with a deal he had with the mayor. With his empire about to crash, if this all ends up in the newspaper, I'm worried about him trying to silence Kelly so it can never go to trial.''

Looked like he'd have to fire up the old Caddy after all. ''I'll try Kelly on the cell phone on my way over to the McGoverns' house.''

But the moment Wade opened his front door to leave, Niles was standing there pointing a gun at him and sneering. ''We're most definitely going to call your girlfriend.''

And Wade no longer needed a lab report to verify that the paint from Niles's car would prove he'd killed Johnny Dixon.

EXHAUSTED, KELLY SLEPT soundly and still only half-awake, she reached groggily for the ringing cell phone. ''Hello?''

''Kelly, it's Wade. Don't—''

At the sound of a loud thunk, Kelly jerked wide awake, fear and confusion washing away her sleepiness. ''Wade? Wade! Answer me.''

She heard several grunts and flicked on her light. It was 7:00 a.m. and her heart pounded with terror as her phone transmitted the clear and sickening smacks of a fist striking flesh. Grunts. Curses.

Oh, God.

She raised her fist to her mouth and bit down on a knuckle. Wade was in trouble. He'd tried to call her, and someone must have jumped him. From the sound of the fight, he was taking a terrible beating and from that she could conclude only one thing: Someone had taken him by surprise and he was no longer in a position to fight back.

She had to do something.

Kelly was reaching for the house phone to dial 911 when a man spoke to her over the phone in a familiar voice she almost recognized. "I have your boyfriend tied to a chair. He doesn't look so pretty anymore." She'd thought she'd been hearing a fight, but in reality what she'd heard was Wade being hit as he sat helpless, and her stomach roiled. "If you ever want to see Wade Lansing alive again, you must do exactly as I say."

"How do I know he's still alive?" she asked, making her tone careless and hard, hoping to counter her trembling from scalp to toes. Despite her fear, she had to stay calm. Stalling for time, she wondered what she should do and how she could best help Wade.

"You just heard Wade talking to you, didn't you?" the man growled with a biting sarcasm that told her to be very careful what she said and how she said it. As much as she wanted to sob, she suspected this man would only respect strength.

"I also heard you hitting him," she countered as she slipped on a shirt and a pair of jeans.

"Well, Wade wanted to play hero. He didn't want to sweet-talk you into coming to rescue him. And I don't have time to change his mind."

She suddenly recognized the voice. Niles! She was almost positive. And her recognition triggered other thoughts. What was Niles doing with Wade and why was he beating him?

Desperately trying not to think of Wade lying somewhere unconscious and injured and vulnerable, her thoughts raced to the conclusion that Niles must have been not just backing the mayor's reelection campaign but working with Daniels. Niles wouldn't want public scrutiny of his business dealings with the mayor, and with his empire on the verge of collapse, he, too, might be willing to commit murder to protect his secrets. The paint on that dented car probably matched Johnny Dixon's. And if Niles would attempt to kill Dixon, there was no reason he would spare Wade.

In the background Wade yelled, ''Don't listen to him.''

She heard another nauseating smack, then gagging, and Niles returned to the phone, breathing heavily. ''We haven't the time for ridiculous heroics. You get your pretty little ass over to your boyfriend's house, right now.''

So he could kill both of them? As much as she feared for Wade's safety she had to make the right decision. Getting herself killed by foolishly running to his side wouldn't help either of them.

She should wake her folks. Call the sheriff. She made her voice sound much younger and girlish. ''I'm scared, and besides I don't have a car. Mine was wrecked.''

''Don't play games with me, woman. Look out your window.''

''What?''

''Just do it.''

She peeked through the miniblinds and spied a man smoking a cigarette in the front seat of a dark van parked across the neighborhood street. In the first light of dawn she could see him stare directly at her as he tipped his cap.

Niles, not the mayor, was having her watched, and

a shiver crawled down her spine. Clearly the two of
them had been working together, since both of them
had used the man in the van to spy on her. And since
she could tie the mayor to attempted murder, even
if Niles had been innocent, just his business dealing
with a killer could put the nail in the coffin of his
crumbling empire. He couldn't afford to let her live.

"My boy will report back to me if you don't follow my instructions exactly."

"What do you want?"

"Take your daddy's car and meet us at Wade's
house. If you try to call anyone or make an extra
stop along the way, I'll know, and your boyfriend
will be history. You've got ten minutes."

"Make it twenty. I'm not dressed," she lied, but
a plan was beginning to form in her mind, a plan
that would take a few precious minutes to imple-
ment.

Niles chuckled. "Fifteen and not a minute more,
or I shoot your friend. Got it?"

"I'm scared." Kelly unzipped her jeans and
slipped them off. She went to her closet and
thumbed through her choices, looking for one particular denim jumper with huge wide-angled pockets. "Can't we work this out like adults? My daddy's
a wealthy man, he'd be willing to pay—"

Niles hung up the phone. Apparently, he wasn't
interested in a deal—which could only mean one
thing. He intended to kill both Wade and her, no
matter what.

Kelly didn't dare use her phone, and tossed it on
the bed to free her hand up to dress quickly. Niles
might have planted some kind of listening device in

her room, or on her clothing, or in her purse. She couldn't risk his man overhearing her—but that didn't prevent her from scribbling a fast and furious note to her folks. She slipped the jumper that she normally wore belted at the waist over her head and glanced at herself in the mirror. Not the effect she needed.

Perhaps a blouse under the jumper would portray the helpless little-girl effect she was going for. Much better. At least she needn't bother with makeup to pull off her deception. Then she parted her hair down the middle, braided each side and tied the braids off with pink ribbons. She slipped white socks on her feet, folded them down to the ankles and tied on an old pair of sneakers. On the way out the door she grabbed her gun and made sure it was loaded.

Not the place to hurry.

She made herself turn back and check her image again in the mirror. Without the belt, the jumper hung loosely and eclipsed her curves. The huge pocket, which now held her loaded gun that she'd grabbed from the floor of the Jag before the tow truck had hauled it off didn't give her much security.

Last but not least, she slipped a note under her parents' door on her way down the hall and banged on their door. She checked her watch, her heart beating so fast that she felt as if she'd just run a mile.

Breathe.

She needed to remain sharp, not tire herself out by tensing every muscle. In retrospect she should have told Niles that she wouldn't come into the house until he proved to her that Wade was still alive. And that mistake might cost her.

She had no time to second-guess herself. No time for regrets. But her biggest fear was that Niles might not keep Wade alive until she got there.

When she pulled her dad's Mercedes out of the driveway and headed out of the subdivision, the van followed her all the way out of town. She did nothing to attract attention to herself, driving the speed limit on the mostly deserted streets. She didn't want to risk doing anything that would cause the van's driver to report to Niles that she wasn't exactly following his instructions.

She parked the car in the driveway. Now what?

Slowly she exited the car, unobtrusively checking the pocket, then deciding to put her hand into the pocket so she could clutch the gun's handle.

"Come right in through the front door." The door opened, but she couldn't see Niles, just his arm.

She hesitated. "I'm not coming inside until I hear Wade's voice."

"Get out of here," Wade shouted, clearly furious that she hadn't listened to him earlier and that she had no intention of listening to him now.

"Satisfied?" Niles asked through the propped-open door.

She wished she could see past the front door so she had some idea of Wade's condition and what kind of situation she was about to walk into. She recalled a Shotgun Sally pillow that her mother had embroidered that said, "Sometimes one must trust oneself."

This was one of those times. She took a deep breath, hoping the added oxygen would not just give her courage but make her wise. Slowly, her heart tip-toeing up her throat, she walked into a certain trap.

WADE CURSED THE BONDS that tied him to the chair, cursed at fate that had let Niles surprise him, cursed at Kelly for stubbornly putting herself in danger. Though his right eye was swollen shut, he could still see out of the left, and Kelly walking through that door almost gave him a heart attack.

How could she be stupid enough to put herself in danger? Was she so naive that she believed Niles wouldn't kill them both? Was she so trusting that she thought she could talk Niles out of his plan?

The bonds that kept his hands firmly tied behind his back and to a chair only served to increase the rage and fear for Kelly that swept through him. She didn't belong in his house, putting herself in danger. And she most certainly didn't belong...in those clothes.

And what the hell had she done to her hair? He tried to blink the blood from his good eye. She'd braided her hair and had dressed herself like a little girl.

Damn. Damn. Damn.

She had dressed herself to pander to Niles's twisted tastes of young flesh, and at the moment of realization, the hot rage inside him froze icy cold. He licked at the cut of his swollen lip, trying to put moisture back into his mouth.

Kelly walked into his living room with the mincing steps of a child, yet just for a moment he caught her vivid blue eyes that glinted with the ferocity of a tigress protecting her mate. Obviously, she had a plan. And no way was Wade going to talk her out of it now, especially after she'd seen the gun Niles had pointed at his head.

The fact that the gun was pointed at Wade and not her didn't make him feel one whit better. Niles would kill him, then Kelly, and the only good thing was that Wade wouldn't have to watch her die. He would never see the life flow out of her or see her drop lifeless to the floor.

What was her plan? Even if she had somehow managed to bring help, she shouldn't have placed herself in danger.

But she was here, and he'd do his best to help, although what that would be, with his hands and feet tied, he had no idea. All of these thoughts had raced with warp speed, and Kelly had yet to come fully inside the living area.

"Shut the door behind you," Niles ordered.

"Okay." She did as he asked, and then Niles flipped on the light.

When Kelly turned back and saw Wade's battered face, she gasped. Her face whitened, and a muscle ticked at her throat. "I thought we could come to some kind of agreement."

"Don't do this," Wade pleaded, earning himself a slap across the face that opened the cut above his good eye.

"What kind of agreement do you plan to make after taking paint samples of my car?" Niles asked her, the gun still pointed at Wade's head.

"Whatever kind you'd like," Kelly responded in a frightened-little-girl voice that should have made Niles suspicious.

What was she doing? Surely she didn't think that Niles would accept her instead of Debbie?

Niles chuckled. "I can get what you're offering anywhere."

"Maybe. Maybe not. I thought what you wanted was to shut me up. Forever. Well, even if you kill both of us, that's not possible. However, if you let us live, perhaps we could make a deal."

Wade shook his head, as much out of frustration as to clear the blood from his eye. "You can't bargain with a man who won't keep his word."

Niles kicked his leg.

"Stop that." Kelly walked toward Niles, but she'd changed her angle slightly, making it impossible for the oil man to keep the gun directly on Wade and watch her at the same time.

Wade fought to keep the blood from blocking his vision, and his gaze dropped to Kelly's hand, which had slipped inside the roomy denim pocket of her dress. Did that pocket bulge more than it should have from just her hand?

Wade didn't know. Fear for her made him lunge against the chair, tipping it over, slamming him onto the floor. He almost blacked out, fought against the stars exploding in his head.

A shot ricocheted nearby, landed on the floor, shooting splinters into his neck. That shot was followed by two more.

Wade tensed, expecting pain, but none came.

He heard a body thud to the floor.

"Kelly?"

"I'm right here." Her hands tugged on the ropes

to untie his hands, and she was sobbing. "I shot the son of a bitch right between the eyes."

Suddenly he was free and gathering her into his arms. "Are you all right?"

"I had to come." Her chest heaved and tears rained down her cheeks. He cuddled her against his chest, turning her away from Niles' very dead body. "I had no choice. I couldn't let him kill you."

He rocked her as she cried. "You almost scared me to death coming here when I told you not to."

"I'm not very good at…taking orders. You'll have to let me make it up to you."

She wanted to make it up to him? She'd risked her life to save him and she wanted his forgiveness? He would never understand her. Never.

But so what? He didn't have to understand her. He only had to love her.

He loved her.

Of course he loved her. How could he not have the courage to admit that to himself after the bravery she'd exhibited today.

He loved her.

But the way he saw it, that meant it was going to be harder to let her go. Kelly McGovern had big things to do with her life and important places to go. He would not be the one responsible for holding her back, for saddling her with a brood of kids that would prevent her from attaining her goals.

He loved her.

And that meant that no matter how much pain it caused him, he had to set her free.

Chapter Fifteen

"Wade hasn't even called me in a week," Kelly complained to Cara and Lindsey over lunch at Dot's sandwich shop.

Cara held up a sour dill pickle and pointed it at Kelly. "Phones work both ways, you know."

Kelly sighed. "I always get his machine."

"Why don't you go over to the Hit 'Em Again Saloon?" Lindsey suggested. "The bar might be his turf, but he won't want to run out the door to avoid you in front of his employees."

"I've considered that plan." Kelly bit into her BLT on toasted rye, chewed and swallowed. "The Hit 'Em Again is not the place to have a private conversation."

"You know what your problem is?" Cara said.

Kelly dabbed a smudge of mayonnaise from her lip. "That I've fallen in love with a man so stubborn he won't admit that he's wrong?"

Cara shook her head.

Kelly tried again. "That I'm not willing to let go of the best thing that's ever happened to me?"

Cara rolled her eyes at the ceiling, and Lindsey

laughed, then tried to smother her reaction with a cough. She ended up almost choking, and Kelly had to pound her on the back. "You okay?"

"I'm fine."

Cara stole the pickle off of Kelly's plate. "Your problem is that you are just as stubborn as he is."

Kelly frowned at the pickle. "Hey, I was going to eat that."

Cara grinned and crunched happily. "Too late."

"And I'm not stubborn."

Lindsey chuckled again. "Yes, you are. You won't give up and he won't give in. You're a perfect match."

"Wade doesn't see it that way." Kelly shoved the second half of her sandwich at Cara. "Here, you might as well have this, too. I've lost my appetite."

"Thanks." Cara tugged Kelly's plate closer. "Your problem is that you want Wade to talk to you."

"Well, duh."

"You're thinking like a woman," Cara added between bites of the BLT.

"I *am* a woman."

"What's your point?" Lindsey asked with a frown.

"Tell us, what's your ultimate goal?" Cara prodded.

Kelly had had more than enough time to think about her answer in the past few days. "A life with Wade. Marriage."

"Now you're talking," Cara said.

"Excuse me? Have you forgotten the man won't even speak to me?"

"Talk isn't what's important here."

"It's not?" Bewildered, Kelly looked at her friend, wondering if she'd put in too many hours of overtime lately, because Cara certainly wasn't making sense. Cara had interviewed Johnny Dixon in his hospital bed and written a page-two story in the *Mustang Gazette* about how Niles Deagen had run him off the road because he'd overheard an incriminating conversation between Niles and the former mayor. Page one had been about the mayor's and Niles's deaths.

"You need to take action," Cara insisted.

"And what, pray tell, would you have me do?"

"I don't know." Cara polished off the last of Kelly's sandwich and washed it down with a glass of sweet tea. "Trying to talk to the man isn't getting you anywhere, so you need to change tactics. Act. Do something."

"Sneak into his bed and seduce him?" Lindsey suggested.

"She already did that. She needs to do something more drastic," Cara prodded.

Kelly had the feeling that Cara was leading her down a twisting, narrow road with a steep cliff that she could easily fall off. Cara had a plan. She clearly just wanted Kelly to think that it was her own idea.

"Think of a Shotgun Sally legend," Cara hinted.

"Which one? There are so many of them, we have no idea which ones are fiction."

"Who cares about the truth? Pick one that will work for you."

"Well, you know that I'm partial to one particular legend about my illustrious ancestor, but do you want me to point a rifle at Wade and force him to say his wedding vows?''

Cara signaled her with a thumbs-up. ''Now, there's a bold idea worthy of page one.''

Cara was still smarting that she hadn't been assigned to write about the mayor's death. But that didn't mean she had to help create the news before she reported it. And urging Kelly to kidnap Wade at gunpoint and force him in front of a justice of the peace might have worked two centuries ago, but not in this day and age.

''Uh-hem.'' Lindsey went into attorney mode. ''May I remind you ladies that holding a gun on a man except in self-defense is not legal?''

''At least I have one sane friend,'' Kelly muttered, because Cara's suggestion had kicked her pulse up a notch. Her thoughts raced at the appealing and oh-so-outrageous idea. ''Suppose I don't point the gun at him? Just carry it.''

''That would be an implied threat,'' Lindsey stated, ''and the law starts getting sticky there.''

''The gun needn't be loaded, either,'' Cara pointed out with a twinkle in her eyes.

Kelly glanced from Cara to Lindsey and shook her head. ''I don't know. This is insane.''

''Do you think Wade is going to let you threaten him into marriage if it's really against his will?'' Lindsey asked pointedly.

No, he would not.

And that's when Kelly had her answer. No more mooning around and waiting for Wade to call. No more sleepless nights wishing she was back in his bed. She was going to act and act boldly. After all, it was in her genes.

She kissed each of her friends on the cheek. "Thanks. You are the best. Wish me luck." She stood from the table, suddenly sure of herself.

"Where are you going?" Cara grumbled. "You didn't even taste your dessert."

"You go ahead." Kelly hurried out the door. "I'm going shopping."

"Of course she is." Cara placed a forkful of cheesecake into her mouth and grinned at Lindsey. "Have you ever noticed that after Kelly goes shopping, there's always fireworks afterward in Mustang Valley?"

"WADE LANSING, you open this door right now," Kelly demanded in a voice that he couldn't fail to recognize.

"Okay. Okay. Don't break down the damn door." Grumpy after a late night at the Hit 'Em Again, grumpier still from missing Kelly and several sleepless nights, Wade padded to his front door barefoot, knowing that another encounter with her would set back his recovery for days.

What was she doing here? He didn't want a reminder of how good she looked first thing in the morning. Or how sweet she smelled after her shower. Or what that smile of hers did to heat him to a fever pitch.

What was she doing here so early in the morning? It figured that she'd wake him up ten minutes after he'd finally fallen asleep. But then nothing about Kelly was convenient. Not the fact that she was Andrew's sister. Most definitely not the fact that even when he closed his eyes he saw her in his dreams. Certainly not the fact that she probably wanted to be around him because it made her feel closer to the brother she had lost. And absolutely not the fact that he wanted her more than he'd ever wanted any woman in his life.

For the first time he admitted to himself the real reason for pushing her away. He was scared. Scared that she would abandon him or die on him, just like every other person who he'd ever counted on. That might not be fair or rational but it was the way he felt.

However, just because he loved her didn't necessarily mean he wanted the torture of seeing her in the flesh. His dreams and memories were vivid enough, thank you very much. Nevertheless, he unlocked his door and kicked it open.

And got the shock of his life.

Kelly stood there in a creamy white lace wedding dress. Her lush breasts filled the bodice, and the early-morning sunlight accentuated a glistening blush on her cheeks and a tantalizing blush in the hollows. Not even the shotgun cocked at her side could dispel the image of her loveliness that made his mouth go dry.

"You…are wearing…a wedding gown."

"How observant of you." Kelly's rich laughter woke him right up and convinced him that he wasn't dreaming. Not even his dreams were this imaginative. Or vivid.

She brushed by him, close enough for him to take in the fascinating scent of spiced lemons with a hint of strawberry. The view from the back was as enticing as her front. The dress swooped low in back, emphasizing her smooth skin, and his breath hitched in his chest.

He didn't want to react to her, but who was he kidding? He had no choice, and his tone came out much huskier than he would have liked. "What do you want?"

"You." She planted the gun handle on the floor and steadied herself with the barrel, cocking one hip at a sexy angle that reminded him of Charlie's Angels. "So we can do this the easy way or the hard way."

"You can't just barge into my house—"

"You let me in," she said so reasonably that he just knew she was up to one of her tricks.

"—and brandish a weapon."

"I'm not brandishing, I'm leaning."

"And the difference is…?"

"Doesn't matter—except in a court of law."

He raised a skeptical eyebrow. "Isn't it a little late to be worried about the law?"

"Huh?" For the first time she seemed confused.

And he had to admit just to himself that sparring with her was much more fun than sleeping and dreaming about her. He allowed a glimmer of appreciation to show on his face. "The way you're dressed you could be arrested for all kinds of things."

"Oh, really?"

"Like getting married without a license."

"I'd like to see you tell that to a judge."

"Okay."

He frowned at her. She'd just given in way too easily. "What do you mean, okay?"

"Okay, as in *yes*. Let's go talk to the judge."

"What are you talking about?"

"You're impossible. I want to get married."

Uh-oh. He'd walked right into that one. He could tell she'd set him up by the pleased gleam of satisfaction in her eyes.

"Where's the groom?" he teased, his pulse racing, because he suddenly knew that he could do this. When Kelly set her mind to something, she didn't change it. When she said forever, she meant it. She wouldn't change her mind or leave him and his mind suddenly cleared like a defroster evaporating fog from a window. He could have her. All he had to do was take the biggest leap of faith in his life.

"I'm looking at the groom."

She wanted to marry him—not have a summer fling. She couldn't have shocked him more if she'd claimed she wanted to enter a convent.

She wanted to marry him. That meant he could have her for a lifetime, not just a few lousy weeks of the summer. That meant she never planned to leave him. Marriage was permanent.

She wanted to marry him, and his heart hummed with joy.

He folded his arms across his chest, thinking hard. "Well, it takes the consent of both parties to get married."

"That's why I brought the gun."

He didn't want to ask if it was loaded. He didn't want to know.

His legs seemed to have gone to jelly and he slid onto the sofa. "We can't get married."

"Sure we can. I got the license yesterday." She sauntered over to him, her hips swaying due to those too-sexy heels. She reached into her bra, removed a piece of folded paper and offered it to him. "After patching you up, Doc already had a sample of your blood."

He marveled at her ingenuity, stunned, shocked and almost stupefied. "And?"

"And nothing." She nudged him with the rifle. "Let's go elope."

Damn, he loved her. When she got all sexy and vulnerable and mad at the same time, she was the most adorable woman. Of course, he had no intention of telling her that—not with her caressing that gun barrel as if it were her best friend. He could think of much better things to do than die of a gunshot wound.

"I can't elope right now," he teased her, but pretended to be deadly serious.

"Why not?"

"My slacks are too tight."

She glanced down at him and chuckled. "I suppose we could take care of that big problem first."

He grabbed her hand and yanked her down beside him. "Good. But we have a few other things to work out." He planted a kiss by her ear. "If we get married, you aren't giving up law school for me."

"If I give up law school, it won't be for you. But I've been considering a career in real estate. I just haven't decided yet."

"And no babies until you finish school."

"You want kids?" she smoothed her hands over his chest and let them dip below his waist.

"Yeah, but not yet." He wrapped an arm around her shoulder, tugged her close and then tipped up her chin to claim her lips. "First, I'm going to let you spoil me in the manner to which I've become accustomed."

"Yes, sir," she teased. "I can tell exactly who is going to be in charge of this marriage."

"You?"

She kissed him and then pulled back. "Oh, did I happen to mention that my wedding veil and your suit are in the car and that the judge is expecting us at noon. The plane leaves for our honeymoon in Hawaii at three. So quit wasting time. Unless you have a better idea?"

He kissed her lips. "Well, there seems to be one important thing you forgot."

"Hmm?"

"You didn't give me time to say I love you."

"That's perfectly okay." She grinned at him. "I already knew that."

* * * * *

*Turn the page for a sneak preview
of the next gripping*
SHOTGUN SALLYS *title,*
LEGALLY BINDING
*by rising star Ann Voss Peterson
on sale in June 2004 in
Harlequin Intrigue…*

Chapter One

Bart Rawlins forced one eye open. Late-morning sun slanted through his bedroom window, blinding him. Pain, sharper than his old Buck knife, drilled into his skull. He gripped the edge of the mattress and willed the room to stop spinning.

He hadn't had that much to drink at Wade Lansing's Hit 'Em Again Saloon last night, had he? Not enough to warrant a hangover like this.

He remembered hitching a ride to the bar with Gary Tuttle, his foreman at the Four Aces Ranch. Remembered wolfing down some of Wade's famous chili and throwing back a few beers. Not enough to make his head feel like it was about to explode. Not enough to make his mouth taste like an animal had crawled in and died.

Damn but he was too old for this. At thirty-five he always thought he would be settled down with a woman he loved, raising sons and daughters to take over the Four Aces Ranch. Instead he was lying in bed with his boots on and a hangover powerful enough to split his skull.

He raised a hand to his forehead. His fingers felt

sticky on his skin. Sticky and moist and smelled like—

His eyes flew open and he jerked up off the mattress. Head throbbing, he stared at his splayed fingers. Something brown coated his hands and settled into the creases of work-worn skin. The same rusty brown flecked his Wranglers.

Blood.

What the hell? Had he gotten drunk and picked a fight? Was a well-aimed punch responsible for his throbbing head?

He pushed himself off the bed and stumbled to the bathroom. Peering into the mirror, he checked his face. Although his nose was slightly crooked from a fall off a horse when he was ten, it looked fine. So did the rest of his face. And a quick check of other body parts turned up nothing, either. The blood must have come from the other guy.

The doorbell's chime echoed through the house.

Who the hell could that be? He tried to scan his memory for an appointment this morning, but his sluggish mind balked.

The doorbell rang again. Whoever it was, he wasn't going away.

Bart turned on the water and plunged his hands into the warm stream. He splashed his face, grabbed a towel and headed down the stairs. He'd get rid of whoever it was so he could nurse his hangover in peace. And try to remember what in the hell had happened last night.

He reached the door and yanked it open.

As wide as he was tall, Deputy Hurley Zeller looked up at Bart through narrowed little eyes. The sheriff's right-hand man had a way of staring that made a man feel he'd done something illegal even if he hadn't. And ever since Bart beat him out for quarterback in high school, he'd always saved his best accusing stare for Bart.

Bart shifted his boots on the wood floor. "What's up, Hurley?"

"I had bad news."

Bart rooted his boots to the spot. If he'd learned one thing about bad news in his thirty-five years, it was that it was best to take it like a shot of rot-gut whiskey. Straight up and all at once. "What is it?"

"Your uncle Jebediah. He's dead."

Bart blew a stream of air through tight lips. Uncle Jeb's death meant there would be no reconciliation. No forgiveness to mend the feud in the Rawlins clan that had started the day Bart's granddad died and left Hiriam a larger chunk of the seventy-thousand-acre ranch. Now it was too late for a happy ending to that story. "Well, that is bad news, Hurley. Real bad. How did he die?"

Hurley focused on the leather pouch on Bart's belt, the pouch where he kept his Buck knife. "Maybe I should ask you that question."

Bart draped the towel over one shoulder and moved his hand to the pouch. It was empty. The folding hunting knife he'd hung on his belt since his father gave it to him for his fourteenth birthday was gone. Shock jolted Bart to the soles of his Tony Lamas. "You don't think I killed—" The question lodged in his throat. He followed Hurley's pointed stare to the towel on his shoulder.

The white terrycloth was pink with blood.

A smile spread over Hurley's thin lips. "I think you're coming with me, Bart. And you've got the right to remain silent."

LINDSEY WELLINGTON adjusted her navy-blue suit, tucked her Italian leather briefcase under one arm and marched toward the Mustang County Jail and her first solo case. She hadn't been this nervous since she'd taken the Texas bar exam. At least her years at Harvard Law School had given her plenty of experience taking tests, but this was a different story. This was real life.

This was murder.

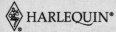
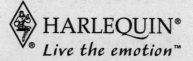

HARLEQUIN®
INTRIGUE®

Steamy romance and thrilling suspense
converge in the highly anticipated
next installment of Harlequin Intrigue's
bestselling series

NEW ORLEANS
CONFIDENTIAL

**By day these agents pursue lives of city professionals;
by night they are specialized government operatives.
Men bound by love, loyalty and the law—they've vowed
to keep their missions and identities confidential....**

A crime wave has paralyzed the Big Easy, and there is only one
network of top secret operatives tough enough to get the job done!
This newest branch of the CONFIDENTIAL agency is called into
action when a deadly designer drug hits the streets of the Big Easy—
reputed to be distributed by none other than the nefarious Cajun
mob. When one of Confidential's own gets caught in the cross fire, it's
anyone's guess who will be left standing in the shattering showdown....

July 2004
UNDERCOVER ENCOUNTER BY REBECCA YORK

August 2004
BULLETPROOF BILLIONAIRE BY MALLORY KANE

September 2004
A FATHER'S DUTY BY JOANNA WAYNE

Available at your favorite retail outlet.

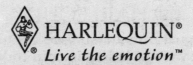

HARLEQUIN®
Live the emotion™

www.eHarlequin.com

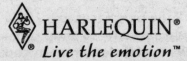

USA TODAY bestselling author

KAREN HARPER

brings you four classic romantic-suspense
novels guaranteed to keep you
on the edge of your seat....

On sale May 2004.

"The cast of creepy characters and a smalltown
setting oozing Brady Bunch wholesomeness makes
for a haunting read."
—*Publishers Weekly* on *The Stone Forest*

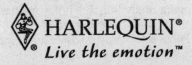

Later in the ev...
settled into th...
change in Matt...

"My feet are so numb I can barely feel them," he complained. He told me that when he tried to stand, he fell over into the snow. "Oh, God!" he wailed. "Help us out of this."

In the darkness, I could feel the movement of his shoulders as they began to shake. Sobbing sounds came from deep within his throat.

"We're never going to get out of here," he moaned. His voice carried an angry, accusatory tone. "Dad, we're going to die here!"

I grabbed for him and tried to calm the spasm. "Listen, we're doing the best we can. We've got to hang on. They're looking for us."

"Okay, okay," he said quietly.

As we lay there, side by side in an isolated cave somewhere on a deserted mountain, I realized that I was perhaps more upset than Matthew. His anger was justified. It was all my fault that we were in this predicament.

MIRACLE
ON THE
MOUNTAIN

A TRUE TALE OF
FAITH AND SURVIVAL

MIKE and MARY COUILLARD
with WILLIAM and MARILYN HOFFER

AVON BOOKS NEW YORK

AVON BOOKS, INC.
1350 Avenue of the Americas
New York, New York 10019

Front cover photo courtesy of Milliyet News, Turkey
Background photo by Tom Stack & Associates
Visit our website at **http://www.AvonBooks.com**
Library of Congress Catalog Card Number: 97-29978
ISBN: 0-380-78979-5

The Avon Books hardcover edition contains the following Library of
Congress Cataloging in Publication Data:

Couillard, Mike.
Miracle on the mountain : a true tale of faith and survival / Mike and Mary
Couillard; with William and Marilyn Hoffer.—1st ed.
    p.   cm.
1. Skis and skiing—Turkey. 2. Skiing accidents—Turkey. 3. Wilderness
survival—Turkey. I. Couillard, Mary. II. Hoffer, William. III. Hoffer,
Marilyn Mona. IV. Title.
GV854.8.T87C68   1998   97-29978
956.3'039'0922—dc21   CIP

First Avon Books Paperback Printing: February 1999
First Avon Books Hardcover Printing: April 1998

AVON TRADEMARK REG. U.S. PAT. OFF. AND IN OTHER COUNTRIES, MARCA
REGISTRADA, HECHO EN U.S.A.

Printed in the U.S.A.

WCD 10 9 8 7 6 5 4 3 2 1

✳

To our friends and associates in the Ankara Community; the friends and coworkers at the Office of Defense Cooperation and the U.S. Embassy; to Major Keith "Sully" Sullivan, who coordinated the overall search effort, and Captain "Fitz" Fitzgerald, who led the ground search; to the many from the ranks of the Turkish and American forces who gave their all in trying to find us; to the countless people from around the globe who encircled our family in prayer; and to Işmail Keklikci and his band of Turkish lumberjacks whom God used to pluck us out of the snow. Most of all, we dedicate this to Yahweh, "the God Who Saves." This is truly His story, one of the many about His countless acts of love and mercy.

✳ Acknowledgments

There are several folks we'd like to thank for helping us with this work . . . people like Pam Jaccard, Cathryn Hoard, Angela Shaw, and Mary Beth Tremblay—who not only were Mary's anchor during those crazy nine and a half days, but later helped recall all of the little details of "what happened when and who said what" to make this story as honest and true to life as possible. There are many others, starting with Neil Talbot and his team in the USAF Academy Public Affairs Office, who assisted in the photo search and in getting the manuscript cleared through DoD channels. We are indebted to Margarete Schmidt and Haldun Armagan at the U.S. Information Agency Office in Ankara for doing a bunch of legwork to put their hands on some of the pictures used in this book and securing permission to use them. We'd also like to thank Captain "Max" Torrens and her assistants in the Incirlik Public Affairs Office for all their help. Thanks to Milliyet News Agency, Istanbul, for their kind permission to use their photos. Most of all, we want to thank Bill and Marilyn Hoffer for their outstanding work "piecing together" our sometimes distant recollections, rough ideas, and best guesses. We think they've created another "work of art" and, best of all, told an honest story that comes straight from our hearts.

✳ Prologue

Lieutenant Colonel Michael Couillard is a C-130 pilot for the
U.S. Air Force. In 1993 he was assigned to the Office of Defense Cooperation (ODC), based in Ankara, Turkey, where he
became chief of operations. ODC's primary mission was to
assist in modernizing the Turkish military. A secondary mission was coordinating U.S. military operations in country with
the Turkish General Staff. Number one among these was Operation Provide Comfort, a program to give air cover to the
Kurds in northern Iraq and to police the "No-Fly Zone"
against the intrusion of Iraqi aircraft. Mike's job was extremely taxing.

Mary Couillard has a master's degree in counseling, but was
not practicing at the time of the Turkish assignment; nevertheless,
her life as a military wife was extremely busy. Utilizing textbooks
rented from a Roman Catholic home schooling company, she
taught the couple's three children—Mark, thirteen; Matthew, ten;
and Marissa, eight—in their apartment in Ankara. She also helped
to organize and manage the Ankara Youth Sports League, which
brought together children from various military and diplomatic
families, as well as youngsters from other countries who displayed
an interest in sports; basketball was her specialty. She was also a
leader of Marissa's Brownie troop.

All of the Couillard's were very involved in church activities.
Together, Mike and Mary had started a small prayer group—
a handful of people met in the church basement on Wednesday
evenings to sing songs of praise and to pray together. With

the help of an Air Force co-worker, Major Wanda Villers, the Couillards initiated a religious/folk music choir. Mike and Wanda played guitar, and various other instrumentalists augmented the choir. The fast-growing group soon included about a dozen vocalists who practiced every Saturday morning at the Couillards' apartment. Mary joined Mike and Wanda in the Ambassador's Choir, so named because it was led by the Slovakian ambassador to Turkey. Although the choir was somewhat secular in organization, it took on a semireligious orientation; practices were held in the church basement, the music tended to be classical and traditionally religious, and performances were almost always held in the church—such as the annual Easter and Christmas recitals. All of the children worked as altar servers during Sunday Mass. Most recently the family had helped to orchestrate a Christmas special with music and a small play. Their involvement in these and other activities had made them known to practically the entire Christian community in Ankara.

When Mike learned of a Sunday outing to a ski resort near Bolu, Turkey, sponsored by the Australian Embassy, he thought it would be a great opportunity for the entire family to spend the day together. Skiing was an activity they had all shared many times. But Mary had volunteered to coach a basketball clinic that day, so she decided to remain behind in Ankara with Marissa. It would be "Boys' Day Out." Mike would treat Mark and Matthew to a day of fun on the slopes. Mary even decided to skip Mass, a rare lapse that always gnawed at her conscience.

The evening before the outing, Matthew took his mother aside and confided, "I don't know if I really want to go on this skiing trip."

"Why don't you want to go?"

He spoke softly. "It's cold and I haven't skied at all this year. What if I get hurt?"

"Oh, Matthew," Mary chided, "this is just going to be a fun day. Mark will ski with his friends. You and Dad will have a good time together."

DAY 1

•

Sunday, January 15, 1995

Mike

Donnell and Chubs started it. We all piled out of the bus as the driver struggled to install tire chains so that we could make it up the mountain. There was a fairly steep slope on this side of the road, and the kids scrambled up and then slid down, laughing and joking. The snow cover had been here awhile, so it contained chunks of ice and packed easily into snowballs. Donnell and Chubs were two of the older teenagers with us, and they could not resist the temptation. Soon snowballs were flying everywhere.

Mark got in some good licks with his friend Bryn. I was watching this and laughing along with them when Matthew took aim and caught me squarely in the shoulder. Roaring in mock anger, I picked up a chunk of ice and lumbered off after Matthew. I chased him all around the bus, caught him, and tackled him into a snowbank. But an attack from the rear diverted my attention. As I turned to face an onslaught from Mark and Bryn, Matthew seized the opportunity to cram a handful of cold snow inside the collar of my turtleneck.

"Hey, that's not fair!" I screamed.

Soon we were all entangled lying in the heavy snow, laughing.

It was an enjoyable diversion, but I was ready to ski, and the morning had already been filled with obstacles.

First of all, the bus fare was about double what I had expected and I realized immediately that I might not have enough cash to get us through the day. I would have to use my Visa card to rent Matt's skis or we would not be able to buy lunch.

The bus had left Ankara early, about 6 A.M., and, since we had skied Kartalkaya Mountain the previous winter, I knew that the area was about a three-hour drive to the north, so I expected to be on the slopes shortly after 9 A.M. But the driver missed the turnoff for the road that would take us up the mountain and meandered for quite some distance before he realized his mistake. He ended up backtracking for about five miles as I glanced at my watch and muttered under my breath.

I glanced over at Bryn's mother, Major Wanda Villers, one of my co-workers in the Air Force Directorate, a component of ODC. I could tell by the expression on her face that she, too, was not very impressed with how things were going. We shared the same personality trait: a certain critical spirit and a low tolerance for what we refer to as "stupid stuff."

Then, as we finally began to head up in the direction of the ski resort, we encountered increasing amounts of snow and ice on the road. The driver gradually slowed his pace and finally slid to a stop, blocking one-half of the two-lane road. As he labored to install tire chains, we all tumbled out of the bus to stretch our legs and the impromptu snowball fight began.

We were chilled and giddy as we climbed back into the bus and waited for the driver to resume our journey. Mark chattered with Bryn. Matt and I visited with Wanda, grumbling about the way the morning had gone. My time working together with the church folk choir had caused our relationship to deepen much beyond the casual acquaintance we shared at work. We could both be rather intense at times and we seemed to have learned to help balance one another. Our conversation soon turned to small talk: upcoming vacation and sightseeing plans, career goals, what we wanted to do on our next assignments, kids. In a freewheeling style we also exchanged stories of our past and where the Air Force had taken us.

The conversation ended abruptly in a cloud of smoke and diesel fumes as the bus engine roared back to life. Soon we were on our way, resuming the slow climb up the mountain.

It was 10:30 by the time we arrived at the Doruk Kaya Hotel on Kartalkaya Mountain, and I was in a hurry. I had my own equipment and Mark had borrowed his mom's, but I had to rent skis and poles for Matt. As Mark and Bryn headed for the slopes, I hustled Matt off the bus, through the hotel lobby, toward the equipment room near the back. Here we found a mob of people huddled about the rental counter. There was no line and no organization. The loudest and most aggressive skier was served first. I tried to be patient, but with each passing minute I grew more vocal. "If we don't get out there soon, we're not going to have much time to ski," I grumbled.

When I finally gained the attention of a clerk, he provided skis and poles for Matt. I left my driver's license as security and I offered my Visa card in payment. He slid it in and out of the machine and we waited for several minutes until he shook his head and said in English, "No, it's not working." Either the machine was not reading my card correctly or the phone lines were malfunctioning. I suspected the latter. This had happened to us on numerous occasions in Turkey, and I was sure that we were well under the limit on the charge card. But I had no choice other than to hand over most of the cash that I had left in my pocket.

"I don't know what we're going to do about lunch," I complained. "And I'm already hungry."

"Me, too," Matt said.

I responded, "I hope Mark brought some of his money with him."

Wanda overheard our conversation and came to the rescue. I was a little embarrassed to borrow money from her, but she was very gracious. "I have plenty of cash with me," she reassured me, handing some over.

"Thanks."

Looking out the back door of the hotel, just outside the equipment room, I could see a good portion of the seventy-three-hundred-foot-high Kartalkaya Mountain, with its several lifts and runs. I knew that just out of sight off to my left, on the other side of a high ridge, were the slopes near the Kartalkaya Hotel, an area our family had skied the previous winter. As Matthew came out the back door, I reminded him of this and we recalled what fun that had been. It had been a sunny day with excellent snow conditions.

We had not, however, skied the slopes that were before us now, so I took a few minutes to orient myself. This other hotel was situated on a fairly steep hill and offered us a choice between two sets of ski runs. The run visible on our left began near the top of the mountain, ran straight ahead for a very short distance, and then curved sharply away as it descended a steep slope and disappeared from view. It apparently terminated somewhere in a small valley that was hidden by the crest of a rolling hill.

Overhead, a chairlift carried numerous skiers upward. I could not see the lift shack from here, but I knew it was situated in the hidden valley. From what I could see of this run, there were some small snow mounds, known as "moguls," and a few steep areas, but they did not appear to exceed the capabilities of an intermediate skier. Although the run began at a sharp downward angle, if we skied far enough off to one side we would spill into a gentler slope. Back in the States, we would call this trail a "blue" run, meaning that it was of medium difficulty, and I was confident that Matt and I could manage it.

To our right I noticed a second path that continued straight ahead, easing gradually downhill, and curved slightly to our right, to the base of another, gentler hill. This slope had several nice, long runs that were the equivalent of our "green" runs in the States, less difficult than the blue run. Instead of a chairlift, this slope utilized two T-bar lifts. Just as the name implies, it involves a T-shaped device, which hangs inverted, connected to a tow cable by a shock absorber built into the top. You do not ride or straddle a T-bar, but remain standing in front of it with the T behind the thighs. As you keep your skis parallel ahead of you, it pulls you up the mountain. Two people can ride together, one on each side of the inverted T.

All three of our children had learned to ski by taking a week's worth of lessons in Breckenridge, Colorado, and there were not many mountains too difficult for their skills. When confronted with more difficult runs, we had learned to proceed slowly, with more frequent and calculated turns.

I was sure that we would ski both of these runs throughout the day, but I thought it might be better to take advantage of the comfort of the chairlift to start with. The top of the slope was steep, but once we began our descent, we could cut over and come down on the gentler side.

I was not surprised to hear Matthew agree. "Let's do the chairlift first, Dad," he said. "I know I can ski down that hill." Matt, like the rest of us, was a little spoiled by stateside skiing, where a chairlift is the norm.

Soon we were out in the cold, fresh, clean air and the bright sunshine, having a wonderful time. We discovered that the lift was built in two segments. The chairlift took us about halfway up. At that point we would have to transfer to a T-bar if we chose to go to the summit. Rather than do so, we simply started down from the midpoint of the run. Matthew wore a ski mask that covered everything but his eyes and mouth, but he found it kind of scratchy, so he removed it.

After we explored that slope we grew more adventuresome, moving over to the run serviced only by the T-bar. To our surprise, riding the T-bar proved more challenging than skiing down any of the slopes. Because of the difference in our heights, we had to situate Matt so that the T was behind his bottom and in back of my knees. A couple of times, as we skimmed upward, Matt accidentally snagged a ski and we found ourselves on the ground, eating snow.

Most of the time we were blessed with sunshine, but on occasion a few clouds rolled in and flurries of icy particles fogged our goggles and stung our faces. This was nothing out of the ordinary and I had come to accept it as one of the stimulating parts of skiing.

The morning was great fun—despite our late start—and both of us soon developed a healthy appetite.

"I want some *tost*," Matthew said.

"Mmm-hmm," I agreed.

What the Turks call *tost* is a sandwich grilled on a wafflelike iron, so that it leaves ribbed markings on the bread. *Tost* often comes stuffed with cheese, salami, sausage, and olives, or any combination of ingredients that one chooses.

We removed our skis and left them outside the lower level of the lodge. Then we walked inside and headed for the restaurant. I was disappointed to see that it was very crowded. If we ate here, we would squander more of our scarce skiing time. And when I checked the prices on the menu I realized that even with Wanda's help, we could not afford a meal here anyway, so we went looking for an alternative.

As we walked through the lodge we encountered Mark, eating Chee•tos and playing cards with his friends. Mark said he wanted to ski with us after lunch.

"Where are you going to be?" I asked.

"I'm not sure," Mark said. "Let's just look for each other at the chairlift."

"Okay." Mark seemed a little confused about something, but I was in too much of a hurry to investigate.

Matthew and I found a snack bar where we could eat quickly. Unfortunately it did not offer *tost*, so we had to settle for a sandwich that was rather like a standard sub, but minus the meat. Matthew pulled the cucumber slices off his and just ate the cheese, tomatoes, and lettuce. We drank cups of *çay* (pronounced "chï"), which Matthew laced with sugar. Hot *çay*, or tea, is the Turkish national drink.

We wondered if this would hold us until dinnertime. "How did you like our lunch, Matt?" I asked. "Did you get enough to eat?"

"Yeah, I guess so," he answered. But after a moment he asked, "Do you think we can get something else to eat before we go home?"

"Sure we can," I said. "I saved some money so we can get a snack to take on the bus or eat before we get on board. We can get some dessert or see if we can find some *tost*."

We looked around for Mark, but he was nowhere to be found. Undoubtedly he was somewhere on the slopes with Bryn.

"You've been skiing great today, Matthew," I said. "Are you feeling okay on those skis?"

Matt beamed at the compliment. "Thanks," he said. "I guess they're all right. Probably not as good as what I had last year. The boots are a little tight and the skis don't seem to go as fast."

"Well, it seems like you got the hang of riding the T-bar again."

"Yeah, I guess so, but I did fall off a couple of times at first. Sorry for knocking you down that one time."

"It's okay. I had to get used to it again, too."

I glanced up toward the summit of the mountain. A few wisps of white cloud had moved across the previously sunny sky, but the top slope did not appear to be particularly challenging or dangerous. Matthew said, "Let's go all the way to the top."

"We've been all over the lower part of the mountain," I agreed. "We've got time for maybe three or four more runs."

We moved off to our left and caught the chairlift that would take us halfway up the intermediate slope. That was as high as we had ventured during the morning, but now we planned to catch the second lift—the T-bar—to the summit. "Maybe we'll see Mark up there," I said, "and he can come up to the top with us."

Matthew nodded.

On the lift, the wind was whipping up a bit. "It's getting colder," Matt remarked.

"Yeah," I agreed.

The view was breathtaking. "Look at those clouds at the top of the mountain," I said. "Isn't that incredible? It just reminds me how awesome God is when I look at how beautiful this earth is. It's really hard to look at the powerful forces of nature and not see His hand behind it all. Kind of makes you wonder how people can look around them and still conclude that there is no God."

Matthew simply nodded. Perhaps I was getting too preachy. He changed the subject, asking, "Do you think it's going to snow today?"

"Well, I don't know. I've seen days like this where the clouds tumble around the top of the mountain for hours without coming down. Then sometimes the clouds roll in so fast it takes everybody by surprise. Remember that time we were skiing at Loveland and it started to snow?"

"Yeah, man, that was fast! One minute it was sunny with bright blue skies and the next there was snow all around us, and wind and—boy, did my goggles get fogged! I couldn't believe I didn't hit something. I fell a few times, just because I couldn't see too good."

There was still no sign of Mark or Bryn when we reached the top of the intermediate slope. It was already midafternoon and the bus back to Ankara was scheduled to leave at 4:30. "They're having fun," I said. "Let's just go on ahead and maybe we'll catch up with them on a later run."

Matthew's brown eyes glanced upward, following the path of the T-bar lift that would take us to the summit. The clouds had thickened, from wisps to powder puffs, but they did not seem threatening. From here the trail appeared to be well marked, and a huge outcropping of boulders provided an easy landmark. Matthew is a good natural athlete and an adequate skier. We had handled much tougher slopes than this. He finally turned toward the short trail that led to the T-bar lift and said, "Okay, Dad."

Only one other person was ahead of us on this lift.

As we rode higher, the weather began to deteriorate. Snow pelted our faces, heavier than the morning's flurries, reducing visibility considerably.

It was about 2:30 by the time we reached the top, and I knew that, despite the snowfall, we could get in some enjoyable runs during the next two hours.

On the left side as we faced down the mountain was a trail labeled *Kolay pist,* or "Easy run." The trail on the right side was designated *Zor pist,* "Difficult run." However, looking down from here, I could not discern an obvious split in the path differentiating them. At least from this vantage point the boundaries of the trail were not very clearly delineated. I applied my limited grasp of the language, asking the lift attendant, "Is this the path to the difficult run?"

The man pointed to the right side of the mountain and responded, *"Bu terafi, kapah"* ["This side is closed"].

Obviously he had misunderstood my question, but I shrugged off the moment of confusion and stared down the mountain. I was a bit apprehensive about the thick stands of pine trees that lay ahead. I noted what I assumed to be the same rocky outcropping that I had seen from below, but the decreasing visibility made relying on it as a reference point risky. Well, I thought, we're up here now, and our alternatives are to ski the direct path of the T-bar lift down—a sort of surrender to the mountain—or find the path that leads to the moderate run. I decided that we could rely on the overhead line of the ski lift as a guide while still pursuing the second alternative. As long as we continued to keep the lift in sight, we would find our way down without any trouble.

The skier in front of us began his run, and I noticed that he was employing the same strategy.

We pushed off. Immediately the sting of rapidly falling snow peppered our faces and worked inside our goggles. We could see only about twenty feet ahead of us. Gosh, I thought, I've got to be careful not to go too far to the right, but I don't want to go too far to the left, either, because that would put us on the easier trail. I reminded myself: Make sure we keep the ski lift in view on our left.

We took the slope in stages, stopping to rest and check on one another whenever there was a bend in the trail. During one break, Matt sounded a bit concerned. "Dad, have we ever skied near so many trees?" he asked.

"Yeah," I said. "If you think back, there were a lot of places where you skied around trees and even through the trees to stay on the trail. Remember last year when we skied at Ulu Dağ and there was that one place where the trail went through a stand of trees so thick you couldn't see the trail from the outside? Then as you kept going, you popped out of the trees right into the lift line for the highest run."

Matthew nodded, but he complained, "The snow's getting too deep. I keep falling."

"We really haven't done much skiing in powder, but there's a special way to do it," I said. "Don't worry. We'll get through this soon and back to the kind of snow you're used to. When you get in the deeper stuff, lean back on your heels. That will raise the tips of your skis a little and you'll be able to keep on going without falling."

Moment by moment, the visibility decreased. It was becoming increasingly difficult to follow the outlines of the trail, and we encountered more and more wooded areas. We had to make frequent choices to go around trees, and some of those choices took us to the right and away from the safer trails. At times we lost sight of the lift.

Suddenly one of my skis scratched across a rock and I fell headlong into the snow. When Matthew caught up with me I warned, "Watch out! There's rocks."

Matthew looked around and noted that there were no other ski tracks. "I don't think anybody else has skied here before," he said. "Maybe we should turn back." His words turned into puffs of icy vapor.

My experience had been that no matter how many twists and turns a ski trail contains, it inevitably leads to the lodge area at the bottom, so, for the time being, I ignored Matt's suggestion and urged him to push ahead. Soon the trail turned back to the left, the ski lift reappeared, and we regained our bearings.

As the snowfall increased in intensity, we once again diverged to the right and lost sight of the lift. We were surrounded by a dense stand of pine trees, and the trail appeared to branch in various directions.

We stopped to assess the situation. About half a mile or more below us was a clearing, like a large, white, snow-filled bowl. A few crude huts were visible. This was not the way back to the ski lodge. If we kept going in this direction, we would wind up amid these sheds and nowhere near the hotel.

I cross-checked my sense of direction with Matt's; there had been times when his had proven more reliable than my own.

"Matt. Think hard. Where did you last see the ski lift? What direction?"

"That way," he said, pointing to the left and slightly behind us.

I agreed.

Matt turned to look at the clearing below us and asked, "What do you think about going to those cabins? Maybe someone there can help us find the way back to the trail."

"They look like storage sheds. Besides, look all around them. There's not a set of footprints anywhere. There's nobody there."

Above us to the left was a mass of boulders. Was this the rocky outcropping I had seen from the summit? I could not be sure. We were disoriented, but I reasoned that we could regain our bearings by moving to the left, toward where we had last seen the ski lift. "All we have to do is backtrack a little and we'll be back on course," I assured Matthew. His eyes were questioning, but he said nothing. "We have to sidestep up that hill and then we'll be where we want to be." I pointed to the left and promised, "The lift's on the other side."

Sidestepping is what a skier does to travel upslope. By pointing the skis perpendicular to the downward slope of the hill, the tendency toward movement is arrested. Keeping your downhill ski and pole planted for stability, you raise your other ski and pole and move it slightly uphill. Then you transfer your weight to the uphill ski and move the other ski and pole. By repeating the process, you move upslope in small, deliberate increments.

Progress is slow, plodding, and extremely taxing even under ideal conditions—when the snow is hard-packed. But here the snow was packed in some places and powdery and extremely deep in other places. Sometimes my ski poles sank down to my wrists without hitting bottom. Sometimes Matthew's four-foot-six frame sank in up to his waist. At times the snow gave way under one ski, causing a quick shift of weight to the other ski, sending us tumbling. On occasion the quick movement caused a breakaway binding to pop, releasing the boot from the ski, and one of our skis slipped back down the hill. The binding is a safety feature to protect vulnerable ankles, but under these conditions it worked against us, making it increasingly difficult to keep both skis on and both feet firmly planted.

After considerable exertion we found ourselves on top of a trailless hill in a deepening blizzard. "We are *too* lost, Dad," Matthew whined.

It was becoming harder to dismiss his concern. I checked my watch. It was 3 P.M., so we still had one and a half hours before the bus was scheduled to leave. I asked, "Now, which direction do you think the lift is?"

He pointed up to the left, where a second hill loomed above us. I nodded in agreement and urged him on. Surely we would spot the ski lift from the top of this second hill.

But from there, we saw only a third hill.

Once more we sidestepped laboriously upward. As we scaled this third hill, I came to a decision. We could not continue to sidestep, for the effort was wearing us out. If we did not see anything familiar from this third ridge, we would simply ski down the mountain. Sooner or later we would find a road, or a fence, or some other sign of civilization. Surely one road would lead to another and, if we persisted long enough, the downward path would eventually run into the main road to the resort. Once we found this road we would have to hitchhike back to the lodge. We still had plenty of time. I was certain we could make it back before the bus left for Ankara.

It was 3:30 by the time we reached that third crest. No landmarks were visible, only blinding white snow. "Don't worry, Matt, I have a backup plan," I said. "We'll just ski downhill from here. I don't think we'll have to go very far to find a road."

Matthew was not convinced. "Dad, we're really lost and I'm getting scared. It's starting to get dark."

He was right. Glancing at my watch I was amazed at how dark it was for this time of day. I knew that the sun had long

ago started down toward the distant horizon, but it was still
well before sunset. The thickening clouds were blocking the
sunlight.

"Matthew, don't be scared, we're not that far off, and if we
go downhill and find a road, it is bound to lead us out, or to
another road that will. You saw this morning that there's a lot
of traffic on that road going up to the top and we're bound to
spot somebody going up or coming down from the hotels."

Matthew continued to resist my optimism. I could tell he
was near the point of tears.

To myself I conceded: We're probably getting closer and
closer to missing the bus. Still, I tried to be optimistic. Surely
the bus would not leave right at 4:30. If we were missing, they
would wait for us. How long? I wondered. An hour? Two? I
tried to calculate a worst-case scenario. How much time did
we *really* have? And how long would it take us to find the
road? How long would we have to wait before we managed to
hitch a ride?

We headed down through the snowy, rocky terrain. The
weather worsened and some of the drifts were five or six feet
deep.

As I negotiated a sudden sharp turn, my right ski caught on
a patch of ice. My boot slipped out of the binding and my
foot plunged deeply into the snow. My body twisted at an
awkward angle, forcing my weight against my right side. I felt
something pop on my right side and I grabbed at my hip.
Intense pain shot up and down my leg.

"What's wrong, Dad?" Matthew asked.

Through clenched teeth I explained that my hip must have
popped out of joint. "I'll be okay," I reassured. "Just give me
a minute."

Matthew was glad for the brief break. As I sat in the snow,
breathing heavily, I tried to mask the effects of the pain, lest
he grow too concerned. I knew that I had no alternative but
to endure this additional problem and push on. Slowly I re-
attached my ski. Then I winced in pain as I used my ski poles
to push myself up.

"Okay," I said after a few minutes. "Let's go."

I pushed off gingerly, testing my hip. Each twisting movement brought a renewal of the agony, but I forced myself forward. Gradually the pain receded a bit, from a sharp stab to a dull throb. After several minutes, quite suddenly, I felt the joint click back into place, and the pain subsided.

Now it was Matthew who found it increasingly difficult to remain on his feet. His skis were not waxed very well. Ice and snow built up on their surfaces, making the trek more difficult. Periodically, the tips of his skis caught on the snow and he tumbled into a drift. His clothes were already soaked.

"I'm cold!" he complained through chattering teeth. "And I'm tired. Please, can't we stop?"

"No, we've got to push on," I barked. "The bus will be waiting for us. They'll take a head count and realize we aren't there. They'll wait around and be anxious to get on the road." I regretted the steely tone in my voice immediately. Matthew was right. We were lost. But I could not yet admit this fact to myself. I reacted by pushing him harder.

Mark

I never did have lunch. When I saw Dad and Matthew walking out of the restaurant I figured they had already eaten. Dad was in such a hurry that I didn't have a chance to ask him for some lunch money, so all I got were a few Chee•tos from my friend Mershan.

After Dad and Matthew left the lodge, Bryn and I got our skis and went looking for them at the lift. Since we could not find them anywhere, we decided to try the highest run. We had been up there in the morning, and it was fun. But as we were riding the first T-bar lift, Bryn dropped his goggles and we had to ski back down to get them.

Still there was no sign of Dad and Matthew.

Once again Bryn and I decided to head up to the summit. This time, when we reached the second, upper lift, we discovered that it was closed. A snowstorm had moved in, so they were restricting access to the top of the mountain. As Bryn and I skied back down toward the lodge, my goggles iced up badly. I did not have a ski mask, and pellets were stinging my face.

At the bottom of the slope we ran into Donnell and Chubs. They were the only two black kids around, so they were easy to spot. And Donnell, even though he is a bit younger than me, is six feet tall. He was laughing. "Chubs almost broke his leg, man!" he said. Chubs had never skied before, and he was falling all over the place.

I wondered a bit about Dad and Matthew. Donnell and Chubs had not seen them all afternoon, either. Then I remembered back to our trip to Disney World, when Dad just sort of wandered off by himself for a while. That's Dad.

The four of us skied around the lower, easy slopes, giving Chubs some pointers. Then we went back into the lodge, played some more cards, and ate a few graham crackers. They were good.

By the time it was near 4 o'clock I was really beginning to get worried, because it was time for the bus to go. Maybe they'll just meet me at the bus, I thought. I gathered my equipment and went to the parking lot. The bus was waiting, warming its engine. I got on, but Dad and Matthew weren't there. I saw Mrs. Villers and said, "Hi, how's it going? Have you seen my dad?"

"No," she said, "I haven't seen him all day."

Now I was really worried. I did not want to stay on the bus and leave without Dad and Matthew. So I got off and just stood in the parking lot, looking around. Then I started to cry.

A man came up to me and asked me in Turkish what was wrong. I can speak Turkish pretty well, but not when I am crying, and I could not explain the problem. That's when my friend Doğan (pronounced "DO-wan") came up. He speaks really good Turkish.

"I haven't seen my dad and my brother," I said.

Through Doğan's translation the Turkish man said, "Let's go inside and look for them."

We went back into the hotel, to the equipment rental room, to see whether Dad had returned Matthew's skis and poles. No, his driver's license was still there.

"What can we do?" I asked. "Can they look for them?"

"Yes," the Turk replied. "We'll get a patrol out there looking for them."

Lots of people started talking and doing things. For a few minutes I just sat down on a bench and prayed. Then I walked outside and stared down at the point where we caught the first T-bar lift. Two people were walking toward the lodge and I prayed that they were Dad and Matthew. But as they got closer, I saw that they were both adults.

Mr. Perry, the man from the Australian Embassy who had organized this trip, found me outside. He told me that people were getting ready to search, but he did not want me to go off by myself and maybe get lost, too. He took me back into the lobby of the hotel. Bryn and his mom were there. Mrs. Villers had gotten my Walkman and a book off the bus for me. She explained that the bus had to leave. But she and Bryn were going to stay with me until we found Dad and Matthew. Mrs. Villers spoke a little Turkish, but not well enough to carry on a long conversation. She explained that the Turkish man who had spoken with me earlier was going to stay on to help translate. His name was Serdar Akkor.

The hotel was going to give us a room.

Mike

Matthew and I were suspended in an icy, white world that had no beginning and no end. The snow cascaded in thick sheets. The wind escalated, severely hampering visibility.

I became increasingly concerned. If I were alone I would simply keep moving. Eventually I would reach the bottom of the mountain and find a paved road or some other landmark. But Matthew was wet and cold and growing weaker by the minute.

We pushed on until our effort was finally rewarded. "Look, Matthew!" I shouted. "We found a road."

Matthew's reaction was almost imperceptible. All he knew was that he was tired. He was hungry. He was wet and very, very cold. "Dad," he said, "I've got to stop. I just can't go anymore."

I thought: I can't let you stop, Matt. If you stop now, I'll never get you going again.

The road was little more than a primitive trail, about ten feet wide, but clearly man-made. It was cut between the meandering path of a stream on our left and a low, rusty barbed-wire fence on a slope that rose sharply off to our right. Somebody has to own this land, I thought. The trail was covered with deep snow. No one had been along here recently—and perhaps it was a logging trail used only in the summer—but it had to lead *somewhere*. Perhaps it would take us to a major road, or to another settlement of cabins, such as we had seen earlier. "The bus isn't going to leave right away," I reminded Matthew. "They are going to see that we aren't back yet, and they'll wait for us."

We began to ski down this path. It quickly leveled, indicating that we had left the sharper slopes of the mountain and were emerging into the flatter areas. We had to adapt to the very different shuffling motions of cross-country skiing, and our muscles—particularly those in the backs of the legs—resisted the change.

I took the lead, but I tried to go slowly enough for Matthew to keep up. I looked over my shoulder constantly, to make sure he was following. As time passed he began to lag farther and farther behind.

I was frustrated. I thought to myself, I wish his skis would go faster. I wish he would try harder. Doesn't he know how important it is that we keep moving? If we stop now we're stuck and the weather isn't getting any better.

I searched within myself, looking for ways to motivate him, alternating words of encouragement with more stern injunctions and even threats. I tried keeping a pace, allowing him to fall behind, hoping it would cause him to move faster. Instead, it seemed to cause him to give up. Frequently I looked back to find him laying in the snow. Numerous times I had to retreat, pick him up, and dust as much snow as I could from his wet clothes.

I tried letting him lead, but he inched forward at such a snail's pace that I invariably rushed past him, sometimes offering words of encouragement, sometimes scolding him.

At least the trees were cleared for us. But our progress remained tough and slow.

Alternatives raced through my mind. The bus would not wait forever, and I reasoned that the organizers of the outing would get the other skiers back to Ankara—I knew that Wanda would take care of Mark—and leave us stragglers to work out our own arrangements. Once we found a main road we could hitchhike back to the hotel to let them know we were all right. First thing, I would call Mary; she would be worried when she found out that we missed the bus. I would have to turn in Matthew's rental equipment to reclaim my driver's license. Then I would have to come up with a way to get us back to Ankara. Maybe there was regular bus service. Maybe Mary would have to come and get us.

Once the sun set the temperature dropped rapidly, and the heavy snow continued. The trail clearly followed the course of the stream, which at some points flowed swiftly. Fortunately, enough moonlight filtered through to give us a bit of visibility. At times it seemed as if the snowfall would stop, but it never did.

Matthew finally gave in to tears. "Matthew, cut it out," I scolded. "We're doing the best we can. If we just keep going, we'll be okay." He responded by crying harder, and I softened. "Matt, I'm sorry," I said. "I don't want to be mean, but we've just got to keep going. If only we can go just a little bit farther, maybe we can see something."

There's a road here, I reminded myself. It's got to lead somewhere.

We pushed on, but Matthew soon tumbled headfirst into another snowdrift.

"Do you want me to see if I can give you a piggyback ride?" I asked. Matthew thought that was a crazy idea, but I decided to give it a try. I hoisted him onto my back, discovering that he felt far heavier than I thought he would. Our combined weight caused me to sink so deeply into the snow that I couldn't move. Again he began to cry and again I shamed him into continuing. I could not admit to myself that we should stop. If we stopped, we had to stay out here for the night. In my mind, that was the cutoff point that meant we were dealing with a survival situation.

"Let's try again to see if I can carry you on my back," I suggested. "This time you're going to have to do some of the work. If you can hang on to me and I don't have to hold you up there, maybe, just maybe I can balance better and use my poles to push us along. But you're going to have to hold on to your poles, also. We don't want to lose those. You may need to use them later."

I crouched low and he clung to my shoulders. I straightened slowly, awkwardly. His skis and poles jabbed at my back and legs. Once again our combined weight pushed me into the snow, and it was impossible to move forward.

We had no choice but to try to continue to ski separately.

Mark

The bus was delayed for quite some time, waiting for plows to clear the road of the fresh snowfall.

I could tell that Mrs. Villers was a little bit worried. She said that she had been to the top slope late in the afternoon and had almost gotten lost herself. She found her way back to the lodge by skiing directly under the lift.

Bryn did everything he could to keep my mind off things. He begged $10 from his mom and we left our hotel room to go downstairs to the arcade. We played video games and shot some pool. I suddenly remembered that Donnell's dad had died from some sort of lung disease, and I said to Bryn, "Oh, Donnell's dad died. He'll talk to me about it."

"Will you shut up?" Bryn snapped. "You're dad's not dead."

We went back upstairs to try to watch a movie on television, but it was pretty dumb and it was in Turkish, so we gave up. Then we played gin rummy and both of us began to cheat really bad, hiding cards in our pockets.

We made up stories about Dad and Matthew: Maybe some Turkish guy had them in his shack and he was giving them really bad food. And he's going to give Dad his World War I Turkish rifle and when they got back we'd sell it and be rich. It was really dumb stuff, just to get our minds off what was happening.

I prayed: Just let them come back. Some of my prayers did not even seem to be in words. It was just a sort of meditation, and it made me feel better.

When the bus was finally ready to leave, Mrs. Villers decided that she had to call Mom. She tried a couple of times but she couldn't get through. That's when I remembered that we were having some sort of problem with our phone, so Mrs. Villers decided to call the Handys' number—Chubs's mom and dad—

because she knew they lived two floors above us and could get Mom on the phone.

At first I wanted to talk to Mom, too, but then I decided I'd probably lose it.

Mary

I was still in my coach's sweats and tennis shoes as I began preparing a Tabasco-based marinade and blue cheese dip for the chicken wings that were such an oft-requested favorite that the page in my Paul Prudhomme cookbook was splattered and stained. Marissa helped me arrange a plate of vegetables and we commented on how fresh and flavorful they were. Turkish produce has not been hybridized into tastelessness. The vegetables spoil quickly, but the selection is very good and they taste great. I made a double batch of popcorn and Marissa set it on the table.

We both scurried about, picking up the apartment before our guests arrived.

The Armed Forces Network was going to broadcast two NFL playoff games this evening, the San Diego Chargers at the Pittsburgh Steelers and the Dallas Cowboys at the San Francisco 49ers. The winners would go to the Super Bowl. It was an exciting sports evening and we had invited our friends Ross and Mary Beth Tremblay and their two children, Caitlin and Sean, to share in the fun. By the time Mike and the boys returned, at about 9 P.M., the party would be in full swing.

Mike has never cared much for football, or any organized sport, but I have loved the game since I was in elementary school. I remember sitting on the couch in the TV room with my twin brother, Ed, who played football. Bart Starr was in his glory and I would badger Ed to tell me what was happening, what the penalties meant, and all the other intricacies of the game. I've been hooked ever since and have passed my love for the sport on to Matthew and Mark. Ross and Mary Beth were fans, too, and it was always more fun to watch the games with enthusiastic spectators.

It was about 7:30 in the evening when I heard a knock on the door. They're early, I thought. "Marissa, would you get that?" I asked. I noted with satisfaction that she remembered to ask who was there before opening the door. This was a basic security precaution for military families stationed in Turkey.

The visitor was our upstairs neighbor, Velma Handy, who announced, "Tell your mother that she's got a call on my phone."

For some unknown reason, our telephone had been disconnected the previous week, even though I had definitely paid the bill on time. I had been struggling for days to straighten out the misunderstanding. I came out from the kitchen muttering, "Oh, that stupid phone company. I'm sorry to bother you, Velma. Marissa, keep on picking up while I take the call upstairs."

I followed Velma up the steps to her third-floor apartment, picked up the phone, and immediately recognized Wanda Villers's voice. I knew that she and Bryn had gone along on the ski trip. "Mary," she began, "Mark told me your phone isn't working and how to get in touch with you. I don't want to worry you but I've put this off as long as I can. The bus is getting ready to leave, and Mike and Matthew haven't come down off the mountain."

"They haven't what?" I asked. "What do you mean?"

Wanda continued, "I didn't call earlier because there was so much fresh snow that they had to clear the road before they would let the bus leave and I was hoping the guys would show up. Now the road is almost cleared and they still aren't back. The bus will be leaving soon."

I was vaguely irritated. Great, I thought, ten minutes after the bus leaves, they'll show up and then I can make the three-hour drive to pick them up. But I glanced at my watch and realized they were not just a little late. They were due back at the ski lodge more than three hours ago. Mike has a well-deserved reputation for cutting things pretty close when it comes to punctuality. My brother even coined the phrase "Couillard-time" to tease him about it, but this was way off the scale.

"Oooo-kay," I said slowly. My heart skipped a beat, but I remained calm.

"Are you all right?" Wanda asked.

"I'm as good as I can be," I said, starting to cry quietly. I asked for more details. Wanda told me that Mark had grown concerned as the scheduled time neared for the bus to leave. He asked a lot of people if they had seen Mike or Matthew but no one could recall having spotted them during the entire afternoon.

"Please don't worry," Wanda said. "There could be a lot of reasons why they aren't back yet. The road was closed and it's possible they missed the trail and ended up below the closed section and couldn't get back to the lodge. We've sent some skiers out to look for them. The manager of the lodge said that Mark can stay behind and Bryn and I will wait with him." She added, "And another guy, Serdar Akkor, who speaks fluent English and Turkish, has also volunteered to stay, to facilitate communication."

I found this news unsettling, but I felt no reason to panic. Mike is an intelligent, highly competent, well-trained Air Force C-130 pilot, and a graduate of the Air Force Academy. At thirty-eight, he was in great physical shape. I knew that he was well qualified to take care of himself and our son. We had been living in Ankara for nearly a year and a half, and he could speak and understand Turkish well enough to get by. In fact, unlike most of the others stationed here, we had benefited from a five-month course offered by the Defense Language Institute prior to our arrival in Turkey. "They'll show up," I assured Wanda. "Before you know it, they'll come walking out of the woods."

Wanda wanted to confirm that it was all right for Mark to stay with her and Bryn.

"Sure, that's fine," I said, and asked her to call if she heard anything further. "I'll stay here," I told her, "at the Handys'."

After I hung up, just as I began to detail this conversation to Velma and her husband, Kelvin, I noticed a group of people arriving at the still-open front door. I assumed that the Handys were expecting company—maybe they were having a football party, too. But then I realized that the visitors were two military couples, Pam and Ken Jaccard and Angela and Ed Shaw. The men were colleagues of Mike; Ken was the Army section chief at ODC and Ed worked with Mike in the Air Force section. We also shared a spiritual connection. Ed was in Mike's Bible study group and I had also seen Pam and Ken attending Mass at our church.

What are they doing here? I wondered. Thank God the men were not in uniform, indicating that they were on official business. They were all dressed casually, the men in Dockers, the women in slacks.

Up until that point, I assumed that I had been the first one notified that Mike and Matthew was missing. But, unbeknownst to me, Wanda had briefed Kelvin when she called and I realized that some other calls must have been made as well. The presence of these couples indicated that the military support system was already in full swing. Is the situation that serious? I wanted to ask. Do you know something I don't know?

I was also a little embarrassed. These people had families of their own at home. There was really no need for them to disrupt their schedules like this on a Sunday night. "Oh, you guys," I said, "how can you be doing this for me?"

I reported the scant information that I had received from Wanda. Angela responded with a hug. "We're here for you," she said. "Would you like us to pray with you?"

I nodded.

"I need to stay close to the telephone," I said, and Velma and Kelvin agreed. We crossed through the dining area and into the Handys' living room. I sat on the edge of a tan couch. Angela sat next to me and Ed knelt on the floor in front of us. They took my hands in theirs. Together, we offered a short prayer for Mike's and Matthew's safe return. At the conclusion of the prayer, I was surprised to hear the familiar muted sounds of Angela speaking in tongues.

For us, praying in tongues is not the sharp, spontaneous pouring forth that is often depicted. It is a subdued whisper in a language like no other I have ever heard. It is as though the Holy Spirit gives you the words to continue praying when your own vocabulary runs dry. I understand that the phenomenon can be confusing—even a little scary—to someone who is not expecting it, or has not experienced it before. But when a group of people, whose voices vary in pitch and depth, come together in this type of prayer, it creates a beautifully melodic harmony, almost like a Gregorian chant.

It made me feel better to realize that Angela possessed this gift.

After we had finished our prayers Pam asked, "What can I do to help?"

"I guess you'd better call the Tremblays and cancel our plans for the evening," I said.

Angela volunteered to go downstairs and clean up the kitchen, pack away the food that I had prepared, and fetch Marissa.

Some minutes later, by the time Angela brought Marissa upstairs, Marissa was beginning to sense that something was amiss. She asked, "When are Daddy and Mark and Matthew going to come home?"

"Well, they're running late," I hedged. "I don't know when they'll be back."

Marissa accepted my explanation without question and busied herself by watching television, even though football was all that was on.

Mike

After some five hours of struggling we were still on the deserted trail and there was no end in sight. Once more Matthew tumbled into the snow. As he lay there shivering and crying, I finally admitted to myself: He can't go on. He's tired. I'm tired. Find the quickest way to make a shelter and get some rest.

Now that we had stopped I was gripped by deep fear. We had come a long way from the top of the mountain and the blizzard had wiped out any sign of our tracks. It would be difficult for searchers to find us. Do something, I commanded myself. It's cold and dark. You've got to work fast.

I glanced around, examining the area.

To our right, up a short but steep slope and across the barbed-wire fence, was a stand of large pine trees that seemed to offer the best available shelter. "Wait here," I told Matthew. "I'm going to find us a place where we can rest."

With shivering hands I removed my skis and crawled up the slope on my hands and knees until I reached the fence. It was only about three feet high, but the wire was covered with large, rusted spikes. Be careful not to rip your clothes, I warned myself. The multiple layers of my ski outfit was my lifeline of protection against cold and moisture. I dared not tear my gloves. Slowly I pushed down on the top wire and lifted my right leg across. But the snow on the other side was deeper than I expected. My right leg slid in deeply, my weight shifted, and once again I felt my hip pop out of joint. Tumbling into the snow, I tried not to cry out in pain.

Adrenaline kept me going. I fought off the intense discomfort, pulled myself to my feet, and glanced around. In front of me was a rocky platform created by one or more large boulders. Atop this was a pine tree with wide, low branches that formed a natural canopy. Beneath the pine tree we could shelter ourselves from the elements and, at the same time, keep an eye on the trail below us.

Biting my lip against the pains that shot through my right leg, I retreated across the fence and slid down the slope to the road, where Matthew sat, shivering and softly sobbing. "It'll be all right," I counseled. "I've found a place to stay. I'm sure we can make ourselves fairly comfortable."

"Okay," he agreed.

We crawled up the slope and encountered the fence. "Be careful not to tear your clothes," I warned. I helped him across and then joined him on the other side, willing myself to ignore my pain.

"There," I said, pointing. "The tree with the lowest branches."

We crawled up the slippery slope of the boulder and inspected the tree more closely. The low branches created a fairly wide and substantial shelter. I was surprised to see that several pine branches were arranged systematically on the floor of this canopy, like a carpet or a mattress. There was a small indentation in the center of the pile. "I wonder if someone else has used this place for shelter," I said. "Anyway, it will do. I want you to lie down on the ground and rest while I fix this up a bit. I'm going to find some more branches, to make this a little softer."

"Okay, Dad."

I tried to work quickly, but movement was difficult. Each step required great care, lest I lose my footing and slide off the boulder. My hip ached. As I tried to rip branches from some of the nearby trees, I discovered that the outer layer of my gloves had frozen into a solid crust, making it difficult to grasp anything.

I realized how ill-prepared I was for this kind of a situation. Most skiers I know never even think of the remote possibility of being stranded out in the cold. I thought of the brand-new Swiss army knife Mark had received for his birthday. Since he had started scouting last year, we had begun to add to his camping equipment. How useful that knife would be to me now, I thought, as I struggled to rip off the green and sappy branches from the surrounding trees. I did not have any matches, nor a lighter. That would be the most helpful thing of all, I decided, for if I had a match, surely I could find something that would burn and I could at least put an end to Matthew's freezing misery.

After considerable labor I was able to spread several additional branches underneath the pine tree canopy to further insulate us from the frozen earth. Then I wove our ski poles into the branches overhead to form makeshift rafters. Breaking off some larger branches from the surrounding trees, I lay them on top of the ski poles to create as solid a roof as I could. Then I broke off many smaller branches from surrounding trees and piled them as thatching on the now fairly substantial roof.

"Okay, Matthew," I said. "You slide in there and try to get warm. I've got a few other things to do."

I made the laborious return trip to the trail and gathered our skis. I thrust mine into the waist-deep snow, a few feet apart, and crossed them in the middle to form an X. Then I trudged down the road, about ten feet, and planted Matt's skis in a similar fashion. I hoped that in the morning the ski resort would send out patrols on snowmobiles or bobsleds, and they would check the roads leading away from the summit. Anyone searching this snow-covered trail would encounter the skis and realize that we were nearby.

Exhausted, I scrambled back across the fence and crawled under the tree next to my son. We prepared for a dismal night on the mountain.

I tried to reassure Matthew. "We'll have to spend the night here but in the morning, when it's light, they'll send snowmobiles to find us. Or maybe if the snow clears we can keep going down the road or at least see where it leads."

We surveyed what we had with us. Our food supply consisted of five pieces of strawberry-flavored hard candy. Mary had bought these for Christmas because she thought the mug they came in was pretty. This morning as I was leaving the apartment in Ankara I had grabbed a handful and stuffed them into my pocket. I also had my watch, my wallet, my comb, a ballpoint pen, and a scrap of paper. Other than four hand-warmer packs, we had no survival equipment of any kind.

I thought back to lunchtime. I had considered having a second sandwich, but had decided not to give in to my impulse. Now I regretted that decision very much.

It was critical to get Matthew dry. His black ski overalls, supposedly waterproof, were soaked as a result of his numerous tumbles into the snow; the outer layer was encrusted with ice. He was shivering uncontrollably. Amid the freezing temperatures, I slipped out of my ski pants and stripped off the jeans that I wore underneath. Fortunately, I had taken few falls and had managed to keep each of my layers remarkably dry. I got Matthew out of his boots and ski outfit and discovered that the jeans and the sweatshirt he wore underneath were also soaked. I helped him strip to his underwear and T-shirt. Quickly I put him into my jeans, stuffed two hand-warmer packs inside his boots, and helped him put them back on. My jacket was big enough so that he could keep his face buried in it, against the warmth of my chest. I was surprised to find that I could get both of us inside and still manage to get it zipped up—sealing out most of the cold. Although my feet were numb I decided to keep my ski boots on to take advantage of their layer of foam insulation.

One of our biggest problems was our wet socks. Mine were more than just slightly damp and Matthew's were soaked. I hoped that the hand-warmer packs would help dry his and that my body heat would gradually dry mine. The boots' plastic outer layer seemed to be more effective at conducting the cold, but I hoped that the foam inner layer would offset this effect.

I lay on my back and tried to help Matthew get comfortable on top of me. I offered him one of the five pieces of hard candy. After he finished it, he was thirsty, so we both gathered a few handfuls of fresh snow and ate it.

"My hands are freezing, Dad," Matthew complained through chattering teeth.

"Okay," I instructed, "I want you to slip your hands up under my armpits. A lot of heat escapes there, and that will help. You can keep them there all night if you want to."

We hugged each other tightly. "I'm sorry I had so little patience with you," I apologized. "But I felt that we just had to keep going. I thought if we could go fast enough we might find our way out tonight, but I know you went as fast as you could."

He said that he understood, and he admitted, "Sometimes I fell into the snow on purpose, just so we could stop." I chuckled inside when I heard this, but I was glad that he had waited until now to confess.

"Keep wiggling your toes, to keep them from getting too cold," I instructed.

"Okay." Soon Matthew fell into an exhausted sleep.

I was bone-tired and my head throbbed. The solid ground was hard beneath my back, and the collection of branches was a brittle, bumpy mattress. My ears became attuned to the sounds of small nocturnal animals—at least I hoped they were small—scurrying about.

I knew that there must be larger animals out here: foxes, coyotes—maybe wolves and even a bear or two. Our Turkish language class had studied the indigenous animal population of Turkey, so I knew these were all possibilities, though I did not know the specific species that inhabited this particular region. I decided that I had to force these thoughts out of my mind, comforting myself with the notion that even the larger animals would be more afraid of us than we would be of them.

Unable to sleep, I replayed the events of the day and remembered ruefully my impatience to get onto the slopes. As it turned out, Matt and I had plenty of time to ski. I mused at how, during portions of our trek, mundane details had preoccupied my thoughts. Even as we skied to the edge of great danger, I was still working on administrative and logistical trivia: How long would the bus wait for us? Would Mary have to drive up from Ankara to retrieve us?

I had a great respect for what the cold could do. I had seen the graphic pictures in my survival classes. I called to mind scenes from a refresher course I had taken at the Air Force Academy Life Support Shop about five years previous—gory pictures of hands swollen to five times their normal size, missing fingers, noses, and ears. I determined to do battle against this monster. We would have to make extraordinary efforts to check each other and, when necessary, warm each other's vulnerable body parts—our hands, feet, ears, and noses.

I removed my watch and stashed it in a pocket. If I left it on it would conduct the cold and perhaps freeze to the skin of my wrist.

Self-pity turned to self-blame. You screwed up big-time, Mike, I lectured myself. I had already broken the cardinal rule of survival training: When lost, stay put so that others will know where to look for you. Instead, we had moved, and I knew that we must have traveled a great distance from the ski lodge. Mike, I thought, look at the mess you've gotten us into. Look at the pain you are causing, not only to Matthew, but to Mary and Mark and Marissa. Silently I prayed, God, help us out of this situation. Please send somebody down this road.

I realized regretfully that I was missing the NFL playoff games and the party with our friends. Then I fretted about my plans for the next day. I was supposed to go with one of my fellow pilots to get visas for Saudi Arabia so that we could ferry a C-12 there. I dwelled on the inconvenience it would cause him to show up at my house and learn that I had not returned from the ski outing.

I drifted in and out of a fitful sleep.

Mark

At dinnertime I talked to the ski patrol guy and he said that the only time this had happened before, it was a German tourist who got lost. He kept moving throughout the night to keep himself warm and they had found him in the morning. That sounded good to me. I was sure they would find my dad and Matthew sometime tomorrow.

Our hotel room had typical Turkish beds. The sheets had a weird, oily feel to them and they tucked them in really tight. On top was a quilt.

I could hear that they were playing really loud music on the outside speakers. It was a kind of Turkish pop music, with a lot of bass, and it seemed to echo off the hills. I wondered if Dad and Matthew could hear it. I hoped so.

Mrs. Villers came up to check on Bryn and me a couple of times. I finally fell asleep, but all I could think about was Dad and Matthew out there in the cold.

Mary

The football game was over and Marissa wondered why we weren't going back down to our apartment. "Mom," she said, tugging at my arm, "let's go."

"Shhh, not now, Marissa, I'm talking," I replied.

Wanda called to report, "They had to call off the search for the night. They've only been able to check the actual ski runs because of the weather and how dark it is. There isn't any more they can do on the mountain tonight." Then she added, "Colonel Fitzgerald will be in charge and he's arriving in the morning. I'll call if there is any more news."

Colonel Ed Fitzgerald was the acting commander of ODC, and I had barely hung up the phone when he called with a military-style report: He was leaving Ankara at 4 A.M.; he would set up a command post on Kartalkaya Mountain first thing in the morning; he would report to me regularly.

It was about midnight when Velma's son Adam—whom everyone called Chubs—arrived home from the ski trip, accompanied by Donnell. Donnell lived in the second-floor apartment between us and the Handys. But his aunt, and guardian, Angela Shepherd, was out of town, so he was staying with the Handys tonight while his Uncle Joe attended a football get-together, similar to the party we had scheduled. We asked the boys for any additional information they could provide. Donnell is not a very talkative kid, but he did say that earlier in the day, every time he saw Mike or Matthew, they were together.

Seeing Chubs, Marissa concluded that her dad and brothers must be home also, and they were probably waiting for us downstairs. Again she asked, "Mom, can we go home now?"

All I could say was, "Soon, okay, soon."

Chubs stepped in to help. "Marissa, you want to play Super-Nintendo?" he asked.

"Sure." They played "Street Fighter." It was a boys' kind of game, but with two older brothers, Marissa was used to that sort of entertainment, and it kept her mind diverted.

As the Jaccards and Shaws prepared to leave, they told me they would continue to pray for us and urged me to try to get a good night's sleep. Pam and Angela said that they would check on me first thing in the morning.

Kelvin set up a mattress on the floor of the TV room, next to the telephone. "Marissa," I said, "we're just going to sleep on the floor here, okay?"

Marissa looked at me with questions in her eyes, but it was way past her normal bedtime and she was too tired to argue. She fell asleep quickly.

Although we did not really know them very well, both Velma

and Kelvin were very supportive and accommodating. Before I tried to get some sleep, we discussed what we could do to get my phone working the next day.

Then everyone settled in for the night.

Lying on the floor next to my sleeping daughter, I worried about how Mark was taking all this, but I told myself: Mark's okay. He's with good people.

But what about my other son?

The Search

Some employers of the ski resort determined to remain out all night long, riding a snow tractor, searching the runs. But the blizzard was too severe for them to venture off the designated slopes.

The lodge manager ordered the loudspeakers turned on and kept at maximum volume. Some were mounted at the tops of the runs, but others were located at various sections of the ski lifts. Music would blare all night long in the hope that the sound would attract Mike and Matthew.

Space heaters in the shacks at the tops of all of the lifts were left running. If Mike and Matthew could locate one of these shacks, they could remain warm throughout the night.

The Turkish National Police were notified and began to check the nearby villages.

Meanwhile, U.S. military forces prepared to do what they could do to rescue two of their own, but there were problems. Since July 1993 the U.S. Air Force had reduced its abilities to conduct search-and-rescue missions in the area. Open hostilities with Iraq had ceased, and the main mission of the U.S. was to enforce U.N. sanctions; therefore, these more routine operations were considered less hazardous and were mainly handled by the Turkish Air Force.

According to the terms of a complex letter of agreement

between U.S. and Turkish authorities, the Turkish Air Force would conduct most peacetime searches, calling for the use of American resources if special circumstances arose. This was logical, since peacetime searches would most likely be attempting to locate Turkish citizens.

On temporary duty at the joint Turkish-American base at Incirlik, Major Keith "Sully" Sullivan was the only available U.S. helicopter pilot with special operations experience, and was personally designated as a "mini-RCC" (Rescue Coordination Center) for wartime and peacetime rescues. On this Sunday night, he was partying. Because no Operation Provide Comfort aircraft were scheduled to fly the next day, the crew members of the 16th Special Operations Wing had received permission to hold a party. Most were taking advantage of the opportunity to indulge in a bit of social drinking.

But when Sully's beeper went off about 10:30 P.M., everyone around him paid attention. Even before he knew the nature of the emergency, Sully directed his assistant, Major Johnson, to select some crews and place them directly into "crewrest" so that they would be able to fly as soon as possible. Then, in the Officers' Club, he met with Brigadier General Carlton, the Operation Provide Comfort Task Force commander. Special Forces Colonel Winslow, the Joint Special Operations Task Force commander, was also present.

The general informed Sully that Lieutenant Colonel Mike Couillard and his son Matthew were missing in the mountains and that the weather was terrible. He asked for Sully's opinion on a course of action.

"I do not have a crew," Sully replied. "Even if I did, they would have trouble getting there. Even if they got there, there would be little they could do until morning."

Colonel Winslow asked Sully how he would then proceed.

Sully suggested that the colonel send two MH-60G Nighthawk helicopters and an HC-130P Shadow, a refueling tanker, to the area as early as he could the next morning. The Nighthawk is an advanced version of the Blackhawk, the Army's workhorse helicopter. The Nighthawk features laser navigation and a FLIR (Forward Looking Infrared) system to peer through darkness. It is also equipped with a probe that allows for air-to-air refueling.

Winslow, a calm and rational man whom Sully knew to be a good delegator, looked directly at the general and agreed that this would be a good approach. He also said that he could send a contingent of Green Berets who were experienced at operations in snow-packed mountains.

The general decided to hold off on calling in ground troops, but he approved plans for an aerial search. He asked Sully what needed to be done.

"I'll notify the crews," Sully said. Noting that Turkish officials would have to approve the air activity, he asked, "Has anyone coordinated with the Turks?"

The general said that ODC officers had already spoken with the Turkish General Staff to clear the way. "It's our people," the general said. "Just us. We'll run it."

Mike

Neither of us slept for more than thirty minutes at a time.

Several times during the night Matthew woke with a start, experiencing a sense of claustrophobia and suffocation. Sometimes his dreams told him that we had found our way back to the lodge and he was safe and comfy at home in his bed. Waking up to this spooky reality caused him to panic, and I had to work to calm him.

Whenever we were awake at the same time I reminded Matthew to wiggle his toes. Sometimes the movement caused us to slip down the slope of the hillside, and we had to crawl back up beneath the tree. We frequently scraped our heads against the makeshift roof.

At some point in the midst of this dreadful night I realized that Matthew was actually too warm in his cocoon. The combined effects of our close breathing brought us to the point of perspiration, so I loosened the zipper on my jacket, keeping him warm but producing a better air supply.

At times the blizzard conditions eased and the area was bathed in moonlight. My eyes were drawn to a reflected glow that pierced through a downslope corner of the floor of our shelter. Like a giant owl's eye, the spot seemed to stare back at me. What is that? I wondered. Matthew stirred and I asked if he was awake. Groggy but somewhat lucid I asked Matt if he saw the spot.

"What do you think that is?" I asked.

"I don't know. It's like some light is coming through the rock but I don't know where it's coming from."

The clarity of his answer surprised me, but as suddenly as he stirred, just as suddenly did he leave me for his dreams. I was alone again with my thoughts.

More storm clouds rolled across the moon, and the glow was gone.

Snow continued to pile up around us.

DAY 2

·

Monday, January 16

Mary

I awoke lying on a mattress on the floor of my neighbors' apartment and immediately turned to stare at the telephone. The realization that it had remained silent all night was disappointing. Marissa slept soundly by my side. She, too, would be disoriented when she awoke and I decided that I would have to tell her exactly what was going on before she heard it from someone else.

Suddenly the words of Psalm 121 were impressed on my mind:

> *I raise my eyes toward the mountains. From where will my help come? My help will come from the Lord who made heaven and earth.*

The message was of genuine comfort to me. My pain came from the mountains, but my strength would come from the Lord, the creator of those mountains.

As I always do, I took advantage of a few minutes of the morning quiet for some solitary prayer and meditation.

I worried that either Mike or Matthew was injured. If Mike had broken his leg or suffered some other affliction, Matthew certainly could not transport him anywhere.

But what if it was Matthew who was hurt? Our younger son has always been a "big guy." He weighed seven pounds four-teen ounces at birth—almost one full pound more than either

Mark or Marissa. By the time he was ten weeks old he weighed fourteen pounds, and all I was doing was nursing him. Strangers made comments such as, "Oh, look at the little bruiser!" The nickname stuck, and soon "Bruiser" was shortened to "Bruise."

Currently, Bruise weighed about eighty-five pounds. We had put him on a low-fat diet after Christmas, but I was thankful now that both Mike and he carried a few "after-holiday" pounds. In any event, if he was injured, I knew that Mike would not be able to carry him very far on skis in the midst of a blizzard. I also knew that Mike would never leave him.

My thoughts were interrupted by the sounds of people beginning to move about in the Handys' apartment. Velma put on a pot of coffee.

The activity caused Marissa to stir and even before she was fully awake I suggested that we go back down to our apartment to change our clothes. Once we were downstairs I checked to see if the phone line had been reconnected, but it was still dead. I splashed some water on my face, freshened up a bit, and helped Marissa get dressed.

"Marissa, I need to talk to you," I said. Trying to keep my voice calm and casual, I explained, "Daddy and Matthew got lost on the ski trip yesterday. They did not arrive back at the lodge when it was time for the bus to leave."

Marissa started to cry.

"It's okay," I said quickly. "You don't need to cry. They're going to be fine. There are people out looking for them and I am sure everything will be all right. Mark and Bryn and Mrs. Villers are waiting for them."

Marissa calmed down a bit, but I wondered what was going on behind her gray-blue eyes, and I knew that I would have to pay close attention to her mood.

Suddenly she asked, "Is anybody lost with them?"

"No."

"Well, why not?" she asked with a pouting expression on her face. "Why should they be the only ones lost?"

That was a good question and I had no answer for it. All I

could say was, "C'mon, we need to go back upstairs to be near the phone."

As Marissa and I emerged into the hallway we almost bumped into Mary Beth Tremblay. Concern was etched on her lovely, porcelainlike face. Her presence here, so early in the morning, told me that the news of Mike's and Matt's disappearance was spreading quickly.

"It was awful of me not to ask what was going on when I got the call last night about the party being canceled," she said. "I should have sensed something was wrong."

"Don't be silly," I assured her. "It's not your fault and I certainly wasn't on top of things. I didn't know what was said to whom last night. I'm just glad you're here. I was going to call you as soon as I got upstairs."

Mary Beth and I had grown quite close. For starters, we were shopping buddies. We had worked as a team to decorate our church for Advent and Christmas, and our families had shared Thanksgiving and Christmas dinners. We had also coordinated First Communion activities for Marissa and Mary Beth's son Sean. I was glad that she was here now.

The three of us climbed the stairs to the Handys' apartment. When I saw that Velma was still in her bathrobe, huddled next to the radiator, I felt a little uncomfortable knowing that people were descending on her so early in the day, disrupting her routine. Velma is a very nice woman, but she is quiet and keeps to herself.

Almost immediately Pam and Angela arrived, a tacit acknowledgment that the military support system was in full swing. Angela asked quickly, "Have you heard anything?"

"No, no." I shook my head.

Pam told me that Ken had left for Kartalkaya Mountain at four in the morning to join in the search. "He just had to do something," she said, "and he felt like he couldn't accomplish anything here in Ankara." All you have to do is look at Ken's face, with a dark mustache trimmed with military precision and the distinguished graying around his temples, to know that he is a take-charge type of guy. As a former battalion commander, he has a very "by the book" personality, so he simply could not sit idly in Ankara knowing that Mike and Matthew were missing. "And it's more than that," Pam added. "His father-neurons kicked in. He's going to re-create the scene and try to figure out what he would do in similar circumstances if one of our kids was with him."

It was wonderful that these military wives were here to help, along with Mary Beth. Angela is model-tall, slim, and carries herself with the bearing of an Audrey Hepburn. Her husband Ed is a health-and-exercise fanatic with a very muscular build. Not surprisingly they had produced two picture-perfect children, and they were devoted to them. Pam, a petite woman with short brown hair, is very extroverted, and I knew that she would be a valuable asset in dealing with all the people who would be swarming about.

Angela kept Marissa occupied and Pam monitored the telephone for me. But I still wanted the spiritual sustenance that I knew I would receive from some of my companions in the various Bible study and worship groups that Mike and I attended in Ankara.

I have always loved the liturgy and sacraments of the Catholic Church. But, through Bible study groups and prayer circles, I formed a deeply personal relationship with Jesus Christ and learned to express my love for Him in ways that were common in the historic church but are not often practiced in the modern Catholic Church. These gifts of the spirit include speaking in tongues and prophesy, and their inclusion in Catholic theology had been blessed by the Pope.

Mike's Air Force assignments had taken us all over the world and wherever we went we found like-minded individuals to join in our devotions. I knew that with a few well-placed phone calls I could set off a chain reaction among our worldwide network of friends. People from the four corners of the globe would reach out to God for the answers we needed.

And, at this moment, I particularly wanted the support of Cathryn Hoard, a close friend from our Monday women's Bible study group. I called her at home, but she had already left for her day. Until recently Cathryn, like me, had been teaching her children at home, but now she was working with a group of other former home-schoolers to establish an English-speaking Christian school in Ankara. She taught about a dozen students, ranging from fourth grade to eighth grade.

Mark

Mrs. Villers called from the hotel lobby to wake up Bryn and me. "It's time for breakfast," she said.

I asked for some hard-boiled eggs, but when I got them I realized that they were barely cooked. I pushed them around on my plate, but I was not very hungry anyway. Mrs. Villers was worried that I was not eating enough, so she finally got some feta cheese for me. It is a part of every Turkish breakfast, and I ate that.

Early in the morning several people from the embassy in Ankara and some of my dad's friends from ODC arrived to help search. One of them was Mr. Mendoza, the father of my good friend Fabian. "Fabian gave me something for you," he said. He reached into his pocket and handed me a small card.

I had seen this card before, at Fabian's house. It had a picture of a saint on it. "Oh, yeah," I said, "thanks. Fabian told me this guy is supposed to help you find what you've lost." I put the card in my pocket.

It was still pretty early in the day when a man came to talk to me. He introduced himself as Colonel Fitzgerald, my dad's commanding officer. He was a big guy, like someone you might see in a war movie. He asked me a bunch of questions, like: "When did you see them last?" "What were they wearing?" I thought that he was kind of abrupt and rude.

Bryn and I spent some time playing gin rummy and then decided that we wanted to go outside for a snowball fight or some skiing. Mrs. Villers said no, but she gave us some money so that we could play a few video games. When the money ran out we went back up to the room and tried to watch whatever was on Turkish TV.

As long as I had something to do the time seemed to go pretty fast, but whenever I thought about my dad and my brother, everything seemed to go in slow motion. In the lobby Bryn and I found a three-dimensional map of the area. We examined it closely, trying to figure out where Dad and Matthew could be. I noticed an area that looked like it was filled with dangerous slopes and cliffs, and that scared me. "I hope they didn't go there," I said to Bryn.

Yesterday I had complained to my dad about the goggles he gave me to use. Now I wished that I had not said anything. I just wanted them to be all right.

I knew that my dad had some candy with him and I also knew how much he loves sweets. I figured that he and Matthew had probably eaten all of it by now.

In my pocket was the Swiss army knife that Mom and Dad had given me as an early birthday present. It was awesome. It had a bottle opener, scissors, blades—everything you could think of. I wished Dad had it with him right now. It wasn't doing me any good.

Mike

It was snowing heavily when we woke to the morning's light.

Matthew was cold and exhausted. There was no way that he would be able to ski down the mountain and there was no way for me to carry him. I simply could not entertain the thought of striking out on my own in search of help while leaving my son cold and alone in the midst of this blizzard.

Our alternative was to rely on the skills of the search team that I knew must be looking for us, but I was sure that they would have great difficulty as long as the snow continued.

Once more I berated myself for allowing us to move so far
from our original position. I estimated that we had traveled a
minimum of five miles away from the top of the ski slope, and
it was quite possible that the meandering trail had led us precisely in the opposite direction from safety. Would a search-
and-rescue team even think to look in this area—wherever
we were?

I had to make our shelter more secure from the elements.
As Matthew dozed, I crawled out from under our makeshift
canopy, surveyed our situation, and decided that I could fashion the branches of the pine tree into a more substantial roof
to ward off the cold winds; I also wanted to raise it so that we
would not continue to bump our heads.

I remembered the mysterious glow that had mesmerized me
during the night. From this vantage point, in the daylight, I
could see what appeared to be a slim crack in the face of the
rock that formed a wall next to the tree we were under. This
crack was near the corner of the floor and this wall, but I could
not discern the source of the "owl's eye."

With considerable effort I crawled across the barbed-wire
fence. The accumulated snowfall of the night had covered up
our skis and nearly obliterated my signal. I had planted them
about one-third of their length, and now the snow was more
than half as deep as the skis. I tugged mine loose and replanted
them as two vertical obstructions along the trail, deciding that
they would be more visible that way, even if they weren't arranged in the skier's classic distress signal. Anyone coming
down this path would see my skis sticking straight up, so I
determined that I could use Matthew's skis to reinforce the
roof of our shelter.

Back at the pine tree I worked quickly as sharp pellets of
snow stung my face, driven by a nasty wind. I used three of
our ski poles as the basis for the new roof and weaved Matthew's skis between them as cross braces. I took the fourth
pole—one of mine, since it was longer than one of Matt's—
and placed it vertically in the center of the floor to help elevate
these braces, thus raising the height of the roof. In the light of

day it was much easier to gather enough additional boughs to create a thicker and more protective cover. By now, Matthew was stirring. I figured my rustling and rummaging about must have awakened him.

I turned my attention to the floor. The brittle pine branches were in disarray and piled high at the topside of the slope. "No wonder we had such a tough time sleeping," I said to Matt. "No wonder we kept slipping down the hill."

I helped him to his feet and directed him to stand off to one side as I worked. Moving quickly, because I wanted to get Matt out of the storm as soon as possible, I tugged at the branches and scraped at the dirt with my gloves, trying to level the surface. I gathered more branches—smaller, softer ones that provided a more comfortable cushion. The extra layer would make our second night more tolerable, in the event that help did not arrive this day. I prayed that would not be the case.

My eyes once more were drawn to the crack in the rock, where I had seen the "owl's eye." From this new perspective, looking down at a lower angle, I could see that daylight penetrated the rock. The small slit on this side appeared to go all the way through the rock to a larger opening. I slid down the sharp incline to inspect further and discovered that the source of the glowing "owl's eye" was a small, hollowed-out area between two large boulders that were sort of fused together. The opening of this tiny burrow was no more than two feet high; it stretched about six feet deep into the rock face. Perhaps what I had seen last night was moonlight reflected on the snow and filtered through this fissure.

It would be a tight fit, but this tiny cave offered much better shelter than the pine tree, and it was shielded from the biting winds of the blizzard. This site, too, appeared to have been used as shelter at some time in the past, for the floor was strewn with pine boughs.

I scrambled back up the hill and announced, "Well, Matthew, we're moving."

At first he misunderstood. "Dad, I'm too tired and sore to ski anymore," he complained. "I can't move any farther."

"Matthew, you know that bright spot on the side of the rock that we were looking at last night? Remember we were trying to figure out what it was? Well, there's a little cave on the other side. We were looking through a little crack to the inside of a cave! It will be much better than sitting underneath this pine tree and I'm pretty sure we can both fit inside without any problem." Matthew's eyes brightened with fresh hope as I offered my hand and said, "Here, let me help you down and you can get out of the cold."

We slipped gingerly down the sharply dropping slope and crossed the fence. I helped him crawl headfirst into the cave and tried to make him comfortable on the mattress of pine boughs. Although he had spent only a few minutes in the elements he was shivering badly, so I stripped off my coat and encased him inside.

Returning to our original site, I tore down the structure that I had built only minutes earlier. With my arms full of skis and poles I made my way back to the barbed-wire fence. I tossed the ski equipment over and eased my way across onto the road.

Moving downslope from the point where I had set my skis, I planted Matthew's skis so that our two sets flanked the cave. Then I inserted the ski poles into the snow at an angle, pointing them in the direction of our new shelter. Matt's rented ski poles had bright orange tips that were highly visible in the snow.

Methodically I tramped through waist-deep snow, creating an X pattern that covered the width of the narrow trail and stretched the entire length—at least fifteen feet—between our two pairs of skis. Survival school had taught me to make the signal as large as I could—the bigger, the better. I surmised that this would certainly be dramatic enough to gain the attention of anyone peering down from a search aircraft—if only his eyes could penetrate the sides of this steep little valley. My training also told me to etch the signal as deeply as possible, so that shadows would highlight it, making it more visible from the sky. I thought about placing branches within these trenches, to

heighten the contrast with the surrounding snow, but I paused
to consider my next move. The snow was increasing in intensity and my strength was waning. Survival involves making a
cost-benefit analysis of every potential effort; priorities must be
balanced constantly. The longer I stood out in the snow, the
more my feet would become vulnerable to frostbite, and I decided that rest and warmth were necessary right now. My
hands and feet were freezing, and I needed a break.

Every movement required intense effort. Once more I waded
through the snow and pulled myself carefully across the fence.
Then I had to crawl up the face of an ice-covered boulder to
return to our original pine tree shelter. I gathered my collection
of branches from the roof and the floor, tossed them across
the fence and toward the cave. I slid down the slope and once
more straddled the fence. When I finally wiggled headfirst into
the cave and snuggled up against Matthew, I was delighted to
realize that the cave was deep enough to provide shelter for
my entire body, even when stretched out. But with the two of
us inside, there was very little room to maneuver.

With considerable effort, I unzipped the coat that Matthew
was wrapped in—my coat—and eased inside. He was able to
zip it up across my back, so that the one coat warmed us both.
We lay against one another, chest to chest, and I thrust my
hands underneath his armpits, as he had done the night before.
The fit was tight and uncomfortable, and made my sore hip
ache even more. With each movement my hands, arms, legs—
and often my head—scraped against the rocky walls and ceiling
of our new home, but the cramped quarters conserved the
warmth of our bodies. Now we were facing parallel to the road,
with our heads upslope and the trail and stream on our left.

Slowly, as I absorbed warmth from Matthew's body, I regained my strength, and when I felt ready I commanded myself: Okay, Mike, get back to work.

Considerable grunting and squirming accompanied my efforts as I slipped out of the coat that covered us both. I tried
to sit up, but banged my head against the rocky interior of the
cave. I had to slither back out in an awkward, feet-first position.

I gathered all the pine boughs that I had tossed down from above. Then I said to Matthew, "Come on outside for a few minutes. I'll try to do this quickly, so that we can get warm again."

As he stood to one side with his back to the biting wind, I started from scratch, pulling the ground cover outside the cave so that the earth was bare. Then I placed some of the thicker, heavier branches on the floor. Methodically I piled softer, smaller branches atop these.

Our attention was diverted by the sound of jet engines, and we gazed upward at the cloud cover. Judging by the sound, it seemed to be a commercial airliner on a regular route, not a search plane. Even if the sky was clear it would have been far too high to spot us on the ground. We listened carefully as the sound crossed directly over our position and then faded from our ears.

Morosely, I returned to my task.

After I had made the cave floor as comfortable as I could, I helped Matthew back inside. Now I was left with some large branches that were devoid of pine needles and thus of no use as ground cover. I tried to weave these into a sort of door. This proved to be a more difficult task than I had imagined and I wondered if the extra effort was worth it. The wind was flowing downhill from behind us and the cave was pretty well shielded from its effects. So I abandoned this task and once again crawled inside and lay next to my son.

"I'm so hungry," he said.

In the cramped quarters it was difficult to maneuver, but I managed to extract our remaining food supply from my pocket. Matthew had eaten one of the hard candies last night. Now we had four left. I was certain that we would be found sometime yet today, but I wanted to be cautious. "Let's each eat one," I suggested. "We'll save the other two until tomorrow—just in case."

"Okay."

We lay there for a while, dazed and worried. Both of us nodded off at times, catching up on the sleep we had missed during the night. Suddenly a scuffling sound alerted us both. "That's somebody coming down the road—in snowshoes!" Matthew said. I scrambled from the cave, banging my head in the process, and hurried over to the road, but all I could see were small animal tracks in the deepening snow cover.

Once more I heard an airplane overheard. This one sounded like a turboprop, flying the same pattern as the jet we had heard earlier. We must be right under a regular air route, I decided.

Mary

The sudden ring of the telephone brought everyone to attention. It was Colonel Fitzgerald, who reported bluntly, "Mary, we haven't found them yet." I was surprised by the brusque, clinical beginning of the conversation, but I realized that this was the critical information I needed to know, and he was not going to waste time in small talk before he gave me the bottom line. It was the military way.

The colonel announced that he had arrived at Kartalkaya Mountain very early this morning to take charge of the search. He said that employees of the ski resort had been out all night long, riding a snow tractor, searching the slopes. "It's still snowing here," the colonel added. "The temperature dropped to about fourteen degrees."

He asked me for a description of what Mike and Matthew were wearing. Since I was the one who shopped for their ski attire, I was able to be fairly detailed in my description. Mike was wearing a red turtleneck, black ski bibs, a royal blue jacket, and a white and black hat. His gloves were navy blue. Matthew wore a black T-shirt, a black sweatshirt blocked with royal blue and red, navy blue bibs, and a black jacket. I had to guess that he was wearing his navy blue cap. As I relayed this information to the colonel I wished that I had been able to convince them to wear long underwear, as I always did when we went skiing.

The colonel assured me that he would continue to report to me personally. I told him that someone would remain near the Handys' telephone at all times until I could get my own phone working.

After speaking with the colonel, my eyes played about the Handys' huge, almost cavernous, sparsely furnished apartment. As grateful as I was for their hospitality, I wished that I were in my own, cozier home, surrounded by familiar things. It was absurd to be without a phone during a time like this.

I wondered how I could rectify the situation and my mind immediately turned to Enis Sonmez, a Turk who worked at ODC. He spoke fluent English, and his job was to help incoming American military families get settled. When we had first arrived in Ankara he had been very helpful. He was so personable and friendly that he had even invited us to his parents' home in a new section of Ankara to celebrate one of the Turkish *bayrams,* or holidays. I had seen him in action, taking care of the logistical details that arise when a family is transferred to a foreign country and is faced with the task of setting up housekeeping. He knew how to cut through all the bureaucratic red tape. I reasoned that if anyone could assist me in getting our phone turned on, it was Enis. When I reached him at his office at ODC he promised that he would do what he could.

He called back only a few minutes later. He said that he had spoken with someone at the phone company. They had found a record of our payment and realized that they had made a mistake in cutting off our service. They promised to restore it as soon as possible. I wondered: How "soon" is "possible"?

Somehow my friend Cathryn heard what had happened. She tracked me to the Handys' number and asked if the news was true. I confirmed that Mike and Matthew were missing, then I added, "I'd appreciate if you would come over and pray with me."

After the call Cathryn told her students what had happened

and they offered prayers for Mike and Matthew. Then, wasting no time, she hurried over to the Handys' apartment.

Cathryn is a petite, brown-haired fireball of a woman, always on the move. Our families had much in common. She and her husband, Andy, were from Los Angeles, where Mike and I had met during our high school years. She attended college in Colorado Springs, where Mike had attended the Air Force Academy, and where our kids had learned to ski. The two of us enjoyed playing basketball against the high school girls' team. Even though neither of us had played competitively since the mid-seventies, we quickly developed a sense of camaraderie and trust on the basketball court. We could predict one another's moves. Our friendship had developed on many levels. The deepest of these was spiritual, and I needed her now.

Shortly after Cathryn arrived, Mary Beth walked over to the bank of windows to the right of the couch and stared north, in the direction of Kartalkaya Mountain. Although there was no snow falling in Ankara, the heavy, gray sky in the distance was an indication that severe weather was still enshrouding the mountain. Mary Beth turned and locked eyes with Cathryn, and I knew that a part of them was wondering when some military official would arrive with bad news.

We needed to pray, but God would not allow us to pray in a despairing manner. Although we knew that He could let the unthinkable happen and still be in control, still be full of grace, compassion, and mercy, He seemed to want us to proclaim His victory and divine protection for Mike and Matthew.

"Just please, God, let them be together," I implored.

Knowing that the continuing snow would hamper rescue efforts, the three of us prayed for the storm to stop.

Afterward I said, "I don't know about you, but I don't feel depressed about this. I feel uplifted and at peace." Cathryn and Mary Beth agreed with me and serenity filled the room. It was good to know that I was not the only one who had that sense of peace. Otherwise, I might have felt I was deluding myself.

The Search

A diverse force of searchers set out to canvass Kartalkaya Mountain. Volunteers from ODC, as well as the U.S. Embassy, were joined by a contingent of Turkish police and troops. Dividing the terrain into grids on a map, they began to systematically check a forty-square-kilometer area (15.444 square miles). Unfortunately, six feet of fresh snow had fallen in the past two days, and visibility was reduced to twenty feet. The temperature was only fourteen degrees Fahrenheit.

One of the search teams found a discarded backpack, but there was no sign of the missing man and boy.

Over and over, Ken Jaccard skied slowly down the runs of Kartalkaya Mountain. Whenever he reached a point where the trail offered choices, where someone—particularly in a blizzard—might stray from the proper path—his brain conducted a dialogue with itself. His daughter Alex was the same age as Matthew, and he said to himself: Okay, if I was with Alex, and we were here and we couldn't see where we were going, which way would we turn? Having this child with me, how would that change what I would do, as opposed to being by myself or with another adult? What speed would I set? What different turns would I make?

Back at Incirlik Air Base, Sully was frustrated, observing sarcastically that things were going "like a well-oiled machine." Crews for the two Nighthawk helicopters as well as the Shadow tanker had assembled in the briefing room at 9 A.M., but the information available to them was sketchy. Their maps were not sufficiently detailed. Sully's crews had maps of the area drawn to a scale of 1:250,000, but for a search of this nature they needed the detail provided by 1:50,000 scaled maps. (One inch on the map equals 250,000 inches on the earth's surface. So by this reasoning, a 1:50,000 is more detailed, and better for rescue operations.) Due to security considerations, the Turkish government would not provide them. The crews would have to fly three hundred nautical miles to reach the area, and the weather was described as "heavy snow and zero visibility." Realizing that the local police radio band was not compatible with the radios on the helicopters, Sully had to request permission to use a different frequency. Then, just before takeoff, Sully learned that the Turks would not allow them to conduct air refueling operations over Turkish land. Not now, not ever! Sully was told. Someone at ODC determined that fuel was available at Bolu, but the Turks would not allow them access to it. Many phone calls later, a backup plan was worked out, allowing the helicopters to refuel at Akinci (near Ankara), but valuable time had been lost.

The Nighthawks, designated as Pony 21 and Pony 22, finally took off at 11:45 A.M., accompanied by a Shadow. Before long they encountered severe weather that extended from fifty feet above the ground to an altitude of fourteen thousand feet. Unable to find their way through the weather, the copters were forced to turn back, arriving at Incirlik about 2:45 P.M. The crews were ordered to rest and prepare to try again early the next morning.

Meanwhile, Sully selected First Lieutenant Simon Gardner to run the ground portion of the search. He would coordinate the efforts of a fifteen-man team of Green Berets from the 10th Special Forces Group who were skilled in mountain and snow operations.

Despite the difficulties, Sully was somewhat optimistic. His crews reported that there was considerable snow on the ground, which would allow the Couillards to leave tracks or some other visible sign. If the cloud cover cleared enough to conduct operations, Sully felt that his crews had a good chance of success.

Mike

Matthew announced that he was thirsty, and this initiated a critical decision. I knew that if we continued to eat snow, it would lower our body temperatures to dangerous levels. "When we want water, we have to go over to the stream," I instructed. The snow had eased somewhat, so I suggested, "Now might be a good time."

I helped him out of the cave. Since his coat was now frozen and useless, I told him to keep my coat on.

Using our ski poles to maintain balance, we slipped and slid our way down to the road.

Before crossing the road we cut to our right so that we would not disturb the large X signal I had created.

By the time we reached the stream I calculated that we had traveled about twenty-five yards. It appeared that the action of the flowing water across the rocks was the only thing that kept the water in a liquid state.

It was difficult to tell where the snow-covered ground ended and the partially frozen stream began. I stepped on what I thought was a rock and immediately sank up to my boot-top in ice-cold water. "Be careful," I warned Matthew. I was thankful that little or no water had seeped down into my boot.

Quickly I worked out a solution. Once I had found a spot that was solid enough to hold my weight, I laid two ski poles down, parallel to the stream. When I knelt on these I found that they provided enough support for me to maintain my balance as I leaned over the water's edge.

I did not want Matthew to get his hands cold and wet, so I pulled off my gloves, cupped my hands, plunged them into the brutally cold liquid, and scooped up a serving of water for my son. White spots appeared on the flesh of my hands, highlighting the calluses on my palms. This, I knew, indicated an early stage of frostbite. Gritting my teeth against the pain,

I continued to scoop up water until Matthew was satisfied. Then I drank myself, lapping up the icy water for as long as my hands could bear the pain. The water quickly gave me what our kids call an "ice-cream headache."

When I finished I shook off as much water as possible and then crossed my arms, thrusting my shivering hands under my armpits, against the fabric of my turtleneck sweater, warming them as much as I could to prevent frostbite from developing beyond the first warning signs. When my hands had recovered from the numbness and pain, we turned to head back toward our shelter.

By the time we made it back across the road and up into the cave we were exhausted, and my wet feet were beginning to freeze. But I was amazed at how quickly my body heat had dried the armpits of my turtleneck.

The plastic outer shells of our boots had turned brittle and seemed to conduct the cold. I began to wonder if they were doing more harm than good and I decided that, here in the shelter of the cave, we could do without them. We pulled off our boots and socks and we both stuffed our soggy socks beneath us, on the bed of pine boughs, to see if our body heat would dry them out. Then I instructed Matthew to maneuver so that he could place his feet against the bare skin of my belly. As he did so, I silently checked his feet, looking for signs of white on the calluses, as they had appeared on my hands. I did not see any of these symptoms, but I was concerned to see some signs of swelling around his toes. The color of the skin was also an alarming gray, broken by patches of redness.

To keep Matt's mind busy as we lay at this awkward angle, and to help him understand the critical tasks we faced, I gave him a bit of a physiology lesson. I explained that the body is designed to preserve the core temperature of its vital internal organs. Blood circulation is greatest in the torso, making it the area of highest body heat. Conversely, since the extremities are less important to sustain life, they receive much less circulation. "That is why your hands and feet, particularly your fingers and toes, get cold first," I said. "They are farther away from the heart and thus receive less blood supply. That makes them more prone to frostbite. What we are attempting to do is transfer body heat from this core—my stomach—to your vulnerable feet."

After about fifteen minutes we switched positions—scraping ourselves in the process—so that my feet could benefit from the warmth of his body.

Checking the condition of our socks, I discovered that mine had dried fairly well. But Matthew's were still soaked, and I did not want him to put them back on. So I folded the ends of the blue jean cuffs over his bare toes and used the safety pins from our lift tickets to fasten them. My jeans were long enough to allow this, but from time to time the pins worked their way loose.

The storm raged about us, obliterating the sunlight, encompassing us in dismal gray.

Mary

Sister Bernadine called. Since our arrival in Turkey, we had been attending Mass at a chapel that we affectionately referred to as the "Vatican," because it was located on the grounds of the Vatican Embassy in Ankara. Our priest, Monsignor Eugene Nugent, who also bore the responsibilities of the Vatican ambassador, spent much of his time working with refugees and others in need of the Church's assistance in this primarily Muslim country. On Sunday mornings, he offered the only English-speaking Mass in Ankara. Sister Bernadine, a sixty-five-year-old dynamo, was the monsignor's right-hand aide. She stood only about four-foot-ten, with close-cropped light brown hair that was turning gray. Originally from Holland, she had lived in Boston for twenty years of her life and spoke English with a pronounced Dutch accent. With the news spreading, Sister Bernadine knew that dozens of friends from the "Vatican" would be anxious to know what was going on, but she also knew that I could not field constant telephone calls. She volunteered to be the conduit of information to the other parishioners and I gratefully agreed. We would speak once or twice a day and she would establish a phone tree to spread the latest reports.

Marissa seemed to take all this activity in stride, busying herself by watching a variety of movies and borrowed videos. Occasionally she sought me out, wordlessly looking for reassurance that everything was going to be all right, and then she would find some means to entertain herself.

As noontime approached we all stared at the maddeningly silent telephone. "I should have asked Colonel Fitzgerald to call at lunchtime with an update," I said.

Pam nodded her agreement.

Mike

Periodically we repeated the foot-warming procedure.

As a boy I had been a Civil Air Patrol cadet and had, of course, learned much more about search-and-rescue procedures during my years as an Air Force pilot. Further, my skiing experiences had introduced me to some of the methods used to search for someone who is lost on the slopes. I attempted to keep up Matthew's hopes by sharing some of this knowledge and assuring him that someone was going to find us.

"Bruise," I began, "I'm pretty sure someone has to be looking for us right now, even with all this snow coming down. Do you remember all these people in red ski jackets when we went skiing in Colorado?"

"You mean the ski patrol guys?" he asked.

"Yeah, that's it. I'm guessing that they must have a ski patrol here, too, and I am sure they are combing the slopes, looking for us. At first they will spend all their time looking in the areas near the resort, but I think that when they don't find us they will start expanding outward, covering all the roads in the area. Maybe that's why they haven't gotten here yet. I'm guessing that they have snowmobiles that they can use to check all the roads and if they do, they'll have no trouble finding us here, with our skis marking our location."

Matthew was somewhat encouraged and wanted to hear more.

"If that doesn't work," I said, "they may start searching from the air, using helicopters or airplanes, and searching in grids, covering every square inch of the area. At first they'll start with a small 'box' centered on the resort, but they will expand this box outward if they don't find us. So I think we have to stay put and let them have a chance to find us. I am very hopeful that they will."

"Okay," he said.

There was a hint of skepticism in his voice. I resolved to remain alert for any mood changes he displayed. Matthew sometimes tends toward pessimism.

Our two biggest tasks were to keep warm and to stay hydrated. The trek over to the stream had been arduous. I thought back to my survival training. Instructors had shown us many photographs of white, waxy flesh on hands and feet. The fact that these spots had appeared on the calluses of my hands indicated that the damage had not yet penetrated deeply into the softer flesh, but it was clearly an ominous sign of danger. I was also concerned about repeatedly trying to pull on our boots over semifrozen feet. I could remember an instructor lecturing, "Once something is frozen, don't mess with it. And if tissue thaws, don't allow it to refreeze, under any circumstance." Each time we put our boots back on we risked violating these rules.

I decided that we would have to strike a delicate balance between eating snow and drinking stream water. We should not eat snow constantly. But we would limit our trips to the stream, doing a "water run" when we had some other reason to go out.

I slipped Matthew inside my overalls—discovering to my relief that the pants were big enough to hold us both. We zipped the overalls and my jacket tightly around us, attempting to gather warmth from one another.

We must have dozed quite a bit, for the day seemed to pass quickly. When we felt the need to urinate, we found that we could crawl just outside the cave and aim the flow downhill, so that we did not have to struggle with our boots.

Mary

Enis worked his magic. When I slipped downstairs to our own apartment, I found that the telephone service had been re-connected. We shifted our vigil from the Handys' apartment to our own home.

Our telephone outlet was located in what we called the piano room. The player piano, a gift from Mike's mother, was the centerpiece of the room, and it was a comfortable environment, featuring a couch in burgundy, green, navy, and mauve stripes that complemented the colors of the Turkish carpet—a Herike "9-mountain flower" design popular with Americans stationed here. The marble mantel over the fireplace held a collection of knickknacks that we had assembled during our various travels. Although this was designated as a first-floor apartment, in fact it was one story above the garage and the building's lobby. One entire wall of the room was a bank of windows overlooking the balcony that allowed us an elevated view of the area. I sat in the moss-green recliner, in front of our makeshift bookcase—a slab of marble sitting atop a radiator—and next to the end table that held the phone. A glance at the collection of family photos on top of our piano brought a painful lump to my throat.

I asked Cathryn if she would assume the responsibility of passing along information to the members of our Bible study groups, and to other friends, so that my phone line would remain as open as possible. She readily agreed. It was about 3 P.M. when she prepared to leave, so that she could report to our Monday Bible study group. The group was nondenominational, and it brought Catholics and Protestants, charismatics and noncharismatics, in a visible testimony of the various manifestations of God's grace. It was a comforting thought to know that Christians of all philosophies would be praying for Mike and Matthew.

Cathryn asked me if I would like for her to return tomorrow to pray with me. I responded with an immediate "Yes." I also asked her to stay in close contact with Norita Erickson, the leader of the Monday study group. Norita is a dark-haired California woman with a bubbly personality. Along with her husband, Ken, Norita had spent many years in the Netherlands working as a missionary with Turkish Christians, and now they lived here. Ken had set up a small shop that manufactured wheelchairs that were sturdy, but lightweight and inexpensive, and thus could be used in the Turkish villages. Both were active in the burgeoning Turkish Protestant Fellowship. Norita believed deeply in the power of prayer and was frequently impressed with scriptural messages.

By now I began to worry that the story was getting news coverage in Turkey. I realized that I had a difficult task to perform and I was at least grateful that I could use my own phone. Concerned that the wire services would pick up the story and publicize it in the United States, I knew that I had to break the news to both sides of the family. Care was required. My dad, Bill Kettler, six-foot-three, is a two-hundred-pound, no-nonsense guy, a retired aerospace engineer who had worked on military contracts all his life. But a few years earlier he underwent quadruple bypass surgery. He had suffered through my mom's death last year, and I did not want him to be shocked further by learning of Mike and Matthew's disappearance from a TV or newspaper report.

Mike's mother was yet another consideration. Cecile Couillard is a retired grocery store checker living outside of Lewiston, Maine. In 1988, while attempting to drive himself to a hospital emergency room, Mike's father had died of a heart attack. During the early morning hours, when it was still dark, the police had arrived to break the devastating news to Mike's mother, Cecile. Now, from thousands of miles away, I had to bring her more upsetting information.

I knew from our years in the military that when bad news has to be delivered, it is best to make sure the recipient is not alone. In fact, this was precisely why Angela and Pam were staying close to me now. But how could I make sure, from some six thousand miles away, that someone was with Cecile when I broke the news that her son and grandson were missing? I remembered that Mike's Uncle Eddie and Aunt Irene lived near Cecile in Lisbon, Maine, and I flipped through my address book, searching for their number. I probably stared directly at it, but my eyes fogged over and my brain spun so wildly that I could not concentrate. Finally, I found the number of Mike's sister Monique, who lived in Colorado. I called and told her, as calmly as I could, that Mike and Matthew had gone skiing the previous day. But they had not come down from the mountain and I needed to inform Cecile before she heard something on the TV or the radio. Before I could ask for Eddie and Irene's phone number, Monique started to cry hysterically. I waited for a moment and then became impatient with her. "You have to get hold of yourself, Monique," I snapped. "I need Uncle Eddie and Aunt Irene's phone number so that I can have them with your mom. Monique, get a grip."

"I'm sorry," she said. "I'll go get it." In a few moments she came back on the line and gave me the number.

"I'm sorry I had to bring you this news," I apologized. "I'm sure they'll be fine, but I have to call your mom."

It was late afternoon in Turkey but nearing lunchtime in Maine when I placed the transatlantic call to Eddie and Irene. After a few short rings the answering machine responded and I left a carefully worded message: "This is Mary, call me when you get home. It's very important." I left my number.

Before long Irene called me back, and I was relieved to realize that Cecile was at her side. The two women had enjoyed a morning of shopping and had found my message waiting when they returned to Irene's home. They knew immediately that something was wrong.

Irene took the news with relative calm and immediately put Cecile on the phone.

When I repeated my brief description of the events, Cecile began to wail and pray at the same time.

Irene took the phone from her and assumed command of the situation on her side of the world. She explained that she was going to take Cecile home to pack some clothes and bring her back. Cecile would stay with Irene and Eddie for however long this ordeal lasted.

I tried several calls to my dad's number in Los Angeles but was only able to reach his answering machine, so I called my twin brother, Ed, in Dallas; Dad had spent the holidays there. Responding to my news, Ed reported that Dad had gone to Phoenix to attend the funeral of a close friend.

My brother was immediately full of questions regarding the search. "What are they doing?" he asked. "Haven't they got helicopters? Are they going to use any special tracking devices, like infrared equipment?"

I did not know, but I assured him that I would ask Colonel Fitzgerald.

Ed agreed to set the family news chain in motion. He would notify my brothers John, George, and Charles and my sister, Kate. Kate would track down our dad and break the news to him as gently as possible. She would also keep in touch with Mike's West Coast siblings, Dan, Cindy, and Jim.

Finally I called our old friends Diana and Paul Freeman, who live in Maryland. We had met them in Arkansas when we all joined the Officers' Christian Fellowship Bible Study, and we had remained in contact ever since. I asked them to notify our other numerous friends who were stationed all over the world, and to start a global circle of prayer.

Mike

As darkness descended, the temperature dropped and the blizzard returned in full fury. Our spirits sagged with the realization that no one was going to find us today. We would have to spend a second night alone on this frozen mountain.

We talked a lot about the other members of our family. "At least we know we're alive, but the guys at home are going to be worried about us," I said.

In the evening at home when we gathered around the dinner table to say grace, Matthew was often the last one to cooperate. We never wanted prayer to be a negative experience, so we tried not to make an issue of it. Sometimes when we prepared for our bedtime prayers, he complained, "I can't think of anything to pray for." But out here the words came easily. "God," he asked with sincerity, "why are You doing this to us?"

It was an obvious question with no readily apparent answer.

Mary

In the evening, Colonel Fitzgerald finally called. After quickly informing me that they still had not found any trace of Mike or Matthew, he asked if either of them had taken a backpack along.

"No," I replied. "Why?"

"Because we found one buried in the snow," he explained.

"No, unfortunately, they didn't have one with them," I said.

The colonel told me about the teams that were systematically searching the mountain and he promised that they would be working through the night.

He assured me that as soon as the weather cleared, they

were going to use Nighthawk helicopters, and he explained
that these were high-tech versions of the Army's workhorse
Blackhawk helicopter. The Nighthawks were equipped with
thermal detectors, infrared sensors, and other special equipment. But he complained that a ridiculous amount of red tape
was gumming things up. Turkish officials would not authorize
air refueling over land, so the only place the helicopters could
refuel was over the Black Sea. Because of the inclement
weather, this would require special equipment. They were trying to work out the details.

Finally he initiated a routine that we would follow. At the
end of each day he would report to me and he would talk to
Pam Jaccard as well. That way Pam and I could compare notes
to make sure that nothing was forgotten or misunderstood.

I worried about Mark. I knew that Wanda would look after
him, but that was not the same as Mom. I also feared that if
Mike and Matthew were found hurt . . . or worse . . . they
would be taken directly to the hotel, where Mark would have
to confront reality by himself. We were a family, and I wanted
us to be together to face whatever we had to face. "I'm thinking
that Mark needs to come home," I said.

"Well, it's too late to do that today," the colonel responded.
"It's getting dark already and they could never get down the
mountain. It's still snowing." And then he added something
that I had not considered. "I don't want to rush Mark into
leaving. He might feel like he is abandoning ship. Although
he's not actually searching, he feels like he's a part of what is
being done here. He's on the team. If we pull him out too
early it might impact him poorly. He might feel like we don't
believe they will be found."

After the colonel hung up I tried to assess the situation as
calmly as I could. What more should I do? What more could
I do?

Five separate spheres of information and activity were swirling. Colonel Fitzgerald would keep me apprised of the search
activities. Pam and Angela were keeping an eye on Marissa
and running my household with military efficiency. Sister Ber-

nadine was the information funnel for the "Vatican" parishioners. Family would be kept informed through an efficient phone chain.

And, perhaps most importantly, the Freemans in Virginia and Cathryn in Ankara were coordinating prayer groups.

With the other women I sat in the kitchen eating a dinner that Angela had prepared. The long day of activity was ending and the darkness over Ankara seemed to creep indoors, causing me to shiver. Mike and Matthew would not be found today. I was warm, well fed, and in the company of friends. They would have to spend a second night alone, cold, hungry, and miserable, somewhere on that desolate mountain.

The friends who had stayed close to me all day had husbands and families of their own to care for. But they did not want me to be alone with Marissa all night long. This dilemma was solved when Norita stopped by, along with Angelina Reddy, another woman from our Ladies' Bible Study Group whom I knew only slightly. Angelina was unmarried, so she volunteered to spend the night in our apartment, so that I would have some adult companionship. In fact, she had enough luggage with her to indicate that she was prepared for an extended vigil; obviously my friends were covering as many contingencies as possible.

Norita visited with me briefly and assured me that she would share with me any scriptural messages that were impressed upon her.

Finally everyone left to return to their own families. Angelina, Marissa, and I were alone, and we prepared for a long night.

We had a telephone extension in the bedroom, but something was wrong with the ringing mechanism, and I had to be able to hear the phone. So I pulled the phone from the piano room into the hallway and placed it on top of an inverted metal pie plate so that I would be sure to hear it when—if—it rang in the middle of the night.

As bedtime approached, Marissa asked if she could sleep with me and I decided to let her, for as long as this crisis continued. At the end of this busy day her mind began to deal with questions that she had shelved earlier. She asked, "Where are Daddy and Matthew? Mom, why is this happening to us?"

"I don't know," I answered, "but we have to wait and see what's going to happen. We have to remember that God's in charge."

I hugged her to me.

We spent a few minutes in prayer. Marissa asked God to protect her father and brother and bring them safely home to us. Soon she was fast asleep.

I needed some answers. "Lord," I asked, "Please tell me what You want me to do. I know You were upset when You found Your disciples sleeping at Gethsemane. Should I spend this night in prayer or should I rest in Your peace?"

He gave me the answer, allowing me to drift into sleep. I awakened twice during the night to engage in silent prayer.

Mike

Throughout the long night we dozed off and on, never sleeping more than thirty minutes at a time. Whenever spasms of cold woke us both at the same time I found Matt very disoriented and frightened. Once he told me, "I had a dream that I was sleeping in my own bed and Mom was making chocolate chip cookies. She said, 'Here, have a glass of milk,' and then I woke up." That story made my own stomach growl.

Matthew drifted back into sleep.

But I lay awake, haunted now by my son's questioning prayer earlier in the evening. It was indeed a temptation to wonder why God was doing this to us. But I knew that I was the one who had gotten us into this situation. Our plight was the result of choices I had made. I mentally kicked myself for having bypassed the crude loggers' sheds that we had seen during the early stages of our frantic run down the mountain.

I had lived a very blessed life. Certainly there were minor problems along the way, but perhaps I had never been faced with a really big trial. Now it had come and I was determined not to crumble.

The story of Job came to mind. When one calamity after another fell upon Job, his wife suggested bitterly, "Why don't you just curse God and die?" But Job refused, and was eventually delivered from his misery.

From my quiet, lonely, icy shelter, I sent a promise to heaven: God, no matter what happens—even if we are to die in this cave—I will never curse You. As hard as it may be to accept, what I want for us both is what You want. Your will be done.

A scripture flashed into my memory:

Yet He slay me, I will always praise Him.

My prayer took on the aspects of a bargain: God, I've been pretty dedicated, I think. We've served You in a lot of ways. We've been leaders in prayer groups, very involved in the church. But I know that in a lot of ways my life really hasn't been as dedicated and totally committed to You as I would have wanted. If we ever get out of this, my life will belong to You in a new way—more than it ever has in the past.

DAY 3

•

Tuesday, January 17

Mary

The first thing in the morning, when I trudged out to the kitchen, my eyes were drawn to the small round table and the five stools surrounding it. Tears welled in my eyes and a lump formed in my throat.

The kitchen stools were symbolic. The move to Turkey had been our fourth in as many years. Once again we faced a long delay before many of our personal effects arrived. Confronted with the task of turning yet another strange apartment into a home, I had found myself beset by lethargy, perhaps exacerbated by the death of my mother shortly after we arrived. Several dreary months passed as I tried to settle in, but I did not feel like nesting.

The kitchen, although large, had precious little counter space. Whenever I walked into it all I saw was a huge, nearly empty, almost useless room with walls tiled in varying shades of olive green and tan. Finally one morning I had decided that I had to do something about it. I would start with furniture. The room was certainly large enough to fashion some sort of eat-in arrangement. I asked my Turkish friend Rumeysa Datillo to accompany me to a local shopping district to see what I could find. Rumeysa is a Turkish woman whose husband Tony is a U.S. Air Force officer who headed the legal section at ODC. Rumeysa is the mother of Mark's friend Doğan, and she lived in the same apartment house as Wanda and Bryn Villers. A petite woman who wore her hair short and dyed it blond, as many Turkish women did, Rumeysa was our "shopping queen." She was a godsend to many of us military wives as she guided us through the complex local customs, wherein haggling over price was expected and even appreciated as part of the game. If we attempted to shop without Rumeysa's help, we paid too much.

On this day, Rumeysa and I returned with a round gateleg table and five wooden stools. Mike had seen similar kitchen furniture in a Spiegel catalog, and he had noted that the stools had been painted with various designs. We decided to duplicate that look; each of us personalized the top of our own kitchen stool. Mine was a bright red, yellow, and black poppy design. Mark, the most artistic of us, painted a beautiful Greek sunburst. Matthew created a tortoiseshell pattern. Marissa painted hers red, outlined it in green, and added black seeds, fashioning a watermelon. Mike's turned out to be a guitar front, with the pick held in place by the strings. This shared activity lifted my spirits. My energy returned and I soon found myself happily creating a home once again.

But now, no one sat on Matthew's tortoiseshell, eagerly awaiting breakfast. Mike's guitar was silent.

I put water on to boil and fled the room as quickly as possible.

Get yourself together, Mary, I ordered. Do something.

Our bathroom had a unique German feel to it. Blue tile stretched from floor to ceiling. A porcelain sink, a large mirror, and shelves flanked one wall. Mike had formed the habit of writing Bible verses on three-by-five cards so that he could carry them around and memorize them. Here on the bathroom shelf, I found two blue and white index cards that had been well handled. In Mike's handwriting I read the messages of Philippians 4:6–7 and Proverbs 3:5:

> *Have no anxiety at all, but in everything, by prayer and petition, with thanksgiving, make your requests known to God. Then the peace of God that surpasses all understanding will guard your hearts and minds in Christ Jesus.*

    Trust in the Lord with all your heart and do not lean on your own understanding. In all your ways acknowledge Him and He will direct your path.

Holding the cards and comprehending their messages seemed to bring me closer to Mike. I stood still for a short time staring at his familiar handwriting. Knowing that he had committed these verses to memory lifted my spirits.

The Search

The Turkish government promised full cooperation, but problems developed along the chain of command. From the standpoint of logistics, this was the worst possible time for American personnel to attempt to coordinate a search. The U.S. ambassador had left Turkey in the beginning of December, leaving his assistant, James Holmes, as the acting ambassador. At about the same time the major general who commanded ODC had also been transferred and Colonel Fitzgerald, at the moment, was only the acting ODC commander, and he was a colonel who had to deal with Turkish officers who carried higher rank. Both men were capable, but they lacked the all-important quality—in the eyes of some Turkish bureaucrats—of status. Thus, there were leadership gaps in both the diplomatic and military spheres.

Despite these obstacles, the ground search continued. Overnight, a twenty-two-man team, under the direction of Lieutenant Colonel David, was transported from Akinci, a munitions site near Ankara, to Kartalkaya Mountain. They now joined a dozen or more men from the ski resort and about ten volunteers from ODC and the American Embassy in Ankara. Beginning at daybreak, they hunted on foot through an area radiating two and one-half miles out from the Doruk Ski Lodge.

More help was on the way. Turkish authorities promised

that about forty Turkish commandos would join the search by tomorrow.

Meanwhile, Captain Timothy E. "Fitz" Fitzgerald (no relation to Colonel Fitzgerald) assembled a fifteen-man team from A Company, 3rd Battalion, 10th Special Forces Group (Airborne). These Green Berets were experienced hands in dealing with mountain terrain and blizzard conditions. Fitz loaded them onto a C-130 Shadow refueling aircraft for a flight from Incirlik to Akinci Air Base, where a bus waited to take them to the mountain.

Back at Incirlik, Sully and Lieutenant Gardner were now an inseparable two-man team. Gardner exhibited such good control of the ground forces that Sully was able to focus his efforts on the air operations. He had the two Nighthawks in the air by 6:01 A.M. Pony 21 and Pony 22 diverted around bad weather and flew toward Bolu, where they had now received clearance to refuel. Penetrating clouds and icing conditions, they landed at Bolu, refueled, and proceeded to Kartalkaya Mountain. They began their systematic search, working as best they could around the clouds that still covered much of the area.

One searcher told a reporter: "He's an aviator and has been through survival training. We're looking through some summer cottages in outlying areas; they may also be in a cave or have built themselves a snow igloo."

Mike

When I woke I guessed that the sun had been up for a couple of hours already. Matthew and I had both dozed off and on through the early hours.

This morning the blizzard conditions were abating, but the mountain ridges were covered with clouds. From our vantage point in this valley, we looked up to them. I hoped that this respite in the storm would aid and encourage the searchers, but I also knew that they would be slowed by the cloud cover, which to them would simply be fog. By now, they should have covered the immediate area of the ski slope. Standard operating procedure would call for them to gradually broaden the search pattern. They would surely find us today.

We ate our final two pieces of strawberry candy, exhausting our food supply.

Matt and I were lying side by side in the cave when we slowly became aware of a sound that was growing in intensity. Is another airliner passing overhead? I wondered.

But before long the sound became stronger, and it turned into a characteristic, rhythmic *thump-thump-thump*. It echoed against the ice-covered ridges off to our left.

Matt's eyes widened in excitement.

"Helicopter!" I said.

Matthew nodded. "Oh, God, please let them come to us," he pleaded. "If they don't get closer, they'll never see us. Please, God, bring the helicopter to us."

It was a desperate cry and perhaps the most fervent prayer I had ever heard him utter. I echoed his words with a silent "Amen!"

From a half-sitting position I reached for my stiff, frozen boots. Bent over with my back against the rocky wall at an awkward angle, I struggled to pull them over my swollen feet. Excruciating pains shot through my legs. These boots were made to attach to skis, not for use as normal footwear. The front and back halves are connected by a hinge. I had to slide the front portion of my foot into the solid toe of the boot, then rotate the back half into place and slide two plastic bayonets into their catches, mating the forward and rear portions of the boot. I labored at the task for what seemed like an eternity but was really about a half hour, suffering with every movement, but the continuing sound of the helicopter blades motivated me.

By the time I finally had my boots on I could tell from the sound that the helicopter was at the far end of its pattern. I could visualize what the pilot was doing. Procedures dictated that he would confine his search to a well-defined "box" on the map. He was zigzagging his way back and forth through that box, climbing farther up the valley that was formed on one side by the ridge on our left. I waited until I could hear that his systematic search procedure was drawing closer to us.

We had been aware of the copter's presence for about forty-five minutes when I told Matthew, "Okay, I'm going out now and I'm going to stay out a while. Maybe they'll come even closer." I reasoned that the activity would keep me tolerably warm, but I knew that Matthew, lying idly in the cave; would suffer without the benefit of my body heat. I ripped off my blue ski jacket, handed it to him, and told him to bundle up. The additional advantage was that my outer garment was now a bright red turtleneck sweater that I hoped would attract the attention of the search crew.

I scrambled out of the cave and looked about, amazed that anyone was flying in this overcast weather. I listened in silence, my ears attuned to every nuance of the sounds. I prayed that the pilot would somehow expand the parameters of his search box.

About ten minutes passed. The sound of the rotor blades fluctuated, growing louder, then fainter, then louder again, but always remaining off to the left, well beyond the road and the stream and over a distant ridge, hidden from view by the low cloud cover.

But suddenly the clouds over the distant ridgeline began to roll back, exposing the treeline along the crest and a backdrop of brilliant blue sky. The helicopter appeared, emerging through the hole in the clouds. It hovered over the adjacent ridge, so distant from us, yet so close. I recognized the type of aircraft immediately. It was a Blackhawk.

"Help!" I screamed at the top of my lungs as I jumped about, waving my arms wildly. "Help! Help!" I knew that my voice could never be heard above the clatter of the helicopter blades, but the screams came naturally. My heart pounded. Our lives hung in the balance of a fleeting glance from just one pair of eyes aboard the craft! I realized that we were in a shrouded area, a deep ravine between two ridges, with tall pine trees all around us. We were difficult to spot.

"Help! Help!" I continued to scream.

The copter searched the area only briefly, then turned away and disappeared back into the cloud cover. The receding sound of the blades left me feeling empty and depressed.

After a time I could no longer hear the distant thumping of helicopter blades. I held my breath, straining to hear, waiting for the sound to return. But finally I reconciled myself to reality. The chopper was gone.

I crawled back into the cave to warm myself with Matthew, and to try to cheer us both. "Those are American helicopters looking for us, Matthew," I reported. "I'm sure that they are going to keep looking." I pointed out the positive: At least this was proof that people were looking for us—not just Turks, but Americans!

We generally had only two or three Blackhawks in the country at any given time, I explained. They were used by the U.S. Army in support of Operation Provide Comfort. Two Blackhawks had been shot down over northern Iraq the previous April, in a tragic and notorious "friendly fire" incident that had claimed the lives of so many Turks and Americans. I knew that the U.S. government was helping to equip the Turkish Army with Blackhawks, but this was more likely one of ours, since the Blackhawk deal was relatively young and the Turks did not yet have many in their inventory. I was dumbfounded and extremely humbled by the thought that the commanders who were coordinating Operation Provide Comfort from Incirlik Air Base were willing to divert a Blackhawk from its primary mission to come and look for us. As an operations officer, it was my job to arrange the details of flight missions, coordinate the schedules and routes, and handle liaison details with the Turkish military. Obviously, a great deal of effort was involved, just in getting this one helicopter out to search—and its presence was a positive sign.

I had assumed that search-and-rescue teams would head out

with snowmobiles and first search all of the trails within the resort area itself. Then I reasoned that after a day or two they would begin to send people down the roads. But I had not really counted on an air search, at least not this soon and in such bad weather.

Matthew's hopes were noticeably elevated. He said, "If those are American helicopters, I'm sure they'll keep looking for us until they find us, won't they, Dad?"

"I'm sure they will, Matt," I responded. "If not today, then tomorrow or the next day."

"Let's pray that they come back today, then," he said.

I let him lead the prayer so that I could get a better sense of what he was feeling. He could express his fears and, at the same time, exert about as much control over the situation— little as it was—that either of us could have.

"Oh, please bring it back," Matthew implored.

I added, "Lord, You're going to actually have to steer that person's eyes to look down in our direction, because it is so hard to see us."

After the prayer I could tell from Matthew's silence that he had fallen deep into thought. "What are you thinking?" I prodded.

"Will they land on the road?" he asked. This was a positive sign of his mood and a welcome distraction from our plight.

I answered, "No, I don't think they could, Bruise. But they have ways of getting us out real quickly without landing. If they spot us they'll lower a basket or a harness while the helicopter is hovering as low as it can. It wouldn't take long to have us both inside. I'll help you get up first and then they can lower it one more time for me."

"Cool," Matthew said, his face brightening. "Just like in the movies. I'd like to do that."

"I think you may get your chance," I said. "Let's hope it's soon."

If only I had some means of starting a fire; searchers would certainly spot smoke from the air. But in the absence of a fire, I did whatever else I could to highlight our position. I took

Matthew's frozen sweatshirt and draped it across the top of a low pine tree just outside the mouth of our cave. We had given it to him for Christmas only a few weeks earlier, and it was one of his favorites. The colorful pattern of black, red, and royal blue stood out against the white background of the snow.

Mary

Pam and Angela arrived on schedule to help me maintain the vigil, but many others decided to help, too. A constant stream of people came and went as the day progressed—military and civilian wives, fellow parishioners from the "Vatican," members of our Bible study group, Turkish friends. It seemed as if everyone we knew in Ankara had decided to join my unofficial support group.

Many arrived bearing gifts of food, and help came from some people whom I did not even know. For example, the wife of the British air attaché sent over her driver with food and a signed card. I had never even met her.

Soon a variety of casseroles, fruits, salads, and desserts filled the kitchen counters; the clear favorite was lasagna. I appreciated every visit, every gift, every attempt to help.

Two men called from the Office of Special Investigations (OSI), the military equivalent of the FBI. They asked me to find good, recent photographs of Mike and Matthew to aid the searchers, and said that they would be over later to pick them up.

Mike's photo was fairly easy to find. I knew that the OSI men would want crisp, clear, full-face close-up shots. At the ODC Christmas party only a few weeks earlier a photographer had taken pictures of each of us individually, so I had a great shot of Mike in his "Mess Dress" uniform, the military equivalent of a tuxedo. As I held the photo in my hand Mike looked back at me, exhibiting his great smile. He looked as handsome as ever. Suddenly a painful thought stabbed at me. This photo was irreplaceable. What if he did not come back from the mountain and I could not get the photo back? Get a grip, Mary, I lectured myself. Do what has to be done.

My quest for Matthew's photo was more difficult. Because we had been home-schooling, I did not have a recent school picture; the latest one I could find was from 1991. We had some vacation photos that showed Matthew, but not very well. I had been telling myself for months that I needed to get some pictures taken—but it was too late now. Finally, I found a photo that Mike had taken of Matthew in the soccer uniform he wore as part of the Youth Sports League. This, too, was older than I would have liked, but it fit the bill better than anything else. And, I realized, I had the negative for this photo in case . . .

Stop it, Mary, I told myself.

The Search

The Doruk Kaya Ski Resort lies seventy-two-hundred feet above sea level. Major Hal Tinsley of ODC told a reporter, "It's hard to get your breath at the top. You're stopping every fifty meters to catch your breath, or dig yourself out of a hole."

Colonel Ken Jaccard was exhausted. He had searched from dawn until dark the previous day, but his sleep had been plagued by restless dreams. He woke very early this morning with a plan, implanted by his dreams. Now, designated as the head of one of the search parties, he led his men across the mountainous terrain, marching nearly shoulder to shoulder. Remembering his dreams, he periodically told some of his search partners, "I just *know* that if we go out and turn *this* way, instead of the way we turned yesterday, we will find them."

But they did not.

Ken's team paid special attention to the areas just off the ski runs where the snow had drifted into deep and dangerous formations. Occasionally one of the searchers fell into an air pocket beneath a drift and others had to pull him out before the snow closed in about him. Ken worried that Mike and Matthew had simply disappeared into one of these.

The search party worked its way down the mountain for several hours. Eventually they arrived in a small village, where someone directed them to the mayor. The mayor explained that Ken's group was the third search party to end up in this village. He also told Ken that when he first heard of the missing Americans he had arranged for someone to go to the outlying cabins that faced the woods in the direction of the ski area. They had lit fires in the cabins, just in case Mike and Matthew stumbled onto them. Periodically, the mayor said, various people from the village had gone out to search, but had found nothing.

Mary

Everyone jumped whenever the phone rang. Late in the morning Pam took a call from Colonel Bob Penar, assistant to Colonel Fitzgerald. He is a tall, lanky, likable Pennsylvanian with a pleasant southern accent acquired from years of assignments in Georgia. As head of the Air Force Section at ODC, he was Mike's boss. And, as Colonel Fitzgerald was directing the on-site search, Colonel Penar was in charge of the "command post" at ODC here in Ankara. Pam called me over to speak to him.

"Mary," Colonel Penar said, "if you've been watching the news you may have heard a report that they've been found." Before I could react he added quickly, "We've already determined that it's not true. It's definitely been proven wrong. So if you hear it, don't believe it."

"No," I replied, "I had not heard that. I'm glad you warned me."

"I'm going to be the person to bring you information from here on," he said. He cautioned me to ignore any rumors or news stories unless they were confirmed by him, or Colonel Fitzgerald, or Jim Holmes, the acting ambassador at the U.S. Embassy.

"Thanks, I understand."

I gained a quick education about the reliability of the media coverage. Norita came over with a copy of a local tabloid that featured a story about Mike and Matthew. We called upon our Turkish friend Emra Başaran to translate the article for us. He was a blond-haired, mild-mannered dentist married to an American doctor based at Incirlik and, as a Christian friend, he was happy to help us out. First Emra was able to determine that the newspaper had misspelled Mike's name and had his age wrong. What followed was a fabricated story claiming that Mike was an Alaskan-trained, James Bond–style commando whose assignment with ODC was so secret that it could not be discussed. The inference was that Mike's and Matthew's disappearance had some mysterious, even nefarious meaning. This was absurd, but it alerted me to the fact that I would have to contend with irresponsible reporting.

At lunchtime, Pam, Angela, Marissa, and I gathered around the television to watch the Armed Forces Network's local news report. The anchorman announced that Lieutenant Colonel Michael Couillard and his son Matthew were lost while skiing in the mountains near Bolu, Turkey. The report featured quotes from an interview with someone who conjectured that, due to Mike's Air Force Academy survival training, his chances for survival were good. But when asked about Matthew's chances of survival, the answer was "unknown."

Pam quickly switched off the television. I was furious. None of us could believe the stupidity of these insensitive comments. I simply could not understand how anyone could assume that Matthew's chances were less than Mike's, let alone voice the sentiment. Mike and Matthew were together!

I walked into the bedroom that Mark and Matthew shared. My hand swiped gently across the spread on Matthew's unmade bed. My eyes glanced at the array of objects that awaited his return—Legos, his plastic reptile collection, a football, a soccer ball, and the cricket set we had bought during a trip to England. But the room was achingly empty of sound and activity. Tears stung at my eyes and a lump in my throat threatened to strangle me but I could not allow myself the luxury of a breakdown.

Angela found me in the boys' bedroom. Closing the door, she sat me down on the edge of Matthew's bed and stared into my eyes. "Let it out, Mary," she urged. "Don't you want to just have a big cry and get it all out?"

My shoulders slumped and my head bent down. I began to sob—hard, breathtaking sobs. A part of me welcomed the relief of tears, but another, more lucid side listened to the sounds I was making. Was I crying or engaged in some uncontrollable hysterical laughter? I did not like what I was hearing. Stop it now, Mary, I lectured myself. Get a grip. You cannot, you must not fall apart now

Mike

The clouds finally rolled back to reveal a deep blue sky and brilliant sunlight. I was now able to take in the complete panorama. Snow-covered pine trees stood tall on the steep slopes that surrounded this valley. The road we had traveled cut a narrow groove into the mountainside. The tops of the ridges paralleled the road on either side of us and I could not see much beyond them. But the brightness and beauty of the scene was in stark contrast to the incessant snowfall and thick, gloomy clouds of the previous days. The bright sunlight brought rays of hope, penetrating to the depths of my heart. A familiar verse came to mind, which now seemed so appro-

priate. I was sure that it was from the Psalms. I did not have
my Bible with me, so all I could do was paraphrase and piece
together the words:

> I cast mine eyes to the hills
> From whence does my help come.
> My help is in the Lord who made heaven and earth.

I had always been struck by the Psalmist's ability to be so
brutally honest with God, expressing utter despair and even
anger, yet always go on to worship his creator. The beauty
of God's creation now filled this place, and it was a great
testimony to His power. The words of that Psalm now became my prayer and I knew that God was here in this valley
to hear it. My help would—must—come from Him and
Him alone.

Although the terrain around us was covered with many feet
of fresh snow, the temperature at the moment was compara-
tively warm, so I used the opportunity to keep Matt busy—
and keep his mind off the failed search effort. I helped him
out of the cave and pointed toward a patch of sunshine where
we could attempt to get comfortable. Since he was barefoot
inside my oversized blue jeans, I needed to protect his feet.
Utilizing his otherwise useless ski bibs, I laid them out on the
snow as a protective mat and helped him crawl on his knees
until we reached the sunny spot. There was, of course, no way
of knowing how long we would be stuck here, so I wanted to
make our situation as optimal as possible. We took some of
the frozen clothes that we had removed after we stopped the
first night and hung them on tree limbs, where they could
catch the sun's rays and perhaps thaw out enough so that we
could wear them once more.

"I think my feet are going to burst," Matthew said.

Soon the snow squalls returned and we retreated to the cave.
Since my major concern was the condition of our feet, I suggested that we squirm backward into the cave, so that our feet
would be most protected from the weather; perhaps this would

warm them. We crawled in awkwardly and found that the angle of the slope caused our heads to be lower than our feet. Not only was this uncomfortable, but it reduced the vital blood flow to the feet. Nevertheless, we lay in this restricted position for a few hours. But finally I determined that there was little or no improvement in the condition of our feet. Deciding in favor of comfort and better blood circulation, we turned ourselves around and crawled inside headfirst.

I suggested that we once more take turns warming our feet against the skin of each other's belly. "Oh, do we have to do that again?" he complained. "I don't want to." But he complied.

As we maneuvered so that he could place his bare feet against me, I checked the condition of his feet. The swelling appeared to be growing. The skin on the bottom of his feet appeared white and waxy, and there were mottled areas of red, like the color one's nose gets when exposed to the cold. There were more of these red areas on the sides and tops of his feet.

I reminded myself that I had to concentrate on a certain few critical tasks. I had to make sure that we kept our feet warm, and I had to make sure that we drank adequate water. In some ways, these were competing issues. There is a significant difference between eating snow and drinking water, even if the water is very cold. The body has to use considerable energy to melt the snow. This would lower our body temperature, retard blood circulation, and increase the danger of frostbite. But getting Matthew over to the stream to drink unfrozen water was a major undertaking. Matthew could no longer get his swollen feet into his boots, and no matter how well I might try to wrap his feet, they would surely suffer greatly.

After our foot-warming session, I eyed Matthew's otherwise useless ski boots and decided that they were drinking cups. "Just stay here," I said. "I'm going to bring you some water."

Once more I labored into my boots and found that the inner lining of foam was more brittle and difficult to handle. The plastic outer shell separated from the insert, and I had to put the pieces of my boots together before I could don them. The linings, having absorbed moisture, stuck to my semifrozen socks and came loose. It was difficult to force the linings back inside. Furthermore, my feet were beginning to swell. Struggling with the boots took a painful half hour.

With one of Matthew's boots in my hand, I slid backward out of the cave, grabbed one of my ski poles, and made my way down to the road. I set Matthew's boot in the snow and gently slid down the icy slope. By now Matthew and I had trampled the snow enough to create a pathway down to the road. The easy way down was to slide in a crouch, with my feet and my backside skimming the slippery surface.

Once more I was careful not to disturb the large X distress signal in the middle of the road.

I found a spot at the edge of the stream where there were enough boulders to support my weight and where I could kneel on my ski pole, lean over, and reach the water. I spent some time drinking handfuls of water and then I scooped up an extra bootfull to take back to Matthew. I guessed that the boot held three or four cups. Water leaked slowly from the hinge, but I discovered that it would soon freeze, more or less sealing the crack.

This is going to be difficult, I realized. How am I going to get back to the cave without spilling this?

With a boot in my left hand and a ski pole in my right, I retreated to the road, crossed, and surveyed the ten-foot slope ahead of me. There was no choice but to make the short climb in stages. I leaned forward, found a relatively flat place in the snow, and carefully sat down the bootfull of water. Using the ski pole for leverage, I crawled part way up the steep and icy incline. Alternately, I moved the boot and myself up until I had reached the gentler slope. Now I was able to move ahead, carrying the boot in one hand and using my walking stick for leverage in the other.

By the time I reached the cave with my precious burden, I estimated that the entire process had taken me about an hour. It was extremely awkward, but vital.

My aluminum ski poles were hollow inside, so I took one and broke both ends off. It served adequately as a drinking straw. Matthew leaned up on one elbow and drank eagerly.

"Thanks, Dad," he said.

Mary

Angela Shaw surveyed the kitchen counters, crowded with casseroles and side dishes. She asked, "Mary, would it be all right with you if I cleaned out your refrigerator to make room for some of this food?"

"Sure, of course," I said.

As Angela set to her task, Pam smiled and confided that she was glad Angela had volunteered for the job. "I don't do science experiments," she said, referring to the prospect of finding something spoiled or moldy.

I had other things on my mind. Wanda had brought Mark home from Kartalkaya Mountain. As I crushed him with a hug, his resolve crumbled and he began to cry. I turned to Wanda and gave her a hug, and she, too, started to cry.

Both of them appeared tired and drawn. They had been in the same ski clothes since early Sunday morning. During the past two days they'd had very little sleep.

Mark quickly composed himself and assumed the task of keeping Marissa busy. I was touched. He knew that he had to be the man of the family right now, and he had decided to be really nice to his sister. They sat in front of the TV to watch a tape of Marissa's favorite movie, *Babes in Toyland*.

Wanda and I had much to discuss. A petite, attractive woman with dark, midlength hair, a small button nose, and a shy smile, she had become a good friend to all of us. Mike had recently recruited her for the guitar choir he had started at the "Vatican." Mark and her son, Bryn, were the best of friends. Bryn, like Mark, was a lanky teenager, slightly taller than Mark, with blond hair, bright blue eyes, and a fair complexion. The boys spent hours together playing Nintendo games and exploring the intricacies of computers. Downtime often found them in-line skating in Bryn's courtyard or playing soccer downstairs at our house with the *Kapeci* (pronounced "ka-pe-jeh")—the doorman or building custodian—and the guards. Wanda told me with pride how hard Bryn had worked during the past two days to keep Mark's mind occupied.

She asked for a sheet of paper and a pen. Then she sketched a diagram of the ski area and offered her opinion that it was possible Mike and Matthew had taken the wrong run off the lift. I was surprised to learn that she, too, had nearly gotten lost in the whiteout at the summit and had made her way down only by skiing directly under the lift, using it as a guide.

Wanda, like Mike, was a graduate of the Air Force Academy and she had full confidence that the team of military searchers would soon find Mike and Matthew. In addition, she had experienced the same sort of survival training as Mike, and she was sure that they would be all right.

As she left to return with Bryn to her own apartment, I thanked her for everything, and as the door closed behind her I offered a prayer that she was right. Our primary hope was God. Our secondary hope was the professionalism and dedication of the troops.

Idly I stepped into the kitchen, opened the refrigerator door, and was treated to an example of Angela Shaw's military effectiveness. Every "science experiment" had been dumped. Every almost-empty item was trashed. Every surface was scrubbed and shiny. Leftovers were tightly wrapped. Everything was labeled. Bottles, jars, and cans were lined up with the tallest to the rear, the labels facing front and center. Spices stood at attention in alphabetical order.

Seeing this, Pam laughed and declared, "Your refrigerator has been 'Shawed.' "

Mike

Matthew frequently brought up the subject of food. "Do you know what I'd like to eat right now, Dad?" he asked. Then he immediately answered his own question. "A nice juicy hamburger with lots of fries and a big Coke!"

"Yeah, that would be good, all right," I agreed. I did not want him to be preoccupied with hunger, but it was a perfectly natural tendency to fantasize about food. I took this as an opportunity to talk about family, hoping that the subject would warm our hearts. Reminding him of the year we spent in Alabama while I attended Air Command and Staff College at Maxwell Air Force Base, I asked, "Remember that hamburger place we used to go to in Millbrook after your baseball games? It was just a hole-in-the-wall place but I think they had some of the best hamburgers I've ever eaten."

"Yeah," Matthew said, "I remember that place! They were good, all right, but I think my favorite was Red Robin."

"You mean in Colorado?" I asked.

"Yeah, I liked all the stuff they put on their hamburgers." Red Robin was a restaurant situated outside the south gate of the Air Force Academy. It featured thick, juicy gourmet burgers with a variety of toppings. Our favorites were the ones with jalapeño peppers and Monterey Jack cheese, and another one with guacamole sauce. These were complemented by giant fries sprinkled with salt and various spices. "Do you think we can go back there someday?" Matthew asked.

"Well, I guess so," I responded. "Would you like to live in Colorado again?"

Matthew grew pensive. "I don't know, Dad," he said. "Not if it's cold like this."

Occasionally we heard sounds of movement, and each time our eyes met instantly, hoping that ground searchers had arrived. But we could tell that it was merely small animals scuffling about.

Mary

Somehow I managed to function.

I am, by nature, extremely extroverted and emotional. Tears come easily. I felt torn apart inside, but I knew how important it was for Mark and Marissa to see me maintain an appearance of optimistic calm. Both Mike and I have degrees in counseling and have been taught to base our reactions on reality. I do not believe in agonizing over yesterday or borrowing trouble from tomorrow. Now I made the decision to deal with the facts as I knew them and not to dwell on the maudlin what-ifs of this mysterious situation. I counted on my faith to help me do that.

Still, when the two OSI investigators showed up for the photos, I found myself reluctant to part with them. Once more I had to berate myself. Mary, I thought, if these photos will help find your guys, great!

To my surprise, the investigators wanted more than the photos. They said that they needed to ask me a series of questions in order to create personality profiles of Mike and Matthew.

I ushered them into the piano room. I sat in my favorite chair. One of the men seated himself in the mauve chair and the other sat on the piano bench. They took turns asking me a variety of what-if questions, and they listened very carefully to my answers. One of them scribbled notes. As somewhat of a mystery buff, I found the process fascinating. I tried to discern why they were asking various questions and what they were really trying to find out.

One of them asked, "Would Mike ever leave Matthew?"

"No," I assured them, "Mike would never leave Matthew. Never!"

Their questions and my answers flew back and forth.

"What would he do if Matthew was hurt?"

"He would take care of him."

"What would he do if they were separated?"

"He wouldn't let that happen."

"If Mike was lost, what would he do?" the man asked.

I had to chuckle despite the seriousness of the situation. Mike was always wandering off. "This is what happens," I replied. "We're at the mall and I'm at the shoe store and he says he's going to the bookstore. But when I go to the bookstore he's not there. I go back to the shoe store—the last place where we were together—and I don't move until he shows up. He'll go around the whole mall looking for me, and I'll be waiting at the last place where I saw him. That's how he operates."

"That's important information," one of the investigators said. "It will help with the search." But his frown told me what I already knew. They did not want Mike to continue to move around the mountain. They wanted him to stay put.

One of the men mentioned that officials had recovered Mike's driver's license from the equipment rental room at the hotel.

That was a poignant, tangible fact, and it brought me back from my fictional mystery to sad, frightening reality.

The men wanted to speak with Mark also, and although he was nervous, I could tell that he was grateful to break away from the beeps and chimes of the Nintendo game he was playing with Marissa. Bless his heart, I thought, he's already endured three or four showings of *Babes in Toyland* today.

They asked Mark to try to pinpoint when—and where—he had last seen his father and brother.

"I saw them around lunchtime," Mark recalled. "I was playing hearts with some of my friends in the lodge and Dad and Matthew came in. I guess I wasn't listening too well, because I thought Dad said something about already having lunch and wanting me to ski with them. But they just kept walking and by the time I got my ski stuff together, I couldn't find them."

"When did you suspect something was wrong?" they asked.

"I waited for them at the bottom of the slope, but they never showed up," Mark said. "Then I joined my friends again, we skied for a while and I kept looking around for them, but I never saw them. I just figured they had gone to the top of the ski lift."

One of the men mentioned that the Turk who manned the top of the ski lift did not remember seeing them.

The investigators handed me a business card covered with printed and handwritten phone numbers. They asked me to call them anytime, day or night, if I remembered anything else that might be important. Then they announced that they were leaving for Kartalkaya Mountain early the next morning in the hope that their information might aid in the search. They also told me they hoped to get the photos and the story in the Turkish newspaper the next day. Maybe someone had seen them and would give us a lead.

Although I had not known Angelina well prior to this crisis, she proved to be a great source of strength. It was so nice to have another adult around in the evenings and first thing in the morning. When she returned late in the afternoon from her day's activities she busied herself with a knitting project, and this caught Marissa's attention. "Can you teach me how?" Marissa asked.

Angelina patiently showed Marissa how to manipulate the long needles. At first it was difficult, because Marissa is left-handed, and she had to learn to transpose the movements. But before long she had the hang of it. Angelina presented Marissa with her very own ball of pale blue yarn.

"I'm going to knit a scarf for my dad," Marissa announced. "I hope I can finish it before he comes back."

The Search

Dividing his Green Berets into three teams, Fitz had sent them out to various areas, exploring out from the edges of the ski trails, searching for signs of Mike and Matthew. Their initial efforts were unsuccessful, but when they returned to the lodge late in the afternoon they encountered a report that someone had found a child's ski tracks. Fitz sent one of the teams back out to check on the report.

Ten of the Green Berets were ordered to return to Bolu for the night, where they would billet with a Turkish commando unit. Fitz remained at the hotel, awaiting the report about the child's ski tracks.

Out on the mountain, the remaining Special Forces team located what did, indeed, appear to be tracks made by a child's skis, but the evidence was maddeningly scant. The tracks started and stopped rather abruptly, and there were no adult-sized tracks nearby. The team conducted an extensive search of the surrounding area, but to no avail.

Were these Matthew's tracks?

Was he alone?

Had the drifting snow simply covered Mike's tracks?

There was no way to know, but back at Incirlik, when Sully heard the report, he believed that they were close to finding the Couillards.

Pony 21 and Pony 22 had been able to cover half of their assigned search areas so far, with negative results. By dusk, they had landed at Akinci and the crews were bused to Ankara for the night.

Mary

Colonel Fitzgerald called with his report of the day's activities. He began with the terse statement. "We didn't find them." Then he detailed the state of the search. He told me about the busloads of volunteers from ODC and the U.S. Embassy who had come from Ankara to help. He described how they were systematically combing the area and how the deep snowfall made the terrain treacherous. And he praised the activities of local villagers, some of whom had joined the search and others who had set out on their own.

He said that ground searchers had investigated ski tracks apparently left in the snow by a child. The trail disappeared. What worried me most was that there had been no adult tracks. Had something happened to Mike? Was Matthew alone? The questions were terrifying, and the colonel made no attempt to calm my growing fears.

Mike

Once more, evening brought despair. Watching Matthew shiver and shake, I tried to take his mind to a warmer place. "Bruise," I asked, "where do you think you liked living the *most*?" Over the past five years my Air Force assignments had taken us to a variety of areas: Colorado, Alabama, Hawaii, Virginia, and now Turkey. I knew what his answer would be.

"Hawaii!" he said.

"Do you remember all those times we would go to the other side of the island?" Our family had enjoyed numerous trips to the beautiful beaches at Bellows Air Force Station on the wind-ward side of Oahu. There were rental cabins, situated at the water's edge, available for military personnel. Many times we had fallen asleep listening to the waves lap at the shore. One of our favorite activities was "boogie-boarding," which is similar to body surfing. A boogie-board is fashioned of some sort of foam material, and is about half the size of a surfboard. You hop on just as the wave starts in toward the shore and ride it on in. Many times we scraped our knuckles or knees as we washed ashore, but that never seemed to slow down the kids. Even little Marissa had been crazy about it. At first I let her ride on my back, but she eventually soloed under my watchful eyes. The waves were not too big, not too small, and the beach was smooth. "Remember when we went boogie-boarding?" I asked Matthew now. "Wasn't that fun?"

"Yeah," he agreed, "and on the way home we would stop at Bueno Nalo for a chimichanga." Although Bueno Nalo was only a hole-in-the-wall establishment located in Waimanalo, not far from Bellows, it was our favorite restaurant on the entire island.

But I was determined to keep our minds off food and attempted to change the subject. "How 'bout all those times we went snorkeling?" I asked. "Do you remember all those times at Hanama Bay?"

"Yeah, and all those colorful fish we saw."

Matthew had learned to recognize the various kinds of fish by their distinctive coloring and had learned their names: the red and white clownfish, the multicolored parrot fish—he even knew the long Hawaiian word for the distinctive reef triggerfish adopted as the state fish. We talked about each of these, with me asking questions such as, "Which was your favorite one?" I knew the answers to most of the questions I asked, but it was a way to keep the discussion moving. Talking about the idyllic Hawaiian climate warmed our spirits a bit. That's what family is all about, I thought. Here was the warmth of love, brought about by the memories of shared fun.

There were other good memories. The star-filled night sky above me brought to mind the many times we had gone camping as a family. I grew up in the mild climate of Los Angeles and have really learned to appreciate the beauty of the outdoors.

Some of the most enjoyable and memorable camping experiences occurred while we were stationed in Arkansas. We were part of an Officers' Christian Fellowship Bible Study, a group made up of people from every denomination imaginable. It was the closest spiritual support group we had ever encountered. We were all in similar places and seasons of life, and the bond of love among all of us was truly a gift from God. This group went camping frequently and gradually we all assumed defined roles. Diana Freeman, for example, took charge of breakfast and now I remembered fondly her wonderful blueberry/buttermilk pancakes.

We had continued to enjoy camping in Colorado during my tour of duty at the Academy. Nothing compared to waking up to hot coffee brewed on an open fire, or hiking through the woods, or singing around a campfire in the evenings. These were happy, comforting memories.

Marissa

One of my schoolbooks talked about guardian angels. My mother had read it to me and we had talked about it for several days. It said that you could name your own angel. My favorite name was John, so that's what I had decided to name my angel.

The book said that it was easy to send John places. All you have to do is pray.

Mary

At bedtime Marissa posed the same tough question she had asked the night before: "Why is this happening to us?"

"I don't know why," I repeated, "but God has a plan and we have to trust Him. He'll take care of us."

Frustrated, Marissa turned away and grumbled, "I knew you were going to say it's some kind of God thing." But then she brightened. "You know what?" she said. "I'm going to ask God to send John to look after Matthew and Daddy."

Mike

Finally Matthew dozed, and I studied his face in the moonlight. A sleeping child always appears innocent and fragile—almost angelic—but now my little boy's vulnerability was almost more than I could bear. His skin seemed translucent, his breathing shallow.

We had, to this point, lived a pretty idyllic family life and none of the kids had ever been in any real danger. Sure, they had taken their share of spills and suffered the cuts and scrapes endemic to childhood, but they had never been seriously injured—not even so much as a broken bone.

We had not sheltered or coddled them. They participated in sports. We never held them back. It all comes back to guardian angels, Mary and I had decided.

My mind went back in time. I had been assigned to the 16th Tactical Airlift Training Squadron as an instructor, teaching new pilots to fly the C-130 and upgrading copilots to aircraft commanders, teaching them to fly from the left seat and helping them learn the decision-making skills required to handle any emergency. We were hosting a barbecue at our home near Little Rock and I was talking shop with a squadron mate. Mary and some of the other women were off to the side, engaged in their own conversation.

The swing set was about a hundred yards away from the patio where we all stood. Mark, then only two, was walking directly into the path of a swing being ridden by one of the other kids. We all saw it at the same time; we watched the scene unfold in frame-by-frame slow motion, unable to reach the toddler in time. Mark was directly behind the swing as it hurtled through the air. We heard the awful *thunk* as the swing seat met his skull. A split second later I was running as fast as my legs would carry me, but it was too late—the damage was surely already done.

As the adults all gathered around him and I swept him into my arms, we were amazed to see that he barely had a scratch on him. Of course, he cried and screamed, which we took as a positive sign, but other than a tiny scrape, he was absolutely fine.

"Angels," I muttered to myself, shaking my head in disbelief. "It's got to be angels."

I snapped back into the present. The angels must be doing double-duty now, I thought. I prayed that God might protect Matthew from serious harm. "God, send your angels to watch over him now," I prayed. "Send reinforcements if you need to, but please, please watch over him."

Throughout my childhood my parents had insisted that we attend church every Sunday, and they had made sure that I went to catechism classes. But during my adolescent years, I began to question what Roman Catholicism was all about. I viewed the Church as an organization that was deeply entrenched in ritual and tradition, with very little substance. I observed people who went to church every Sunday and then honked and screamed at each other as they drove home.

One of my teachers once told me, "You know, the devil is out to get little Michaels because, ever since Michael the arch-angel threw him out of heaven, he's been mad." Her supposition was that anyone burdened with the name of Michael had a penchant for trouble, and I spent much of my adolescence bearing out that prediction. I had heard the gospel message, but had not really acted upon it. My relationship with God was confined to moments when I was in trouble and called upon Him for help.

Such superficial Catholicism pervaded my life, and I even exploited it during my early time at the Air Force Academy, when I developed the habit of frequently attending morning Mass because it excused me from the breakfast formation.

But in 1975, during my sophomore year, one of my classmates, an ex-Catholic, suddenly asked me, "If you were to die today, where would you end up?"

I responded, "Well, I'm a pretty good person, and I've even been going to morning church."

"How do you know that you're good enough?" my friend countered. "How do you know that you are deserving of heaven? How do you know that you won't end up in hell?"

As the discussion continued, my friend's words, and the obvious influence of the Holy Spirit working upon my heart, brought me to the realization that neither I nor any human being deserved God's favor. Only the atonement provided by Christ's death on the cross could ever bring me to true righteousness. It was on that particular day that I truly gave my life to Christ, and I had done my best to live out the commitment ever since—although some days were better than others.

I realized that I had missed something in my Catholic upbringing: the concept that organized religion is not as important as a personal relationship with Christ. I felt that I had missed God's invitation to encounter Him in the vital, loving, person-to-person manner that He intended. I had become lost in the tradition and ritual and had missed "the person."

Over the ensuing years I searched in directions other than the Catholic Church. While still at the Academy, I became involved in groups such as the Officers' Christian Fellowship and the Navigators, two groups that employed an evangelical approach toward the Air Force cadets. Once I attended a Bible study meeting during which, suddenly but quietly, some of the others began to pray in an incomprehensible gibberish. I had heard of this "speaking in tongues." Supposedly it was a manifestation of the presence of the Holy Spirit, but it sounded very weird to me and I wondered, Is this God or Satan speaking here? Nevertheless, my skepticism was tempered by the sense that these people genuinely loved the Lord.

After graduation I married my high school sweetheart, Mary, and was assigned to flight training at Williams Air Force Base in Arizona. Mary and I both became involved in an evangelical, nondenominational Bible study group that included a number of charismatic Christians who exhibited the gifts of the Holy Spirit, such as speaking in tongues and prophesy. We remained wary, but interested.

Ultimately we were assigned to Germany, where we joined an Assembly of God congregation and, finally, received the baptism of the Holy Spirit and came to understand the beauty of such close communion with God.

The pilgrimage came full circle when, reassigned to Little Rock, Arkansas, we became aware that a charismatic movement within the Roman Catholic Church had received the blessing of the Pope. After a period of emotional adjustment, we realized that the liturgical service of the Mass, augmented by the gifts of the Spirit, was the right mixture of religious expression for us. I felt as if the Holy Spirit had touched my heart. I found that the Mass came alive for me as never before, providing a worship experience that enhanced my personal relationship with the Lord. The liturgical prayers that I had heard so many times before now jumped out at me and I was struck with their powerful expression of praise and their profound meaning.

Our early experience in the Catholic charismatic prayer group Light to the Nations was that of immense personal and spiritual growth fueled by the fire of God's love and gifts of the Spirit. I bought a used guitar from a friend and taught myself a few simple chords—enough to play a small selection of songs. Soon I was in the music ministry and learned the tremendous power of God-anointed music to lift me up when I was down. My heart longed to offer God the worship He deserved. Mary, a singer since early childhood, joined in.

I believe that my stronger gift was the one of prophesy, not in the sense of predicting the future, but simply allowing myself to be used as a vehicle to proclaim a message inspired by God. Often, when I was inspired to say something during a prayer meeting or Bible study session, I realized that it was a particular message to someone in the room who needed that inspiration. Sometimes I am inspired to read a particular scripture that, unknown to me at the time, addresses an individual's private, critical concern of the moment.

My mind drifted for quite some time as I reflected on the past. Gradually, though, my thoughts shifted back to present realities. As the hours of the night wore on, a swirl of negative images invaded my imagination. I was extremely concerned about our fingers and toes. If I was going to come back somehow incomplete or maimed, perhaps I did not want to come back at all. Far, far worse was the possibility that, through my actions, we might lose our son. If that terrible nightmare were to become a reality, I did not think I could ever look Mary in the eyes again.

DAY 4

•

Wednesday, January 18

Mary

I awoke about 7 A.M., with Marissa and Mark still sleeping by
my side. Lying in bed, I spent a quiet, reflective half hour
in prayer.

After I got dressed I walked into the piano room and picked
up Mike's Bible from the telephone table. I read some scripture
and offered an additional prayer.

Angelina stirred. We were learning to savor this quiet time
before the storm of visitors and ringing telephones descended. I took my usual position in the chair next to the
phone and Angelina sat across from me on the mauve-col-
ored chair.

Angelina told me that during the night her thoughts had
been led to Zephaniah 3:14–19, which begins:

> *Sing oh Daughter of Zion, shout aloud, oh Israel! Be
> glad and rejoice with all your heart, oh Daughter of
> Jerusalem.*

The passage ends with the words:

> *The Lord your God is with you, He is mighty to save. I
> will rescue the lame and gather those who have been
> lost . . . at that time I will bring you home.*

The reference to "the lame" caused us to speculate that either Mike or Matthew was injured, perhaps suffering from a broken leg. Tears flowed down my cheeks as I reread the scripture, but the message was so positive I knew that God would rescue them and bring them home.

Mike

We were shivering in the cave, half dozing, when the sound of another helicopter galvanized me to action. This one was close!

A rush of adrenaline propelled me outside. There was no time to struggle with my boots, so I quickly wrapped our scarves around my feet. I grabbed Matthew's ski bibs and tossed them outside the cave, hoping that their thin layers of plastic would provide some protection from the snow cover. Then I squirmed my way outside and stared at the sky.

From the noise, I could tell that the pilot was following the upward slope of the mountain, paralleling the creek, the fence, and the trail. The weather was clear, and the sound was coming directly toward us!

It appeared over the treeline, no more than a hundred feet above the ground, and it was slightly off to one side of our position.

I leaped into the air and waved wildly. I shouted my lungs out, even though I knew that the crew could not hear me.

It was another Blackhawk and this time I could see a large American flag painted on the side of the cargo door. As it flew directly across from me I grabbed the metal ski pole Matthew had used as a drinking tube and banged it wildly against a rock, hoping unrealistically that someone could hear the noise over the sound of the engines and the din of the giant rotor blades. I even wondered whether they had some kind of sonar equipment that could detect the sound of a metal pole banging on a rock. But the copter continued along its path up the ridge, disappearing quickly. I stood still for several minutes, deeply disappointed and yet marveling at the wondrous sight of the American flag.

I thought: He was so low—*so low*—that if I had been able to find a stone to throw, I might have been able to hit him. If not for the sun's reflection on the windshield, I probably could have seen the pilot's eyes.

I looked down and saw that the scarves had unraveled from around my feet and the slippery plastic ski bibs had slid away. I was standing barefoot in the snow but, in my excitement, I was unaware of the pain and cold.

I scrambled back into the cave and said, "You'd better warm my feet."

Matthew nodded and tried to hide the fear and disappointment in his eyes. "They didn't see us," he said. The words came hard and his voice quavered. His shoulders slumped. He cast his eyes downward in a futile attempt to hide the tears that began to flow as he prayed from his heart, "God, please send them back and make them see us. They've got to look down here and see us."

I nodded and swallowed hard. "It was really close," I said. I explained that the people inside the helicopter really could not see directly below them. They were looking off to the side. "Because they only made one pass, I'm not even sure they were searching this area," I said. "This might be the path they take to refuel." I added lamely, "Maybe they'll come back any minute."

We were heartened by the fact that the searchers were, indeed, Americans and were using such sophisticated equipment to try to find us, but we also realized that we were two tiny needles in a giant white haystack.

"I'm really getting worried now," Matthew said.

Once again, I wished that I had brought along a supply of dry matches. A fire would keep us warm and also attract the attention of the helicopters.

What can I do? I asked myself. What resources do I have?

Checking my wallet, I realized that my Sprint calling card,

with its shiny, silvery surface, could function as a mirror. I held it in both hands, with my thumbs on the bottom and my index fingers on top, and practiced. I managed to catch the sunshine and flashed a signal against a nearby rock. Then I angled it upward so that the reflection would, if we were very lucky, attract the attention of a searcher.

Periodically the faint sounds of distant rotor blades returned. They remained off to one side, closer to where I'd assumed the ski resort must be. I figured that they must be searching on the other side of the ridge to our left. The valley we were in must be just this side of that ridge, outside of their search grid, at least for now. The sounds remained distant.

Mary

Calls came in constantly from all over the world as the news was passed along by various members of the prayer and Bible study groups we had joined over the years during several military tours of duty. We had maintained correspondence with these good friends, and they rallied behind us now. Some called to tell me of a scripture that had been impressed on their minds; some reminded me of past prayers that had been answered. Still others called to report dreams or visions. Three of them told me the same thing: Mike and Matthew were close to a road and a fence. Should I share their insights with Colonel Fitzgerald the next time I spoke with him? Would he think that I had a screw loose? Then I decided, Oh, well, who better to be a little wacko than a woman whose husband and son have been missing for days?

Cathryn told me that she found that she was awakened off and on throughout the nights. "I think God is calling us to sleep in shifts, and pray in shifts," she said. She told me that she had contacted a Turkish convert named Hulya and asked her to pray for Mike and Matthew. Hulya was known for her spiritual knowledge and wisdom. Many Turks have visions; it is accepted in their culture. When Hulya became a Christian, this was one of the gifts she brought with her, and Cathryn wondered whether her particular insights could offer us guidance.

In fact, Hulya said that she had experienced a vision of a young boy, alone in an airplane, staring out the window.

"Did you know that Mike is a pilot?" Cathryn asked her.

Hulya was surprised. "No," she said.

Cathryn said that she thought that the vision meant that Matthew was safe in his father's arms.

Sister Bernadine made her regular call to me so that she could pass on any information to the "Vatican" parishioners. She told me that she had awoken in the middle of the night and felt compelled to go over to the church. For some time she stood in front of the Blessed Sacrament and prayed. She said that God had a message for me: He would answer our prayers. She was sure that Mike and Matthew were going to be okay.

Then she informed me that Monsignor Nugent was going to say a special Mass for Mike and Matthew tonight. "Do you want to come?" she asked.

"I don't feel that I can leave," I said. "I want to remain close to the telephone. But I'm glad to hear about the Mass." The more people praying, the better, I thought. Especially at Mass.

I turned my attention to other concerns. Fortunately, we were surrounded by so many people that Mark's and Marissa's needs were met during the day. Marissa is an exceptionally social and inquisitive youngster, always on the move. Her attention was easily captured by the variety of activities swirling around her.

But it was Wednesday now, and some of the novelty was wearing off. Marissa needed to see some of her friends and Mark needed a break from his self-imposed duty of shepherding his little sister. Marissa complained, "It's my house and it's my phone. It's not fair that all these other people can answer the phone and I can't."

"I know it's not fair," I agreed. "But it's what we have to do right now."

Cathryn sided with Marissa. "Marissa needs a change," she said. Cathryn's daughter Joanie and Marissa were very good friends, and Cathryn offered to take Marissa to her home for the rest of the afternoon and into the evening.

I was reluctant, but finally agreed, and when I saw how much this pleased Marissa, I decided that I would also allow Mark to go over to Bryn's apartment.

Idly I rummaged through the contents of Mike's blue and white sports bag; Mark had brought it back from the mountain. I noticed a package of peanut butter cheddar crackers that was still unopened. They should be eating those! I thought. I also found Mike's black and white hat that he usually wore. Uh-oh, I thought. I'll have to update the searchers on that.

The Search

One of the helicopter teams spotted what appeared to be a ski pole leaning against an abandoned building. A ground team was sent to investigate, but a thorough search of the area turned up no evidence of Mike and Matthew.

Meanwhile, Major Jeff Willey of ODC complained of the difficulties brought about by the weather. "It's very difficult to walk, to make any progress in the snow," he grumbled. "It's like walking in water, only more difficult."

Fitz was also grumpy after a frustrating night. After his final four-man Special Forces team had returned after inspecting the area around the child's ski tracks, they were all exhausted. Fitz wanted everybody fresh for an early start in the morning, but the hotel rooms were all full. They were given permission to sleep on the floor of the hotel bar, but were not allowed to lay out their gear until midnight. Then, this morning, they lost two hours of search time waiting for their ten compatriots to arrive from their overnight billet in Bolu.

Mike

By early afternoon the sky was clear and the sun was shining brightly. Some of the snow began to melt and drip from the branches of surrounding trees. Streamlets of flowing water formed shimmering icicles. I hoped that Matthew's frozen sweatshirt might thaw and dry out.

Matthew was quiet and I was alone with my thoughts. In my head I could still see the glorious sight of the American flag, painted across the side of the helicopter. A Blackhawk is a large aircraft and this flag covered fully twenty-five percent of the side. The insignia had been added to the Blackhawks after the tragic shoot-down over northern Iraq, to aid American fighter pilots in identifying friendly choppers. The more I recalled the sight of that flag this morning, the more thrilling it seemed.

A memory came back to me from my days as an Air Force Academy cadet. A portion of our survival training included what we were told would be a three- or four-day simulated prisoner-of-war exercise. Of course the instructors were not allowed to really harm us, but they slapped us around a good bit and otherwise made the experience as realistic as possible. We were kept in tiny cells, impervious to daylight, so that we lost all track of time. They woke us at odd hours for rude interrogation sessions. Then, at one point, they placed laundry bags over our heads and marched us blindly outdoors. What was coming next? we all wondered. How long had we been here? How much longer before the ordeal was over? They pushed us together into a line and told us to remove the laundry bags from our heads. Suddenly we found ourselves in the sunshine, staring at a large and glorious U.S. flag, the signal that the exercise had ended. The sight of the flag brought a surge of patriotic feeling, and I realized that I had experienced the same sensation this morning. Although no one in the Blackhawk had seen us, I had seen the unmistakable evidence that proclaimed: *Our guys are looking for us.* Once again, at this moment, I was proud to be an American. I knew that every effort would be made to find us, and it was great to realize that we were part of this special "family."

The thought was inspiring, and I realized that I had to try to do more to aid the searchers. I had to find some way to make us more visible. Perhaps our vantage point was just too hidden, and perhaps there was a much better spot nearby. I could not know unless I looked.

How long do we sit here? I asked myself. My training had taught me that it was best to stay put, but that conflicted with my personality. If I know that I can do something about a situation, I do it. My mind went over and over my actions during the first day, and I concluded that, yes, I had done everything that I could possibly do. Days of snow had followed and by the time the weather had cleared we had both sustained some frostbite on our feet. Matthew could not move on his own, and I had already tried to carry him. That did not work. So we really were pinned down. But how long do I stay here? How long?

With a break in the weather, I decided that it was time to at least explore the immediate area, to see what might lie across the ridge where the copters seemed to be concentrating their efforts. I was certain that was the direction of the ski slope. Maybe, from that vantage point, I would be able to see something familiar. Maybe I could spot a helicopter searching over a finite patch of terrain, giving me a clue as to the direction and the distance we had traveled from the resort. Maybe, if I could find my bearings, I could strike out early the next day and still have time to make it back to Matthew before nightfall.

The stream lay in that direction, so I could drink some water before I began the climb, and I could leave a boot there to bring back water for Matthew. I told him what I intended to do and assured him that I would be back before dark.

Matthew was unresponsive. I wondered if he had understood my purpose, so I explained my plan to search for landmarks and perhaps get our bearings. "I think the ski area is that direction," I said. "We've seen helicopters over that way, and we've heard them over that way. Maybe I'll be able to see it from there. And even if I can't, I'll be able to get a better idea of the terrain. Maybe I can spot a road." I reassured him that I would not leave him. "I'll follow my tracks in the snow and return in a couple of hours," I promised.

Finally, with a more confident "Okay, Dad, I'll be fine," a faint smile, and a solid head nod from my son, I decided it would be okay to leave him alone for a little while.

Once again I endured the complicated and cumbersome ritual of donning my boots.

Now I was a bit anxious about leaving. The days were short and the sun went down early in this little valley. I simply had to get back to Matt before dark. The internal tension mounted as I tried to hurry myself into action.

Reasoning that the exertion of my trek would warm me sufficiently, I left my coat with Matthew. But I took one of his empty boots for water and my unbroken ski pole, which I could use as a walking stick to aid in my trek. Finally I grabbed the broken ski pole to use as a sipping tube when I reached the stream.

I made the familiar trip down to the trail. I stopped at the stream, dipped my broken ski pole beneath the surface, and drank my fill of water, enduring the recurring "ice-cream headaches." Leaving Matthew's boot and the sipping tube by the side of the stream, I straightened up and scanned the area for the best crossing point.

A bit downstream I spotted a series of rocks that I thought would provide a sufficient natural bridge. I made my way across these slowly, laboriously, concerned about falling in and soaking my boots and clothing. The surfaces of the boulders were coated with ice, making the footing treacherous. My hard plastic ski boots made the situation even worse. Several times I had to reach out with my ski pole to maintain balance.

Once across the stream, I headed upslope, making my way through deep snow and across fallen limbs. Large boulders and tree stumps impeded my progress and forced me to weave back and forth. Sometimes I sank up to my armpits in the snow. My boots were designed to be latched to skis, not to hike across difficult terrain. The tops of the boots cut into my shins as I climbed, and the deep snow made every step a monumental effort. Soon my calf muscles were burning from this awkward exertion. I worried that I would not have enough stamina for the return trip. But when I glanced back I realized that I was creating a deep trench that would make the return much easier. Also, gravity would be on my side.

As I climbed, I pondered our situation. I was increasingly concerned about how long it would take the searchers to expand their "box" outward. Should I venture out for help? It seemed that the scales were balancing more in favor of this alternative. Survival training had taught me to stay put—but for how long? And what would the searchers find if and when they finally arrived?

I attempted to maintain a straightforward course, but the terrain forced me to divert first to the left and then to the right. This was far more difficult than I had imagined. Instead of climbing a single ridge, I was churning my way through a series of smaller slopes and valleys. I tried to alternate my diversions, first to the left, then to the right, so as to maintain a zigzag path that would keep me on course in the general direction that I wanted to go. This brought back memories of our family sailing together in Hawaii, when I learned the art of "tacking" at a forty-five-degree angle to either side of the predominant wind as a means of keeping the boat on course.

The presence of so many tree stumps told me that loggers had worked this area. That realization raised my spirits a bit. Perhaps they would return to cut more timber. But then I reasoned that they probably did their work in the summertime. Still, the sight of the stumps was comforting. Somehow, they connected me to humanity. These trees had been felled by someone. People had been here.

At one point during the climb, when the going got really difficult, my right foot plunged deeply into the snow and lodged in an icy hole. The sudden shift threw me off balance and I winced in intense pain as my hip once more popped out of joint. "Damn!" I yelped. I felt a tinge of guilt as I heard my curse echo through the canyon. Worse than the pain was the worry that this recurring injury might reduce my ability to do whatever I had to do to get us through this ordeal. But a strange mixture of thoughts ran through my head. Would this hip injury really matter? I wondered. If I'm going to die, it really isn't that important.

I shrugged off the strange jumble of emotions, bit my lip against the pain, and forced myself to continue.

After several hours of plodding, I reached the top of the ridge. I gasped for breath and glanced about anxiously. Daylight was beginning to fade, bringing hues of blue and gray to a panorama of ridges and valleys filled with snow and trees. It was breathtakingly beautiful, and for a moment I marveled over the mix of feelings. Here I was in the worst situation of my life, and yet I could still appreciate the glorious sight.

There was no sign of the ski resort—or anything else that was familiar to me. None of the terrain features I had seen while we were skiing were visible from here. But between the ridge on which I now stood and the next ridge on the horizon in front of me lay a low, narrow valley. Far off, in a small clearing well below my vantage point, I spotted a cluster of what appeared to be tiny cabins. My eyes strained to see signs of human activity, but the village was a long way off and many trees blocked my view.

Although it was clearly too late on this day, if I set out early in the morning, could I reach the cabins and make it back to the cave before nightfall? I wondered. I estimated the distance to be at least five miles, but it was hard to gain a perspective. I could see that the terrain would take me up and down a variety of slopes and valleys, and I was fearful that I would lose my sense of direction when I descended into the lower patches of trees.

And what if I did reach the village? What if there was no one there? I was so weakened by hunger, thirst, and cold that I might not have the ability to return. And if there were people at the cabins, could I direct them back across a series of ridges to find the exact spot where Matthew was stranded?

There were too many uncertainties. I could not risk leaving Matthew alone overnight.

I would not do that.

Turning my back on the bittersweet view of the cabins, I began to retrace my course through the tracks I had made on the way up. Because of the trail I had left, and because most of the trip was downslope, it did not require as much time or effort, but I was already exhausted. I was aware that the more I trudged about, and the more wear and tear I delivered to my ski boots, the less protection they would offer. Each difficult step increased my danger of frostbite.

Somehow I made it back to the stream and across without falling in. Again I drank my fill from the stream, quenching an intense thirst generated by the long hike. I filled Matthew's boot with water and negotiated the difficult last few feet across the road and up the steep incline to the cave.

Matthew complained, "You were gone a while." He left unspoken the fear that I might not return. He drank the water gratefully and quickly maneuvered his position so that I could warm my frozen feet against his skin.

The Search

Pony 21 experienced a mechanical problem and had to return to Akinci. Sully arranged for a C-12 to ferry maintenance personnel from Incirlik to Akinci to repair the problem. But it appeared that Pony 22 would be on its own tomorrow.

Mary

After spending three days searching Kartalkaya Mountain, Pam's husband, Ken, returned to Ankara and came over to brief me. To my surprise I learned that three other men had gone with him. Two of them, Mike Björk and Neil Townsend from the American Embassy, were men I knew from the Youth Sports League. The third man was our neighbor in the apartment directly above us; Joe Shepherd—Donnell's uncle and guardian—had taken leave from his duties as an agent of the Drug Enforcement Administration to join in the search. He had gone on Monday morning with the first crew of volunteers, but I had known nothing about it. It was a really warm feeling to realize that all three of these men, who were not from Mike's unit, were willing to go to the mountain and use their skills in an effort to find my husband and son.

Ken described for me in detail what was going on. He said that they searched from dawn until dark for three full days. Even though they were exhausted, none of them slept well. Several had dreams that suggested areas to search, but all of these had proven fruitless.

He told me how his search team had skied its way down to a Turkish village, and how they were impressed with the willingness of the local people to look for the lost Americans. This was the type of behavior that I had come to expect from the Turks. In our sixteen months in this country we had found the Turkish people to be very hospitable. When you go into a shop, someone is certain to offer you *çay*, the Turkish tea. In restaurants, the waiters would hover over you to make sure your needs were met.

My father had come to visit us the previous April, and we had traveled western Turkey from Antalya to Istanbul. Sometimes the villagers were a bit wary of an American family riding in a Toyota van, but once we began to speak a bit of Turkish to them, they were eager to help us. In friendly conversations, they directed us to the special attractions of the area. And when Mark would ask in Turkish about the score of the night's ongoing soccer match, we were accepted into a special brotherhood that only happens when you appreciate a country's national sport.

Colonel Fitzgerald reported by phone on the results of the day's search. First he spoke with Pam, and then I took the phone.

The colonel noted that only a single helicopter would be available tomorrow. "But we only have one map, anyway," he grumbled.

I told him that three different people had relayed to me the impressions they had received that Mike and Matthew were somewhere near a road and a fence.

He took this information calmly and, surprisingly, not in a patronizing manner. He said that he would relay the information to the searchers. But he grumbled, "There are lots of roads and fences out there."

Then he told me a frightening and pessimistic story about one of the searchers who had fallen into a snowdrift that came up to his armpits and had to be pulled to safety by his fellow searchers. The colonel also reminded me that dangerous areas on the slopes were not roped off; it was possible that Mike and Matthew had skied over the edge of a chasm, into oblivion. "If that's the case," he said in his efficient, military style, "we might need to think about coming back to look for them after the spring thaw."

I was stunned. My eyes widened in disbelief. It had only been three days, and he thought that they were dead already? Because of my experience in the Civil Air Patrol I felt that I could have survived this long. Mike would do much better than I and he had Matthew with him to help share body heat. I asked myself: What is this guy thinking? Do I want someone like him searching for them when he has no faith in their being found alive? I was mad now. How could he be so insensitive? He had just spoken with Pam. She had left the room to go to the kitchen. I searched my memory to recall if she had responded to a similar statement. I did not remember any odd reaction from her, such as turning away to shield her reaction from me. He must not have said the same thing to her. Should I tell her what he said? For him it was, perhaps, a realistic assessment of the situation, but did he really need to share it with me?

After the call I moved about the apartment in a daze, but I could not bring myself to discuss the colonel's macabre assessment with anyone. Did I really have to face the possibility of life without Mike and Matthew? I ordered myself: Put it out of your mind. Say a prayer. Carry on.

Mike

Later in the evening, after I was once more settled into the cave, I began to notice a change in Matthew's conversation. "My feet are so numb I can barely feel them," he complained. He told me that while I was gone he had crawled out of the cave to urinate. When he tried to stand, he fell over into the snow. "Oh, God!" he wailed. "Help us out of this."

In the darkness I could feel the movement of his shoulders as they began to shake. Sobbing sounds came from deep within his throat.

"We're never going to get out of here," he moaned. His voice carried an angry, accusatory tone. "Dad, we're going to die here!"

I grabbed for him and tried to calm the spasms. "Snap out of it!" I ordered. More calmly I added, "Listen, we're doing the best we can. This isn't going to help. We've got to hang on. They're looking for us. We know that—we've seen them a couple times now."

"Okay, okay," he said quietly.

As we lay there, side by side in an isolated cave somewhere

on a deserted mountain, I realized that I was perhaps more upset than Matthew. His anger was justified. It was all my fault that we were in this predicament.

After he was quiet for a time, Matthew asked, "Dad, will I still be able to play sports or ski if I have an artificial foot?"

The question caught me off guard, but I replied quickly, "Sure. But I don't think that's going to happen. Let's not assume the worst. I think your feet are still okay."

In truth I was not so sure, and I used this somber discussion as an excuse for another session of foot-warming against one another's belly. This time Matthew did not complain.

Marissa

Joanie and I were just playing around when I told her that Matthew and my dad were missing.

"Whoa!" she said. "That's kind of cool. Maybe they'll be in a movie or something."

I had not thought about that.

"Let's play like we're lost in a snowstorm," Joanie suggested.

"Okay."

Mark

Mom let me go over to Bryn's house for a while. We were eating Spaghettios and watching the movie *Teen Wolf* when our friend Doğan came over to ask, "Did you hear the news?"

"What news?" we asked.

"I just heard that some terrorists have them," he said.

I really didn't believe that, but I thought: Well, if that's true, at least they aren't freezing somewhere.

Mary

The sharp ring of the telephone once again interrupted my thoughts. It was Rumeysa, our "shopping queen." "Have you heard the news on TV?" she asked. "Some terrorist group has them."

According to the news report, someone who identified himself as a member of a Lebanese terrorist group had called the U.S. Embassy as well as several Turkish news agencies, claiming that his group had kidnapped Mike and Matthew. They were demanding the release of a member of their group who was being held prisoner in an Israeli jail in exchange for the safe return of my husband and son.

I reminded myself that I could not believe any news unless it was confirmed by Colonel Fitzgerald or Mr. Holmes from the embassy, and it was useless for me to try to watch the report on Turkish television. Could this be true? I wondered. Could this explain why the searchers had not found a trace of Mike or Matthew—not a scarf or a glove or a hat? My mind was reeling. If this story was not true, then Mike and Matthew were still out there freezing. But if it was true, then some "bad guys" had them. What would a terrorist group do to them?

Then I thought: Oh, no! Mark and Marissa might hear this. What will they do if they hear? I knew that I had to gather them around me. Mary Beth agreed to pick them up.

I called Mark at Bryn's apartment and asked, "Have you heard any rumors?"

"Doğan came down and told me some terrorists have them," he said, "but I don't believe any of it. I'm not sold on it at all. Do you want me to come home now?"

"Yeah," I said. "Mrs. Tremblay will be there to pick you up shortly." I was overwhelmed with Mark's exhibition of maturity. He had made the offer to come home. I did not have

to "out logic" him. It was a great relief, because I knew that
I did not have the energy.

Wanda took the phone. She was upset that Doğan had
"spilled the beans" to Mark, and that she had been unable to
get the situation under control before the rumors had been
sent flying.

I then called Cathryn, who had not been watching television
and therefore heard nothing about a terrorist threat. She said
that she would make sure Marissa did not hear anything until
Mary Beth arrived. Since Cathryn spoke fluent Turkish she
said that she would watch the local news, find out all that she
could, and report back to me.

When the kids arrived home they must have felt as if I had
put them under house arrest. "Marissa," I said, "there has
been a report on the TV that some terrorists have kidnapped
Daddy and Matthew. We don't know whether this is true or
not. If someone does have them, at least they're not out in the
cold. I don't want you to worry, because we don't know anything for sure. Does this make sense to you?"

Marissa asked, "What's a terrorist?"

I explained to her as best I could. She grew teary-eyed and
demanded a hug.

I told both Mark and Marissa that I would not allow either
of them to leave the apartment until I figured out what was
going on. Nor would I allow them to watch any news.

Marissa grumbled about having to leave Joanie's but then,
with the innocence of youth, found something to play with.

Banished from television viewing, Mark retreated to the
study and sat in front of the computer. He had previously
watched a *60 Minutes* segment about the Palestinian terrorist
group Hammas that showed them burning the American flag.
The people who claimed to have Mike and Matthew said they
were from Lebanon, so Mark began researching Lebanese terrorist groups on our CD-ROM encyclopedia. Within minutes
he called me into the room. Standing behind him, I looked
over his shoulder at a map of the Middle East. We studied the
image on the screen and talked quietly about whether it would

have been possible to get Mike and Matthew out of Turkey and into Lebanon. Was someone just capitalizing on information that had appeared in the newspapers and on television? Or had they waited until they had gotten Mike and Matthew to Lebanon, so that they could make the claims from the security of their homeland? There was no way to know.

Cathryn checked in regularly, helping to translate the bits of information we could gain from Turkish TV. But we learned nothing new. It was similar to what happens in the United States when there is breaking news. Reporters have about three facts that they keep repeating. There was no official confirmation but plenty of informal speculation. The Armed Forces Network was not reporting the story.

A part of me wanted to believe the terrorist story. If it was true, at least it was an indication that Mike and Matthew were still alive. I thought: Maybe they have something to eat and drink; maybe they're out of the cold.

The phone rang off the wall. One of the calls was from my friend Mrs. Tu, who worked for a radio station. She said that her station confirmed the calls, but they had no way of knowing who it was from or whether it was authentic.

Finally Jim Holmes called from the U.S. Embassy. He told me what I already knew. Yes, the calls had come in. No, none of the information was confirmed. He promised to call me back in the morning with more details.

Later that evening Monsignor Nugent and Sister Bernadine arrived at our apartment. They told me that the chapel had been full for the special Mass for Mike and Matthew. I was pleased with this show of support from our spiritual community.

"Would you like Communion?" Monsignor Nugent asked.

"Oh, it's so nice that you came over to do this," I said. "I just felt like I really couldn't leave here."

Receiving the Sacrament at home, under these circumstances, was even more special than usual. I felt much like I did when I was very young, when Communion was new to me and every encounter with Christ in this form was almost mystical. As a mere seven-year-old, the sacred feeling of Christ coming to me in His flesh was nearly incomprehensible and extremely awe-inspiring. Time had dimmed this feeling, but this night it returned.

I thought: God is present for me. Here. Now. When I so desperately need Him.

DAY 5

•

Thursday, January 19

Mike

I awoke during the middle of the night to the sound of distant drumbeats, and hope stirred within me. For quite some time I tried to guess the origin. It was a sound similar to what I had heard during Ramazan, the Muslim holy month of fasting. (Many other Muslim peoples use the term "Ramadan.") During this time, most Turks eat nothing during the daylight hours, and the drums signal the hour before sunrise, when they may still take food. In Ankara the previous year, drums such as these woke us at 3 A.M. during Ramazan.

The mysterious pulsating sound continued, sometimes growing faint, sometimes increasing in intensity. How far away are they? I wondered. How far away are *we?*

I attempted to get a bearing on the direction of the sound, but it seemed to vacillate, as if the sound waves were blown about by changing wind patterns. Am I really hearing this? I wondered.

I searched my memory. It can't be Ramazan, I decided. Ramazan is in early spring and even though the dates move around on our calendar, based on the lunar "Arabic" calendar, this surely must have been a bit too early. But what else could it be? I knew from my time in Saudi Arabia that strict Muslims adhere to the call to prayer five times a day. Did the villagers have a similar signal for their call to prayer, or did they perhaps have their own special rituals? I knew that the villagers were far more conservative than the urban residents, and I theorized that this might be some sort of cult ritual.

When Matthew woke, I asked, "Do you hear those drumbeats?"

He was sleepy and his mind was foggy. He strained to hear, but he shook his head no.

Mary

Early in the morning Angelina again offered me a few messages of uplifting scripture that had come to her the night before. She mentioned her belief that God must be "working on Mike." It was a phrase I knew well. I believe that God has a purpose for the trials we endure. Life experience has shown me that we grow and learn at least as much from the rough spots as we do from the smooth ones. Was it patience He was trying to teach us now? If it was, I could hear Mike saying, "Okay, God, what are You trying to teach me, because I'd sure like to learn it real fast!"

Angelina's statement cued a memory. I shared with her the story of what we went through a few years earlier, when we were stationed in Hawaii. After only eight months at the assignment, Mike's unit was deactivated, ending what we had anticipated to be a three-year tour of duty. Our heads were in a jumble. We did not know where we were going or when. Mike was looking into assignments in Hawaii, Singapore, St. Louis, and numerous other locations. He engaged the Lord in serious prayer about this issue, but still struggled with the uncertainties and his apparent lack of control over his future—and our future. He had theorized: "God must be working on me." One night, as we attended a prayer group meeting, Mike responded to the call from a visiting evangelist to come forward for prayer. When Mike stepped forward he said nothing, but waited on the Lord to speak through the man. The evangelist had said, rather cryptically, "If you think you are having trouble now, just wait!"

Now that prophesy was upon us.

Mike

As daylight arrived we remained in the cave, huddled together, hoping to hear the sound of another chopper.

Matthew asked, "How long have we been out here?"

The question caught me by surprise. I had no answer. What day was this? Three days? Four? I could not be sure. Although pocketing my watch on the night we were lost had been a matter of survival—to prevent frostbite due to the cold conducted by the metal watch and wristband—I wondered if subconsciously the action had served another purpose.

By removing my watch from my wrist and keeping it tucked in my jacket pocket, I had put away my means of keeping track of the days. All I needed to do was take the watch out of my pocket to see what day it was, but my mind refused to allow me to do so. What did it matter? What could that information do for us? A day-by-day, hour-by-hour, minute-by-minute tracking of the time would only deepen our misery and intensify our tendency toward despair.

The Search

Sully's first reaction was that the terrorist scenario might be good news for the Couillards. The tracks that the searchers had found on Tuesday had led nowhere. The air search had discovered nothing and the crews were starting to tire. If the terrorist story was true, then at least the Couillards were still alive. He thought: That's better news than I have.

Sully now faced a difficult task. He was asked to provide his professional opinion as to how long the air search should continue. Although he attempted to maintain a businesslike attitude toward a search-and-rescue mission, he always found himself personally involved. He had to steel himself now, to make sure that his emotions did not color his opinion.

Responding to a reporter's inquiry, Colonel Fitzgerald discounted the terrorist threat. "The group wanted to take advantage of the incident," he theorized. He asked rhetorically, if terrorists had actually kidnapped Mike and Matthew, why did they wait so long to announce the fact and make their demands? In fact, they had not acted until Mike's and Matthew's disappearance had been reported in the press.

The colonel returned his attention to the search, but in truth he was losing hope. This was probably the final day that Nighthawk helicopters could be committed to the search. The aircraft were needed back on their primary mission, Operation Provide Comfort.

To make up for the loss, the colonel tried to cut through the Turkish red tape. A Turkish Air Force general said that he would try to send a couple of Hueys from Izmir Air Base. A Huey is a smaller, potbellied helicopter that was the workhorse for U.S. forces prior to the development of the Blackhawks and Nighthawks. Hueys were being phased out of the U.S. arsenal, but America had been supplying the Turks with these surplus helicopters for some time.

A new force of five hundred Turkish commandos was ready to join the effort and the colonel made plans for a massive ground search.

One *final* search.

Mary

Fairly early in the morning Jim Holmes called from the U.S. Embassy to confirm what Turkish television had reported the previous night: A terrorist threat had been received. According to Mr. Holmes, the caller, who spoke Turkish with a heavy

Arabic accent, said that he was from a group that called itself the Lebanese Freedom Fighters. He claimed that members of his group had kidnapped Mike and Matthew and were holding them until their demands were met. The caller said that the American man and his son were in good health and that he would be able to offer proof that his people had them. The prisoner whom they wanted freed was a Lebonese Shiite Muslim identified as Haji Ali Drani.

Mr. Holmes explained that both U.S. and Turkish officials suspected that the call was a hoax. The timing made everyone suspicious. No one had claimed responsibility for the missing pair until it had become common knowledge, reported in the newspapers and on TV and radio. And, in fact, the caller had asked for the release of the wrong man. The prisoner in question was Mustafa Dirani, the uncle of Haji Ali Drani. The previous May, Mustafa Dirani had been snatched from his home in eastern Lebanon by Israeli raiders. Although he was not a member of the notorious Hezbollah terrorist organization, he was sympathetic to their cause and was believed to have been involved in the capture of an Israeli airman. For its part, Hezbollah was denying any involvement in the claimed kidnapping of Mike and Matthew.

Mr. Holmes assured me that both Turkish and U.S. authorities would investigate the terrorist threat thoroughly, even though they tended to discount it. He reassured me that this new development would not affect the continuing search effort on Kartalkaya Mountain.

When Cathryn arrived to check on me, I admitted to her, "I never thought I'd say, 'I hope my husband and son are in the hands of a terrorist group.' " But it was true. The alternative picture in my mind was that Mike and Matthew were freezing to death somewhere in the mountains.

Mike

We heard the whirring of helicopter blades coming close and again I rushed outside in my bare feet. Energized by the possibility of rescue, I found the strength to wave and scream. I used my Sprint card to try to flash a signal, but I knew that the chances were slim that anyone would notice. Just like the helicopter that appeared yesterday, this one flew directly overhead. Searchers would be peering off to the side and would be unable to see anything directly below them.

I calculated that we were about a mile outside of the search area. The rescuers simply did not expect us to have traveled this far in the backwoods wilderness amid blizzard conditions.

After I crawled back into the cave I pondered the wisdom of making another arduous trek to the top of the ridge. If and when another chopper came along, I would at least be closer to the search area. But to do that I would face the painful ordeal of pulling on my boots and struggling through the ice to reach the vantage point. I would have to wait indefinitely, with no guarantee that another helicopter was on the way, risking further injury to my feet. And the ridge was covered with trees, making it difficult for anyone to spot me from the air. In the meantime, Matthew would be alone, freezing in the cave.

Then I turned my attention to the ridge located above our cave on this side of the barbed-wire fence. It was directly opposite the one I had climbed yesterday, but it was somewhat lower and appeared to spread out on top, forming a high plateau. The route to the top was not as long as it was to the ridge on the opposite side, and I decided to give it a try.

But I quickly realized that this route was even more difficult. I zigzagged along the path of least resistance until I encountered a huge, fallen tree. There seemed to be no way around this obstacle, yet its ice-covered trunk was too broad for me to climb across, especially in my weakened condition.

Mary

Christine Lane was a recent graduate of the Air Force Academy, a sharp young lady with a solid career future in the military as an OSI investigator. She was also a Roman Catholic and we knew each other from the "Vatican." Possibly because of this, she was assigned to interview me and gauge my reactions to a series of possible scenarios. She called and asked if it was a good time for her to come by. "Fine," I replied. "Where else would I be?"

When she arrived we went into the piano room to talk. It was a bright sunny day and light streamed in through the windows. Christine stands about five-foot-four and she has shoulder-length sandy brown hair and a lovely, ivory-toned complexion. Her gentle appearance belied the fact that she was well trained and in control of the situation.

She stood with her back to the piano. "I hate to do this," she began, "but I have to ask you these questions. I have seen your family at the 'Vatican' and I have always admired your relationship, but it's part of my job to ask you these questions." As she spoke she occasionally glanced away. She found it difficult to maintain eye contact. "Mary," she asked, "could there be another woman in Mike's life? Could he possibly have run off with Matthew?"

My mind said, Let's get real here, but I knew that Christine was just doing her job, and I knew that I had to give her a straight answer.

"Let me tell you about last Saturday night," I began. "Mike and I walked to the grocery store together, hand in hand, up the street and around the corner. He told me that not only was he in love with me, but that I was his best friend as well. It was not the kind of thing you say to someone when you're planning to take off with one of your kids the next day."

Christine nodded and smiled, and noted my answer. As the

conversation progressed she became more confident and comfortable. The OSI, she explained, was going to conduct a standard "Missing Persons" search for Mike and Matthew. They would trace any use of Mike's phone or credit cards to make calls or obtain money. They would see if there was any record of anyone attempting to get access to the base using his military ID. If they found anything, they would trace it backward to see if they could get a lead on Mike's and Matthew's whereabouts.

It seemed like a good idea, and for a passing moment I thought to myself: What an interesting job Christine has. Then reality returned. She asked me what documents Mike carried in his wallet.

She copied the information carefully. Mike's driver's license had been recovered from the equipment rental room. But in his wallet he would have his military ID card, Visa card, and Sprint calling card. He had photos of the kids. There was his flying license, his ID card from the Federal Aviation Administration, and perhaps his ODC badge. "And he always carries a copy of his orders into Turkey," I added. We searched through our family business records and copied down account numbers.

At the completion of our half-hour interview Christine returned to her office and began to search for any use of Mike's documents during the past five days. When she contacted an official at the U.S. headquarters of Sprint, she ran into a stone wall. The man informed her that he could release information only to the person or persons who held the account. Since the account was only in Mike's name, he could not cooperate.

Frustrated, Christine called me. "Okay, Mary," she said, "I've got the Sprint official on the phone and he wants to know just why you think you should be able to get this information."

"Because I'm his wife!" I shot back.

She passed on my response, came back on the line with me, and whispered, "He's chuckling because he says that's exactly what his wife would say." Still, he refused to release any information.

I told Christine to tell him to check his billing records. I was the one who handled our business affairs and the account might reflect that payments came in from Mary Couillard, not Michael.

Several minutes passed. Then Christine relayed to me that the Sprint official also found this response amusing. But he still insisted that the matter was out of his control. I asked her if she could get him to say whether or not the card was being used, without revealing specific information as to who was being called. No, the official said, he could not.

Christine finally aborted this annoying conversation and told me that she would quickly seek a subpoena forcing Sprint to turn over the information. That was fine with me. I knew that if Mike were able, he would have called me, but the possibility existed that Mike and Matthew had found their way to some remote village that did not have telephone access. Or perhaps someone, somewhere, had found his wallet and used the card. Any report of telephone activity would give a new impetus to the search and provide a point of reference.

Mike

A second Blackhawk did come by later in the day. Once more I jumped outside and tried to attract the attention of the searchers. Once more I failed.

Returning to the cave, I found Matthew unresponsive. He no longer wanted to talk about the excitement of the helicopter sighting, and I was concerned that he was beginning to give up hope. I had to find some way to distract him from our plight. "You know where I wish we were now?" I asked.

He shook his head slowly.

"Remember that cruise we took? Wasn't that neat?" The previous October, Mary's sister, Kate, and her husband, Elliot, had come to visit us and we had enjoyed a five-day Mediterranean cruise. "The water was warm," I reminded him. "Can you believe it's only been a few months?"

Matthew finally brightened at this memory. "We had a pretty good time snorkeling on that cruise, didn't we, Dad?" he said.

"Yeah, I guess it's hard to compare to Hawaii, but we did see some pretty neat fish." I reminded him of the little dinghy with a small outboard motor that he was allowed to pilot. "Did you like being able to drive the little motorboat around those times we stopped and docked?"

"Uh-huh!" Matthew's brow crinkled, and he asked, "Do you think we can have a boat someday?"

"Of course. I'm sure that after this we may be looking for a warm place to live and it is very possible we might want to have a boat there. Do you like that idea?"

"You bet!"

This has to be a good thing, I realized. We had shifted our thoughts from the extreme cold—and from the increasingly hopeless feeling of our situation—and spoken of the future.

Mary

A month earlier, a city-wide prayer meeting had been scheduled for this night. Under ordinary circumstances, we would have attended. Now the fact that this service had been planned ahead of time appeared to be a clear case of divine intervention. I could not go, of course, but I knew that Christians throughout Ankara would be praying for Mike and Matthew all evening.

Still another OSI investigator arrived. He advised me not to answer my telephone directly. Instead, he asked Pam and Mary Beth to screen my calls and instructed them to be on the alert for contacts from strangers. He gave them a list of procedures to follow:

If you get a call from someone claiming to have hostages:

STAY CALM—TRY TO KEEP THEM TALKING

Try to get evidence:
   "WHY SHOULD WE BELIEVE YOU?"
   "WHAT IS THEIR CONDITION?"
   "WHAT DO YOU WANT?"

Ask about identification:
   "WHAT CAN YOU TELL ME ABOUT THEM?"

Listen for:
   Background noises
   Accents
After you hang up, write down everything you remember.

If you speak to a hostage:
STAY CALM—TRY TO KEEP THEM TALKING
Ask: "HOW ARE YOU?"
   "ARE YOU HOT/COLD?"
   "DID YOU HAVE A LONG TRIP?"
   "WHERE ARE YOU?"
Listen for:
   Background noises
   Accents
After you hang up, write down everything you remember.

Not long after the OSI man left, a strange phone call did
come in. Mary Beth took the call and immediately began making notes. A man was on the line speaking English, but Mary
Beth could hear someone in the background chattering in
Turkish. The caller wanted to know, "Where are the other two
children?" When Mary Beth did not respond directly, the line
went dead. She reported this to me immediately.

I was truly frightened. "None of the newspaper stories mentioned that we had three kids," I said.

"Yes, but Mark and Bryn were in one of the pictures taken at the search scene," she reminded me.

"Oh, yeah," I said, "but I don't think anyone has ever written about Marissa or about us having three kids. How would someone know that? Why are they calling? Who are they and how do you think they got our telephone number?"

Mary Beth simply shook her head in bewilderment.

"Do you think they know where we live?" I said.

She had no answer, and I could tell that she was picking up on my fear. We were military wives, and this was a tension that always ran beneath the surface of our lives here in Turkey.

I realized that, whether or not the terrorist claim was true, our family was now well-known in a country where Americans—particularly those in the military—have to be careful. I thought back to the orientation we had received when we arrived at this assignment. For example, we were taught to routinely check under our cars to make sure there were no bombs. We always made sure that we knew the identity of a visitor before opening the apartment door.

Were we targets now, singled out by the media attention?

I gathered Mark and Marissa about me and told them that, through no fault of their own, they were grounded. "Since we don't know what this business is all about, I'm going to have to insist that you stay at the apartment."

Mark began to argue, "But I want to be with my friends. You have your friends here all day and I don't have any of mine."

Marissa picked up the theme, whining, "I want to go to Brittany's."

"Now, listen," I said in a stern tone, "I'm going to tell you something. I don't want to scare you, but you have to know what is happening. We just got a phone call from someone who wanted to know where the other two children were. There has been no mention of Marissa in the papers. No one should know this. I don't feel safe about you leaving the apartment. Daddy and Matthew are—we don't know where—and I can't be worrying about you guys, too."

Marissa was upset and needed a reassuring hug. Mark joined in the embrace and said, "Okay, Mom, we'll humor you!"

Last night, when I ordered Mark home from Wanda and Bryn's apartment, I had asked him to do just that. Hearing my own words come back at me brought a smile.

Late in the day Colonel Fitzgerald called with another negative report. He explained that the Nighthawk helicopters were needed for Operation Provide Comfort, so they were being forced to cut back on the air search. But they were trying to persuade Turkish authorities to send a couple of Hueys from a Turkish base at Izmir to continue the airborne patrols for another day or two. I knew that the Huey was the smaller predecessor of the Blackhawks and Nighthawks. I also knew that its technology was inferior.

The colonel explained in a matter-of-fact tone that the Hueys could at least scout out the territory further so that the searchers might have better leads when they returned to Kartalkaya Mountain after the spring thaw. The fact was, he said, they were close to quitting. They were now ready to make one final, massive ground search, augmented by a special group of five hundred Turkish commandos.

All of this was very alarming, and I wondered if I should just go to the mountain myself and try to force everyone to look harder. But I knew that this was out of the question; there was no way that the authorities would allow it.

The colonel's call left me drained. Emotionally and spiritually, I could not accept his "spring thaw" scenario, but it was impossible to force the echo of his statements from my mind. Finally, I could keep it in no longer. I drew Pam aside and told her what the colonel had said.

She was incredulous and very angry. She had spoken to him several times on the telephone as well and kept detailed notes on their conversations. He had said nothing to her about giving up and returning after the spring thaw, and she was livid that he would say such a thing to me. When Pam's husband, Ken, arrived to keep company with us for the evening, she recounted the colonel's words to him. Ken was incensed. He immediately

went off somewhere to make a private phone call. I never
learned who he spoke to, perhaps Colonel Fitzgerald, perhaps
Mr. Holmes, perhaps both. But he must have communicated
our anger and frustration. After he returned from his conversations, I never heard the "spring thaw" theory again.

I was glad that Ken was here. I grew up with four brothers
and have always been comfortable around men; I enjoyed
sports and masculine things. I realized that during most of this
week the apartment had been nearly devoid of men. Ed and
Ken had come that first night with their wives, Angela and
Pam, but that had been it. Why had none of the Air Force
section officers come by? Many of them had joined in the
search for the first few days, but what about now? I realized
that Ed was home with the kids so that Angela could be with
me. And Scott Marble was manning the ODC "command
post" desk all night. But what about Mike's buddy Hal? He
and the others should know that I would like to see them.
Could they not face me?

These thoughts led me to comment, "Ken, it's so nice to
have a guy around. Being constantly surrounded by all these
women is sort of like a hen party."

As soon as the words were uttered, I regretted them. I could
tell that I had ruffled Pam's and Angela's and Mary Beth's
feathers. I was so grateful for their support and for the sacrifices they had made for me. Hurting their feelings was the last
thing I wanted to do. I tried to smooth things over. It was all
right; they knew that I was preoccupied.

About 8 P.M. Mary Beth took a call and began speaking in
broken Turkish. Pam stood at her side with a notebook, ready
to record what she could of the conversation. I paced the room,
sharing questioning looks with Pam.

After a few moments Mary Beth covered the receiver and
said, "It's a woman speaking Turkish but I can't understand
her. What should I do?"

I was the only person in the room who was more fluent in
Turkish. Mary Beth whispered, "Maybe you should speak with

her, Mary. Just don't identify yourself." Pam nodded in agreement.

The other women huddled around as I grabbed the phone and said, *"Merhaba?"* ("Hello?") I listened for only a moment before my face broke into a grin. I covered the receiver and said, "It's the maid! She wants to know if she should come tomorrow. I told her no."

None of us realized how tense we had become until we started to breathe and laugh at the same time. We hugged each other and retold the story as if none of us had been there. Clearly the laughter kept us from crying in frustration.

Jim Holmes called back from the embassy and Mary Beth recorded the time of the conversation as 8:50 P.M. Speaking calmly and compassionately, he reported, "I want you to know that we've gotten a call from the people claiming to be holding Mike and Matthew. The caller says there's a videotape and still photos to prove that his people have them. We have instructions to pick up the material at a particular site, and we have people on the way. I just wanted you to know in case you heard anything on the news about this. I'll call you back as soon as I know anything."

I appreciated his candor. "I feel honored, actually special and surprised, that you are telling me this, that you are letting me in on this."

He explained once more that he did not want me to hear about it some other way.

"Thank you, Mr. Holmes," I said.

"I'll call you with any new information."

By now both my dad and Mike's mother, Cecile, were hooked into the system operated by the military's Casualty Affairs Office, which had branches all over the world. An Air Force member contacted them each day to keep them apprised of the latest developments. This was a relief to me because it was hard to keep reporting to them, "No, they haven't been found."

But, because of this new development, I felt that I had to call them in person, and I also decided to contact my twin brother, Ed, and my sister, Kate, so that they could pass the messages along. I wanted them to know that, yes, claims had been made, but the authorities were discounting them. From their end, they told me that the American media were picking up on the terrorist story and calling them, asking for interviews and comments. I cautioned them all about letting the media get its collective foot in the door. "You can do something for them, but what can they do for you?" I asked. I was happy that the story was being covered in Turkey, because Mike's and Matthew's photos were all over the place and someone might spot them. But our family in America might do better if we protected our privacy.

As we waited for Jim Holmes to call back, we all passed the time by working on a complicated jigsaw puzzle that depicted ornate Ukranian Easter eggs on a black background. No one wanted to bring up the subject of the terrorists.

It was 10:25 P.M. before Jim Holmes reported, "Our people went to the pick-up site, but there was nothing there. They're going to a second site now, but it will take awhile. We're beginning to believe that the tapes and photos don't exist. I won't have anything more to report until the morning, so why don't you try to get some sleep?"

I thought that this was probably an impossible suggestion, but in fact I was able to sleep.

Mike

As darknesss descended, so did my spirits. Matthew drifted off to sleep, leaving me alone with my thoughts. It was increasingly apparent that we were outside of the search area, and I had to consider the possibility that we would not be found, that perhaps there was a very real chance that we would die out here.

I recalled people who had hurt me in the past and I forgave them. I asked God to forgive me for all of the ill thoughts and feelings that I had harbored toward others. I knew that I had been totally forgiven by God. Small sins that I had fretted about in the past now seemed inconsequential. It was a bouyant feeling, even in such close proximity to death, to have the assurance of salvation.

During my college years I had read a book entitled *Life After Life,* which documented the near-death experiences of many individuals. I was impressed with the consistency of the accounts: the out-of-body sensation, traversing a tunnel, seeing the light, and being overcome with peace and joy. The message was clear that death was leading us toward the wondrous presence of God.

Later, I read another book that offered a different picture. For some, the near-death experience seemed to place them on the verge of entering hell. Again, the experiences were somewhat consistent. People described an intense suffering within themselves: grief and remorse over wrong choices and an incredibly harsh feeling of utter "aloneness." Even the biblical account of the physical pain of being eternally burned was there. People described a universal suffering of being trapped in this "lake of fire" with no way out. As one might expect, when these victims of traumatic near-death experiences revived, they expressed great relief at having a second chance. All were profoundly affected and left with a fear of what might have been.

As a Christian, the prospect of death did not inspire this fear, for my future was secured. I believe that my life is hidden in Christ, that by the virtue of what He has done through His death on the cross and His resurrection from the dead, I, too, would rise to a new life once I perished.

As a military man, I had often wondered how I would react in a combat situation. Would I hold up under pressure? How would I handle real and present danger if my life were on the line? And, as a Christian, I had heard numerous stories of persecution which took place in communist and totalitarian regimes in our day. I wondered if I would be strong enough and true to my convictions and beliefs under the threat of death.

Now I was in combat, a mortal combat against the elements. And I was, by the grace of God, at peace. Even if it meant ultimately we would die. Because of my strong faith in God my protector and Christ my shepherd, the prospect of my own death did not bother me.

The greatest valley was not death itself; it was the road that would lead to death. I dreaded the thought of seeing Matthew suffer the long, agonizing journey ahead as our bodies slowly deteriorated. What scared me even more was the thought that I might die first, leaving him to face the end of his ordeal alone.

I offered the most painful prayer of my life: Please, God, should Your plan be to take us home, by Your grace and mercy, take Matthew first. And if it is possible, spare us a slow, agonizing death. Please take us quickly.

DAY 6

•

Friday, January 20

Mary

"When I called you last night I told you the agents were on their way to the second pick-up site," Jim Holmes reported by phone. "But when they got there nothing was found." He paused long enough for my mind to process this information. Then he continued, "The Turkish police have picked up a man who they believe initiated most or all of the phone calls." The man's name was Murat Mercan. "He has been arrested before and is known to them for other hoaxes," Mr. Holmes explained. "They spent the night interrogating him."

I almost chuckled at that statement, for I had some idea of what it must be like to be interrogated by the Turkish police. The Turkish police do not read someone his rights.

"They now believe that no group is involved in Mike's and Matthew's disappearance," Mr. Holmes said. "The embassy believes that the Turkish findings are true, but because we still have not closed every avenue, we will continue to follow up on any leads we have."

I thanked him and once again he expressed his concern. "We'll be with you through this whole thing, Mary. We'll sort it out."

Someone in the room commented in an offhand manner, "At least they extended the deadline by another twenty-four hours."

Deadline? I thought. What deadline? This was the first I had heard that the terrorists had set a deadline. And what did they plan to do once the deadline passed?

My immediate reaction was to shine interrogation lights in my friends' faces and scream, "Spill your guts now. I want all the facts."

Someone explained that the original threat was that Mike and Matthew would be killed if the Arab was not released in forty-eight hours.

"How dare you keep this from me!" I screamed inside. "When did the clock start ticking on this? What was the original deadline? Where are we now?" These thoughts drove me crazy until I realized that my friends probably were not in the loop, probably unaware that the deadline information had been specifically kept from me.

When my mind quieted, I tried to calculate how many hours had passed since I had first found out about the terrorist threat on Wednesday night. When had Rumeysa called with the news? About 7 P.M. So a full day had passed and now another night. Twenty-four hours plus twelve hours. How much time before the next deadline was reached? What then?

It was all so crazy, and I knew that my hysteria was counterproductive.

I just won't think about it, I decided. What good will it do if I know when the next deadline is? I'll just make myself sick watching the clock. This whole terrorist thing is probably just a bunch of hooey anyway.

One by one my caretakers were falling prey to some kind of bug or virus. Mary Beth had stocked the apartment with tissues, but they were being used for blowing noses, not wiping tears. Tension, lack of sleep, and abnormal schedules were taking their toll. Angela was truly sick and needed to be at home, taking care of herself. I realized that all of these women had done more than their fair share and it was time to turn from my extended family to my immediate family for support. I thought of my sister, Kate.

Being the only girls in a family of six children, Kate and I had shared a room as we were growing up, and we had always remained close. She was only fourteen months younger than I and although I have a twin brother, Kate and I had developed a more twinlike relationship over the years. I needed my sister.

For days I had been waited on and catered to. Someone was always there to answer the phone. Well-meaning friends brought tons of food. Various people cared for Mark and Marissa; my apartment, like my refrigerator, was "Shawed" from top to bottom. I appreciated all of the support, but I could not stand my own idleness any longer. I had to accomplish something. Since it was January and we would soon have to face the yearly grind of preparing the tax return, I decided to assemble the necessary paperwork.

I was in my bedroom, shuffling through files, when Angela, Pam, and Mary Beth entered and closed the door behind them. All three of them appeared very serious. Obviously, something was up. I had not heard the phone ring, so I decided that whatever they had to say could not be devastating.

Pam spoke first. "Mary," she said, "we've been asked to approach you with the idea of your returning to the States with Mark and Marissa to wait this thing out."

"They're crazy!" I snapped. "I'm not leaving. They can't make me leave."

Pam knew me pretty well. "I had a feeling you'd say that," she responded.

"Look," I said, "I do have an idea for you. Just this morning I was thinking about all of you. You have done so much for me that you are all getting sick. I was thinking of asking my sister to come over. Do you think that will keep the 'powers-that-be' happy?"

The consensus was that it would have to do. I was not going anywhere, and they all knew it.

Mark pestered me for permission to go visit Bryn or Fabian. When I snapped at him, he began to grumble, but he stopped himself and said, "I know, I know: 'Just humor me.' "

Laughing at his gentle sarcasm, I offered a compromise. Fabian and Bryn—and anyone else he wanted to see—could come over to our place this evening.

Mike

Throughout the long day we heard the sound of a helicopter, quite distant from us. I tried to remain ready, in case the sound came closer. I had finally been able to get my socks somewhat dry, so I wore them, and I had Matthew's ski bib arranged near the mouth of the cave so that I would not have to struggle with my boots.

Late in the day the helicopter finally approached our position. I jumped out of the cave, screamed, waved, and banged the broken metal ski pole against a rock. Once again the rescue workers failed to look in our direction. Once again our hopes were dashed.

Other than that brief moment of hope, the day offered no consolation.

By now the experience had taken on a surreal quality; we were suspended in time and the edges of reality began to blur. Matthew was quiet, weak, and sullen. I found my own spirits sinking further.

The distant drumbeats continued to provide an absurd, rhythmic background to our plight. "Don't you hear those drums?" I asked Matthew.

He shrugged.

"You don't hear that?"

"Dad, don't be silly."

Trivial things did not matter. Under normal circumstances I often shower two or three times a day—first thing in the morning, then after my daily workout, and sometimes before going to bed. Shaving is an important ritual. But out here, the only thing that was critical was survival.

The condition of my hands was beginning to concern me. My gloves had been scraped and cut so many times that they absorbed increasing amounts of moisture that the thin inner insulation could not fend off. It was difficult to keep them thawed and dried. At times the gloves became so caked with ice they were useless. The lack of protection was beginning to show in my hands. In the days prior to the ski outing, I had suffered a cat scratch and a paper cut. Under these conditions, they festered. The paper cut, especially, was opening up like a knife wound. At times my fingertips felt numb and my guitarist's calluses had taken on that ominous, slightly waxy appearance.

I noticed that when I crawled out of the cave to urinate, near the end of the process my body issued a thicker fluid, as if the urine were mixed with a milky substance. At first I thought this was a seminal fluid and I reasoned that it was part of the body's natural ability to prioritize; perhaps it was shutting down a nonessential function. But Matthew was experiencing the same phenomenon, and he was too young to produce semen. I did not know what this symptom indicated; I only knew that it was ominous.

By now I felt that I had given the search teams enough time to find us, and I constantly second-guessed myself. Maybe I should leave this place, I began to think. Maybe the only solution was to strike out in search of help. The thought of leaving Matthew alone here in the cave was a somber one, but if I did not do something soon, what was to become of us? We might survive, but we would be in bad shape.

And we might not survive.

Each time I contemplated Matthew's features, so innocent and weak, I condemned my own foolishness. I was his father, supposedly his protector, and I had brought him to the point of death.

Both of us are introverts; we did not have a deep, burning need to constantly converse. We dozed so frequently that our conversations took place in bits and pieces. But I knew that, sooner or later, we had to discuss the reality of our plight. I did not want to lie to my son. I wanted to prepare him for what might happen, but I did not quite know how to do it.

The Search

"With every day that passes, we are aware their chances for survival are diminishing," Colonel Fitzgerald told a reporter. He explained that three hundred soldiers had combed twelve square miles. All they had discovered were a child's ski tracks on Tuesday, and traces of a fire sometime later. He said that the search would be called off Sunday and that teams would return to the area in the spring.

Back at Incirlik, Sully spoke with Major Johnson, commander of the 16th Special Operations Detachment, and he talked to the air crews. He checked their reports and confirmed that they had covered each of their assigned search areas at least three times. Even though Sully knew that the crews were working with inadequate maps, he had flown with them and characterized them in his mind as "ultimate professionals."

This was a heart-wrenching call. During the entire week he had committed his every moment to the search, and he told someone that the negative outcome was "the biggest failure of my life." He was in pain as he advised Brigadier General Carlton to suspend the aerial portion of the search until such time as the ground parties turned up something.

Mary

I called my sister, Kate, and asked if she could come to Turkey to help me get through this ordeal. She was very willing, but she said that she needed to check with her boss first. Kate works in Executive Compensations at Hughes Aircraft Company. This was the time of year when Kate's department had to inform the executives about their bonus packages, stock val-

ues, and other key considerations. It was the worst time for
Kate to leave.

The terrorist threat had caused Mike's and Matthew's disappearance to become an international news story, and it
was getting a bit crazy for all of our relatives back home.
My dad found reporters and camera crews camped out on
his lawn. He angrily ordered them to leave and the evening
news coverage showed him slamming the door in their faces.
In Lewiston, Maine, Mike's mom, Cecile, was approached
for a comment but, heeding my advice, she said nothing at
first. Then the reporters started seeking out other relatives.
Since both Mike's mom and dad had ten siblings, there were
plenty of cousins, nephews, nieces, and others who found
microphones thrust in their faces. When Cecile heard a report that Mike was born in Maine—he was actually born in
California—she decided that she had to speak out in order
to keep the facts straight.

As a result of the attention, I was receiving communica-
tions from various people around the globe. Many of them
were people we had known and prayed with over the years,
and many of them sent along scriptures that had been impressed upon their minds. Each message carried hope and
revived my faith that God was watching over Mike and
Matthew.

Nevertheless, dismal signals also came. Christine informed
me that the chief of the Turkish police theorized that Mike
had intentionally left the country, taking Matthew with him.

"Why in the world would he do that?" I asked Christine.

"The chief thinks that it's for financial gain," she replied.

The theory was preposterous, of course, but I realized that
if the chief could sell this idea it would save face for the owners
of the ski resort, who had not properly delineated the trails. It
would also quash the publicity about foreign terrorists operating in Turkey.

Christine said that when OSI investigators had dismissed the
chief's theory he had stormed out of the meeting muttering,
"We're not responsible."

This was maddening information, and I stormed about the apartment for a while, trying to control my anger. Finally I went to the bedroom to resume my task of assembling our tax information; it was the only way I could think of to keep myself busy.

Suddenly I was aware that Angela had sought me out again. It was clearly time for another speech. She began, "Mary, they are wanting to get your feelings about doing some kind of service on Monday."

I was immediately suspicious. Who did she mean by "they?" This is not good, I thought. "What kind of service?" I asked.

Angela explained that her husband, Ed, would be the one charged with planning the event. "He's thinking about calling it something like a Service of Hope," she answered.

I immediately relaxed. Ed Shaw is a strong Christian and I knew that he would arrange things in an appropriate manner. "Okay, that sounds good," I said. "What are they planning to do?"

Obviously this had been in discussion for a while because plans were already under way. "Ed is trying to get the monsignor to speak," Angela continued, "and he has been asked, or told, that he needs to have some kind of Turkish Muslim religious representative speak also."

This made me a bit uncomfortable. I'm thinking to myself . . . as a Christian I'm called to spread the Gospel. In okaying this service am I now going to spread the teachings of Mohammad? "And just what is this guy going to say?" I asked. "Who is he? Will he be the head of a mosque?"

"No, I don't think so. I think he will be somebody from the government religious office, a professor or somebody."

"Why is this necessary?" I wanted to know.

"Well, people feel that since there are so many Muslims intimately involved in the search, it's just the right thing."

This was not exactly as I would have wished, but I saw the logic, and I knew that it was the politically expedient thing to do. "Okay, I'll buy that," I said, nodding. But I added very quickly, "There is something I have to make very clear. I am not going to participate in any kind of death-oriented memorial service. Mike and Matthew are not dead. I know it in my heart. I won't participate in anything focused that way. Make certain that Ed and the others are aware of that."

Mike

Finally Matthew voiced his fear, asking, "Dad, what would it be like to die?"

I took a deep breath. Please, I prayed silently, let me say this right. Bits and pieces of scripture that referred to death and the afterlife filtered into my mind. Echoes of sermons I had heard and pages from books I had read surfaced in my memory. "Well, Matthew," I began, "I'm not sure any living person knows what it is like to die, but I did read a book once that told stories of people who believed they had died."

"How do they know they really died?" Matthew wanted to know.

"We can't be sure about that but many of these stories told about people who had drowned or had heart attacks or had been struck by lightning. Their hearts stopped beating for a time before they could be revived. For some it may have been seconds, for others many minutes. But they all told similar stories; it was like they had gone through a tunnel or passageway of some sort. On the other side, maybe death, they described a feeling of great peace, and most said they found themselves encountering an all-loving being, maybe God Himself. Maybe they were knocking on heaven's door. I'm not sure."

Matthew listened, wordlessly willing me to continue.

"I've also read about some people who had the same experience of going through that tunnel, but finding only suffering and fire on the other side."

"Were they in hell?" Matthew asked.

"I'm not sure, but some of it does seem to agree with what the Bible says about heaven and hell. We'll talk about that in a minute, okay, but I'm not sure we can put a lot of trust in those stories because we don't really know how long our brain can keep working when our heart stops. Looking at it scientifically, we could say that maybe what happened to these people was a function of brain waves that continued after the heart stopped—sort of like a dream. What's so puzzling is that their experiences seem so universal, so similar. Did they really die? We can't be sure. Some say you are dead when your heart stops beating. Others say you are dead when your brain no longer functions. I would say that a person is dead when his spirit leaves his body, and nobody can see when that happens."

Matthew seemed to be digesting this slowly, so I paused and let his thoughts catch up. Then I continued, trying to tie into what I knew he had learned at Sunday school and at home in our studies of religion. "Remember how you learned that we have a body that will one day die—but your spirit, the part of you that makes you Matthew, who you are, your personality . . . well, that part will never die? That part of you will go on to heaven or hell when your body dies."

I had given Matthew a lot to chew on, so I paused and let him think about it. Then I asked, "Matthew, did you follow all of that?"

"Yeah, I think so, but I don't want to go to hell. It would be awful to be burning forever."

"Yes," I said, "I can't think of a much worse picture than that, but maybe the worst part of it is that in hell you are forever separated from God. Maybe that's why it's so awful and maybe part of that burning is from not being able to taste God's love ever again."

Matthew's mind was racing now. "How can I be sure I won't go to hell?" he asked.

"Well, first of all you have to understand that there is nothing we can ever do to earn God's love. God is so good and so pure and holy that even our best behavior isn't good enough. Did you ever have a day when you could say you didn't do anything wrong or think anything bad about anybody?"

Matthew considered this silently.

"Pretty hard to do, isn't it?" I asked.

"Yeah, I don't think I ever had a day like that," he admitted, shaking his head.

"Well, the good news is that you don't have to be perfect. God loves you anyway. But you can't stop there, Matthew. God hates sin so much that it can't just be left alone. It will end up killing you. Sin separates us from God and will kill us if God doesn't do something. Remember in the Bible where it says, 'The wages of sin is death'?"

Matthew nodded.

"Sin kills. So what did God do? He sent His Son and let Him be killed in our place and then He raised Him up—that's why we celebrate Easter, because the day Jesus was raised from the dead, He made it possible for us to live. With God. Forever. Without having to worry about our sins anymore. Remember where it says that God loved the world so much that He gave His only begotten Son so that all who believe in Him should not die but have everlasting life?"

"Yeah, so all we have to do is believe in Jesus?"

"Well, sort of," I continued, "but Jesus Himself said that even the demons believe and tremble. So just believing isn't really it. Maybe a better word is 'trusting'—trusting Jesus to save you because, by His dying on the cross, He paid the price for your sins. Do you remember when you gave Jesus your heart years ago, while we were living in Colorado?"

Matthew's mood brightened. "Yeah, that's it, then—that was good enough!"

"Sure was," I affirmed. "If you gave Jesus your life and trusted Him to save you, I don't believe He will ever let you go."

"Dad, I want to be sure. How can I be sure?"

"Well, you said that prayer when you were very young and maybe you don't remember just how important that prayer was or what it did. Would you feel better if I prayed with you now just to make sure it was real?"

"Yes."

I believed that Matthew had made a heartfelt confession years ago, but I once again led him in the sinner's prayer, this time matching the words of the prayer to his new, more mature understanding:

> *Dear Jesus, I confess that I'm a sinner—even my best efforts aren't good enough to earn Your love. Without Your help, my sins will kill me and I will die forever. But because God loved us so much He sent You to pay the price for our sins. You died on the cross and He raised You up, snuffing out sin's power to kill. So now I trust You, Jesus. I give You my whole heart and my whole life and if I should die on this mountain, I trust You to raise me up to live with You and God the Father forever.*

No tears flowed and, because of the darkness, I could not see Matthew's face, but the tension in his body left and I could tell that a certain peace had come over him. I could not give Matthew hope that we would walk off this mountain, but I had restored his assurance and hope that even in death, we would live.

We talked about what heaven would be like. "It could be that we'll suffer getting there," I said quietly, "but we're going to a good place." I remembered some descriptions from Revelations and the gospels. "Matthew, in heaven there will be no more crying, no more suffering or pain. That's one thing we all have to look forward to. No matter what we have to go through to get there, we're going to a place that will have none of that. Heaven is a place where we will continually praise God. Jesus has promised us, 'In My Father's house are many rooms,' and He has prepared a place for us. He's already paid the price for our sins, so we don't have to worry about where we are going."

Mary

I read unspoken messages into Colonel Fitzgerald's daily report. The Turkish commandos were gearing up for one last big push during the weekend. But after that only a small contingent of U.S. Special Forces troops would continue the work. By Sunday night, if there was nothing new, the search team leaders would meet with embassy officials to decide what more, if anything, they could do.

Equally depressing was a paragraph in today's edition of *Stars and Stripes,* the newspaper for overseas U.S. military personnel:

> *Pentagon spokesman Kenneth Bacon says, "Our operating assumption is that they were lost in the snow." Skiers have disappeared in the Doruk area before, and their bodies have always been found in the spring after the snow melts.*

Having faith during the good times is easy, I reminded myself. It is during times of fear and despair that we are tested.

Cathryn and Norita came over at about the same time and had some news to report from Hulya, the Turkish convert. Hulya said she felt that either Mike or Matthew had some sort of problem with his leg—perhaps a sprain or a break—and was unable to walk. I knew that if Matthew was the one with the injury, Mike would stay and care for him. But how could Matthew take care of his dad if Mike was injured?

Hulya also had a vision of a stone cavelike structure on the mountain. This was a real possibility, for the searchers were specifically seeking out caves to see if Mike and Matthew had taken refuge in one of them.

I asked Cathryn and Norita to pray with me, specifically asking God to guide the search teams this weekend, so that they would at least find some evidence that would cause them not to give up.

The three of us prayed quietly for a time, but I had to fight hard against the despair that tried to encompass me. Afterward, Cathryn randomly opened her Bible and found herself staring at a passage from Luke 18, the parable of the persistent widow. She read it to herself and then eagerly read it aloud:

> *Then Jesus told His disciples a parable to show them that they should always pray and not give up. And will not God bring about justice for his chosen ones, who cry out to him day and night? Will He keep putting them off? I tell you, He will see that they get justice, and quickly. However, when the Son of Man comes, will He find faith on the earth?*

As she read this we all questioned ourselves. Had we truly been steadfast and persevering in our prayers? Or had we slowly allowed the world's doom and gloom to overtake us? Had we forgotten who our God really is? We determined that this passage was a gentle rebuke. We could not give up. We had to keep pounding on God's door.

Cathryn said, "I think God wants us to keep praying and asking him to save Mike and Matthew."

"I agree," I said. "This is like the scriptures we have gotten all along—uplifting, encouraging. We have to keep praying and just believe that God will answer us."

Mike

Matthew slept.

But as the hours of another long night passed, I found myself involved in a strange internal dialogue, as if I were two people, bantering back and forth, contemplating the situation, trying to decide what to do.

I realized that my earlier response—that I would rather die than return home less than whole—was supremely selfish. My family needed me, and I should be willing to make whatever sacrifices were necessary. But what could I possibly do? Matthew and I were lost in the wilderness, like the wandering tribes of Israel, and there was no pillar of cloud by day, or fire by night, to lead us out.

I thought of the pain for those who would be left behind, Mary without a husband, Mark and Marissa without a father. We had encountered several children who had been in that situation, and we knew that it was tough. Some were emotionally scarred, consumed by an irrational anger at the father who had left them behind.

My strength was failing fast. Hunger was no longer an issue. I was accustomed to the bitter cold, and my feet were so numb and frozen that they felt little pain.

The real agony was in my soul.

DAY 7

•

Saturday, January 21

Mary

Angelina woke up singing "Come on and Celebrate"—and so we did. When Cathryn arrived she picked up Mike's guitar and we sang:

> *Come on and celebrate! the gift of God.*
> *We will celebrate the Son of God who loved us and gave us life.*
> *We shout your praise, oh King,*
> *You give us joy no one else can bring.*
> *We give to you our offering of celebration praise.*

As we sang other hymns of praise and victory, the room took on a pep-rally atmosphere of "Let's get together and remember what the Lord has told us!" We praised God and thanked Him for keeping us hopeful.

We wanted to give Him the glory.

Once more we remembered the words from Zephaniah that Angelina had been led to earlier in the week:

> *Sing oh Daughter of Zion, shout aloud, oh Israel! Be glad and rejoice with all your heart, oh Daughter of Jerusalem. . . . The Lord your God is with you, He is mighty to save. I will rescue the lame and gather those who have been lost . . . at that time I will bring you home.*

Mike

"When are they going to come and look for us?" Matthew asked. "Why aren't they coming?"

These were painful questions with no easy answers. I tried to remain positive, pointing out that the continued presence of helicopter activity was surely a positive sign. They *were* looking for us. It was just a matter of time before they expanded the search area wide enough to find us. But even as I attempted to cheer my son, my own spirit grew more frail. I hoped that he could not detect this, but I knew that he might.

"Should we try to ski out again?" he asked.

"I don't think you could do it," I declared.

He nodded his head weakly.

I was increasingly concerned about our deteriorating physical condition. Every time I ordered Matthew to warm his feet against my stomach I surreptitiously checked their appearance. The swelling seemed to be increasing, and the skin of his feet had taken on a sickly gray pallor. Each time I struggled to put on my own boots I pulled back the edges of my socks, and noted that my own feet were getting worse.

Both of us had cuts and scrapes on our hands that refused to heal; in fact, they were turning into open sores.

Now I was convinced that we were, indeed, going to die. I thought: I'm a Christian, but Christians and other good people die all the time. We don't understand why we have to suffer, but we do have to accept God's will. It seemed that God's will was for Matthew and I to die together on this mountain.

The Search

The search teams were now comprised of U.S. military personnel from Incirlik Air Base, ODC, and the 39th Munitions Storage Group, as well as more than four hundred Turkish soldiers. They lined up shoulder to shoulder and, beginning at the lodge, prepared to trudge over every square foot of the search area.

Hadum Armagan, press spokesman for the U.S. Embassy in Ankara, said, "The chances are diminishing. The search will continue at least until Sunday afternoon, unless something is found."

Mary

I was surprised by a call from Debbie Erdahl. She was the mother of Matthew's best friend, Jared. We often joked that the two boys were practically joined at the hip, but Debbie had remained silent throughout the week. "I was wondering why I hadn't heard from you," I said.

"I didn't want to tie up your phone," she explained.

Thanking her for her consideration, I detailed the latest news or, more accurately, lack of news. Then I asked, "How's Jared?"

The sound of crying came over the phone line. "He's got hives all over him," Debbie said. "He's so worried about Matthew . . ."

Ed, Ken, Pam, Mark, Marissa, and I spent much of the day working on some wooden jigsaw puzzles that I had purchased at an after-Christmas sale from Lands' End. We sat on the

Doşemaltı carpet, and our conversation was often light and
breezy.

Angelina had been staying over at night so that I would not
be alone, but during the day she was at work. Now, on the
weekend, she was with us, and I sensed that she thought I was
spending too much time talking idly, playing with puzzles, and
sometimes even joking. Maybe she's right, I thought. Maybe I
should be spending more time in prayer. But I knew that the
activities were helping to keep me sane. I knew that God knew
my deepest desires.

Mike

I had faced death in the past and was surprised at my analytic
approach to it. We were flying out of Little Rock Air Force
Base in Arkansas. I was in the pilot's seat of a C-130 undergo-
ing low-level tactical training, leading a formation of three
other aircraft toward a drop zone that was about five miles
distant from, and directly lined up with, the runway at the air
base. It was an odd situation: a flight instructor sat in the
copilot's seat, checking my performance and offering instruction, but on this particular exercise, two additional pilots—
flight evaluators—stood behind him, checking his performance.

Suddenly the loadmaster's voice blared over the intercom:
"Oh, we've got some fluid loss back here. I'm going to check
it out." Moments later he reported, "We've got fluid spraying
all over back here." He went on to describe a high-pressure
leak emanating from one of the hydraulic lines in the area of
the aft ramp and door. This is the large door in the back of
the aircraft used to airdrop heavy equipment; it had its own
hydraulic system and its own lines, but booster and utility lines
also ran past this area to power the plane's elevator and rudder.
The loadmaster said that the leak was coming from the booster
hydraulic system. This was not a major problem. The booster

system works in unison with the utility system to power the flight controls. Most of their functions were redundant. With the booster system malfunctioning, we might find it a bit more difficult to actuate the controls, but the utility system alone was more than sufficient. Following standard procedure, we switched off the booster system so as to stop the fluid from spraying out.

Using caution, I suggested that we relinquish the lead of the four-plane formation. "Let's get it down," I said. The instructor agreed.

It was a low-threat emergency, but of course the tower cleared us for an immediate landing. Then, shortly after we lowered the flaps and the landing gear, the loadmaster reported, "We're losing fluid in the utility system, too! The reservoir is going down." There was panic in his voice. If both systems went out, we would not be able to control the aircraft.

"I'm taking it," the instructor said. Since he was the more experienced pilot, this was the automatic and correct response. I busied myself on the radio, apprising the tower of this new situation. Since we were already on our glide path and fully configured for landing, the instructor decided to switch off the utility hydraulic system to prevent further loss of fluid. His plan was to turn it back on during the final stages of the approach—but he did not tell the rest of us what he was doing, and we were all too busy to notice that the flight controls had frozen into place.

There may have been a bit of "up" in the elevator, for the nose of the plane rose slowly, causing us to lose critical airspeed. We should have been moving forward at more than 120 knots, but the airspeed indicator was falling toward 110. The instructor and I pushed hard on the yokes, trying to bring the nose down.

What happened next was not clear. One of us may have unknowingly pushed against the trim switch that is located on the yoke. And the trim is activated by electricity, not hydraulics. We were only a thousand feet above the ground when the trim engaged, activating a small tab on the elevator, which pushed the nose of the plane down.

Suddenly we pitched over into a dive, heading toward the ground at about a thirty-degree angle.

I was aware of people in the back of the plane and even some on the flight deck screaming in fear. The two flight evaluators behind us leaned forward, and all four of us tugged at the frozen controls. A strange, detached, analytical thought crossed my mind, simply noting: We're going to die.

We were only about two hundred feet from our deaths when the instructor, in desperation, switched the utility hydraulic system back on. We leveled off quickly and landed safely only minutes later.

When that near tragedy had occurred a dozen years earlier, I knew that there were angels on board.

I prayed that angels were with us now.

In an analytical frame of mind, I compared and contrasted these two experiences that had brought me face-to-face with death. In both instances, I was unafraid.

But there were key differences. On the C-130, the others were all professional airmen, who made adult career decisions that logically took this possibility into consideration. This time I had a far different "passenger" on board, an innocent child who was merely along for the ride and depended on me to make the critical choices.

Perhaps the greatest contrast was this: In the C-130 incident, I did not have time to consider the ramifications. Had I died then, it would have been over in a matter of seconds. But this time I—we—might have to suffer a long, agonizing death, and there was far too much time to consider the effects of all this on those whom we would leave behind.

Mary

Throughout the day dark thoughts attempted to intrude. I was walking from the back of the apartment when the thought crossed my mind: What will we do if they don't come back? Mentally I went through the checklist: The military will get us home and settled, take care of the funeral—we have good insurance. I have a master's degree in counseling. I can get a job—

—Snap out of it, Mary, I told myself. They are not dead. You don't know that. You'll deal with that if you find out it's true, but don't go down that path. It's not functional. It's not faithful.

"I need to pray," I announced. "Who wants to join in?" At the conclusion of our prayer sessions, my faith and hope were renewed and the dark thoughts were chased away for a time.

Mike

I decided to take care of some unfinished business, in case my condition deteriorated so badly that I could not use my hands.

I twisted my body around until I was sitting near the mouth of the cave, where there was sufficient sunlight. I fished the ballpoint pen from my jacket pocket. In my wallet I found an old, one-page leave slip, my official permission to be absent from my base at ODC. I had taken it along on our trip with Elliot and Kate last October. In case I was hurt and needed medical attention, the leave slip, along with my ID card, would provide the necessary information. Fortunately I had not gotten around to cleaning out my wallet. The back of the leave slip was blank. I unfolded it and arranged my wallet beneath it as a tiny desktop.

"Matthew," I said, "I'm writing a note to our family, just in case they don't find us. I want to make sure something gets written down. Do you have some stuff that you would want to say?"

He thought for a moment and replied, "What are you going to say?"

I told him that I was going to explain what happened, so that everyone would understand how we got ourselves into this predicament. And I had very important thoughts to leave with Mary, Mark, and Marissa. "Do you have anything that you want to add to that?" I asked. "Do you want to tell your brother and sister anything? Do you want to tell Mom anything?"

"Tell Mom she's a good cook," he said quickly. More slowly he added, "Tell them that I love them. Tell Marissa that I wish I hadn't fought with her so much."

With a huge lump in my throat and tears welling in my eyes, I wrote:

> *My darling wife, Mary:*
>
> *How I grieve at leaving you behind. I hate to come to that conclusion, but after 8 days (I think) and the 3 helicopters that flew overhead and despite my frantic waving did not spot us, it seems more and more the path the Lord is calling us on. Oh to see your smiling face again and to taste the sweetness of your lips. You have been more than a best friend—a great lover, fantastic mother (Matthew put in a word for good cook—he's been chattering about food since we ended up here). You have been that special person in my life who I could always count on, who I knew would always be there, no matter what. You have been my counterweight, matching each other's weaknesses with our strengths. I'd say we made a great team! Matthew has been a real trooper. The hardest part of this whole ordeal is watching him suffer. He wants me to relay to all of you*

how much he loves his family and especially wanted Marissa to know how much he loves her, and wishes he had not fought so much with her.

Mark, I want to encourage you to stay on the right path. You have come to an age where the temptations are more abundant, and the peer pressure is greater. There are always consequences for wrong choices. Sorry to start with a lecture, but I have so many dreams for you and I'm so proud of how far you've come already. I am very proud to be your father. By the way, being without a father won't be easy, but I know your maturity will help you—and remember you have another Father which can never be taken away. Call on Him when you need Him. Son, I love you with all my heart. Thanks for your patience when I was less than nice.

Marissa, you are a special person! I have not always known what to do with all your energy and sometimes even the impulsive expressions of your love for me. I'm sorry, and let me say right now, that I love you back! I love your enthusiasm for life and I pray it never dies. You are more than pretty on the outside—you have a beauty of heart that is hard to find. I love you, my daughter.

As to how we got here: the visibility at the top of the run was so poor and I was confused by a sign denoting a split in the trail, we ended up in the trees. Thinking we could make our way back, we took what must be a logging road—I expected to run into road or civilization—nothing. Got dark. Had to stop and make shelter. Much snow next several days—went scouting over ridge and could see cabins, maybe 5 miles, but couldn't leave Matthew alone.

Mary, my heart and soul forever: Mike

When I was finished I folded the note and placed it carefully in the inside lapel pocket of my coat, next to my heart.

Mary

My sister, Kate, called back with welcome news. Despite the fact that it was the busiest time of the year in her department, her boss was very understanding and told her that she could take a leave of absence. Since Kate and her husband, Elliot, had visited us only a few months earlier, she already had a valid passport and visa. She would leave Tuesday morning, L.A. time, and arrive in Ankara on Wednesday.

As evening approached, Mark asked to go to the movies with his friends. I did not want him to leave, but I knew that he was stir-crazy. I told him yes, if he promised that he would go straight to the theater and come directly back home. "You are not to discuss anything about Dad or Matthew being lost," I lectured. "Someone may overhear you, realize that you are an American, and start asking questions." Mark nodded and I continued, "If someone does approach you and asks you if you know anything, just give them the basics. Mike and Matt are still missing and the search is continuing. Try to end the conversation as soon as possible. Do not identify yourself or let them know that you are part of the family. You especially will not go with anyone else anywhere, and you have to promise me that you will take extra care in all that you do."

"Okay, Mom, okay," he said.

Then I used a technique that by now was very familiar to all of our children. I asked him to repeat to me what I had just said. When I was confident that he had heard and understood my warnings, I told him that he could go.

Colonel Fitzgerald had nothing new to report this evening. He told me that the massive search by more than five hundred Turkish troops had found nothing. "They will be out again tomorrow to finish what they started today," he said.

This was the last big push, I knew. The Special Forces troops were still out looking, but would they stay past Sunday?

I had to face the possibility that the search would be called off by the following evening.

I found myself thinking a lot about my mom. She had died of cancer in 1993. Although I was reconciled to her passing, I wished I could talk to her now. I missed her. Silently I asked: Mom, do you have any pull up there in heaven? Please do what you can.

The words of hope from Zephaniah encompassed me:

"I will bring you home.

"I will bring you home."

Mike

For no apparent reason I woke in the middle of the night. Easing my way out of the cave, I was suddenly overwhelmed by the sight of the brilliant night sky. I lay on my back in the snow and stared in awe.

Framed in the moonlit branches of snow-covered pine trees were billions of stars, so many that they blended together across the sky. There was no moon, and we were so far from the lights of civilization that the Milky Way seemed like a bright pathway to Paradise. Points of starlight poked through gaps in the branches, creating the illusion of a Christmas tree. The radiance was stunning.

I lay still for quite some time, overcome by a sight that outshone the beauty of anything I had ever seen.

After several minutes, God began speaking to my heart. Old Testament words came to mind: "Abraham, look at all those stars. Your descendants are going to number more than all these stars you see."

It was as if we were suspended between heaven and earth. Here we were, caught in this impossible, cruel, and painful place and at the same time witnessing the majesty and beauty that God has created. I was torn. To which home do I want to return? I wondered.

Perhaps it was a similar night in ancient times when God used Abraham's senses to remind him of the reality of His promise that Abraham's descendants would be as countless as the stars. Now He used my senses to underscore His promises to me. I was embraced by peacefulness and God chose this moment to speak to me—not audibly, but within my spirit. It was as if He said: "Look, Mike, do you remember My promise to Abraham? Well, I made a promise to you, if you'll remember. And when I give you a promise, I will never break it. I will not rest until the promise I made comes to pass."

It came back to me. One and a half years earlier, shortly after I had arrived for my assignment in Turkey, I succumbed to the stress of new responsibilities in an unfamiliar environment. For that entire time I handled the jobs of two people. It was a tough period, and I temporarily and stupidly tried to rely upon only my own strength to get me through. Then, during a group meeting I asked everyone to pray for me, to help me remember to rely upon God's strength. Norita, one of the leaders of the group, was inspired to refer me to Jeremiah 29:11–13. In that scripture, I found a personal promise. During these past days of tribulation, I had forgotten all about it, but God brought it back to my mind now:

> *I alone know the plans I have for you, plans to bring you prosperity and not disaster, plans to bring about the future you hope for. Then you will call to Me. You will come and pray to Me, and I will answer you. You will seek Me, and you will find Me because you will seek Me with all your heart.*

These words, which had encouraged me during the previous year, now came alive to enkindle a spark of hope within me. As I pondered these words it struck me that they applied directly to my life here on earth, that God chose to prosper my days here and now. It seemed God was saying that He was not done with me yet, that He still had plans for me, and that He knew intimately every detail of these plans.

I thought: Gosh, it's hard to believe I am going to die here if the Lord has promised me prosperity. God is going to take us through this. He's *not* going to let us die out here!

Lying outside under the canopy of stars, I felt the message clearly. And as I crawled back into the cave and snuggled next to my sleeping son, I pondered the implications.

After a time, my mind made the next leap: If God is going to get us through this, then I'm going to do the best I can to help Him do it. I will not give up.

I did not know what I would do, or could do, but I had to do something.

As I fell back asleep I felt the warmth of a loving God who cared so deeply for me, who chose this way of sharing His love for me at a time when my heart had been darkened with gloom.

DAY 8

•

Sunday, January 22

The Search

The hundreds of Turkish commandos arrived to continue what was described as a "last-ditch effort" to find Mike and Matthew.

Mary

Last Sunday Marissa and I had played hooky from church and I still had a tinge of guilt about that. We would not miss church today. Ross and Mary Beth offered to drive us.

Ever since the terrorist theme had been introduced, Christine had cautioned me to vary my patterns and routines and not be predictable in my movements. So we decided to leave early and take a circuitous route to the "Vatican." We also wanted to be in our seats before the rest of the congregation arrived, so as to reduce the number of well-meaning "I'm so sorry" comments that would inevitably be offered. Since this was the only English-speaking Mass available in Ankara, we wondered if any representatives of the media would be there.

We took seats on the far left side of the chapel. This was not where our family usually worshipped. Since Mike led the choir and I sang in it, we usually sat opposite this spot on the right side, near the organ and piano. This new location gave me an entirely different view of the service. We all prayed quietly and fervently. A few parishioners approached and offered words of concern and hope. I was touched by the realization that the entire Christian community of Ankara was deep in prayer for Mike and Matthew.

Throughout the service, I felt many eyes riveted in our direction. This was a debut of sorts—my first public appearance since this ordeal began—and I felt naked and exposed. Back when I was in high school I once had a genuine panic attack, and now I was concerned that all this attention would cause me to repeat the experience. I prayed for strength.

Tears welled in my eyes. Mark put a protective arm around me.

I knew that many well-meaning people would want to speak with me after the service, but I did not know what I could or would say to them. There were many people here whom I had never seen before. Who are they? I wondered. Are they all friendly?

Fortunately the Jaccards had anticipated my concerns. During the singing of the final hymn, they escorted us out the side door and back into their car. Once we reached home we persuaded Ken to create his "famous" omelettes.

Mark

I was happy that we were back at home with friends now. Life was almost normal. Colonel Jaccard said that we could each pick the ingredients we wanted inside our omelettes.

Jess and I hung out and talked. We didn't know each other real well but we had done stuff with the youth group, and now with Dad and Matt gone our friendship was growing.

Alex and Marissa were being their creative selves. They began to plan a magic show for later in the day—complete with a disappearing act and pulling a rabbit out of a hat.

I thought: Too bad Dad and Matthew aren't here.

Mike

Once again we had rested intermittently, waking at intervals to warm our feet, then slipping back into a dazed, troubled sleep. By the time I was aware that morning had arrived, the sun had been up for a while. Last night's vision came back to me, bringing with it a calm resolution.

It must have been about 10 A.M. when I became aware of the *thump-thump* of rotor blades. It emanated from behind our vantage point in the cave, from the high side of the mountain. This sound was somewhat different than before. I scrambled outside the cave in my bare feet just in time to see it pass directly overhead. I jumped and waved in despair as it disappeared in the distance.

This helicopter was different, a smaller, clumsy-looking Huey. It was American-made, but I could tell by the paint scheme that it was not currently used by one of the American service branches. It was undoubtedly a retired piece of equipment transferred from our inventory under the terms of the U.S.-Turkish Defense and Economic Cooperation Agreement. Some Hueys were still flying in the States, but most of them had been replaced by the newer Blackhawks. I assumed that this Huey was now a part of the Turkish military, or perhaps it was under the aegis of NATO.

But whoever was operating it, the copter had been on track. It was clearly searching for us, and I waited many minutes, hoping that it would return.

Once again disappointed, I retreated within the cave to thaw my feet.

"Maybe he's just going for fuel," I said to Matthew. "Maybe he's going to come back along the same route." But in truth I realized that the appearance of the Huey was a negative. Since it was not a Blackhawk it made me wonder whether the American searchers had given up. Perhaps they had been

forced to return the Blackhawks to their primary duty, and the
Huey indicated a kind of marginal effort to keep the search
going. I did not discuss these thoughts with Matthew; I did
not tell him that this was a different type of helicopter.

Strangely, despite this latest instance of plummeting hopes,
I could not contain myself. Somehow, in spite of—or perhaps
because of—this occurrence, I was stirred to the very core of
my being. The melody of a favorite song flowed freely and I
refused to be silenced. As I struggled into my boots, simple
words with a profound meaning poured from my mouth:

> "I love you Lord and I lift my voice
> To worship you. Oh my soul rejoice!
> Take joy my King in what you hear,
> May it be a sweet, sweet, sound in your ear."

Matthew stared at me as if I were crazy, but I believed the
words were anointed of God, certainly in what they had meant
to me over the years. Now, at this moment, as I began to
praise God, the hope that had been planted in my heart the
night before took root and sprouted. Like the stump of Jesse,
out of the ashes of my own reconciliation with death grew a
tree of towering hope for the future.

The key problem was that our location was not very visible.
Since it was still very early in the day and there was at least a
chance that more helicopters would fly past, I decided to try
once more to climb the ridge that was off to our right. I had my
Sprint card ready; maybe it would be visible from that location.

I knew that the exertion would tax me. But I now began to
see my body as an expendable resource. I would spend myself
in an effort to survive and would deal with the results later. If
I did not survive, any injuries I sustained would not matter
anyway. My dislocated hip was an unimportant inconvenience,
and I considered the condition of my feet to be another. I
knew that each time I put the boots on and the longer I trudged
around in them, I was damaging my feet, but I would deal
with that later—if there was to be a later. For now, I had to

do what I had to do. I had to search for landmarks, make myself as visible as possible, bring water to Matt—I had to do whatever it took to survive.

This would be one last try. I had to find some way to get across the huge fallen tree that blocked the route to the top.

Once more I set out, wading through snow, ignoring the pain, ignoring the ice. Before long I reached the massive tree trunk that barricaded the way.

I rested, gathered my strength, and formed a plan. Laboriously, I arranged several rocks as stepping-stones. Standing on top of the pile, I tried to climb onto the broad tree trunk, but my legs were too weak and I stumbled back into the snow. Again I tried, and again I stepped back. Finally I was able to lunge for a branch and pull myself up and across the massive log. Now I could wade through the deep snow and up the final, steep slope of the ridge.

A gift awaited my eyes. Snowcapped trees glistened in the morning sunlight. Icicles hung from the branches and sparkled with the rainbow colors of a prism. Despite our desperate situation I marveled at this sight, truly enjoying the splendor of the moment. I had always loved mountains and tall pine trees. One might think that after all these days of tribulation, I would be repulsed by the panorama of a snow-covered landscape. Instead, I was dumbfounded.

From this vantage point I spotted another group of cabins, somewhat closer than the cluster I had seen from the ridge on the other side. The cabins resembled Alpine chalets and appeared to be well cared for. I estimated that they were about two miles away. I thought: Gosh, that's close enough!

Small ridges and patches of woodland blocked my direct line of sight, but the trail appeared to head from our location directly toward this settlement. It was still morning, and I thought it might be possible to reach these cabins by skiing the trail on down the mountain; I was sure I could make it before nightfall. Maybe there would be people there, and food, and warmth. I thought about attempting to strap Matthew onto my back, but I had tried that before, on the first day, without success. Now,

many days later and much weaker, I knew that I did not have
sufficient strength. This trek up to the top of the ridge had
already exhausted me.

If I did attempt to get to the village, I knew that I would
not have the strength to make the uphill return trip. But surely
there were people there. A hope popped into my head and I
wanted desperately to believe it possible: Maybe someone
would have a snowmobile! Then they could retrieve Matthew
quickly, surely in a matter of minutes. It would be easy enough
to direct them back along the trail until they found the skis
planted in the snow. They would find him easily and speed
him back to me.

But how could I possibly attempt to reach the village if it
meant leaving Matthew alone?

My mind returned to its original objective: to wait for the
return of the Huey, or perhaps another Blackhawk.

For a time I could see the Huey off in the distance, orbiting
in a search pattern above what I assumed was the ski area,
several ridges beyond us. I thought: Boy, it seems like a long
way off. Had we really traveled that far? Or had the copter
expanded their search area—but in the wrong direction?

I waited and prayed that the Huey would return, even if it
was just to refuel. From this location, I was certain that I could
make myself seen. One pass was all I would need. But the
waiting proved to be in vain. After a while, the Huey
disappeared.

Mary

All day long a variety of people arrived, many of them bearing
food. The weekend had freed them from their jobs and other
responsibilities, and they now wanted to show their support.
Men and women milled about, talking quietly, introducing

themselves to one another. Some gathered in small prayer groups.

Some of us continued to work on the puzzle, and I found myself blurting out unanswerable questions. "How could they just fall off the face of the earth without a trace?" I asked. My previous training with the Civil Air Patrol told me that Mike should be making SOS signs and other maneuvers to signal their whereabouts. "Not a scarf. Not a glove found. Why?" I babbled to no one in particular.

Cathryn suggested a prayer and, for the first time, some of our military friends who were not part of our Bible study group joined in. I prayed that those hundreds of soldiers who were going over every inch of the mountain would find Mike and Matthew today. I knew that this was the final, aggressive push to find my husband and son.

During the afternoon my twin brother, Ed, called with the suggestion that the searchers use metal detectors in the snow-drifts around the parking lot of the ski resort. His concern was that if Mike and Matt had been taken by terrorists and simply discarded the ski equipment, we would not discover this fact until the snow melted, months from now. I decided to pass the suggestion along to Colonel Fitzgerald when he called.

It seemed as though every time I put the receiver down, the phone rang again. After speaking to Ed, I received another call from the States. It was Tom Stuart. He and his wife, Rose, are Mark's and Matthew's godparents. I knew Tom as a man who had, on many occasions, successfully interpreted God's messages, and his words now gave me immeasurable comfort. "Mary, I've been praying fervently," he said, "and I've been impressed with the knowledge that Mike and Matthew are still alive. They will come back to you," he promised.

He gave me a scripture, II Timothy 4:18:

And the Lord will rescue me from all evil and take me safely into His heavenly kingdom. To Him be the glory forever and ever. Amen.

Although the verse spoke about going to heaven, Tom believed that God was speaking to us about rescue.

"Yes," I agreed, "so many people have that same sense. No one—not one person—has had the sense that they are dead."

Mike

Time ticked by slowly as my eyes continued to search the horizon. A half hour passed. Then another, and another. The sky remained clear, but no helicopters appeared. This world was deserted, and deathly quiet. Tension built within me until my heart was ready to burst.

The more I waited, the more my eyes were drawn to the cabins below. Sometimes I blinked my eyes, to make sure that the village was not a mirage.

You've got to make a decision, Mike, I thought. If you wait much longer it will be too late to go.

I calculated that it would take me between one and a half and two hours to reach the cabins. That would still give a search party sufficient time and daylight to come back for Matthew.

Once more my mind split into two factions and conducted a critical debate:

It's downhill, and it's close enough for me to make it. . . .

But it's too far away to return, uphill. . . .

Surely there are people there. And I can direct them back up the trail to Matthew. There would still be plenty of daylight left. . . .

But what if no one is there? Matthew would be stranded here. You can't do that. . . .

If you do nothing, you and Matthew will both die. Probably soon. Your bodies will freeze. In the spring you will thaw and rot and eventually someone will find your remains. . . .

You can't leave Matthew alone. . . .

If you wait any longer, you won't have the energy to reach the cabins. . . .

You can't leave Matthew alone. . . .

It has to be now. . . .

You can't leave Matthew alone. . . .

You have to do something!

Finally I realized that I could not make the decision on my own. I would propose the idea to Matthew and hope that he readily agreed that I should go. If he reacted in a negative manner, I would have to make a careful decision, gauging the depths of his fear. A simple "No, I wish you wouldn't" would give me an opportunity to persuade him of the logic of the plan. I had my answers ready: "If I don't go, I'm just not sure how long it's going to take these guys to come out this far. This is one of my last chances to do this, because I don't know how much longer I'll have the strength." If Matthew was in a reasonable frame of mind, I was sure that I could persuade him.

But if he acted hysterically, I might have to scrap the idea altogether.

The trek back to the cave was much easier than the climb, for I could slide down boulders and jump downslope over the fallen logs. A rush of adrenaline helped.

Back at the cave I found Matthew nearly asleep and clearly despondent. I tried to formulate my words in a positive, cheery manner. "Matthew," I announced, "I've seen some cabins and I'm really thinking of going there. What do you think? Do you think that's a good idea? Do you think you will be okay?"

He replied, weakly but quickly, "Yeah, I think that's a good idea. Because I'm not sure they're going to find us here."

The decision was made, and I could not afford to waste additional emotional energy. Suddenly I was all business. I carefully went over a set of instructions: "The first thing I want you to do is not leave this cave. I want you to stay put, no matter what happens. I'm going to go to these cabins and I think there are people there. And I'm not going to have any difficulty telling them how to come back and get you. So I think I'll get there in a couple of hours and there is still going to be plenty of daylight left for them to come back and get you."

The sun was bright, and I reasoned that once I began skiing the exertion would generate enough heat to keep me warm even without a coat. In addition I reasoned that my black ski bib and red turtleneck would heighten my visibility from the air. Most importantly, I knew that Matt would need it more than I. "I'm going to leave my coat," I said. "I want you to keep that coat zipped around you. Keep your legs covered and keep those feet covered. Zip it up and bury yourself in the coat, and don't get out of it. Don't let yourself sleep too long. Wake up every now and then, check yourself, warm the cold parts of your body—especially your feet."

I again reassured my son that somebody would be back for him as soon as possible. "I love you, Matthew," I said. "Please pray for me."

With my stomach full of knots, I strapped on my skis. Is this the right thing to do? I wondered, but I forced myself to banish the thought quickly. Since I had broken one of my ski poles to use as a drinking straw, I grabbed Matthew's solid, shorter set of poles and started down the trail, using the half-walking, half-shuffling motion of the cross-country skier, pushing with my feet, pulling with the ski poles.

Despite my attempts to concentrate on skiing, my mind still rang with the refrain: Is this the right thing to do? Is this *really* the right thing to do?

Almost immediately I realized that I had overestimated my strength. The skiing was fairly easy and in most places the snow was no longer very deep, but I had to bend my knees and crouch awkwardly to use Matthew's ski poles. I could not believe how quickly I was winded. My muscles ached and burned. As a swimmer, I had known this sensation, but only after an extended workout. I had also experienced this feeling after a very long day of skiing. But how could I be this tired after traveling such a short distance?

I had only traveled for fifteen minutes before I had to stop. I doubled over and drew in great draughts of cold, moist air.

As soon as I felt strong enough, I plodded forward. At times the pathway crossed the stream, and I had to ford carefully, lest I soak my boots or, worse, fall in and drench all of my clothing. At most of the crossing points the stream was narrow enough so that I could span it with my skis and slide across.

The sensation of exhaustion continued to overcome me. I was forced to stop every ten or fifteen minutes, and my rest breaks grew longer and longer. Whenever I rested, I remained standing, bent over at the waist; I dared not sit down.

And yet, as I forged ahead, a strange mixture of elation and exhilaration filled me. My brain and body were not in sync. Although I was physically taxing myself to the limit, I was ecstatic with the realization that, instead of sitting and waiting, I was finally doing something. I was actively involved, performing the most constructive task I could think of to get us out of this mess. The countryside surrounding me was bathed in the brilliance of the sun. Around me was some of the most awesome beauty I had ever seen: snow-covered branches shimmering in the sunlight, rainbows of light glowing from icicles that hung from the branches. Birds trilled their joyful songs. When I remembered the cross-country ski trips Mary and I had taken, it was hard not to be hopeful.

It was a strange sensation to find this terrain—which had been so cruel and full of danger—now so compellingly beautiful. Despite the hard work and the undercurrent of concern for Matthew, I was enjoying myself. Filled with hope that people would be in those cabins somewhere up ahead, I could not ski fast enough.

After about two hours I was near collapse, but I was certain that I was approaching my goal. I just had to keep moving. By now the sun had slipped across the sky and was beginning its slow descent toward sunset. I calculated that there were about two hours of daylight remaining. I had to find somebody—and soon.

Someone has to get to Matthew!

Time stood still. It was as if the cabins in the distance receded away from me as quickly as I was moving in on them.

My senses were alive. I squinted my eyes to see more clearly, anticipating my first glimpse of the settlement. Would I see a snowmobile next to one of the cabins? Perhaps there would be a sled or some other form of transportation. What a beacon of hope that would be! I needed a tangible sign of the presence of people.

Finally, through the heavy branches of the trees, I spotted what appeared to be power lines overhead, and I hoped they also carried a telephone cable.

A short time later the cabins came into view. I examined the cabins from a distance, as if I were a detective looking for clues, formulating a plan. There were perhaps twenty or twenty-five buildings standing on several patches of open fields that were separated by low, split-log fences. My eyes scanned the nearest cabins first, looking for signs of activity, signs of people living within. I realized that none of these wooden structures had smoke coming from its chimney, but I would not allow myself to believe what that reality implied. I dismissed this by convincing myself that a fire would not be necessary in broad daylight.

Skiing closer, I began to form a better impression of the true nature of these structures. What had appeared as alpine lodges in the distance now struck me as crude, roughly cut wooden huts. Most were smaller than I expected, about the size of house trailers. The split-log and clapboard exteriors conveyed a rustic flavor. This was no resort, but probably a logging camp or some sort of mountain village. There were no signs of recent activity. No snowmobiles. No sleds. No footprints. The power lines I had seen in the distance turned out to be one single wire, most likely electricity, dashing my hopes that a phone would be available.

Once into the clearing, I found myself facing several small cabins. Two somewhat larger structures stood way off in the background. The clearing was covered with several feet of fresh snow, but I could see that someone had plowed the access road leading to the two largest cabins prior to the latest blizzard.

"Yardım!" ["Help!"] I called out. I tried to rush forward, but the snow-covered ground beneath me was soft and muddy and slowed me down. It felt as if I were struggling through a marsh.

Reaching the first tiny shack, I was dismayed to find the door locked. Through the frosted window I could see that the interior was barren—and had been for some time.

Don't waste your time, Mike, I advised myself. You can't check all the cabins. Go to the larger ones. They are bound to be better equipped. I had to reach within myself one more time to muster the strength I would need to get to these farthest cabins. Unfortunately, they were uphill from here.

I skied onward in a slow shuffle. *"Yardım!"* I yelled. No one answered.

Crossing field after field toward my objective, I came across some animal tracks. They appeared to be made by a relatively large animal, perhaps a dog or a wolf. They had to be somewhat fresh because of the blizzard. I wondered if they were made by the giant Kangal sheepdogs indigenous to Turkey. The Kangals' primary mission is to ward off wolves. They wear spiked collars around their necks to protect that vulnerable area from attack. What would I do if I encountered one or more of them now? I wondered. An animal that size could do a lot of damage to clothing, and to flesh.

Ignoring that threat, I worked my way forward, focusing on the largest cabin, skiing straight ahead until I ran into one of the split-rail fences. I turned myself backward and, using care not to snag any part of my clothing, hoisted myself up to the top rail and swung my legs and skis around and over.

A series of small creeks ran through the fields, leaving the ground soft and muddy. I forced myself to move cautiously, so as not to slip or fall. Several times I eased backward over more of the split-rail fences.

Confronted with a barbed-wire fence, I decided to detour to avoid the danger of ripping my pants or injuring myself on the sharp, rusted spikes.

Finally I reached the tall wooden fence that stood directly in front of the largest cabin. It was too high to climb over, and the gate was blocked by a snowdrift.

"*Yardım! Lutfen!*" ["Help! Please!"] I called.

My voice echoed off the surrounding ridges. My heart sank with the dawning realization that I was still very much alone. I clung to the hope that the people who lived in these huts were simply gone for the day, working, and would return at night.

I pushed against the gate, but it would not budge. Removing my cumbersome skis, I planted them in the snow and proceeded on foot.

Turning to my left, I waded through the heavy snow toward the second-largest cabin. About a hundred yards in front I came upon a stone structure with a water spigot and two basins. Possibly the lower basin was for animals to drink from. People could use the upper basin to fill containers for drinking and cooking. But I wondered whether this structure was associated with the Muslim ritual of washing. Throughout Turkey, spigots and basins similar to this were found near the entrance of a mosque so that one could wash hands, feet, and face prior to entering. There was no mosque here, but I reasoned that even the smallest village must have some sort of designated place to worship; therefore the ritual washing would be necessary.

Under normal circumstances, out of deference to Islamic custom, I would never trespass upon a religious site, but these were not normal circumstances. Unashamedly I climbed up on the structure, knelt on the ledge, and bent down low enough to drink the fresh spring water that flowed from the faucet. I drank until I could hold no more, once again producing a throbbing headache.

With my thirst quenched, I trudged the final hundred yards to the front door of the cabin. In my awkward ski boots I labored up a small wooden staircase and tried the front door. It was locked. The front door had a pane of thick, frosted glass, too opaque for me to see inside. For a few moments I debated whether or not I should break in. Certainly these village folks were poor and I did not want to damage their prop-

-ty. But I needed to get to whatever was inside. Maybe I
-ould pay for the repairs, I thought.

But I decided to investigate the rest of this area first. Maybe
- could find a door that was unlocked or easy enough to force
-pen without breaking a window.

I trudged around the outside of the building to the back
-de, the side that faced toward the trail I had taken, toward
-e cave where my son lay—waiting for me. How long would
-e have to wait?

On this side I discovered a set of stairs leading to other
-ooms. I was able to see inside well enough to realize that the
-ont and back sides of the building were divided like a duplex
-partment. But this door was also locked securely.

I stumbled back down the porch and around to the front of
-e house, where I had seen another door under the steps lead-
-ng in to a basement-level floor. Next to the door was a small
-ottle of kerosene. This door was secured by only a flimsy lock.
-mashing it open, I found myself in a storage area containing a
-ariety of heavy construction materials, but there was nothing
-hat I could use to improve my situation. Several sinks and
-enches were piled on the floor.

The realization grew that I was in a ghost town, probably a
-ummer camp for loggers. And summer was a long way off.

I checked a nearby set of storage sheds. Through cracks in
-he exterior I could see that they contained mostly wood. I
-ried to force these locks, but none would give.

Finally I decided that I had to get inside one of these houses.
- returned to the first porch just above the basement door.
-Jsing a ski pole, I shattered the lower left corner of the glass
-n the door and reached through to turn the doorknob. I found
-nyself in a hallway that led to two rooms.

I moved through the hallway and into the first bedroom on
-he left side. My eyes were drawn immediately to a woodstove
-n the corner; a matchbox sat on top. Quickly I checked the
-est of the building, to see if there were any signs of life. There
-vas a second bedroom, sparsely furnished, also located on the

left side of the hall. The bunks were cold and hard, but the one in the first room held a fairly thick woolen blanket.

There was indoor plumbing, but the water supply was turned off. Located on the right side of the hallway, opposite the second bedroom, was a very crude bathroom. It contained a large utility sink like the ones I had seen in the basement, a crude shower with no curtain or door, and a typical Turkish toilet—a porcelain "hole in the ground" with footpads on either side of the base.

I continued to the end of the hall and found that it took a sharp turn to the right, into a small, narrow corridor leading to a utility closet that held nothing useful. In the corner of the corridor was another small woodstove. A shelf above it held an empty kerosene lamp. There were no matches.

Taking the blanket to the larger, better-furnished second bedroom, I searched for food. A box containing several cubes of sugar had been left on the small table, alongside a knife and mirror, as if a man had shaved himself as he sat here.

This sight brought a mosaic of thoughts. I pictured a simple man, sitting at this table, shaving himself with the knife while perhaps a pot of *çay* brewed quietly in the background. Perhaps that scene took place this very morning and I would encounter this man when he came home for the night.

In the cupboards I discovered a small supply of Turkish tea leaves, a jar with about a cup of brittle macaroni noodles, and a vial of cooking oil, so old or cold that it was like a solid white chunk of congealed lard. There was a dirty bottle that would hold water that I could bring in from the outdoor spigot. There was a shallow pan that might be sufficient for boiling the stale macaroni—if I could get a fire started.

I checked the stove in the corner of the first bedroom and found to my delight that it was stoked with wood and bits of old newspaper. My mind raced: A fire would help me get warm; I might be able to cook the macaroni and brew a hot cup of tea. More importantly, chimney smoke from this apparently abandoned cabin might attract the attention of the helicopters.

But the matchbox on top of the stove held a single wooden atch that appeared old and brittle. Unless I found other atches, this would provide my one chance to start a fire, so decided to wait until I searched further.

Back outside, I trudged around the cabin to the porch on e other side of the duplex. Peering into the window of one the rooms, I now spotted an encouraging sight: another ove, another matchbox. Frantically I punched through the ass with a ski pole and unlocked the door. Lunging toward ie stove, my heart nearly stopped as I fumbled to open the rize. My eyes did a double-take as I stared into the empty ox.

In the next room, I found only an old, worn-out bench. 'here was no food, no matches, nothing. It had been a long, ng time since these cabins had seen life.

Weary and worried, I stumbled back outside and made my ay around the house and back onto the front porch. I took ie small jar of kerosene that I had found near the basement oor and brought it into the first bedroom. I placed the jar of erosene near the stove and the single, precious match. I dou-le-checked each of the rooms, but found nothing that would e of use.

There's not a lot here, I thought. I turned my gaze back to ie other cabin, the largest one in the settlement. Maybe it's etter over there. Maybe there's food, more blankets, and, most ritical of all, more matches.

I knew that I could not force my way through the gate, and ie fence was rather high. A glance at the sky told me that aylight was fading, and I could not stumble my way around iis settlement in the dark. I was desperate to find at least one iore match, to give myself two chances to start a fire. Mus-ering my final reserves of strength, I gathered all the empty ontainers I could find, so that I could fill them with water on iy way over to the next cabin.

Slowly and deliberately I waded through the snow once gain, forging my way toward the other cabin. I had been in iy boots for hours now, and my feet ached to the point of numbness. The tops of the boots dug into my shins, makir each step excruciatingly painful. I kept my eyes focused on t goal, willing myself to ignore the pain. From time to time wondered what damage I might be doing to myself, but I w aware that there was no choice. I had reconciled myself to n injuries and to the prospect of coming back less than who' The goal now was survival.

Halfway to the cabin, I stopped at the spigot to fill the con tainers. Once more I drank all I could hold. Again, the i water caused my head to pound. I left the bottles here, plan ning to collect them after I finished rummaging.

As I continued toward the tall fence, I tried to figure out way to get inside that cabin. I pushed and pushed against t gate, but it would not budge.

I tried several times in various places to climb the fence, b it was no use. Looking about, I could find nothing to stand c so that I could vault over the top.

Working my way around the perimeter of the fence, headir toward the back of the house, I saw that the fence appeare to get progressively lower. I found a gate that opened into t backyard. It was locked; however, it was low enough to clim and its horizontal logs offered a foothold.

Finally I was able to hoist myself over. As I dropped to t ground I sank into the snow past my knees. The fence w not that much lower here, I realized—the snow was deepe With great effort I worked my way from the backyard to t front door of the cabin. Through its window I could see large front room with almost nothing inside it. A single cha sat next to a fairly large window at the front of the house.

By now I was past the point of worrying about doing an damage in this village. I shattered the glass on the door an moved inside.

I surveyed as quickly as I could and found nothing of us It was clear that this village had been stripped and abandone for the winter.

It struck me that these two larger cabins were fairly simila perhaps even made by the same builder, as they both ha

lentical windows and the doors on each had the same
osted glass.

Having found nothing of use, I stepped outside and waded
rough the snow to the backyard. Retracing my path to the
ate, I clambered back over and followed my own tracks to
ie cabin where my single match awaited. On the way I picked
p my water bottles. Disappointed by the lack of resources, I
onsoled myself with the fact that, at least for now, I had plenty
f water.

My senses focused on the task of building a fire. If only I
ould get a fire started, everything would be all right.

Weak and wheezing, I prepared the stove. I used some of
ie kerosene to soak the wood and paper in the stove. Holding
iy breath, I struck the old, brittle match. A slight spark flew
·om it, but it did not catch. I tried repeatedly, until all the
ulfur was rubbed from the tip.

There would be no fire.

Consciously attempting to build my strength, I gobbled a
ew of the sugar cubes. They left me thirsty, and I drank a bit
f water.

I wanted to consume as much sugar as possible, and devised
 more efficient way. I put some sugar into the bottom of a
mall tea glass, splashed some water on top, and stirred the
nixture with a small spoon. Despite my most vigorous efforts,
he sugar would not completely dissolve. It was simply too
old. When I drained the glass I found grains of sugar clinging
o the bottom. I added more water and drank, chewing on the
·ranules as I did.

In frustration, I lay on the floor and tried to clear my mind.
Despair grasped my spirit; I had done everything in my power
o save us, but it was not enough.

And now my son and I were separated. I'm not going to be
ble to get back to him, I realized. There was no way I could
;et back. And even if I could, would that be the smart thing
o do? There was a much greater chance that someone would
ind me here, rather than at the cave. Maybe it was better to
tay here and hope that I was found soon enough to save

Matthew. This was a realistic conclusion, but the fact that
was now in a better position than my son produced an intens
conflict within me.

I agonized with worry. I was more concerned, at the mo
ment, with Matthew's emotional state than his physical condi
tion. I had promised him that someone would be back befor
nightfall, and I had not adequately prepared him for the possi
bility that we would be separated. I wept the most bitter tear
of my life.

Mary

Colonel Fitzgerald's call began as all the others had. "W
haven't found them." Then he continued, "I'm going to com
off the mountain tomorrow morning so that I can attend th
Service of Hope. I want to stop by your apartment and brin
you some pictures that we took so you can see for yoursel
what it's like here. What is a good time for you?"

We settled on a one o'clock meeting and then I told him o
my brother's suggestion to use the metal detectors.

He dismissed it. "The search is basically over," he declared
"The Special Forces contingent will stay indefinitely, and Stev
Tolbert will take over as the search coordinator."

At least Steve knows Mike, I thought.

The Search

Even as Colonel Fitzgerald pulled out most of the troops and
prepared to head back to Ankara, even as the five hundre
Turkish commandos returned to their base, others were unwill
ing to give up. A contingent of fifteen U.S. Special Force

oops, under the command of Captain Tim Fitzgerald, vowed
o stay on. These quiet professionals of the 10th Special Forces
roup would be aided on Monday by helicopters from the
ATO Operation Land Southeast. Captain Fitzgerald noted
hat the most frustrating part of the week had been the inces-
nt snowfall, which systematically covered up any evidence of
here Mike and Matthew might have headed.

Still, he remained optimistic and relished the thought of hav-
g more control of the search procedure. He said, "Maybe if
e expand our search to cover some of the locations out and
way from the immediate area, we can find them."

Mike

the bedroom of the cabin, I collapsed onto a wood slat
unk, covered by a thin mattress. I tried not to scream out in
ain as I pulled my boots from my feet. I wrapped myself in
e woolen blanket, but I was still shivering, from cold, from
ar, and from grief.

A strange thought hounded me. What kind of man would live
such a sparsely equipped hut? What kind of man shaved him-
elf with a knife in front of a tiny table mirror? I imagined a large
urly Turk who spoke no English. Would he return in the dark
f night, tired and cranky from a hard day's work? How would
e react when he discovered the shattered pane of glass in the
indow of his front door? What would he do if he found an in-
ruder sleeping in his bed, under his blanket? Would he give me
me to formulate a few sentences of explanation in Turkish, or
ould he go for his knife and ask questions later?

Beneath the woolen blanket my feet began to thaw, and that
ensitized the nerve tissue. Pain kept me awake most of the
ight.

"Take care of Matthew," I begged God. "Don't let him give
to despair. Give him the strength to hold on."

Mary

Cathryn arrived about 8 P.M. to find the house filled with the usual group of people: Pam and Ken Jaccard, Angela and Ed Shaw, Mary Beth Tremblay, Jessica and Alex, and, of course, Angelina.

Cathryn repeated that she thought God wanted us to keep on like the persistent widow and not give up hope. She also said, "Every time I pray it seems as if God is saying, 'They're in my hands. I will take care of them.'"

Even as our prayers continued, a U.S. Embassy spokesman told Reuters News Service, "Unfortunately, we can only assume they are dead. The search is over."

Again the phone rang. Mary Beth screened the call and handed me the receiver. I immediately recognized the voice of Helen Garity, a member of our prayer group during the brief time we were stationed in Fairfax, Virginia, studying the Turkish language prior to our move here. "The prayers are continuing," she told me. "I want you to know that two women from our group have had visions of Mike and Matthew in a cave. They are fine," she assured me. I could almost see her characteristic warm, broad smile as she spoke to me in gentle, motherly tones.

I told her that one of our Turkish friends had reported a similar vision, and in my mind I could see Helen's short dark hair bobbing as she nodded her agreement.

Helen went on to tell me that, although she was sure that both Mike and Matthew were fine, she felt compelled to pray for Mike at this very moment. "Not for his physical safety," she explained, "but for his spiritual and emotional strength. He's going through something right now, and I will continue to intercede for him."

Marissa

Everyone crowded into the kitchen so that Alex and I could present a magic show. We did about ten tricks. We had a curtain rigged so that we could sneak into and out of the pantry and we threw flour into the air to make smoke so that we could disappear and reappear.

We did the show once, but it was not quite perfect, so we asked everyone to come back for the second show. This time we used more flour and it went everywhere, even into the fluorescent light in the ceiling. Everyone clapped and cheered. It was such fun.

I wished I could make Daddy and Matthew reappear.

Matthew

"Dad!" I called out.

There was no answer.

"Dad!"

Was this a bad dream? I wondered. I knew that I had been asleep. But now it was dark and I thought I was awake. Did Dad really leave me here alone? Where is he now? He said he would be back in a few hours. He *must* have found *somebody*.

"*Dad!*"

DAY 9

•

Monday, January 23

Mike

Throughout the night I drifted in and out of sleep. My feet were thawing, and each throb of pain woke me. I used this as a way to maintain my watch. Each time I woke I lay very still and listened for sounds.

Once again I was startled by drumbeats. It was the same sound I had heard before, perhaps announcing the call to prayer for nearby villagers. Could this be a good sign? I asked myself. Are there people living nearby? It took minutes to clear my head and to realize that I was alone, huddled under a blanket in a woodcutter's shack on this frozen mountain. Where is that sound coming from? I wondered.

I anticipated the possibility that the men who lived here would return, perhaps late into the night. This was an illogical conclusion that I desperately wanted to believe, despite all the evidence that it had been some time ago—weeks? months?—since these cabins had seen human activity. I was torn by a strange mixture of hope and fear: hope that I would be found; fear of what they might do when they realized that I had broken in. Would I wake in time to explain?

Drifting back into sleep, I was soon haunted by a strange dream. When fresh spasms of pain woke me suddenly, I was certain that I had been in deep conversation with someone, but that person had no name and no face.

Slowly I swung my feet off the edge of the bed and screamed aloud. Searing pains ran up my legs and attacked my spine.

In the dim predawn light I looked at my feet and found them more reddish than before. They were horribly swollen. They had partially thawed throughout the night and the return of circulation was accompanied by agony.

Rays of sunshine now poked over the horizon, and the drumbeats had returned. I twisted my head to look out the window, trying to identify the source of the sound. But the glass was covered by a thick frost.

Since my feet had thawed, I knew that it would be foolish to attempt to walk; this was when I could really damage them. In addition, even the slightest touch brought immediate and intense pain, and I doubted that I could stand up if I tried. I crawled on my hands and knees to the edge of the bed, so that I could press my face against the cold, dirty glass. My eyes tried desperately to penetrate the thick frosted surface for any signs of human existence, but I could not see out.

Using the knife, I attempted to scrape away some of the ice and frost. But it was so cold inside the cabin that, with every labored breath, I exhaled white puffs of moist air that quickly condensed and froze to the glass. It was no use.

The sound of the drumbeats was very strange, buzzing inside my head. I realized that whenever I moved, the sound changed its orientation. Finally it dawned on me that the rhythms I had been hearing were not drumbeats at all, but the sound of my own pulse, pounding in my ears.

I've got to get back to Matthew, I thought. Maybe the sugar water has given me strength.

But the slightest movement brought instant torture; my feet burned as I tried to stuff them inside my brittle boots. Finally I gave up in despair. It would be impossible to get back into my boots, impossible to stand, impossible to ski. The only way to get back to Matthew would be to crawl on my hands and knees.

Although the temptation was great, I tried not to doze. Yesterday I had seen the signs of a plowed road and, of course,

here had to be some way to bring people up to this camp.
That now became my hope. I managed to maneuver myself
off the bed and into a chair that sat in front of the table. This
offered me a view of the window.

Matthew

The sun was shining when I woke up. It was so cold in the
cave that I decided to see how it would be in the sunshine. I
remembered that it had been kind of warm when Dad and I
sat outside, so I decided it would be worth the effort, at least
for a little while.

The warmth of the sun on my face comforted me, and I felt
myself being hypnotized.

Mary

Norita came over to pray and sit with me. She told me about
a conversation she had with Hulya over the weekend. Hulya
had received two visions and one of them troubled her
deeply—she said that she had seen Matthew being tortured. In
her second vision she had seen Mike's head staring out of the
window of a wooden cabin.

Was this evidence that terrorists had them? I wondered. All
the evidence indicated that the terrorist threat was phony. "Do
you really think someone has them, or do you think it is more
of a spiritual battle?" I asked. "Do you think they are just
getting to the breaking point and are tormented because they
haven't yet been found?"

Norita thought for a moment before responding. "Hulya
really felt like it was humans holding them," she said, "but I

guess it could be a spiritual attack. Mike is a strong believer and a servant of God. I would not put it past Satan to be torturing them."

I forced the thought of Matthew being tortured from my mind. It just did not seem possible, but I knew that I was too involved to be clearheaded about this.

"Well, Mary," Norita continued, "let's pray that whatever is torturing them will be bound and removed from them."

We prayed in tongues and intermittently in English, using the name of Jesus to bind this evilness as we are given the power to do in scripture. At the conclusion of our prayer session, I felt peaceful. I was no longer concerned with the specter of torture, and I was far better equipped to handle the next task.

Pam showed Colonel Fitzgerald into the piano room. A tall, good-looking man with chiseled features, wearing the casual uniform of olive-green trousers and a starched, light green shirt, he could have come from Central Casting, under the heading "no-nonsense military officer." We shook hands and I offered him a seat on the couch. I sat in the chair to his left.

He spread out a map on the table before him and pointed out the ski areas and the lifts where Mike and Matthew had last been seen. "We've pretty much concluded that they must have gone to the top," he said, "since we are having so much difficulty finding them." I agreed with that assessment because I could picture them skiing the lower slopes all morning and, after lunch, accepting the challenge of the toughest slope.

"Okay," he said, pointing, "this is the area we covered first. When we do a search, we focus a lot of our efforts in this small area around the site, and if we don't find anything we expand."

I nodded.

"This is where we found the ski tracks and this is where the fire was found." He went on to detail the helicopter activity.

Then he pulled out a stack of color photographs of Kartalkaya Mountain and its surrounding terrain. "I want to show you what it's been like up there," he said.

I knew that there had been a great deal of snowfall, but I

was unprepared for the otherworldly vision now before me. In some of the pictures fully shrouded trees blended into the snow-covered earth against a backdrop of icy white sky. I could barely discern the horizon. The entire area looked like some primitive, pristine planet that had never been touched by humanity.

In one photograph, Colonel Fitzgerald stood before a tree so thickly covered with snow that its branches were forced to the ground, appearing to melt into the landscape as a series of white, icy mounds. Waist-high drifts of snow surrounded the colonel, causing this large man to appear insignificant against the majesty of nature.

Pointing to one of the pictures, he said, "They could have skied off something like this and ended up in twenty feet of snow, not to be found for a long, long time."

He thinks they're dead, I realized. I don't think they're dead. We will agree to disagree.

After about a half hour of this lecture that seemed clearly designed to cause me to abandon all hope, Colonel Fitzgerald glanced at his watch. "I have to be going," he said. "I will see you at the Service of Hope."

I do not believe that he comprehended the irony of his words.

Mike

As the sun crossed the sky, it melted away some of the frost on the windows, and I kept my eyes glued to the white landscape. My ears were tuned for the sound of any approaching traffic. On numerous occasions I thought I heard the rumble of a bus or truck, but after several false alarms I realized that my senses were playing tricks on me. The roadway, somewhere out there at the edge of the clearing, remained deserted.

All day long I tortured myself with a variety of "what-ifs."

Was there another way I could have done this, so that I didn't have to be separated from Matthew? I asked myself. Maybe it would have been better to have stayed put. I had made many decisions during the past week, and all of them seemed to have turned out wrong. Why did I insist on skiing the most difficult run? Why did I not turn back immediately, the moment I realized that we had lost our bearings? Why did I not stop at the first set of sheds we had seen? Why did I not have matches with me? But most of all: Why did I abandon my son?

I prayed: God, You've got to have mercy on us. I've done everything I know how to do, and it's still not good enough. You've got to help us, because I really believe that if You don't do something, we're going to die here. Matthew's going to die alone in the cave and I—

This was unbearable. I seriously considered crawling the several miles back to the cave. Reason and emotion were in deep conflict. Although this cabin was barren and freezing, I knew that my chances of survival were somewhat better here than in the cave. And the chances were greater that someone would find me here—which meant that Matthew's chances of survival were increased if I remained here and left him alone.

Could I somehow get back to Matthew? Was there any way to drag him back to these cabins where we could both wait out the cold until the searchers arrived? I knew this was impossible, but my rational conclusion did absolutely nothing to ease the agony in my heart.

Yesterday I had tromped about the village, leaving discernible tracks in the snow that might be spotted by a searching helicopter crew. But if they found me, I wanted them to find me quickly. I cried out to my wife: "Mary, I wouldn't want to face you without Matthew."

Mary

What does one wear to a "Service of Hope"? Anything but black, I decided. I settled on a paisley print skirt, white blouse, and navy blue blazer. Mark balked at the idea of getting dressed up until we compromised. He did not have to wear a suit—just a nice pair of slacks and a white shirt. Marissa put on a floral dress and her bright pink Lands' End jacket.

Ed Shaw arrived to escort us to the gymnasium, and I was surprised to see that he had obtained the use of the general's limousine, as well as a Turkish driver. Mark, Marissa, and I got into the backseat and Ed sat in front, next to our driver. The kids were fascinated by the vehicle's special features and began fiddling with the pull-down reading lights. I reminded them that this was one of those "best-behavior" times.

As we drove toward the DOD (Department of Defense) school, where the service would be held, our driver, mindful that we should vary our route, attempted to enter the Turkish side of the base, but we were turned away. We were forced to backtrack and enter at the main gate. A few people were milling about, but I did not recognize any of them.

I had been to this gym countless times with Mike and the kids for sporting events, but I had no idea how this service would be arranged.

Colonel Fitzgerald, now in his dress uniform, appeared and escorted us into the gym. Okay, Mary, I instructed myself, let's put on a smiling face and thank everybody. I was amazed to see at least three hundred people crowded into the bleachers. Many of the faces were familiar, but their expressions were not. Eyes were downcast, shoulders slumped. I had been too busy with my own concerns during this ordeal to realize how much it had touched the lives of both military and civilian families in this community, as well as the Turks at ODC and throughout the city. So many people had become personally

invested. I thought: These people are so nice to come an
support us and pray with us. I'm going to smile and let ther
know that I appreciate it.

But the room was deathly quiet. As I walked across the har
wooden floor, I felt that the bleachers were a wall of depres
sion, a somber gray. They've all given up, I realized. What ar
they going to think if they see me smiling?

The experience took on a surreal quality. A makeshift alta
had been set up on the main floor. Framed photos of Mike an
Matthew were placed in front of a larger picture of Kartalkay
Mountain. Pots of gold and brown chrysanthemums had bee
arranged around the speaker's podium. That's kind of funer
alish, I thought.

Jim Holmes and his wife, Connie, greeted us and ushere
us to a row of folding chairs. We sat facing the altar an
podium, with our backs to the bleachers. Good, I though
Now, if I cry, nobody will see me.

Colonel Fitzgerald began the service by announcing, "Th
search is continuing, and the search will continue. They ar
an integral part of the community. We hope that they are safe.
Although the Turkish commandos would no longer be in
volved in the search, the colonel said that a small continger
of U.S. Special Forces would continue the effort. Unfortu
nately, there was no good news to report, and something i
the colonel's demeanor communicated that he thought th
searchers were now wasting their time.

Monsignor Nugent is an excellent speaker. He is alway
clear, easy to understand, and has a calming but firm deliver
In his address he declared, "It is hope that keeps us goin
when all the odds are stacked against us. Being a small commu
nity, we have all viewed the tragedy as a personal one. Th
tragedy could've struck any one of us. By reasoning alone w
will never understand why it struck this family." He cautione
"We shouldn't have false hope," but he added in a triumphar
tone, "but, as Christians, our hope is in Christ Jesus, dead an
risen!" I was excited about these words because they affirme

ae message of faith that I wanted to communicate to all
aese people.

Next, a Muslim official from the Ministry of Religion ad-
ressed the audience. He spoke in Turkish, and I could not
nderstand much of what he said. He ended by looking directly
: me and intoning, *"Başina sağ olsun."*

I wished that I knew what he was saying.

After the service my mind was a daze of conflicting emo-
ons. I stood in a sort of receiving line as scores of people filed
y to embrace us and offer their words of hope and solace. I
ried on many shoulders. It was the first time I had seen Neil
'ownsend and Mike Björk since the search began, two men
om the Ankara Youth Sports League who had been the first
o begin the search. Although we knew them only marginally,
aey had taken the time and gone to the effort, and their partic-
pation touched me deeply. I also met Serdar Akkor, the bilin-
ual "Good Samaritan" who had stayed at the ski resort to
elp Wanda converse with Turkish authorities. Through the
og that shrouded my mind I was able to take notice of Mat-
aew's best friend, Jared Erdahl. As his mother had told me,
is skin was covered with painful, itchy hives.

Later, a Turkish acquaintance filled me in on what the Mus-
m speaker had said. He began his address by noting, "Like
ay Catholic friend before me, we believe in *kader*," a God-
irected fate. He said that the Turkish people were more than
illing to help, because they believe that when one person from
ae community is lost, then the community is not complete. He
rayed that Allah would bring the family back together soon.

"What did he say to me at the end?" I asked.

"Başina sağ olsun," she said. The literal translation is "Health
o your head." She lowered her eyes. "That is what Turks say
hen someone dies."

Mike

Over and over I debated the point: Should I try to get back to Matthew? How could I allow myself, miserable as I was, to be in a more comfortable situation than my son?

Yet I was forced to cling desperately to logic. I *had* to stay here. It was best for both of us.

This dilemma caused the deepest pain that I had ever experienced.

And I felt myself growing weaker and weaker.

Matthew

I'm not sure how long I slept, but when I woke, the sun was ready to set and I was in cold shadows. I crawled back into the cave and gloom really took hold of me. I could hardly stand it.

After a while I realized that my eyes could not seem to focus on the scene outside, and I knew that something was very, very wrong. My heart pounded against my chest.

The picture slowly came into focus: trees, snow, a lake's edge. Then I saw a body, lying half in the water and half on the shore; bones appeared beneath rotten flesh. I looked at the man's face and saw that it was Dad.

I woke with a start, my mind still confused. A dream, I told myself. It was only a bad dream.

I tried to force myself to stop shivering, then I realized that I wasn't shivering because of the dream, but from the cold.

My dad was gone and that was a bad dream that was *real*.

Mary

fter the service, Ed drove us home. The kids could not wait
o get out of their dress clothes, and Marissa was looking for-
ard to a promised movie outing with Norita and her children
is evening. *The Lion King* had finally made its way to Ankara.

Throughout the late afternoon and evening, people came
nd went, and a few phone calls from well-wishers in the States
ame in as well. Angela arrived, bringing with her the mums
at had been used at the service. Usually I enjoy flowers, but
ese were not welcome; they still had a funeral feeling to them.
was harboring very mixed feelings about our Service of Hope.
was grateful for the support and outpouring of affection, but
isappointed that it seemed to be devoid of a real spirit of
ope and optimism. "Put the flowers in the kitchen," I said.

Marissa chose this moment to show off for Ed Shaw.

Sometime earlier we had learned from our good friends Rod
nd Sabra Wells that their daughter Allison had won a full
Javy ROTC scholarship to Bryn Mawr. When Allison first
tarted with ROTC she could barely manage one chin-up.
owing to improve her strength, she had installed a bar in the
oorframe of her bedroom. Whenever she went in or out, she
rced herself to practice. Eventually she could do more chin-
ps than anyone else in the ROTC unit, male or female. Re-
embering that story, I had given our children a similar,
nsion-type bar for Christmas. It was installed in a doorframe
t the far end of our long hallway.

Marissa was too short to reach the bar from the floor. Some-
mes she used a chair to boost herself high enough to grab
e bar, but at other times she crawled up the door casing like
monkey until she could grasp the bar. That was her method
day. She did chin-ups but wanted to prove she could do ten
a row. Eventually she decided she had done enough and

just relaxed her arms, though still hanging from the bar. B
she hung on to the bar so long she lost control.

A bloodcurdling scream suddenly echoed through the apart
ment. Ed, who had been watching from a vantage point nea
the kitchen, sprinted down the hallway, scooped up Marissa
and brought her to me in the piano room. She squirmed an
cried in pain. Cuddling her, trying to calm her down, I asked
"Well, what did you hit?"

"My head!" she screamed.

"What did you hit it on?" I asked, thinking that it must hav
been the floor.

"I hit the wall."

"Oh, bummer," I allowed, "the wall's cement. But don
worry, you're okay."

Within minutes Marissa was calm and dry-eyed, and off an
running again. I put the incident out of my mind.

I was setting the table, preparing for dinner, trying to decid
which of the dozens of dishes we would sample, when Mariss
found me in the kitchen. "My eyes are kind of weird," sh
complained.

"What do you mean, 'weird'?"

"I don't know, they're just kind of sparkly or something."

"Are you tired? Do you want to take a nap before th
movie?"

"Okay," she agreed.

I tucked her into bed, thinking: This is really great. Th
movie doesn't start until 8:00, and if she takes a nap now sh
won't be tired and cranky at the theater.

By 7:30 Marissa was still fast asleep. I woke her and fed he
a light snack. Then Norita and the kids left for the movie.

I called my sister, Kate, to check on her arrival time and t
tell her that I would not be meeting her flight. Ed had volun
teered to do that for me, and I gave her a brief descriptio
of him.

Pam approached me and said, "You know, Mary, since you
sister is arriving tomorrow and we're all kind of wasted anyway
I think we're going to take off. You can probably use som

quiet time to yourself by now, anyway. Angelina will stay the night though."

I agreed that some solitude would be welcome.

Late in the evening, when Norita returned with Marissa in tow, I asked, "How was the movie?"

"It was great," Norita said, "and the music was wonderful. But Marissa got sick twice during the movie."

"Did you get to see the movie at all?" I asked.

"Oh, yes. I thought you should know, though."

"That's really odd," I said. "Earlier tonight she said her eyes were acting weird."

Angelina overheard the conversation and she asked tentatively, "Didn't you tell me she hit her head earlier this evening?"

Reality struck like a bolt of lightning: Bumped head. "Sparkly" vision. Sleepy. Nausea. What an idiot I am, I thought. I let her go to sleep!

I put Marissa on the love seat and called a friend of mine, a nurse, to detail what had happened and ask for her advice. She cautioned me that Marissa should be seen by a physician and gave me the name and phone number of an English-speaking doctor. Within minutes Marissa and I were in a taxi heading for the hospital.

The hospital personnel were helpful and friendly, but my mind was in such a jumble that even the easiest decisions seemed impossible to make. Once again, our communication network must have been in gear, because I suddenly looked up to see Ken Jaccard standing there. I was grateful beyond words for a reassuring presence in this strange and worrisome environment.

The doctor took a medical history and decided that Marissa should have an X-ray taken. This was inconclusive, so he proposed that she undergo an MRI examination. While we were waiting for the procedure to begin, she once again became sick to her stomach and vomited. She appeared tired and a bit disoriented. A nurse appeared and placed a small vial of smelling salts under her nose.

"Whoa! I feel so much better now," Marissa said.

Fortunately, the MRI did not indicate any problems. The doctor instructed me to take Marissa home for the night, but to wake her every hour. If I noticed any problems I was to come back immediately.

Ken drove us back to our apartment.

A difficult night ensued.

I woke Marissa periodically, asking, "Who are you? Where are you?"

"Mom, stop it, leave me alone," she complained. She was obviously sensible enough to know that it was sleep time.

It was 5 A.M. before I finally got to sleep myself.

DAY 10

•

Tuesday, January 24

Mike

The pain of the thawing process plagued me throughout the night. Each time I woke, I cried out to myself—and to God: "Where's my son? How's he doing?"

The only answer was the maddening sound of the "drumbeats" pulsating in my ears.

Mary

This was the first morning that none of my friends came over to keep me company. Only Angelina was there, and she would be leaving soon to run some errands and to attend Ladies' Bible Study. I wanted to go, too, but I had to wait for Christine. She was coming to drive Mark to the OSI offices, where the Turkish police wanted to ask him another round of questions.

For the rest of the world, the Service of Hope was the signal that it was time for them to return to the routines of their own lives. For me, the lack of visitors, the quiet time, was welcome. I moved about slowly, taking my time getting dressed, thinking about what the searchers might be doing this day—those few who were left. Mark was getting ready for his appointment.

After Marissa's difficult night, she was still sleeping soundly, and I thought: Oh, to be a child!

Cathryn called and told me, "I was in the Word this morning and I was led to read Daniel 9. It details how the prophet had identified with the sins of his nation. I read the following chapter and I felt that the Lord was speaking to us in verse. . . ."

"Hold on," I said. "Let me find the verse, so I can get the whole idea." I got Mike's Bible and turned to Daniel 10.

Cathryn continued, "In chapter ten, Daniel asked God to help him understand the meaning of a certain dream. The answer did not come immediately, and Daniel prayed and fasted for three weeks. Finally an angel appeared and explained that he had been dispatched immediately to answer Daniel's prayer, but a powerful demon—the prince of Persia—had opposed him. Only when the archangel Michael had come to his aid had the demon been overcome."

I replied, "Yep, that sounds like all the other Words we have been getting: 'I have heard your prayers. I have sent an answer. It just hasn't gotten to you yet.' "

This was what had happened to us, Cathryn believed. God had answered our prayers from the beginning, but unknown, unseeable demons were keeping us from receiving or comprehending the answer. Cathryn was still certain that the answer, when it finally arrived, would be a message of victory.

I took great comfort in this.

Matthew

When I woke up I had a song running through my head. It was a tune from Queen, called "Bohemian Rhapsody." I had sung it many times with Mark and Marissa. We really liked it because it was so catchy, and I sort of liked the harmony of all the singers in it.

Suddenly I realized that I was singing it out loud. Very loud.

That's kind of strange, I thought, but since there's no one out here to hear me, no problem. As I continued to sing, the music comforted me, and I thought of a lot of good things about my home and family.

Then I realized that Dad was not coming back.

I crawled out of the cave and I grabbed the sweatshirt that Dad had left hanging on a branch. It was icy and cold, but I beat it against the side of the cave, harder and harder, until I got tired.

It was still pretty early in the morning when I crawled back into the cave and went back to sleep.

Mike

I lay in bed for some time, shivering beneath the blanket, marveling at how cold it can get inside a cabin. My fuzzy mind worked slowly on the solution to my most immediate problem; I was thirsty and I had used up all of the water that I had brought inside. I knew that I could not get back into my boots. I could crawl on my hands and knees out to the spigot in the yard, but it was a long way off. Finally I decided that I would simply go out to the porch, fill up pots and pans with snow, bring them inside, place them on the windowsill, and see if I could get the snow to melt in the sunlight. If not, I would simply eat a little at a time to satisfy my thirst.

It took considerable time and effort to crawl about the cabin, gathering my collection of four pots and pans and dragging them to the doorway. I pulled the door open and straddled the threshold, with my knees in the snow on the porch and my feet still inside the cabin.

As I reached back for one of the pots I suddenly thought that I heard . . . something. Is my mind playing tricks? I wondered. Is this really a sound, or am I wishing the sound? Is it an echo off some canyon? What is it, really?

The noise grew fainter, then louder. I dared not move, lest my ears lose contact.

Perhaps a minute passed, perhaps two before I allowed myself to believe that this was not another audio mirage, like the drumbeats. No, this was real. And finally I realized that I was hearing the sound of a diesel engine, speeding up, slowing down. There was a vehicle out there, somewhere, negotiating the curves of a mountain road. And it was getting louder. It was approaching!

My eyes scanned the landscape in the direction of the sound. After another minute or two I caught a glimpse of white. It was the roof of a minibus! The roadway was cut below the surrounding terrain, so I could not see the entire vehicle, but I guessed that it was one of the tour buses I had often seen in this country, and it was probably taking a group of skiers up the mountain. I was terrified that it would simply drive past this deserted village and disappear.

A jolt of adrenaline surged through me. I waved my arms and screamed in Turkish, "Hey! Hey! Help! I've had an accident! Help! Please help!" I grabbed a couple of pots and banged them together as loudly as I could, screaming at the same time. If this bus did not stop, I would lose my one and only chance of being found.

My eyes followed the white roof, willing the bus to turn into this settlement.

"Help! Help!" I screamed. "Hey, over here! Hey! Hey!"

I could not believe my eyes when the white roof took a slow turn and pulled directly into the clearing. It followed the previously plowed lane, its tires packing down the fresh snowfall, until it reached the fence surrounding the largest cabin. it stopped about a hundred yards away, directly facing me.

"Help! Please help!" I shrieked. I banged some more pots together for emphasis.

For what felt like an eternity, nothing happened, no one moved. Are they going to help me? I wondered. Or have I scared them off?

Then the bus door opened and men began to step outside,

slowly, warily. They were a rough-looking lot, dressed in heavy wool sweaters, in varying shades of brown. Some had gloves. Most wore wool hats that resembled ski caps. Many of them were bearded. One or two were carrying axes, and I realized that they were not tourists or skiers, but Turkish lumberjacks. Was this their village? Is this where they were headed after all?

A few more men got out, but no one approached. They simply stared at me, with expressions of confusion on their faces.

I was afraid that I had frightened them by acting as if I were a madman. I decided to speak to them in Turkish, using a phrase that I knew well, even if the words were not literally true. "Help!" I yelled. "I've had an accident."

None of them moved. None of them spoke.

I tried again, speaking more slowly and calmly: "Can you help me? I'm lost. Please help me."

They began to chatter to one another, but remained at the side of the bus.

"I've lost my son," I implored.

Finally one of the woodcutters moved forward, following the path that I had previously etched into the knee-deep snow. Others straggled warily behind him.

The leader came to within five feet of where I was kneeling on the porch. He stood only about five-foot-five, but he was a rugged old man with a brown, leathery face. He stared at me through wise eyes and then his face broke into a wide grin. He said, *"Yarbay."*

His comment astonished me. *Yarbay* was the Turkish word for "lieutenant colonel." Did he know who I was? No, I thought. There must be someone in the group who is retired from the military and still uses the term as a nickname.

But when he asked in Turkish "Where is your son? I have seen you in the newspapers and on TV every day!" I realized that he did, indeed, know who I was!

The others chimed in, *"Yarbay. Yarbay!"* They gathered around. Hands reached out to touch my face, as if to see whether I was real. They spoke so quickly to one another that I could not understand much of what they were saying.

The leader called for calm and asked again, "Where is your son?"

I spoke slowly, taxing my language abilities, augmenting my limited vocabulary with gestures. "There's a road that goes out that way," I said, pointing. The man grunted. As I attempted to describe the stream and the fence, he nodded in understanding. "Go up that road," I said, "probably five or ten kilometers. You will find some skis planted in the snow. On the left side, go up the hill and you will find the . . ." During my eighteen months in this country I do not think I ever needed the Turkish word for "cave" but, as if a gift, it came to me instantly.

"I don't think you can get there with a truck," I added suddenly. I tried to ask "Do you have a snowmobile?" but I botched the attempt. I blended two words that I knew, "snow" and "automobile," hoping they would translate well enough to be understood.

I repeated my description of Matthew's location two or three times. The old man managed to assure me that they would find Matthew, but I could not comprehend his description of his plan. Behind him, the others continued to jabber excitedly, augmenting their words with sweeping hand gestures. They seemed to look at me as if I were their trophy. Each of them took his turn pumping my hand in congratulations. Someone wanted to tend to my feet, attempting to rub vigorously on the now-thawed flesh. I put my hands on his and stopped him immediately, shaking my head and saying, "No, no, no. Let the doctor do that."

One of the men stepped into the cabin and retrieved the blanket I had used for the past two nights. The men wrapped me in it and carried me into the bus, laying me on the floor in the center aisle. I was vaguely aware that about half of the group remained behind. The others piled into the bus and we drove off, down the mountain in the direction from where they had come, away from Matthew.

The bus bounced down the road.

One of the men leaned over and asked, "Do you want some bread?"

I felt obliged to accept the offer and was rewarded with a slab of Turkish flat bread, similar to pita. It was delicious—we had enjoyed this bread many times during our travels to various Turkish villages—but I was more thirsty than hungry. "Thank you," I said. "Do you have some water?"

The man brought a jug of water and helped me raise myself up to drink.

The leader of the group introduced himself as Işmail Keklikci, and announced that he was sixty-five years old.

But I could concentrate on nothing other than Matthew. I could not begin to rejoice or relax—or make conversation—until I knew that my son was all right.

Matthew

Dad had told me not to leave the cave, but it was so scary inside. He wasn't coming back. No one is going to find me here, I realized. I've got to crawl out of here and go for help. I tried, but I could hardly move at all.

I lay back down in the cave and I felt myself falling asleep again. Suddenly I heard a group of birds making a lot of noise. I shook my head. Wait a minute, I thought, that's not birds, it's people!

"Hey!" I screamed.

"Whoohoo!" someone yelled back.

Before I knew it, someone was there, peeking into the cave. Then some other men were there, carrying shovels. They were all chattering in Turkish and I couldn't understand what they were saying.

But they wrapped me in a blanket and carried me piggyback down the road to a logging camp and put me in a truck. I didn't know where the truck came from. And I didn't know where the two-way radio came from.

We drove off quickly. They fed me a Turkish breakfast of salty white goat cheese, black olives, and bread.

Mike

I lay on a bench that ran across the back wall of an office known as the Turkish Forest Center, surrounded by excited men. All about me, everything appeared to be happening in slow motion. Is this really happening? I asked myself. Am I imagining this?

A Turkish boy, not much older than Matthew, spoke fairly good English; he had obviously been recruited as an interpreter.

The loggers and others in the forestry office seemed to be jockeying for position in the local political hierarchy; each wanted to claim his proper share of credit for this remarkable rescue. Işmaıl Kıklikci introduced me to some of his companions: Sedat Aslan, Murat Bayram, and Adem Bozoglu. They managed to convey the message that they had left their tiny village of Keşkiali Yaylaşı prior to the arrival of the blizzard. The snowfall had been so deep that they were unable to work for ten days. The only reason they had found me was that their boss had ordered them back to work.

Someone offered me hot tea along with the advice, "Don't drink it too quickly."

But all I wanted was the sustenance of my son. Did I give them enough information to go on? I wondered. What if they wander off onto another trail? No, it had not snowed since I had made it to the cabins, so I was confident that my ski tracks would be very easy to follow. My biggest worry was Matthew's condition, after being alone in the cave for two days. I had no idea what to expect. I knew that one of his feet was in bad ondition and I wondered how well he was able to take care f it. And what about his hands? Were they frostbitten by ow? After two nights away from him, I prepared myself for ie worst.

Would he be coherent, or would he have lost it? I had not repared him for the possibility of being alone for two nights, ecause I'd had no idea that was going to happen.

I asked myself: If I had known it would be a two-day separaon, would I have left him? I answered: Probably not.

Across from me a Turk operated a shortwave radio. He iade several transmissions to various offices, and finally a call ime in from a rescue team. He turned, grinned broadly, and)oke to me slowly. In Turkish he said, "They have found)ur son. He is all right. They are bringing him here."

It had taken the men less than an hour, which really surrised me. I must have given them good directions, I iought.

I could not wait to see Matthew with my own eyes, to make ire that he was okay. Nevertheless, a deep sense of relief assed over me. Thank You, God, I prayed. Thank You. You ave fulfilled Your promise.

Tears flowed freely down my cheeks. Seeing this, the young terpreter said, "Oh, no, don't cry."

You don't understand, I thought. You have no idea of what e went through, and of the feelings that were unleashed ithin me just now.

"Your son is really okay," the boy added. "He's going to e fine."

I nodded, but I knew that this young Turk simply did not omprehend my tears of joy.

Mary

It was about 10 A.M. when Rumeysa called. "They are found They are okay!" she said. "They are saying it on TV!"

I warned myself: This is not Mr. Holmes or Colonel Fitzger ald. This is the woman who told you about the terrorist threa that turned out to be such nonsense. "Okay, Rumeysa, than you very much," I said. "But I have to wait until I hear officially." The calm tone of my voice surprised me, and I kep my thoughts hidden: What if it is true? My heart wants t jump for joy.

Don't get excited, I told myself. It could be another false fin

Within minutes several other friends called with simila news. I thanked them all, but held my emotions in reserve. did not turn on the television, for I would not understand th reports anyway. But I began to think: If this is true, I'd bette get dressed.

It was difficult to finish this task, because the phone contir ued to ring. With each caller I reminded myself: Do not le yourself get excited. If it's not true you will reach the lowe low you can imagine.

I jumped each time the phone rang, hoping desperately tha it would be the official word.

Mike

The radio operator thrust the receiver's handset at me. The cor nection was poor, but I could hear a female voice ask, "Mike?

"Who's this?" I replied.

"This is Wanda." She added quickly, with a note of disbe lief, "Is this really Mike? What's my last name?"

Her question exasperated me and I said sharply, "Wanda, ock it off!" She's got to be joking, I thought. Why are we aying this little game? I said, "This is Wanda Villers, right?"

Her voice cracked. Through tears she explained, "Mike, you ve no idea what we've gone through. You have to forgive e, but we've just had so many false leads."

I could not imagine what she was talking about, but I would on learn what everyone had gone through on the other end this drama.

"We're going to call Mary," Wanda said.

Mary

his time—finally—the voice on the other end of the telephone e was that of Colonel Penar. "Mary, they found them!" he outed. "They're okay. Wanda has talked to them. It's true!"

"Praise God!" I shouted, and sighed at the same time.

Tears poured from my eyes as I listened to the details. Colo-l Penar said, "Mary, we're going to patch a phone call rough as soon as we can. We are also making arrangements get the family together. I'll have to call you back on that e. Just sit tight. They have some frostbite, but otherwise ey're okay."

Mark

was Christine who had asked me to talk to the Turkish police ain. I really didn't want to. I had already told them every-ing I knew. But I kept thinking: Well, if I don't do what they ant and Dad and Matthew aren't found, I might always regret It's only for half an hour.

The men wanted to know what Dad and Matthew wer wearing, when was the last time I saw them, how did th mountain look that day—every question they asked was or that I had answered before.

When the interview was over, as we were walking down th hall away from the office, Christine suddenly ushered me int one of the side rooms and told me to wait for her. There w a strange tension in the air, sort of like electricity. What's goir on? I wondered. What don't they want me to know?

As we were driving home, Christine said, "Sorry abou that." But she did not explain anything.

The attendant outside our apartment grinned broadly whe he saw me approaching with Christine. "Oh! they foun them," he said.

Of the several security guards who worked here, this ma was the one I didn't like because he was so gruff and mear looking. I did not trust him, so I mumbled sarcasticall "Oh, sure."

But when someone opened our apartment door, Mom wa standing in front of me with a huge smile on her face. "The found them!" she shouted.

Mike

Navy Captain George Allison, the acting second-in-comman of ODC, came on the line and we discussed details. Arrang ments were under way to fly Matthew and me to the bran new U.S. military hospital at Incirlik Air Force Base. And the would use the ODC's C-12 to fly Mary, Mark, and Maris there to join us.

It was not long before the phone was back in my hands an I heard Mary say, "Hi, cutie!"

The connection was poor and we had difficulty understand

ing one another. I also had trouble speaking over the lump in my throat.

"Are you okay?" she asked.

"Yeah, I'm in good shape. There's some frostbite, but otherwise I'm fine."

"What happened?" Mary asked.

"There was a whiteout and we got lost."

"How's Matthew?"

"He's okay. We were separated for a few days, but he's okay."

Increasing static made further conversation difficult, but I knew that we would all be reunited soon.

After the call I found myself relaxing a bit. Matthew had been found. The rest of my family was on the way. But the thought rolled around in my head: Maybe they're just saying Matthew's okay so I won't worry. I'll just assess that for myself, thank you very much.

"They are on their way," the radio operator said, referring to the crew of loggers who had rescued Matthew. "They are about ten minutes away."

I was too excited to remain lying down. I pulled myself to a sitting position, oblivious to pain.

The loggers must have been checking in via two-way radio, for the operator continued to give me a blow-by-blow account of their position.

Word had spread throughout the area. I was surprised to learn that this forestry office was located at yet another ski resort. Many of the Turkish skiers were milling about outside this office; some had their faces plastered against the large-paned window, seeking a glimpse of *"Yarbay."*

It seemed like an eternity, but it was only another few minutes before the radio operator reported, "They are just about here." I could hear a fresh flurry of activity outside. Turning my head toward the window, I saw that the crowd of spectators had reoriented its attention toward the road. A tan four-wheel drive sport utility vehicle had arrived. I caught a brief glimpse of a strong Turk reaching into the backseat and cradling a blanket-clad figure in his arms. The crowd gathered around and blocked my view. Within moments the young Turk entered the room, surrounded by a throng of chattering people. Others yelled at them to move out of the way.

Finally the man reached the bench next to me. He laid down his burden and unfurled the blanket.

In an animated, singsong, childlike tone Matthew trilled, "Hi . . . Dad!"

I put my arm around him and felt fresh tears spill down my cheeks. "Hi, Matthew," I said. Words failed me. For several minutes I just hugged and kissed him. Finally I was able to ask, "How did you do it? How did you get through that?"

He had no answer for me. He was working hard to hold back his own tears, and my hug was what he wanted most.

"Gosh, I'm so proud of you," I babbled. "I really didn't think you were going to make it. There is no way for me to describe how proud of you I am at this moment. I really am amazed and impressed that you hung in there."

His feet were covered by thick woolen socks given to him by the lumberjacks. I decided to let the doctors take those off, later. But I was desperate to know, "How are your feet? Are your feet okay?"

"They hurt a little but I think they're okay."

I dismissed any further thought about that for now, realizing there was nothing I could do about it anyway. Regardless of his condition, I had my son back. Nothing could dampen my joy—and my thankfulness to God—in this sweet reunion.

"Mom knows we're okay," I said. "I talked to her, and they're all going to come see us."

Somehow, the eyes that looked at me from the thin, pale face had changed. I realized that this was not the same kid who had gone skiing with me ten days ago. His eyes were wiser now. I was struck with the thought that our relationship would never be the same. What happened on that frozen mountain had changed us both. There was an unspoken

camaraderie—and I knew that he felt it, too. We had perse-
vered against insurmountable odds. Through our persever-
ance—and with the help of God—we had challenged death.
And we had won.

The Search

Sully happily issued instructions to send an Army Provide
Comfort C-12 to transport Mike and Matthew from Bolu to
the 39th Medical Group Hospital at Incirlik. The ODC's C-
12 prepared to bring Mary, Mark, and Marissa from Ankara.

Mary

Everything happened so fast. I suddenly realized that I had not
told Marissa! She heard the commotion at the doorway and
came over to us. We grabbed her and hugged her as the joyous
words tumbled out of our mouths: "They found them!
They're okay!"

Mark, Marissa, Christine, and I were dancing together in joy
when Norita appeared at the door. I assumed that she had
heard the news on television. But she had not, and she shrieked
with joy. "I just knew it would be today!" she said. "Daniel
nine or eleven. God impressed it upon me."

"No," I said, "it has to be chapter ten. Cathryn called this
morning and said chapter ten is the one that God showed her."

"Anyway it was verse four," Norita said. "They were supposed to be found today."

"What do you mean?" I asked. "I thought it was a verse
much further back. Let's get a Bible and look it up."

We moved into the piano room and looked up Daniel 10.

Sure enough, verse 4 pointed out the day that the angel finally got through with the answer to Daniel's prayer:

> *On the twenty-fourth day of the first month I was on the bank of the great river, the Tigris . . .*

I caught my breath and glanced at a calendar. Today was January 24.

God had just gotten His answer to us. And, oh, what an answer it was!

✳ Epilogue

Mike

Matthew and I were flown from Bolu to Incirlik Air Force Base for treatment of hypothermia, dehydration, and frostbite. The pediatrician at Incirlik, Captain Barbara A. Rugo, a dark-haired American with deep dark-brown eyes and a ready smile, was surprised to find Matthew sitting up and joking. When he asked for a Coke and fries she decreed, "You're going to be okay."

Once Matthew's feet thawed, rather large blisters appeared on his feet, filled with fluid. But doctors determined that he would not lose any toes.

Both Captain Rugo and the internist, Captain William Thomas, determined that both of us were in better condition than they would have thought. Matthew had lost ten pounds and I had lost about fifteen, but we took quick action to remedy that situation. Our frostbitten limbs improved quickly; the prognosis for a full recovery was good.

Colonel Penar jokingly told the press that when I was fully recovered, "We'll give him a shave and put him back to work. His chair is waiting. The work is piling up."

The entire nation of Turkey seemed to be celebrating the *Mucize,* the "Miracle," along with us. We learned that the village where I was found, Aladağ Orman Bölgesi, was fully eighteen miles west of the Doruk Kaya Hotel. The nineteen woodcutters who found us became local heroes. Turkish authorities from Bolu gave each man a watch and enough material to fashion a new suit. The management of the Doruk Kaya Hotel rewarded each man with the Turkish equivalent of $85. The U.S. government had a well dug in the village.

We spent the next three months receiving various treatments, first at Incirlik, then at Wilford Hall Medical Center in San Antonio, Texas. It was here that I learned more about the mysterious milky fluid that had appeared in our urine. It was creatine phosphate, a substance found in muscle tissue. The fact that it was appearing during the latter stages of urination was an indication that our muscle tissue was breaking down. In fact, our bodies had started to feed on themselves. Doctors were concerned because this sludge can clog the kidneys and render them nonfunctional.

Matthew lost half of one toe and the tip of another, but is as fast and agile as ever on the soccer field. I healed more slowly than Matthew—I had to have a skin graft on my left foot to replace frozen tissue—but have suffered no adverse long-term effects.

I have now been reassigned to the U.S. Air Force Academy in Colorado Springs and am a glider instructor.

Mary

On January 24, 1996, Mike coaxed me into going on a day trip to the Ski Cooper resort in Colorado, to celebrate the first anniversary of the rescue. Before going, I re-treated our ski clothing, to make sure that it was waterproof. Mike loaded his fanny pack with "power bars," hand-warmer packs, extra socks, a knife, a compass, a signal mirror, cotton balls soaked in petroleum jelly, a candle wrapped in cloth, and a generous supply of matches.

It was early afternoon by the time we arrived. It was snowing like crazy and a cold, miserable wind howled about us. But we

gnored the elements and took a lift to the top of one of the
ifficult slopes.

After we skied down the mountain, we decided to warm up
n the lodge. As we sipped hot tea, Mike looked over at me
nd said, "Well, we did it. You ready to go home?"

Amazing and Inspiring True Stories of Divine Intervention